Alexander Fullerton, born in Suffolk and brought up in France, spent the years 1938–41 at the RN College, Dartmouth, and the rest of the war at sea – mostly under it. His first novel – *Surface!*, based on his experiences as gunnery and torpedo officer of HM Submarine *Seadog* in the Far East, 1944–5, in which capacity he was mentioned in despatches for distinguished service – was published in 1953. It became an immediate bestseller with five reprints in six weeks. He has lived solely on his writing since 1967, and is one of the most borrowed authors from British libraries.

Praise for Alexander Fullerton:

'The research is unimpeachable and the scent of battle quite overwhelming'
Sunday Times

'The prose has a real sense of urgency, and so has the theme. The tension rarely slackens and the setting is completely convincing'
Times Literary Supplement

'Impeccable in detail and gripping in impact'
Irish Independent

'Has the ring of truth and the integrity proper to a work of art'
Daily Telegraph

'You don't read a novel by Alexander Fullerton. You *live* it'
South Wales Echo

By Alexander Fullerton

SURFACE!
BURY THE PAST
OLD MOKE
NO MAN'S MISTRESS
A WREN CALLED SMITH
THE WHITE MEN SANG
THE YELLOW FORD
SOLDIER FROM THE SEA
THE WAITING GAME
THE THUNDER AND THE FLAME
LIONHEART
CHIEF EXECUTIVE
THE PUBLISHER
STORE
THE ESCAPISTS
OTHER MEN'S WIVES
PIPER'S LEAVE
REGENESIS
THE APHRODITE CARGO
JOHNSON'S BIRD
BLOODY SUNSET
LOOK TO THE WOLVES
LOVE FOR AN ENEMY
NOT THINKING OF DEATH
BAND OF BROTHERS
FINAL DIVE
WAVE CRY
THE FLOATING MADHOUSE
WESTBOUND, WARBOUND

The Everard series of naval novels

THE BLOODING OF THE GUNS
SIXTY MINUTES FOR ST GEORGE
PATROL TO THE GOLDEN HORN
STORM FORCE TO NARVIK
LAST LIFT FROM CRETE
ALL THE DROWNING SEAS
A SHARE OF HONOUR
THE TORCH BEARERS
THE GATECRASHERS

The SBS Trilogy

SPECIAL DELIVERANCE
SPECIAL DYNAMIC
SPECIAL DECEPTION

The Rosie Quartet

INTO THE FIRE
RETURN TO THE FIELD
IN AT THE KILL
SINGLE TO PARIS

SINGLE TO PARIS

Alexander Fullerton

timewarner
paperbacks

A *Time Warner* Paperback

First published in Great Britain in 2001
by Little, Brown and Company
This edition published in 2003 by Time Warner Paperbacks

A CIP catalogue record for this book
is available from the British Library.

ISBN 0 7515 3234 7

Typeset by Palimpsest Book Production Limited
Polmont, Stirlingshire
Printed and bound in Great Britain by
Mackays of Chatham plc, Chatham, Kent

Time Warner Paperbacks
An imprint of
Time Warner Books UK
Brettenham House,
Lancaster Place
London WC2E 7EN

www.TimeWarnerBooks.co.uk

SINGLE TO PARIS

Chapter 1

Head down, pedalling, pumping hard, a lot of the time getting along faster than the nose-to-tail mass of Wehrmacht trucks, transports and cars pounding towards the Seine. Maybe they'd get over it, maybe not – depending on bridges, whether any were still standing. She'd heard bombing, and aircraft had passed over high; the RAF and the USAF had the skies to themselves, apparently, whatever was left of the Luftwaffe wasn't getting a look in anywhere. Rosie was keeping her head down as much as anything so as not to meet the eyes of the same truckloads of German soldiery alternately passing her or being passed by her every few minutes. This was a defeated rabble, even though some of them didn't seem to know it. An astonishing amount of the heavy stuff had been abandoned on the grass verges for lack of fuel, vehicles' former occupants in files and straggling groups, some despondently trying to hitch lifts but mostly resigned to the futility of that – plodding northward, following the greenish khaki flow and *not* now singing bloody *Deutschland Uber Alles*. Although a lot of the diehards still apparently thought they'd win – or had been told to think so: that they'd make a stand and be heavily reinforced between the Seine and the Rhine, hold on there while Hitler's indiscriminately murderous 'secret weapons' turned the tide back for them. They did *look* beaten, though. Tended to perk up when their eyes fastened on her – if she happened to be looking up at that moment: French girl, pretty one at that, on her own and pedalling *their* way, apparently escaping just as they were. It was what she'd told the *Feldgendarmes*, Boche military police, who'd stopped her a few miles back when she'd been finding her way through the outskirts of Evreux and demanded to know where she'd come from and was going; she'd panted, 'Escaping, is what!'

Out of breath, leaning on her bike, fumbling one-handed for her papers – *good* papers, for a change, ones they wouldn't fault, at any rate not quickly or easily; it was almost a let-down when after she'd got them out that the bastard didn't want to see them. He'd asked her, 'Escaping to where, exactly?' Quite friendly, easy-going, as if she might have been one of *them* – which was a concept to make one retch. She'd told him, 'Rouen. To find my child and mother-in-law. I have other friends there too.' Indicative of having no friends anywhere behind her, where the Allied armies were advancing and where she'd been landed from a Wellington at dawn and then been brought on by an advanced detachment – patrol – of the 51st Highland Division, part of Montgomery's 1st British Corps. They'd dropped her with her bicycle in the Forêt d'Evreux, this very young-looking lieutenant warning her that whatever military personnel or vehicles she might encounter from there on northward were sure to be Hun. Rouen was due north from there, distance roughly 65 kilometres. She had the map clearly enough in mind. The lieutenant had proposed – ostensibly joking, but sounding hopeful too – 'See you in town, perhaps?'

'In Rouen? When d'you think you'll get there?'

'Week or so. Depending of course on—'

'I'll be gone long before that. But – thanks, and good luck.'

'Oh, good luck to *you*!' There'd been a growl of support for that, from his sergeant and the other two. He'd added – begun to – 'In whatever it is you're—'

'Bye.' On her way then, with a quick glance back; echoing in her mind that word *whatever*, and answering it with *Saving that kid's life, please God*. Two lives actually, and a lot of others which in the longer term might be dependent on them. She was thinking on and off about that all the way to Louviers, which was about half-way – at least would have been if all had gone as she'd foreseen, if there hadn't been a traffic snarl-up of immense proportions around a *very* slow-moving re-direction of traffic to the right. The first sign of it had been a sudden reduction to snail's pace – for all of *them*, not for her; she'd been passing them when they were crawling, and pretty soon they weren't even doing that, had stopped, while she'd penetrated far enough up the congested road to get some idea of what was happening. There was a stink of burning, a choking, eye-watering haze of it; it wasn't only a matter of traffic being diverted, but also a road-clearance operation, vehicles that must have been hit earlier in the day by Allied aircraft still being dragged away into nearby fields, mainly by half-tracks. Many of the wrecks were still smouldering, while of these others some were being diverted and some weren't. In any case she decided to make her own diversion – westward, pedalling away into the back streets of Louviers, finding herself among other cyclists and a drift of pedestrians thronging down the streets she'd come by, she guessed heading that way for a close-up view of stalled, retreating Germans. A fine sight for them, after four years of occupation, but maybe not all that wise – such a concentration and no way of escape from the blocked major roads: if the RAF should happen to pay another visit now they'd have an absolute field day of it – as they had been doing all over Normandy for weeks now, so one had been told in London. It was a noisy, happy French crowd though, with no Germans anywhere in these back-streets: there would have been Louviers-based ones, but they must already have evacuated. A blockage of farm-carts was developing on the western edge: people from outlying villages and farms flocking to see the rout. But the traffic they'd been diverting eastward, she realised, visualising the map, wouldn't have far to go before it hit that southern loop of the Seine – at or near St Pierre-du-Vauvray for instance. There'd be an intact bridge there, she supposed – otherwise they wouldn't be sending them that way at all. The diversion would also turn them well away to the east of Rouen itself, where with bridges down – again, courtesy of the RAF – there must be a degree of chaos. This process would take *some* of it away in any case: thinking back to the view she'd seen of it, it could be that they were diverting every second or third truck, or just those of certain weights – trucks for bridges like horses for courses. For her anyway, the best thing from here on would be to stay on minor roads and country lanes; one might get along better and certainly more comfortably – as well as more safely, in the event of further straffing from the air. In any case there was no practical alternative to heading north-west, eventually getting around *that* southward loop – the one in the vicinity of Orival.

Lengthening the journey somewhat. And getting into Rouen on the city's left bank, which would be OK, there was bound to be *some* way of getting across – for a cyclist or pedestrian, anyway. Navigating meanwhile by the sun, which was currently behind her right shoulder and burning hot through the light summer raincoat she was wearing over a blouse and cotton skirt. She could have done without the coat, but she'd have had to stop and cram it under the string that was holding her scuffed cardboard suitcase on the rear carrier: *could* have, but it was protective colouring, this garment, shapeless enough and drab-coloured and French-made – at least had a Marseille supplier's label in it – and about right for August temperatures when nights cooled and there was a likelihood of showers. It was also useful on account of the large inside pocket that held all her papers in buttoned-up security, so that her handbag, slung with its long strap slantwise from a shoulder, didn't need to be opened, drawn attention to – containing as it did a Beretta .32 automatic pistol, possession of which would earn one an automatic death sentence. Its spare clips were in the suitcase. Shifting the bag now – change of shoulder, bag on the other side . . . This lane was straight and tall-hedged with very flat green fields visible through gateways, higher ground beyond, and the only other moving object at this moment was a stack of hay a couple of hundred metres ahead of her and moving steadily north-west. There'd be a tractor the other side of it, of course: a *gazo*, burning green wood or charcoal in a 20-gallon steel cylinder glowing at its tail-end. Head down again, legs pumping, muscles burning. It was a long time since she'd biked any great distance – and in the intervening months she'd been knocked about rather a lot. It was a shock to be doing it now in any case – to be back in France at all, when only last Thursday, August 10th – this was Thursday the 17th – just a week ago she'd radio'd her last message from a place called St Valery-sur-Vanne, reporting completion of that task (including the death of an individual whom she'd gone there to kill) and asking to be picked up the next night from a field code-named Parnassus: which should have been her last job for Special Operations Executive, so that all her thinking from there on could be concentrated on a man called Ben: Australian, lieutenant-commander in Coastal Forces – meaning motor torpedo boats and gunboats – who loved her and whom she loved – well, loved fit to bust, couldn't wait to be back with and this time *stay* with. Even though he did at this moment think she was dead: that wasn't *his* fault. But consequent to all that, and in contrast to expectations which she'd been living on for quite a while now, she really hadn't believed the soft-voiced Chris Brierly's warning: 'Intention is to turn you round and send you straight back in, Rosie. All right to call you Rosie?' She hadn't believed it, hadn't *wanted* to believe it; she'd met this Brierly before but only once and very briefly; he'd been an agent but had been pulled out of the field and stayed out, on SOE staff in Baker Street, for some reason – loss of nerve maybe, you wouldn't blame him if that was it, some stuck it and some didn't. Telling her this last Sunday/Monday as the Hudson roared up into moonlit sky over the surrounding Forêt d'Othe and set course for Tempsford. 'Actually all I know – you may be able to guess at what's behind it, but for me the sum total is it concerns two agents, the *chef de réseau* and his pianist, from Nancy. You were there with them recently – in Nancy?'

Organiser – or *chef de réseau,* meaning head of group – Guillaume Rouquet, and pianist Léonie Garnier. 'Pianist' meaning radio operator, which happened also to be Rosie's own specialist function. Rouquet and Garnier were only their field names of course. She could see them in her mind's eye: Rouquet – real name Derek something – English, tallish, brown-haired, with a narrow, bony face; and Léonie *petite* – tiny, really – with dark hair, blue eyes, ivory-pale skin, neat little pianist's hands. She was a few years younger than Rosie, maybe 22 or 23, and she'd said her mother – French – had a dress business in London.

Rosie had asked Brierly, 'They in trouble somehow?'

'I'm afraid they are.' Long intake of breath, close to her ear in the cabin's lurching darkness. 'Fact is, the Gestapo have them.'

Silence. If you could call the steel-decked interior of a Hudson battering its way through the night sky 'silent'. In Rosie's mind, unuttered, a groan of, 'Oh, God, *no* . . .' and the immediate reactive question, also unspoken, whether they might have been caught through having been involved with *her*. Aware incidentally that her hand was resting on the worn leather handbag which Léonie had given her only a couple of weeks ago in the flat in Nancy; and a second question pushing through: how could sending *her* back into France help *them*? Wordless, gazing at the dim close-up shape of this virtual stranger through the surrounding thumping, howling darkness: accepting that there'd be no point pressing for further information which he didn't have – *and* knowing a great deal more than he did about being in Gestapo hands, having been in them herself on more than one occasion.

In Rouen, as it happened, the first time. First and *worst* time. A year ago, almost exactly. More recent experiences had been bad enough and lasted longer, but what had happened in Rouen was still the theme of recurring nightmares.

At Elboef – from her mental photography of the map she *thought* that was the name of it – she was amongst the Gadarene swine again, one stream of the stinking heavy transports lumbering from the right and another infiltrating on a major road from the south-west. Ordinary Boche soldiers were being used as MPs to sort it out, merging the two columns, and it looked as if they had yet another losing battle on their hands. Rosie with her head down, weaving through, actually not scared of being stopped and questioned, having to show papers, a hazard which at some stages in her previous missions had been a source of fairly acute anxiety – definitely frightening, when she'd been conscious of having really rotten papers. Her fear this time was of being stopped and turned back, prevented from getting to Rouen or even just delayed. It was on her own insistence that she was coming this way, and it meant losing at least one day – real destination being Paris; her reasoning had been that going straight there – Paris, where reportedly they were being held . . . at least, had been a few days ago – might well achieve precisely nothing. If you didn't know where to start – which she would not have; whereas in Rouen there was an old trail which, touch wood, one should be able to pick up.

Get through this lot and on to the river-bank, track or pavement or dirt road running along it – if there is one . . .

A shout behind her. *Feldgendarmerie* . . . She yelled back, *'Oui, d'accord!'* Flap of the hand – to whatever that one had yelled after her. Noting *en passant* that in side-roads and open spaces here and there many more trucks and transports had been abandoned. She was bumping and rattling over railway lines: couldn't be far from the river now. Should have stopped in open country though and had a snack, she told herself – having a loaf of bread, some cheese and a bottle of water in the basket here. She'd taken a few swigs of water but hadn't mustered the resolution actually to stop. Nerves – the imperative to keep going: knowing what an extra minute – let alone a day – could mean to those two. Aware too of how much time had already been wasted – having called for the pick-up on Thursday night, and Special Duties Squadron not having had an aircraft available in that sector until the Sunday. Her frustration *then* had had nothing to do with *this* business, had been solely at the delay in getting home to Ben.

A glimpse of water ahead, as she turned a corner. Bike jolting over cobbles. Down at the end there, turn left; with luck might find oneself passing the Roches d'Orival and Saint Aubin. Then – what, 15, 16 kilometres? Less than 20, anyway. St Etienne, then into the southern approaches – Rouen's Rive Gauche. Might stop at Ursule's – and if she was there and said it was all right, hadn't filled quite *all* her rooms with prostitutes . . . Worth a try anyway. From Ursule – who was a nice enough woman, with friends in the Resistance, happened to have inherited a large house and to make ends meet took her customers where she found them – only insisting they didn't pursue their profession on her premises – from her one might discover which bridges, if any, were still standing, what were the hours of curfew now, locations of checkpoints and any new Boche regulations or places or areas to avoid. Thank heavens she'd paid Ursule all she'd owed her: might well not have, in the throes of that very sudden, panicky departure a year ago. It might also be as well that she was using the same alias she'd been using then – Jeanne-Marie Lefèvre. She'd opted for this not with any thought of Ursule in mind, but for a more vital reason; although in other ways it had been a difficult decision, mainly in that it would still be the name on her Gestapo file. One of the names on it, at least, she'd used others since. It had been her preference, anyway, and her briefing officers had had to go along with it. Monday afternoon to Wednesday evening had been all she and they had had, and that sort of detail had had to be settled right at the start so that SOE's master forgers in their house on the Kingston bypass could get to work on the really excellent papers which she now carried, identifying her as Jeanne-Marie Lefèvre, date of birth 10th September 1916, husband killed in the French army in 1940 leaving her with a daughter – Juliette, now four and a half, whom allegedly she'd left in the care of the child's paternal grandmother on a farm near St Saven, district of Nantes. Whereas in reality she was Rosie Ewing, *née* Rosalie de Bosque, born in Nice in 1918 of a French father (deceased) and English mother (extant, in Buckinghamshire) and since February 1941 she'd been the widow of Squadron Leader Johnny Ewing who'd been shot down into the English Channel in that month, only a few days before she'd gone into training as an agent of Special Operations Executive. The passport-sized photo pasted to Jeanne-Marie's identity documents was undoubtedly of Rosie Ewing, and shown on the documents in black ink over Nazi rubber stamps on the documents were the relevant facts and figures: hair brown, eyes hazel – *noisette* – height (in centimetres) 5 feet 4½ inches and weight (in kilos) 112 lbs. The child was a complete fiction, she'd never had one.

Besides the excellence of her papers, another factor in her feeling of comparative security this time was that she was not carrying a radio-transceiver. On each of her deployments before this she'd had one, latterly an 'A' Mark III in its specially fitted attaché case, and that had always been a hazard. Essential, until now, because it had been her job, she *was* a pianist – and her briefing officers in the SOE-run country house this last weekend had assumed she'd take a set with her on this jaunt too, but she'd dug her heels in, pointing out that it was unnecessary since she was to be on her own with a single purpose, little time in which to accomplish it, and effectively beyond anyone else's help. She'd told them, 'If I make a mess of it, you'll have no time to send anyone else. Who would you send, in any case?'

That was the point, really. She had the personal contact, and there was no one else who did. Which of course was why they were lumping her with it in the first place. If she'd ducked out they wouldn't have known what the hell to do, and you could have written those two off, they'd have had no chance at all. Didn't have much *this* way. And while in the briefing-officers' minds there were valid and urgent military reasons for wanting them out double-quick, before Gestapo torture broke either of them, in Rosie's own private mind there was a strong personal motivation – a desperation to find them and get them out *before* the bastards began using their whips or pliers on them.

Having been there oneself. Knowing how it was, or could be, and to a large extent identifying with them – with Léonie in particular, of course – and remembering all too well that if that session in Rouen a year ago had lasted another half-minute she'd have told them everything and anything they'd wanted to know.

Chapter 2

Arrival at Tempsford hadn't been all that joyous. She'd allowed herself daydreams of Marilyn being there, even bringing Ben out with her. Marilyn Stuart, 2nd Officer in the Wrens – tall, blonde and as slim as a mannequin, but much more importantly a tremendously good friend – had been Rosie's Conducting Officer, i.e. sort of mentor-companion, during the months of SOE training, had seen her off on each of her deployments and had usually been there to welcome her back; in the course of this last one she'd even flown out as Baker Street's special courier for a late night/early morning clandestine conference in a wood near St Mihiel. Which in fact was where they'd last seen each other: so that her *not* being there on the ground at Tempsford when the Hudson had put itself down in the pre-dawn glow on Monday had been . . . disconcerting.

Because she'd always been there when needed. And this *was* a lonely business. Very much alone in the field, you looked forward intensely to reunion with your friends.

The man who had met her, introducing himself as David Hyatt – a major – and sending Brierly and an orderly ahead to the car burdened with Rosie's gear – suitcase, transceiver and an 'S'-phone – asked, 'Did he mention what we've got lined up for you?'

By 'he' he'd meant Brierly, presumably. It was a dawn full of strangers as well as disappointments. Rosie had asked him, 'Are you from Baker Street?'

Baker Street being the location of SOE's 'F' Section – 'F' for France. Hyatt had told her, 'No. The other lot. St James's.' Meaning not SOE but SIS. Secret Intelligence Service, and adding, 'We're in partnership on this one. *Did* he tell you?'

'A suggestion that I should go straight back into the field, you mean?'

'Rather more than a *suggestion*, actually.'

'Only if I accept it. Do you know how long I've been *in* the damn field?'

'Yes. As it happens. We're well aware of the grisly time you've had, too. Left for dead at one stage. Baker Street only very recently discovering you *weren't* dead, they'd even put you in for a posthumous G.C. – which *won't* now be posthumous, of course – and three cheers for that . . . The story as I've heard it is – heck, flabbergasting. So – yes. I take your point. Only we hope that in all the circumstances . . .' A hand on her arm: 'Exhausted?'

'Slightly.' Depressed, too – somewhat. 'Are we going to Gaynes Hall?'

'No – Fawley Court.'

'Do you know Marilyn Stuart?'

'Yes. Not well, but—'

'I'd thought she'd be here to meet me.'

'Involved elsewhere, I was told, circumstances beyond her control, but she was supposed to be getting back tonight – last night – and she'll be joining us at Fawley. Rotten for you, I'm sorry. Anyway you're entitled to a good long sleep – meal, hot bath . . .'

'When does the de-briefing start?'

'Re-briefing, more than de-briefing. Well . . . soon as you're rested, fed and fit. Here we are now.'

Brierly drove the car, a black Humber, and Hyatt sat in the back with her. Rosie asked him as they got going, 'One more question – please?'

'Many as you like.'

'In respect of Guillaume Rouquet and Léonie Garnier –

why me? What can I do that anyone else can't?'

'Ah. Well. You'll recall doing a job for us – for SIS, that is – a year ago. You did it in parallel with your SOE activities – in Rouen?'

'So?'

'You made contact with a woman by name of Jacqueline Clermont, and in her company you also met a German, member of the SD who was calling himself a sergeant – name of Gerhardt Clausen?'

'Jacqueline's boyfriend.'

'*One* of her boyfriends. You may remember he went around in civvies. It was fairly obvious he was only passing himself off as a sergeant. For whatever reason . . .'

'Didn't they all wear civvies – SD and Gestapo – until the landings in Normandy?'

'In Paris I believe they did, yes. Didn't all call themselves sergeants though, did they? And it's fairly obvious he's nothing of the kind. Good-looking chap, eh?'

'Jacqueline was certainly keen.'

'Although he'd introduced her – handed her on, you might say – to a colonel of engineers, Hans Walther, then top dog in the construction of rocket-launching sites. She spent weekends with him in Amiens, didn't she? Which is why we asked you to recruit her as an informant.'

'Has she stuck to the deal we made?'

'Walther was replaced – recalled to Germany months ago. Unfortunately. Fortunately for Clausen though, who's had her to himself again.'

'So the deal I made with her went phut.'

'Well – yes, but while it lasted, Rosie—'

'The evening I met Clausen – very briefly, thank God – he was on his way back to Germany. To Berlin. He'd been away somewhere, come back to Rouen to pack up and say goodbye. Jacqui was going strong with Walther then, but it was obvious Clausen was planning to spend those last nights with her – a Thursday and Friday, I think it was – and she wasn't by any means averse to it. My presence in her flat that evening choked him off, rather. Which might have saved my bacon – I mean, his mind wasn't on anything but Jacqui, he didn't question her account of me.'

'And she's back with him now. He's in Paris – wielding considerable authority.'

'She in Paris with him?'

'Some of the time. Still has the hairdressing business in Rouen, I gather. In Paris rather as she was with Walther in Amiens, one supposes. But – sticking to the point, your question – the Gestapo's been pulling out of Rue des Saussaies, and the SD out of Avenue Foch, and Boemelbourg himself – know who he is, do you?'

'Elderly homosexual, second-in-command at Rue des Saussaies.'

'Yes. More precisely, head of SD Counter-Espionage Section IV. In which capacity he's left Clausen a free hand with Courtland and di Mellili. *So*—'

Rosie cut in: 'Mind if we stick to calling them Rouquet and Garnier?'

'I don't mind, no, but—'

'If I'm to be sent back into France – those *are* the names they're using—'

'Yes. Point taken. But regarding Clausen, what I was about to say – he can play it any way he likes – have them shot, ship them east—'

'Wouldn't get much out of them *then*.'

'No. And his brief would be simply to get results – by whatever means . . . That old pansy must have a good opinion of him, obviously. The other prisoners we knew of have already been cleared away to the camps, poor devils – Germans don't want walking, talking evidence left for us to find – but those two—'

'They can't have had them more than a week.'

'Less. Just days. Our information's extremely fresh. Which does give us some chance – we *hope*—'

'Information from what source?'

'Might we leave that sort of detail to later, when we get down to the nuts and bolts? The answer may well surprise you – but if we keep shooting off at tangents—'

'All right.'

'Thing is, Clausen must be pretty well on his own. For instance, Rue des Saussaies is guarded by *Milice* now. Although Oberg – *General* Carl Oberg – heard of him?'

She hadn't. And her head was fairly splitting. Hyatt telling her, 'Head of Gestapo for all France. He's still in Paris, or was a day or two ago. So was Helmut Knocken, *Standartenführer* – Boemelbourg's superior, technically. You see, we're off on yet another tangent – and you *are* whacked, aren't you . . .'

She'd got the general feel of it, though: why they were roping *her* in, or hoping to – the possibility of re-establishing contact with Jacqueline, and through her getting to – or *at* – Gerhardt Clausen.

But *then* what?

End up sharing a cell with Léonie? Hearing the guards coming, the crash of their boots and clink of keys, she and Léonie both hoping to Christ it wasn't *her* that was going to be dragged out this time?

She'd been there. In the Gestapo prison at Fresnes for instance. Didn't need to exert any powers of imagination to know how it was, or could be again.

Didn't have to take it on, either. While the car wound its way through the quiet English countryside to Fawley Court she was beginning to think she wouldn't. She *was* exhausted, and dispirited – by Marilyn's absence, let alone by the collapse of what had perhaps been extravagant hopes of Ben being here too. Although she could still see the crazy image as she'd daydreamed it, the moment of reunion – herself clambering out of the aircraft and Ben loping towards her across the airfield – bawling her name, arms spread to grab her, snatch her up . . .

She'd slept, woken as the car crunched over gravel in the forecourt. New faces then in the growing daylight, quiet voices – mainly women's, those of FANYs who staffed this place. Hyatt's quiet, 'Get her to bed. She's out on her feet.' Bed like an enveloping cloud in which she'd dreamed again of Ben, but not happily at all; he had the Stack woman with him – *Lady* Stack, former wife of a former motor gunboat CO of his, and before that his own (Ben's) mistress. An English Jacqueline? But she'd quite liked Jacqueline: and *loathed* la Stack . . . There *was* a degree of confusion in it. But Marilyn had let her know – certainly implied – that in the interval when they'd all thought she (Rosie) was dead, Ben had resumed – what was the phrase – 'keeping company' with that bitch. All right, if one had been dead, what the hell, who'd care? It was only rather sickening that he'd have been so ready to *accept* the notion that they'd killed her – and so damn quick to—

But la Stack would have been pursuing *him*.

Hyatt had said something about waking her at noon so she could get a bath before lunch, after which they'd start the briefing, but in the event Marilyn had arrived in mid-forenoon, taken charge and let her sleep until about 1 pm. The two of them had lunched on their own then, and she'd told Rosie that Ben was in Norway or on his way there, in a motor gunboat on some urgent mission. Norway being still thick with Nazis, of course.

But why should this be so – when surely he was in that job in London still? He'd twice been wounded in MGB actions on the French coast, was supposed to be unfit for sea duty, and they'd put him back in his old job in St James's, the one he'd had when she'd first met him.

'Isn't he still walking with a stick?'

(So would *not* have come bounding across the airfield like some great kangaroo . . .)

'Yes, he is. Or was a fortnight ago. I gather this is a special operation, mounted in a hurry; they're short-handed at the moment, and by all accounts he's a very competent navigator – which they needed. Anyway, you know how he is, your Ben . . .'

'Straining at the leash. Speaking of which, what about Joan Stack?'

'Rosie, I honestly don't know. Nor does anyone else. We *have* had . . . well, spotters out for her.'

'He still doesn't know I'm alive, then?'

'I don't think he can. To start with he was out of town – had a few days' leave, we heard—'

'With la Stack?'

'No reason to assume so.'

'But plenty of reason to *guess*?'

'Rosie – when he gets back from Norway—'

'If that's where he *really* is.'

'It is, I promise you. I've spoken to his boss. Believe me, Rosie darling—'

'Believe *you* all right—'

'And if I *could* have been here earlier—'

'I know. I know . . .'

'The thing to remember at this meeting now, Rosie, is that if you don't want to go back in, you damn well don't have to. I'll back you to the hilt, I won't *let* them persuade you against your will. Nobody'd blame you for a moment for turning it down. Come on, let's get some food in us.'

Head down, pedalling doggedly, and the bomb-shattered southern outskirts of Rouen closing in around her. Traffic not thick at all, mostly bicycles and a few *gazos*. Nothing German, as far as she'd seen yet. They'd always been thicker on the right bank than the left, of course. She was on Rue d'Elboeuf now, with Sotteville les-Rouen off to the right somewhere and Rouen-St Sever ahead. She'd recognise the corner when she came to it – if it was still there. There'd been a lot of bombing. This was the industrial side, presumably the main target area.

If she got to the church – St Sever – she'd know she'd come too far, missed the turn.

But she hadn't. *There* . . . Corner house intact, although its neighbour was a heap of rubble. Old-looking rubble, weeds growing all over it. Then the café she'd used once or twice: Café Saint Sever, they'd been lucky too. Now the next right, then left: spotting it and free-wheeling across the road to it, bumping up on to the pavement. It was a narrow-fronted, three-storied house which a century or so ago had been one half of a convent. Occupied more by tarts now than novices. She hung on to the bike while leaning to press the bell: bikes being valuable items in France, costing as much as cars had before the war and tending to get stolen.

Door opening: Ursule herself, in a skirt and striped shirt. A smell of onions. Rosie smiled up at her: 'Ursule.'

'It's – Jeanne-Marie?'

'Well done. And you're looking marvellous!'

'Don't look too bad yourself. But you left in the devil of a rush, didn't you?'

She nodded. 'Without saying goodbye. Sorry. *Force majeure.*'

'*Force Boche* . . .'

'Quite. I left the rent money though.'

'Of course you did. And you want a room now – that it?'

'For one night – probably.'

'One night or longer, suit yourself. Same room, same rent. Bring the machine inside. Come far?'

'Far enough that my legs are dropping off.'

'Well. Top floor again, I'm afraid—'

'I'll manage . . .'

Alone, she sat on the iron-framed bed and ate the bread and cheese while massaging her calves. Recalling Hyatt's comment, 'Adding at least a hundred kilometres to the journey, that way. Worst thing's the delay – you'd need a night in Rouen, day two getting into Paris—'

'Maybe more than one night. Depends on whether Jacqui's there or not.'

'And there you are. If she isn't, could be a *fatal* waste of time.' Frank Willoughby – balding, twitchy, SOE staff, a colleague of Marilyn's – shaking his head decisively. Decisively as *he* saw it . . . Rosie said to Marilyn, 'Via Rouen is the only way I'd consider going. Arriving blind in Paris, relying on luck and some unknown *résistant*—'

'Dénault's as good a contact as you could have. Gaullist FFI – one of their most effective ones – with chaps he can call on all over Paris.' Willoughby assured her, 'He'll have Clausen tracked down for you in no time at all!'

'How?'

'Well – for instance – pick him up outside Rue des Saussaies or Avenue Foch, wherever the action is, and trail him to where he's living. Correction – where *they* are living. Then you either drop in on Jacqueline when he's out, or with our friends' help watch the place until she shows up. Or if he's around too much and she goes out on her own . . . huh?' He'd glanced at Hyatt as if inviting congratulations; added, 'She could be up and running within hours.'

'If it's as easy as that, why haven't you put this genius on to it already? Why bring me into it at all?'

'Rosie.' Hyatt, blunt-featured but patient. 'It's only forty-eight hours since we had the tip-off about these two. And *you* are the obvious person to make contact, so it had to be discussed with you – as we're doing now. Wait a minute – there's more. Getting on to this chap any sooner would have meant going off at half-cock: that's one thing; another is that with so many *réseaux* blown now, radio links aren't . . . well, aren't exactly guaranteed secure. Whereas your contact with him would be personal, face to face and a password, no possibility of interception. It's a *very* sensitive issue, this, you realise. Another directly related point is that having located Rouquet and the girl, this same chap is the one you'll be relying on for – well, for whatever can be done about it.

Depending on where they are and how heavily guarded.'

'And the general state of affairs in Paris by that time.' Willoughby cutting in again. 'It's already chaotic. The only trains running in and out of any of the stations are troop trains – no food getting in, and no fuel – so electric power at best only a few hours a day; communist elements of the Resistance pressing for a rising *now* – to forestall the Gaullists of course—'

Rosie asked Hyatt, 'What's the military situation? When are we or the Americans likely to get there?'

'Not as soon as you might expect. Eisenhower's bypassing Paris, to the north and south. Here, I'll show you.' A map – one of several on the table – which he unfolded. Leaning over from behind her and Marilyn, but pausing then: 'Re strategy, have you heard of the landings this morning in the South of France, on the coast between Nice and Marseille?'

'Yes. Marilyn was telling me.'

'American and Free French troops mostly. Our contribution's paratroops. Anyway – Ike doesn't want to get bogged down in Paris. Street fighting's a slow and costly business, and one of his biggest problems is fuel. Food too – his own armies' rations, let alone feeding a population of that size. He needs every gallon of petrol he can get, and the answer to that problem is to take and occupy Le Havre and all ports north of it double-quick. Front line's still being supported by supplies through the Normandy beachheads – we need Antwerp and Rotterdam a hell of a lot more than we need Paris. So – British 21st Army Group fighting its way via Rouen and taking in Le Havre, and the US 12th Army Group mainly to the south here – what they're calling "the long right hook". This lot from the south driving up the Rhone valley'll link up with them somewhere around . . . oh, Dijon, thereabouts. Paris in the middle of all that, but for the time being having to be left to look after itself, since what really matters is to break through the Siegfried Line and to the Rhine and over it.'

Willoughby put in, 'So the Germans in Paris will be

surrounded anyway, left as it were to wither on the vine.'

'But' – Hyatt, back on his chair, pointing again at the map – '*en route* to the Rhine, the enemy'll be trying to hold on in the region of Nancy-Metz-Saarbrücken-Strasbourg. In which area all Resistance and Maquis forces' locations, organisation and arms dumps are known to Rouquet and his pianist.'

'Yes.' Rosie nodded. 'Oh yes . . .'

She wondered again how those two had been trapped. In particular whether it had been anything to do with her. She hoped to God it hadn't. Looking across at Hyatt: 'Question I asked you in the car, if you remember—'

'The source of our information?'

'You said I'd be surprised.'

'You may be, too. Yet another old connection coming home to roost. Remember Pierre Cazalet?'

'Do I *not*! The perfume king – or queen.'

Marilyn put in, 'I remember in your debriefing you told us he had Hermann Goering's portrait in his drawing-room.'

'He does have – did have – some very highly placed friends.' Hyatt nodded. 'Including one I mentioned in our conversation earlier – Carl Boemelbourg, head of Gestapo Counter-Espionage, who has the same deviant sexual tastes as Pierre Cazalet. Which has helped to make our Pierre fairly safe – and very, *very* useful to us.'

Willoughby agreed: 'Oh, rather.'

'Our man, Frank, not SOE's.'

'But we've used him.'

'Only on our say-so. *We* directed Rosie to him, for instance, when she was doing that job for us. Doing it darned well, too. Anyway, Cazalet's gone *au vert*. Gave us notice the day before yesterday that he's ducking out – by then *had* ducked out, God knows where, and won't be surfacing again until the tumult and the shouting dies. Can't blame him, really – if the Boches don't have it in for him, the Resistance surely will. Of course we can clear him, if or when it comes to any sort of trial, but meanwhile—'

'Might get lynched.'

Rosie had said it. Having had similar thoughts about Jacqueline – a year ago, and resurrected now. Hyatt nodded. 'Hundreds will be. Thousands. Not only in Paris, all over France.'

'But *he* gave you the news of Rouquet and Léonie having been caught – only the day before yesterday?'

A nod. 'Guess who he had it from?'

'Boemelbourg?'

'Go to the top of the class, Rosie. Boemelbourg in a farewell chat or get-together prior to departure for Berlin. Mentioned to him that they'd arrested this pair in Nancy and brought them to Paris, that the info they possessed was of potentially great value and he was leaving them in the hands of Gerhardt Clausen, a young officer whom he held in high esteem. I'd guess that such a full spillage might have come from Cazalet asking him something like, "But if you and most of your boys are pulling out, Carl, what the heck?"'

'Clausen's not one of *them*, is he?'

'Far from it, surely.'

Rosie said drily, 'Ask Jacqueline. How did Cazalet get this message to you?'

'I'd better not tell you that . . . Oh, I suppose I can. A diplomatic channel. Totally reliable.'

'Neutral?'

'Of course. But now, where were we?'

Marilyn reminded him, 'We'd accepted that if Rosie's going to take this on at all, she'll go in via Rouen.'

Chapter 3

Rue de Fontenelle: long, straight and narrow, with old timbered house-frontages. This was the river end of the street where it ran north from the Quai du Havre. She'd crossed the Seine by a footbridge rigged on floating pontoons, close to the damaged or anyway closed-to-traffic Pont Jeanne d'Arc; there was a checkpoint manned by *Milice* at each end, but she hadn't been required to show her papers. The *Milice* were unspeakable: a force of paramilitaries set up by Laval as the Vichy security force in the then unoccupied south and which since then had spread all over. In many respects they were worse than their German counterparts: brutal, stupid, viciously anti-Semitic, and no matter what they got up to – murder, robbery, rape, protection rackets – the ordinary French police couldn't touch them.

On Rive Droite she'd mounted her bike and ridden west along the *quai*. There were barges tied up all along the Pont Guillaume-le-Conquérant as if repair work might be in progress or contemplated.

Jacqueline's *salon* was two blocks from the river, as she remembered it. Actually at this end of the third block – after crossing Rue St Jacques. Dismount before that, get a good look while passing, then turn and come back to it on that side. The place *might* be shut: depending on Jacqui's routine now. When she'd been spending her weekends in Amiens she'd shut down here from Friday noon to Monday noon. This was Thursday of course; and midweek, if she was spending any time at all in Rouen, might be the most likely. On the other hand, if civilian-carrying trains between here and Paris weren't running: although her boyfriend might provide road transport . . .

Didn't want to find her here, in any case. Only wanted to know where to find her in Paris. And the time now – 4.45, closing time probably 6 o'clock. She could see the place now: remembered those blue-striped curtains and the gilt sign over the door. The windows above were those of Jacqui's flat, which had its own street entrance up an alleyway at the side.

No way of telling whether the shop was shut or open. No lights showing – all right, probably wouldn't be, there'd be a lamp or two, no more than that – and no bicycles tethered to the railing on that side. Again, wouldn't be – unless they belonged to staff. Anyway, cross now – as if turning at the intersection with Rue Racine, but then head back towards the river – while unobtrusively checking on surroundings and movements. Why be taking this much trouble? The answer was – habit, when in the field. Training, experience, and an interest in remaining alive and free. One could have been recognised, followed – or for instance Ursule could be working for them now. You couldn't be *certain* of anything or anyone at all. Remembering David's – David Hyatt's – last-minute advice: 'Don't get to thinking that because it looks like they'll soon be booted out of France it's all over bar the shouting. They're still in place and will be for a while yet. Get caught and sent to Ravensbrück, Rosie – it's the same old Ravensbrück – you get sent there to be killed.' Another memory struck then: as she edged her bike over into the roadway, waiting then for a *gazo* to pass, as if intending to mount when it had done so but actually staying clear of a trio of SS troopers occupying the full width of pavement; remembering that she'd asked Guillaume Rouquet, 'Do you loathe them as much as I do?', and that he'd answered, 'Only the way you'd loathe cobras if you were in a house infested by them. Once we've cleared 'em out I doubt I'd give much thought to it.'

He might have changed his mind on that by now, she thought; might be viewing them much less philosophically. But was there a hope in hell, truly, of finding them – let alone getting them out?

Yes. Had to be. Bloody well *had* to be.

One of the SS had stared at her, was smirking back at her over his shoulder. The others then also looking round: laughing, clapping him on the back – the silly, barking laughter of brutish creatures *lacking* humour. Rosie seeing the start of it, then only sensing and bearing its continuance: having endured the same sort of thing often enough before. Waiting, watching other cyclists pass – and a pony and trap, two *gazos* – until the simple-minded oafs had gone out of sight and earshot. If they could only guess how utterly she detested them – or what she was here for – or that a year ago she'd killed one of their officers with a kitchen knife.

The Gestapo had it in her file, of course. Had photographs of her as well. If the file still existed . . . Frank Willoughby had mentioned during the re-briefing that in Paris in both Rue des Saussaies and Avenue Foch (numbers 82, 84 and 86, *Sicherdienst* headquarters) the Gestapo and SD had been burning files in their courtyards. That might be a blessing; although it was on the cards that they'd only been getting rid of paperwork from cases already closed, in which case files like her own might be retained. While in the same line of supposition, what might be the odds on rounding a corner and coming face to face with the Gestapo officer by name of Prinz – short, thick pig of a man, really quite Himmler-like – who after presiding over a series of extremely painful but ineffective preliminaries had stroked her bare breasts with one hand while advancing a pair of pliers towards her nipples with the other.

She'd know *him*, all right. Anywhere, any time. In fifty years' time or as long as she lived she'd know him.

Leaning her bike against the railings outside Chez Jacqui, she looped the chain through and padlocked it. Brushing herself off then, conscious of her own scruffiness and aware that Jacqui's customers tended to be well-heeled, well-dressed – therefore collaborators, or the wives of collabs . . .

Who'd have it coming, very soon. She pushed the glass door open and went in.

Jacqui had a male employee now. Slim, dark-haired, swarthy – Spanish-looking. He was stooped over one of the two customers who were being worked on. Three chairs, one unoccupied; odour of soap, scent, powder. No Jacqui. The other woman was being attended to by a girl in a light blue smock which matched the young man's jacket. She might be the one called . . . oh, Estelle, who'd been Jacqui's assistant here a year ago. It *was* her: very ordinary-looking, mousy-blonde, pudgy-faced, shapeless. Complete contrast to Jacqui, a contrast which had been heightened, Rosie remembered, by their having worn identical blue smocks – like the one Estelle wore now.

The customers were staring at her in their mirrors. Middle-aged, selfish faces showing resentment of this intrusion.

'Help you, mam'selle?'

Foreigner: *might* be Spanish. Rosie looked at the girl: 'I know you, don't I? It's some time since I was here, but – Estelle, isn't it?'

'How clever to remember. I likewise remember madame. I hope madame is well, and—'

'An appointment?'

She looked at the man, frowning, left it a second or two before telling him, 'It's Mademoiselle Clermont I came to see. Is she not—'

'In Paris, madame. She comes and goes, we don't know until we see her. The trains now, you know, they're—'

'Has she opened a branch in Paris?'

The two women looked at each other as if that was funny.

Rosie heard a murmur of, '*One* way of putting it.' Estelle began, 'No, madame, but she—'

'Comes and goes.' He'd cut Estelle short again. Telling Rosie, 'In her absence, I am the manager. My name is Joao. If you would care to leave with me your name and where she might find you if she so wishes . . . Madame' – addressing his customer – 'I am sorry to neglect you.' A glance at the clock and then at Rosie: 'If you'd excuse us?'

'Perhaps you'd give me an address or 'phone number in Paris?'

'Not possible. I regret . . .'

'Estelle – surely she'd have left an address with you?'

'Unfortunately not, madame. I'm truly sorry, but—'

'In Paris you might try the Hotel Meurice.' Estelle's customer had said it, watching her amusedly in the mirror. 'Or the Raphael or Trianon. I'm sure someone in one of those—'

'The Majestic or the Crillon, don't forget *them*!'

That had come from her friend, and they were both sniggering. Rosie shrugged: 'Don't get it. Never mind. I'll look in again, Estelle – but if you see or hear from her before that—'

'Of course, madame. I'm sure she'll be overjoyed . . .'

All five of those great hotels were among those taken over by the Germans as offices, messes and accommodation. The Meurice for instance, on Rue de Rivoli, was Staff Headquarters and residence of the new commander of Greater Paris, a General von Choltitz. Hyatt had told her yesterday, 'He flattened Stalingrad and razed most of Sevastopol. Sevastopol was his big thing. More recently he's had an army corps in Normandy. Very tough cookie, reputedly. One might deduce that the intention is to hold on to Paris at all costs – alternatively to destroy it – since the choice of that individual would have been made by Hitler personally, must reflect *his* intentions. Especially since after last month's bomb plot he distrusts practically all his generals.'

What those women had been implying was that wherever Jacqui was, she'd be with Germans. And the secrecy over her whereabouts meant she didn't want to be tracked down too easily. Understandable, considering that when the Boches pulled out or were driven out and the Resistance – FFI, *Forces Françaises de l'Intérieur* – came out into the open, known or identifiable collaborators would be in for a hard time – like being hanged or torn to pieces. As in the case of Pierre Cazalet, of course; and it was something Jacqui had been aware of a year ago, had been a factor in her agreeing to become an informant, establishing herself as an agent of British Intelligence, a claim which London would support.

Try the same line again. It was still entirely valid. In fact more so. Unlocking her bike, Rosie was thinking that on her own, away from the rather unpleasant Joao, Estelle might be more forthcoming. Knowing that she, Jeanne-Marie Lefèvre, was a friend of Jacqui's. They *must* have some way of contacting her in an emergency. The bombing for instance: one stray bomb in Rue de Fontenelle would be enough to set the whole street ablaze: wouldn't she want to know about it, have her moments of anxiety meanwhile? Anyway – 5 o'clock now – about an hour to wait. You'd get warning by seeing the customers leave first. There'd be cleaning and sweeping up to do then, and with luck those two wouldn't leave together; it was a fair bet that Joao would be the first out, leaving most of the chores to Estelle.

Six-twenty. Both those women had left, clacking away on their articulated wooden shoes. Both wobbly, overweight, well dressed and able to afford Chez Jacqui prices, almost certainly therefore the wives of collabs. Rosie was on the south side of Rue St Jacques, in the doorway of a derelict stone-built house; she had a slantwise view across the intersection to the Chez Jacqui shopfront. When passers-by had seemed to be taking interest in her she'd made a show of checking the time – *again* – and looking anxious, pondering whether to go on waiting for the bastard or give him up, go home . . .

She *was* anxious. A lot depended on Estelle. All of it, in fact, the whole justification for coming via Rouen, and chances of achieving anything in Paris. By the time they'd finished even Frank Willoughby had come to see the sense of doing it this way: but it was still a gamble.

Movement over there, where for a few moments she had not been looking. She'd been studying the remains of a poster exhorting young Frenchmen to join the LVF – *Légion des Volontaires Français.* Most of it had been ripped off the curve of stone wall, but as much as was left was recognisable; one had seen them everywhere, earlier on . . . But that movement had been the opening of Chez Jacqui's door – and emergence now of Joao. Standing there looking up and down the road, then turning back to push the door open and shout some instruction to Estelle. He'd now shut it again and was walking quickly northward, hands in pockets and leaning slightly forward. Habitual posture maybe for a hairdresser. In any case it saved trouble that he was going that way: she'd been ready to push her bike across this street and up into Rue Vieux Palais. Moving now in any case: a stout man in a suit who'd passed twice in the last ten minutes, both times taking obviously predatory interest in her, must have turned back again and this time would probably have addressed her. Was following, in any case – same heavy steps, scrape of heels. So if she turned at the next crossing and started back, as she'd been intending—

Tell him – waiting for a friend. *Be so good as to leave me alone, m'sieur . . .*

Tarts didn't push bikes around with them – did they?

Chez Jacqui's door jerked open again. Estelle, in a black-and-white checked jacket – and a perfectly timed appearance. Rosie called, 'Estelle!' and started over. 'Estelle – so glad to see you! That creature there following me . . .'

Creature had turned on its heel, was shambling back into

Rue St Jacques. Estelle primly indignant: 'I'd give him a good piece of my mind! Were you waiting for me, or—'

'Sort of. Came back up this way in the hope – might strike lucky. Couldn't talk freely in front of those others, could we? Especially Joao. What is he, a Spaniard?'

'Portuguese. We don't get on very well. Mademoiselle Jacqui found him in a salon in Paris where he was the star. She pays him very well, of course, but I don't think he likes it here and he has a dreadful temper.'

'Didn't Jacqui think of letting *you* run the show?'

'Well – no, she—'

A black Citroen – petrol-powered, therefore either German or *Milice* – swung out of Rue Racine close ahead of them, its engine slowing – more than it had already for the corner – and the driver braking, but then changing his mind: shifting gear, accelerating down towards the *quai*. She asked Estelle, 'You were saying – Jacqui didn't . . . what, think you were up to it?'

'She thought I was too young – that when I'm a little older I might become her manageress, and she'd like that, but—'

'Let's hope what's-his-name decides to go back to Paris, then.'

'I'm not sure I *could* do it. For instance, the control of staff, since one would need at least one other—'

'Might Jacqui come back? Does she still have her apartment over the shop?'

'Yes. When she's here she lives there, but – I don't know. The way the war's going – she doesn't agree with me, but surely the Allies might be here quite soon – and there'll be a great battle for Paris, won't there? Even for Rouen?'

'Perhaps. Although it looks as if the Boches are getting out. The roads today – heavens, you should have seen it! There'd been air attacks as well – in fact I was very lucky . . . Look, what about a coffee – or some supper? Come to think of it, I'm famished – and it would be nice to have your company, Estelle.'

'Well—'

She was checking the time. Rosie went on, 'Trying to remember – a café I used to eat in – on Rue Guillaume-le-Conquérant?'

'You mean the Brasserie Guillaume. Yes, that's not far – if we aren't *too* long—'

'It'll be my treat, of course . . .'

Vegetable soup, bread, cheese, so-called coffee. She persuaded the old waiter to allow them second helpings of the soup and more bread to go with it; as far as she was concerned it had been a fairly spartan day. The weekend too – they fed one well at Fawley Court but it had been a hard grind – until late on Monday, then all of Tuesday and literally from dawn to dusk yesterday, followed by take-off from Tempsford after moonrise. While here and now the question was whether by playing the sympathetic friend of Jacqueline Clermont she was going to worm an address or telephone number out of Estelle. Alternatively give up, push on to Paris empty-handed, with one *more* day down the drain.

Smiling at Estelle, at something she'd said. There couldn't be more than a year or two between them, but she was really very unsophisticated – young for her age and fairly dim. It was conceivable that if Jacqui had said her address in Paris was not to be divulged, Estelle would die at the stake sooner than divulge it.

'This is *so* kind of you.'

'Oh, shush!'

A giggle. 'Truly. And coming as such a surprise makes it even nicer. I'm looking forward to telling Mademoiselle Jacqui—'

'Better still, let *me* tell her.' A hand on Estelle's, on the iron table. 'Seriously – I mean privately, just between the two of us – you do have an address for her, don't you?'

'No – no, she—'

'It's very much in *her* interest, Estelle, that I should get in touch with her. For reasons which it's difficult – well, embarrassing – to go into—'

'But I couldn't – honestly . . .'

Eyes wide with alarm: and one knew now that she *did* have an address. Not, 'I haven't one, I swear it' but 'I couldn't give it to you, honestly.' And the fact that she was so upset about it. Rosie sighed. 'I'll risk the embarrassment – you've simply got to understand why it's vital. I should talk to her in Paris right away.' She was virtually whispering. 'Jacqui has a . . . well, a very close friend, let's call him – who's a German. I could tell you his name but I think you must know it. Huh? Must have known about him – Estelle?'

A nod: eyes down. 'It's why she doesn't want – well—'

'To be tracked down. Yes, I realise. On the other hand those women in your *salon* know all about it anyway – so what's the difference? I swear to you – if Jacqueline could have known I was coming, she'd *certainly* have wanted you to give me her address!'

'Yes. I suppose. But—'

'You said there'll be a battle for Paris, and you may be right, but there'll certainly be a rising *in* Paris, by the Resistance. I don't want to frighten you, but they won't only be killing Germans, they'll be hunting down collabos, won't they.'

'But she is *not* a—'

'In their eyes she is, and that's what matters. Those customers of yours knew all about Amiens a year ago, didn't they? Now *another* Boche lover – and SD, at that!'

No answer. Rosie followed up quickly: 'I can help her, you see. You might find it difficult to swallow, but I swear to you it's the honest truth. She may not realise how close the danger is – and *he's* not going to tell her – nor when the time comes will he be there to protect her. Even if that concerned him. *He'll* be all right – on his way with all the rest of them – but she'll be left, won't she . . . and with the mob out in the streets. I've come a long way to try to help her because I *have* to, I *owe* it to her!'

'You'd go to Paris now?'

'Of course!'

'But she made me *promise*—'

'First, this is to save her life. At least, save her from serious harm. Be clear about that. Second, I won't tell her I got the address from you. D'you have a telephone number, by the way?'

'No. She calls *us*. How else might you have got the address?'

The girl wasn't all *that* stupid. Rosie whispered, 'From another source which I can't discuss with you. Nothing to do with Rouen – I won't have been here, you won't come into it at all. If I haven't been here, how *could* you? But I can't discuss it, except to say she'll know what I'm talking about. The source of my information, I mean. Look – I'll tell you. *Strictly* between you and me, in the past year Jacqui has rendered certain services to the Resistance. I've been involved in it too. So happens, only a few people know about it, and none of them are in Paris, so I'm her witness – d'you understand? She may have to go into hiding for a while, but – *please*, Estelle . . .'

Chapter 4

Ben came up quickly from his chart-room into the gunboat's bridge. All four engines had stopped; he'd heard the skipper's order and the clink of the telegraphs only seconds before the abrupt cessation of that thunderous roar, and by the time he was in the bridge MGB *600* was already rolling more noticeably as she lost way, silence as well as fog closing in around her. The fog was no thicker than it had been when he'd gone below ten minutes earlier, but there wasn't a damn thing in sight.

Which of course was the answer. Nothing in sight even astern, where there should have been. OK, so it was still dark in any case – dark*ish* – but they'd had the Norwegian launch *Ekhorn* following at a distance of about a cable's length – 200 yards – with her bow-wave plain to see – through binoculars, at least – and now damn-all, only the heaving surface of the Norwegian Sea with the fog lying on it like oily wool. If the *Ekhorn* had been anything like in station – two or three cables astern, say, if she'd only dropped back a bit – she'd have been up with them by now, surely. Visibility was about a cable and a half, two cables at most, and the reason for stopping would have been (a) to let the Norwegian catch up, (b) to listen, get a bearing on the sound of his engines.

Mike Hughes had glanced at Ben and shaken his head. Glasses at his eyes again then, continuing the search. He'd been CO of this motor gunboat in the Dartmouth flotilla when Ben had been her navigating officer – a bloody age ago – running agents and cargoes of weaponry on moonless nights to French Resistance groups in Brittany. Had landed Rosie once – *and* brought her off again. Never guessing how temporary a blessing that would prove to be – Rosie having been shot dead beside some railway line in Alsace a couple of months ago.

All right, so this was no time for wallowing in private misery. It just happened to be there all the time – in or at the back of any other thinking. They'd only broken the news to him three weeks ago, at a meeting in the SOE building in Baker Street: there'd been a girl called Lise present who'd been with Rosie only seconds before they'd shot her down. Rosie had made a target of herself so that Lise could get away.

With no way on now, *600* was rolling hard. Mike Hughes pushing back his battered, salt-stained cap. 'Could've sworn I heard her – just as we stopped engines . . .'

'Thought I did too, sir.' Nick Ball, that was. In the Dartmouth flotilla days he'd been a sub-lieutenant and MGB *600*'s boat officer, meaning that one of his jobs had been the rowing ashore in a dinghy of agents and cargoes, and bringing off agents who were returning. He was a lieutenant now and Hughes' second-in-command; there was a lad by name of Cummings in his old job. He'd added, 'Could've been aircraft passing, I suppose.'

Hughes said, checking the time, 'Give it two minutes, then we'll check back a mile or two in case he broke down.' *He* referring to the *Ekhorn*'s skipper – Nils Iversen. Glancing at Ben then: 'We know where *we* are, I take it?'

'Near enough.' The joky question hardly merited a 'sir' in response. Ben did put one in occasionally – after all Hughes was the gunboat's captain, despite he and Ben being of the same rank now, both lieutenant-commanders. Mike was older anyway, had been a solicitor in practice before the war when Ben had been struggling to become a painter, keeping the wolf from the door in Paris by taking on any work he could get, such as washing dishes in those very grand hotels – which one had heard were now all occupied by the creatures who'd killed Rosie. He added to Hughes, 'In forty minutes, fog permitting, I'd have expected to pick up the Ytteroerne light-structure. However Ytteroerne's pronounced.' Looking round at Jens Vidlin, the Norwegian who'd be their inshore pilot and contact-man with shore-based agents. Short, stocky, bearded, in a woollen hat, sweater, baggy trousers stuffed into seaboots: didn't talk much, probably because his English was so limited, didn't correct Ben's pronunciation of Ytteroerne either. Ben checked the time and told Hughes, 'Your two minutes are up.'

'Right. All engines slow ahead. Bring her round to port, Cox'n. Course, Ben?'

'Two-six-four, sir.'

Chief Petty Officer Ambrose spun his wheel anti-clockwise. He was another old hand in this boat; had been coxswain – as a petty officer – in Ben's day, was now a Chief PO with (Ben had noticed back in Lerwick) a Distinguished Service Medal.

Hughes said, 'We'll stay at these revs.' Ambrose easing wheel and rudder as *600* swung. Possible outcome of this manoeuvre might be to find the *Ekhorn* and either take her in tow or stand by her while her crew completed repairs – very swiftly, one might hope. Daylight wasn't far off, the fog might lift quite suddenly, and if the *Ekhorn* was still immobilised she'd be natural prey to German aircraft. All right, *600* could put up a reasonably good defence – but not for ever, not if the *Luftwaffe* decided really to get into it. The *Ekhorn* had only a couple of Lewis guns. You were 180 miles from base – Lerwick in the Shetlands – and with the nights in these latitudes still too short for comfort, the intention had been to make a quick dash over and be tucked away under camouflage inside the fjord well before the dawn.

Might not be achievable now.

They all had their glasses up, searching. Ben, Hughes, Ball, Cummings, Vidlin too, as well as lookouts at the bridge's after end. The 291 radar wasn't in operation – wasn't much use anyway, certainly couldn't be relied on, and this near to the coast might have been detectable. MGB *600* was making about ten knots on her four engines at these low revs, the sea curling away in a great V from her bow but its surface hardly broken, only a light-coloured sizzle of it close to the boat's stern. Despite which she was still making enough racket to be audible at least a mile away. Which was what made one think the *Ekhorn* must be lying stopped. While a sideline to the risk of being caught by enemy aircraft was that *600* was carrying a deck-cargo of 100-octane petrol in drums, for the *Ekhorn*. It was a large part of the reason she (*600*) was here at all; the intention was for *Ekhorn* to lie up in a number of different locations along this coast over the next two or three weeks while Nils Iversen made a survey of German guard-posts and defence arrangements – from here to maybe as far north as Kristiansund – and she wouldn't have had anything like the endurance – fuel capacity – without this additional reserve.

You'd be serving other purposes as well. Landing weapons and explosives for the Norwegian Resistance, and bringing back to Lerwick two escaped prisoners and some SOE or SIS agents who were in hiding, awaiting pick-up. The escapers were in particular danger, as the Gestapo were hunting them. MTB crewmen, one Norwegian and one British, a telegraphist – who if they hadn't managed to escape from some nearby prison camp would already have been shot – as presumably their shipmates *had* been.

By order of the Führer. Men landing on the coasts of occupied countries, or captured in territorial waters, were to be shot out of hand as 'pirates', even when in uniform and engaged in legitimate military operations.

One certainly didn't want to hang around.

'Five minutes gone, sir.'

Ball had said that. Hughes told Vidlin, speaking slowly and clearly for the Norwegian to understand, 'We go on into fjord.' Pointing north-eastward. Even at this speed *600* was rolling quite hard. Vidlin shrugging, gazing out into the fog and shaking his head, worried for his friends. Hughes added, 'Sorry. Nothing else for it.' To Ambrose then, 'Bring her back to oh-eight-four, Cox'n.'

'Oh-eight-four, aye aye—'

'Half ahead all engines.'

Ball jerked the telegraphs over, the engine-room responded and you felt the surge of power as the inner pair of engines joined in and the revs built up, driving her back up towards her cruising speed of 21 knots. Ben checking sea and sky, quality of light and fog. Telling himself they might just make it. Even poor old *Ekhorn* might. Depending on how badly lost or broken down she was, and how alert the Krauts might be. Then for *600*, how efficiently Jens Vidlin piloted her in between the holms and skerries, and how good a lying-up place it turned out to be when you did get in there. MGB *600* was carrying a considerable bulk of camouflage netting lashed down on her forepart, and another lot aft (with Vidlin's 16-foot, double-ended Norway fjord-type dinghy secured upside-down on top of it), but if patrols were active, and with the locations of lookout-posts unknown – after the four months of no darkness, therefore no visits by either Norwegian Navy or Shetland Bus craft – hence the need for an up-dating survey by Iversen and his crew; you'd need all the camouflage you could get.

He told himself, on his way back down to his little chart-room, that the *Ekhorn* – Norwegian for 'squirrel' – *might* be perfectly all right. Might for instance have gone off course and passed them while they'd been motoring slowly back westward: ahead of them now, wondering where the hell *they'd* got to . . .

Chart-work now. Starting from where they'd been at the point of stopping, and estimating the time and distance lost, the small northerly drift of current and the fact that both turns had been made to seaward. Finding the entrance to one particular fjord on this rock-bound stretch of coast, rock-littered and islet-studded, you needed a fairly high standard of navigational accuracy. Before long, he thought, pencilling a new dead-reckoning position on the chart and extending their course from it, soon enough one *might* – depending on the fog, which admittedly was rather like wanting to have one's cake and eat it – *should* spot that Ytteroerne lighthouse or light structure – not light, none of those lights were lit – and having spotted it, touch wood, not long after that be able to put Vidlin's nose to the ground, so to speak, at a point where he'd feel himself at home.

After getting his knee smashed, Ben's desk job had been in the offices in St James's Street of a naval department called NID(C), which amongst other things controlled the Dartmouth-based gunboat flotilla's clandestine operations in landing agents and munitions on the Brittany coast. The departmental head was known as DDOD(I), which stood for Deputy Director Operations Division brackets Irregular, and his brief was to cater for the sea-transport requirements of both SIS and SOE.

Ben's immediate boss, a commander by name of Charlie Cranmer, had drifted into his office a few days ago and asked casually, 'Care to put in a spot of sea time, Ben?'

Everyone in the department knew he'd been putting in application after application to get back to sea, and in the same endeavour given up using a stick and made efforts not to limp. Cranmer also knew of Rosie's death and its effect on him.

Ben had glanced at the calendar. 'Not April Fool's day . . .'

'Remember Hughes, your CO in MGB *600*?'

'Of course.'

'He's at Lerwick – with *600* – on temporary detachment to help out in an emergency that's arisen. You know of the so-called Shetland Bus operations?'

'Heard of them – that's about all. But they use fishing-boats, don't they?'

Running agents and cargoes into Norway and bringing out refugees. They were fishermen, not Norwegian Navy men, highly independent characters, splendid seamen who knew the fjords intimately.

'They're reorganising. Have been since the season finished in the spring. Season of the midnight sun closes them down for the summer, you know. As it happens, the fishing-boat operation's more or less had its day – they lost five boats and crews last winter and early spring, Jerries are making it almost impossible by banning the larger legit fishing craft – so theirs stand out like sore thumbs – and so on. They're switching, believe it or not, to US Navy sub-chasers – small enough for the fjords, fast enough for the long hauls, well able to defend themselves – in fact ideal. Three have arrived so far – from Miami, brought over as deck cargo and put together on the Clyde, American base at Roseneath. That's where the Shetland Bus lot are now – retraining, pretty fundamentally of course. Norwegian Navy personnel seem to have got themselves in on the act too. So on this particular job, MGB *600*'s filling the breach. With not much doing on the Brittany coast now – as you know – also since she's just completed a major refit—'

'This particular job being?'

'Escorting a Norwegian-manned launch – Shetland Bus people, one gathers – to some fjord about a hundred miles north of Bergen, landing the usual sort of cargo – also cased patrol for the Norwegians' use – and bringing off some escapers. It's not the season yet for such shenanigans, but at a pinch they reckon it can be done.' Ben had seen Cranmer touch the wooden arm of his chair. Adding then, 'The bit about escapers is from SIS, who had it from their man in

Oslo – hue and cry along that coast, urgent to get the blokes out double-quick, et cetera.'

'Where do I come in?'

'Hughes lacks a navigator. Over the scrambler from Lerwick he mentioned this, and asked, "Don't suppose Ben Quarry's around and at a loose end, is he?"'

'Kind thought, too. But Lerwick's a fair stretch, and if it's so urgent—'

'Sleeper tonight to Aberdeen, and fly from there. Little machine takes two passengers – head-in-air, Biggles stuff – Aberdeen to Sumburgh. That's on Shetland.'

'And is it OK? Does the Old Man know?'

'Knows and approves. Reckons a break might do you good.'

'Well, good on him! On you too, you must've—'

'A short break is all it will be. It's a one-off, obviously – just helping out. Your rank and experience, after all . . .'

He'd picked up the Ytteroerne light structure at a range of about three miles, recognising it by the sketch in the *South Norway Sailing Directions* and coming round at once to due north to stay clear of rocks shown on the chart. Vidlin had agreed: that was Ytteroerne, sure. But those rocks weren't anything to worry about, you had deep water there, could pass within an oar's length of them. Same on the west side of Frojen – a smallish island – and Bremanger, a large one, mountainous – on the north side of which was the way into Nordfjord. Dawn was about to rear its ugly head by this time, but mercifully the fog still hung around; in the bridge they were all living through their eyes, searching with binoculars not only for the *Ekhorn* but for enemy patrols. In the plot – chart-room – Ben had the windows covered and a spotlight on a gooseneck bracket pulled down low to the chart; there was virtually no spillage of light even into the rest of the little closet-sized compartment.

He'd had Rosie in here with him, twice. Once soon after

they'd sailed from Dartmouth, and then again for 10 or 15 minutes before bringing the boat in to land her at a Breton pinpoint called L'Abervrac'h. Getting to know her again, picking up the threads – trying to, in just minutes, after not having seen her for a whole damn year. Hadn't known she was coming with them until she'd shown up, escorted by Marilyn Stuart, just before departure time. Rosie's curvy little figure contrasting with the beanpole beside her – charming beanpole, attractive enough in her way, but . . . Rosie just happened to be – well, quietly sensational. Should be thanking God, he recognised, for having known her even for the short time – times – they'd had together. Known, loved, been loved by her. Absolutely bloody wonderful, every single minute – as long as the times had lasted, as long as you'd had reason to hope – pray – they'd start again.

Vidlin said – beside him at the chart and pointing with a pencil-tip at Nordfjord somewhere near its entrance – 'Here, OK.' Pencil tracing the length of it, then: 'Here, no good.'

'Right, cobber.' Looking at him – at the brown, spaniel's eyes. Brown eyes, weather-tanned face, shaggy blond head and beard. Ben was re-growing his own beard, at least, he'd begun to. He added, 'Won't be going that far up anyway.' He tried again: 'There, *not* go.'

'*Ekhorn* go. I say not good. I *knowing* this.'

'Because of patrols and lookout posts.'

'Sure. Here,' – the fjord entrance – 'to here' – the head of the fjord, roughly – 'kilometre, *so* many.' Pencilling figures on the margin of the chart: 80, 90 . . . Stab of a blunt forefinger: '*Ekhorn* here maybe. Trysker I think *here*.'

'Trysker meaning Germans?'

'Sure.' A thin pencil line across the width of the fjord. '*Ekhorn* finish, huh?'

If she wasn't finished already. But that was a point Hughes had raised in discussion with Nils Iversen – that escapers were more likely to be safely embarked if they made their way to the seaward ends of fjords or better still offshore islands. If the rescuing boat had to put itself at the wrong end of a fjord which might then become very difficult to get out of, it wasn't improving the escapers' chances any more than its own. Iversen had said he agreed, but on this trip for some reason had no option.

His business. Not Mike Hughes', and certainly not Ben's. The Norwegian knew a lot more about it than either of them did. But then, Jens Vidlin wasn't exactly a stranger to the business. Ben shrugged mentally; until one knew what had happened to the *Ekhorn* one couldn't be sure the question was going to arise in any case.

He reached for a packet of Senior Service, offered it to the Norwegian. 'Smoke?'

Shake of the head. Clink of the bridge telegraph then, on the heels of Hughes' voice ordering the inners stopped. On the outer screws only therefore, and revs falling sharply: *slow* ahead on outers. Ben on his way up – into half-light and the lingering fog, Hughes and Ball hunched with glasses at their eyes, Bremanger a towering dark mass to starboard and Hughes telling Ben, 'Patrol – *there.* Trawler, coming out of *our* fjord, cheeky sod.' Then: 'Come five degrees to port, Cox'n.'

Holding her bow-on of course to minimise her exposure to the German. End-on, there'd be very little for him to see. You could thank God for the fog, and thank Vidlin for the fact that they were so close in, in the shadow of this mass of rock shielding them from light in the eastern sky. Without the Norwegian's advice about the steep-to nature of the coastline Ben would have taken a wider sweep at it. Engine-noise meanwhile had fallen considerably: not only from lower speed and the centre engines out of it, Hughes must have told his PO Motor Mechanic to engage the dumbflows – silencers. Only a *muffled* thunder now. Ben had the trawler in his glasses: definitely a trawler profile, with a gun mounted conspicuously on its foc'sl. Probably a four-point-one. Moving slowly from right to left with a flicker of white at the forefoot – making six or eight knots, he guessed. The big question now was which way it would be turning, having cleared the fjord. If to starboard – away – fine, but if to port – well, rather less so. MGB *600*'s guns would all be manned – Ball had been passing orders, and there'd been a swift movement of men on deck – and the German wasn't likely to come off best; but the last thing one wanted here and now was a scrap of any kind. Besides which, when you were below your draught-marks with the weight of 100-octane in drums all over the upper deck, it wouldn't take more than one hit from that gun—

'Stop both outers.'

Getting too close. So now just drifting. With your fingers crossed, begging that bloody thing to turn away to *starboard* . . .

Chapter 5

A hundred and forty kilometres, ninety-two-and-a-half miles: the figures clicking around in her head as she rode, encouraging herself with optimistic estimates of distance covered but having to make a couple of rather chancy detours to avoid the worst blockages of slow-rolling or actually stalled *Wehrmacht* transport. Those were in the first few hours out of Rouen – Louviers for instance, which she remembered from the day before as particularly bloody, and around Vernon, beyond which for a longish stretch she was blinded by the sun still low and in her eyes – and reluctantly accepting that rather than 92 miles it was going to end up as 100 at the very least. With, from time to time, rumbles of gunfire, she guessed at no great distance. Apart from that it was like a re-run of yesterday – could have been the same trucks, same exhausted-looking soldiery staring out grimly over their tailboards. Maybe grimmer, closer to the reality of their situation, fewer of the shouts and offensive gestures. She'd started out soon after first light, actually within minutes of curfew lifting – as advised by Ursule, who'd been up at cock-crow in her purple dressing-gown to provide a breakfast of porridge, ersatz coffee and an apple; she'd also sold her half of a large cabbage and a chicken – by no means cheaply, but that didn't matter, as she had plenty of SOE money in the lining of her suitcase; it was a scrawny old bird that might have died of old age and/or starvation. She had those and her water bottle in the panier on the handlebars, wrapped in old copies of *Le Matin* and the more overtly collab paper *Aujourdhui*, which Ursule told her had ceased publication – as had several of the weekly rags including *Au Pilori*, *Signal*, *Je Suis Partout* and all those other filthy tracts with their savage anti-Jewish and anti-Gaullist diatribes. It was heartening to think of all those proprietors and editors on the run, vanishing (or hoping to) into the *paysage* – or the sewers, which might well be their rightful home. These week-old copies, though, she'd have had with her when she'd left Paris to forage in the countryside for sustenance for her little girl and the old woman, whom she'd left half-starving in some rented hovel in Montmartre. There was a café there, the Chien Bleu, which was where she had to meet her FFI contact, Georges Dénault, who had red hair and a limp and worked in the ticket office at the Gare de l'Est. It made sense to plant the child and its grandmother in that same district; until she got there they – and the chicken – would be her cover, notionally. And once she *had* got there, she'd be scouring the streets for them. It was an uncomplicated, believable and reasonably flexible cover story.

A third diversion pushed her into more of a detour than she'd expected. By way of Beynes, and southward then it seemed interminably, over a railway crossing to a place called Le Pontel where at last she was able to turn east again. At the intersection where she'd been forced to divert southward, Boche tanks had been deploying on both sides across the hayfields. If one had had a transceiver – and of course a battery for it, which travelling by bike one would *not* have had – might have stopped in some copse or ditch and told someone about it. Anyway . . . all of 10 or 12 kilometres to cover before getting to Le Pontel, which when she got there she found was yet another interlocked confusion of Boche transport – in which she had the best of reasons not to get held up, one being the strong possibility of air attack: and very much as she had at one stage yesterday she found another way out, a minor road leading – again – more or less east. This had turned out to be another wide detour though: as she began to appreciate when after another dozen or so kilometres she found herself passing St Cyr, not far short of Versailles. Needing, if she was going to make it into Paris by way of the Porte d'Auteuil, to head up north-eastward – making more for St Cloud than for Sèvres. Anything to the left, therefore . . . Reason for entering via Porte d'Auteuil being that it would bring her in close to the Bois de Boulogne and the 16th *Arrondissement*, in which Jacqueline's flat according to Estelle was in a cul-de-sac off Rue de Passy. She had a name for the house but no number, and there'd be 2 or 3 kilometres of road to search unless she struck lucky early on. The name of the house was Le Clos de Fretay, which sounded fairly grand. If the route she had in mind worked out – she'd studied it on the map by candle-light at Ursule's this morning, a map published recently by the War Office and based on a pre-war street guide – she'd be starting at the top end anyway: Porte d'Auteuil, then Boulevard Suchet all the way to the Ranelagh Gardens, and from there due south. *Should* then be near enough on target. Intention being only to locate the house so as to be able to go straight to it later – tomorrow, early. Secure one's base first – primarily, find the Chien Bleu in Montmartre and get in touch with Georges Dénault, Hyatt's FFI man, and find some lodging – possibly that same pub. Pinpoint Jacqui and Clausen first, anyway, then to Montmartre – 7 kilometres as the crow flew, say perhaps 10 by bike.

And thereafter use the Métro? As long as it was running. Willoughby had said the last they'd heard was that on most lines there was a train about every 15 minutes *when* the power was on, on which you had to take your chances: an example of which was that the few theatres still open were using candles on stage, and cinemas had all shut. Re lack of Métro, though, in terms of the days ahead, to bicycle 5–10 miles when one had *not* covered 100 miles since dawn mightn't be so terrible.

Think about that in the morning anyway. Having been stiff enough *this* morning. Mightn't be able to bloody *move*.

After circling Versailles, she set a course north-eastward: facing about an hour of that. Thinking in terms of setting courses derived naturally from Ben, and brought him back to mind: not that he was ever far out of it. Wondering again what the rescue mission might be, in Norway; and how they'd let him, semi-crippled as he still was, go back to sea on anything, anywhere, in any capacity at all. Needing a stick just to get along a London pavement, how could he get around a motor gunboat crossing the Norwegian Sea?

I'm not dead, Ben. Won't get to be, either, if I can help it. Mind you come back in one piece, you bastard!

(Epithet justified by a vision of the Stack woman also awaiting his return.)

Through lack of concentration towards the end of that hour she almost missed a further course-alteration to the right which would surely have brought her to the Porte St Cloud. Telling herself that she wanted Auteuil, not St Cloud; but seconds later – at the last moment – realising that *would* be the best way and swinging off too late, entering the turn-off pretty well in the middle of the road, even somewhat over on the left, having then to dodge back across a lot of horn-blowing and waving fists, probably screams of rage. It paid off anyway – a kilometre ahead, no more, she was coming to the great river and to a bridge. Pont St Cloud? Go left there, then: over the bridge and—

Damn. Control point. Poles on trestles, and *Schutzpolizei* stopping vehicles. All right, didn't *matter* – thanks to her papers and the chicken. Which she'd noticed was beginning to smell a bit. Then as she got nearer she saw they weren't stopping bicycles. Perhaps because they were all *Schutzpolizei*, had none of the usual back-up of gendarmes and were thus short-handed. She looked questioningly at one of them as she passed close to him, letting him see she'd be quite happy to stop and show her papers if he wanted her to. He didn't, anyway; and she rode on through – then did have to stop, waiting to turn left; after which the river was on her left, and with this bit of the map in mind knowing that ahead of her was Longchamp and the Bois de Boulogne. Longchamp being on the great park's western side. A kilometre or maybe two. Paris in front of her and the sun a glow of heat up there on her right. Chicken warm to the hand, inside its wrapping of newsprint. Traffic surprisingly thin here. Plugging on and keeping her mind on what mattered now – not making any more daft mistakes. Reminding herself that after passing Longchamp and turning left from Porte d'Auteuil, the steeple-chase course would be about 3 kilometres ahead – eastern side of the Bois, so that by turning on to the Boulevard Suchet she'd then have it on her left all the way to Porte de Passy. Then right-handed, for a change – leaving Suchet, turning down into the Ranelagh Gardens, eastward down through the middle of them . . .

Getting towards 5 o'clock. Had been on the road therefore for 12 hours. Felt like it too. Pedalling slowly now, looking for culs-de-sac. Rue de Passy houses tended to be set well back from the road. As yet, though, not even one cul-de-sac. Several intersections and side-roads leading off at various angles.

There . . .

She'd passed it. High-walled and with tall double gates at the end of it, one of them standing open, the house creeper-covered and also tall, behind some kind of monument – statues, she thought, but had gone too far, had only caught a glimpse of it and was having to wait now to let a *gazo* van pass. Then, U-turn. Grey ivy-covered wall, and a thicket of trees on its other side, right up to the corner of the cul-de-sac into which she rode slowly. Looking for but not seeing any house name. On this one gate half of a coat of arms was visible, surmounted by half a coronet: the other halves of both were on the part that was open.

Dilemma: whether to accept that this was the house – so turn back out into the road and ride on, next point of aim Montmartre – or to nose around a bit, make sure.

The open gate inclined one to take a closer look.

Fine house. Light grey stone façade, beautifully proportioned windows, attractive wrought-iron balconies, slate roof with a graceful curve in it. A number of enormous chimneys. At ground level here, balustraded steps under an ornate *porte-cochère* leading up to double doors – what looked like mahogany. She was inside the gates by this time, still on the bike but stopped with one foot down on the gravel, seeing that the driveway encircled an area of grass with an ornamental pond and fountain which if it had been running would have been sluicing down on three nude stone girls grouped with their backs to it, arms linked and breasts uplifted.

If the fountain had been running, might have been tempted to join them.

Hold on, though. Beyond and to the right of that group – a dark grey Citroen Light Fifteen, close to the right-hand front corner of the house. The kind of Citroen that had always been Gestapo officers' favoured form of transport. That colour, too, as often as not – grey or black. She'd seen quite a few of them in recent years, and if she'd spotted it sooner wouldn't have come this far in.

So drift off. Unhurriedly but wasting no time. It would be Clausen's, obviously; he must have come home early. He was SD, not Gestapo, but that made no difference; Gestapo and SD worked hand in glove, and it was the Gestapo chief Boemelbourg who'd delegated to Clausen the interrogation of those prisoners.

As soon as she'd seen the car she'd dismounted, was on the point of dragging her bike around in order to remount and take off – job done, this was the love-nest all right – when a voice called, 'Allow me to drive out first, mam'selle?'

She'd looked round, startled. Gratingly high voice from a

tall and – at first sight and at that distance of 15–20 yards – perhaps rather good-looking man. Fashionably cut light grey suit, trilby hat. Tall, wide-shouldered. But that awful voice . . . He was on the steps, descending slowly, watching her as she obligingly slanted across to the side of the drive that was blocked by the closed half of the gate, where she'd be out of his car's way. Not that he was exactly hurrying to get into it – whoever the hell he was. He certainly *thought* he was something, was her impression. But two other men had got out of the car – must have been sitting there all this time, watching her. She'd seen enough of them in one glance to feel uncomfortable: they were thugs, bodyguards or somesuch.

The high voice again: 'Have you come to the wrong address, perhaps? Can I direct you?'

'No – thank you—'

'What are you doing here?'

Challenging, even threatening expression. Definitely was French. Some Boches spoke the language well, but usually with some of the dregs of their own harshness in it. This one's accent in fact was brashly Parisian, working-class. He certainly wasn't hurrying to the car. The others were waiting beside it but he was approaching *her*.

'Well?'

A *Milice* colonel, or somesuch? But he – *they* – would surely have been in uniform . . .

She shrugged. 'Only visiting. Is there some reason for your interest, m'sieur?'

Whatever authority he carried or thought he carried, it was better to seem aloof than nervous or too respectful. On the other hand her own accent was definitely not working-class, and one didn't want to seem over-conscious of that difference. The other two – one at the front of the car, the other holding a rear door open – were more roughly dressed and had coarser features. Both wore leather jackets. The high-voiced one had glanced round at them, now looked back at her. A smile: 'Don't worry, they won't hurt you.' He laughed

– presumably at that would-be reassuring statement – like a dog-owner whose animals did frighten people at first sight. Then: 'Visiting, you say?'

'Yes. If it concerns you – looking for a friend who I believe lives here.'

'Name of?'

'Well.' Instinct told her that it was actually important not to seem scared. Very much like facing untrustworthy dogs. She shook her head: 'It need really be no concern of yours, m'sieur.'

'Name of this friend?'

That *had* been a threat. A shout, and higher-pitched than before. Reminiscent of interrogations in quite different circumstances and surroundings; and it would be natural now to show – confusion, at least. Shaking her head again, bewildered: telling him with a quick glance at those others – who were alert now, if they'd been dogs they'd have been growling – 'As you're so insistent, m'sieur – it happens I'm looking for Mademoiselle Jacqueline Clermont. Who I'm sure you wouldn't—'

'I know her very well. And of course, if she's a friend of yours – what's your name?'

'Jeanne-Marie Lefèvre. But *is* she—'

'Up there.' A gesture towards the upper part of the house, as he came right up to her. He'd been closing in towards her all this time. She didn't like his face – rather long, pointed nose, small round eyes . . . Telling her, 'Up two flights and there's a bell-push.' He put his hand out: she tried to touch it only lightly, but it closed on hers. 'If you're a friend of Jacqui's – well . . .' Smiling – his manner altogether softer, an implication of 'then you're a friend of mine.' Asking her as she got her hand back, 'Have you come far on that thing?' A slightly humorous enquiry, perhaps faintly contemptuous, but with none of the previous bullying tone. And looking at her mouth – as men tended to. *Damn* him. She told him – giving him the story she had ready for Clausen – 'From

Nantes, to start with, and from there to Dijon, where some people I've been looking for might have gone, but hadn't, so now it's Paris.'

'No difficulty getting here from Dijon? No military interference?'

'Not really.' Pausing, as if wondering why she was answering his questions. She shrugged: 'In fact to come by this route I found my way round by way of Fontainebleau and – oh, Sèvres, then Porte St Cloud.'

'Just like that. With the Americans as close as Rambouillet. Did you know?'

'A truck-driver did warn me. Well – Rambouillet, no, I didn't. I suppose that *is* close.' Shake of the head: 'Certainly I didn't see any.'

'But you got lifts along the way?'

'Only that one – from Fontainebleau to Fresnes.'

'Fresnes, huh?'

Where the prison was. Run by the Gestapo. She'd been an inmate not long ago. Looking now – she hoped – as if it meant nothing to her, Fresnes only a place she'd come through and which the truck-driver might have named. She was aware that this creature still hadn't bothered to tell her who he was. Ask Jacqui – ask her, 'Who's that schizophrenic hanging around down there?' A thought then – that he *might* be, that the other two might be not his bodyguards but his keepers. He'd been stooping over her, crane-like, during this exchange, but straightened now, checking the time.

'We'll meet again, perhaps. Jacqui won't put you up, you know.' Looking at her tatty suitcase on the carrier: having already given the old raincoat the once-over. 'Do you have somewhere to stay in Paris?'

'Yes. In Vincennes.'

'Better hurry, then. If you want to be off the streets before curfew – which I'd advise.'

'May I ask who you are, m'sieur?'

'Oh, just a friend of Gerhardt Clausen. And thus also of

Jacqui's, naturally.' A hand to his hat: 'A pleasure meeting you – mam'selle.'

She wasn't going anywhere near Vincennes. Had thought of it as a possibility during the Fawley briefing, through remembering two middle-aged ladies, sisters, whom she'd met on a train arriving in Paris a year ago, after landing in Brittany from Ben's gunboat. Having elicited that she was a stranger in the capital they'd very kindly offered her a bed for the night and added after she'd made excuses, 'Well – any time', giving her their address and surname – which she'd kept in mind, thinking it might one day come in useful, and that it mightn't be a bad idea to lodge with people who had no contact with anything illicit. But Vincennes was definitely too far out from the centre, especially if one couldn't count on the Métro running.

She'd have to call on Jacqui now, though – since that man would most likely mention to her (and Clausen) that he'd met her. To have been here and *not* called in on her old friend, after coming so far out of her way to do so – well, Jacqui was no fool, and Clausen had to be fairly sharp. Brief call, therefore – make contact, break ice (if any) and arrange later meeting.

Not *much* later. Thinking of Léonie, as she settled the strap of Léonie's bag more comfortably over her shoulder. She'd chained her bike to the iron balustrade under the *porte cochère* and taken her suitcase off it, to bring that up with her too. The chicken could take its chances. The Citroen had driven out – fast – its leather-jacketed driver either needing to make up time or showing off.

As either of those two might. That stupid look: brutes with the mental age of children. Tyres spurting in gravel *would* appeal to them. While as for the tall one . . .

Friend of Jacqui's?

Very spacious hallway, marble-tiled and with small stained-glass windows that didn't let much light in; beamed ceiling and wide central staircase. Climbing it, she wondered whether that one's business was actually with Jacqui or with Clausen. Logic suggested the latter, but with no other car out there, Clausen presumably *not* at home . . .

Climbing: and feeling it in her legs. Two whole bloody days' cycling – on top of a lot else, in recent weeks and months. At Fawley Court one hadn't really foreseen the extent of it, with so much else to think about, as there had been. And in any case, really no alternative; plus the fact that on previous deployments one had made even longer trips.

The landing on the second floor wasn't carpeted or furnished as the one below was. There was only a pile of empty wine-boxes near the top of the stairs, no doubt put there to be collected. 'Saumur', she saw stencilled on one box, and 'Graves' on another. The door from the landing to the flat was of plain, new-looking wood. On closer inspection, oak: and definitely new, with that sawdust smell.

Pressing the bell, she heard it ring – faintly, as at some considerable distance – and then no other sound. Jacqui did have to be in there, though; the man with the high voice would have had no reason to say she was if she wasn't.

Might be in the bathroom – following his visit?

Nasty mind, Rosie.

But *something* stank, with that one. Merely to have that type of car – and manner.

Female voice, thin through the timber of the door: 'Who is it?'

'Jacqui?'

'Who—'

'Remember Jeanne-Marie Lefèvre?'

No answer. She tried again, after a pause: 'Or someone called Rosalie?'

A bolt was withdrawn; then maybe another. A year ago she'd given Jacqui her own real name, Rosalie, as a password to be used by any other agent calling to pick up whatever intelligence Jacqui might have gleaned from pillow-talk in Amiens. A key turned, finally, and the door opened by about six inches, coming up against a chain.

'Jacqui.'

'I really will be damned . . .'

'May I come in?'

'Not stay long – unless you want to meet Gerhardt again?'

'I *can't* stay long.' The chain was off and she was in. 'Would he remember me, d'you think?'

'Don't know. But he has a good memory. And you haven't changed at *all*, Rosalie.'

'Haven't I, indeed? Certainly *you* haven't.' Smiling at her darkly Mediterranean good looks. Her mother had been (or was) Italian. Lovely figure – in a green summer dress that hadn't been designed to hide it; longish dark hair swept back, marvellous eyes and beautiful skin. 'As ravishing as ever. Incidentally, though, I'm Jeanne-Marie, not Rosalie. Truly, Jacqui, you're sensational.' Susceptible to flattery too, she remembered. The door was already shut again, locked and bolted, Rosie asking her, 'Is all that really necessary, even in the sixteenth *Arrondissement*?'

'Anywhere, one needs to take precautions. Do you know there've been killings on the streets every day this week? I'm sure you *would* know. Unless – tell me where you've sprung from?'

'You can guess, I'm sure.'

'London, again?'

A movement of the head: neither affirmation nor denial. Asking her, 'Colleagues of mine did visit you after I'd left, didn't they?'

'*One* did – three, four times. But then Hans was recalled to Germany. You must know all about that too, surely. I ceased to be of use to you at that point – uh?'

'Actually I wouldn't know, I was elsewhere by then – in fact from the day after I last saw you. Did – *he*, you know, the one I met—'

'Gerhardt?'

'Did he ever question you about me?'

'Not that I recall. One knew that you might be back – selling your cousin's perfume, all that . . . What are you here for now? How did you find me, anyway?'

'One other question first: did you say anything to Gerhardt about Pierre Cazalet being my cousin, or that I worked for him?'

'I'm sure not. As I said, you weren't really a subject of conversation. Nor would Cazalet have been. We had only two days before Gerhardt was leaving for Berlin, you know.'

'You had other preoccupations. May I sit down?'

'Please. But if he comes—'

'I've come a long way on a bicycle and my legs are – hell.' Leaning forward, massaging them. 'I've some distance to go yet, too, really do need to push on. If he does come, Jacqui, my story is that I'm in Paris to find my little girl. Remember, I'm a widow? I'd left the child with its grandmother and I believe they're now in Paris, so—'

'Why *truly* are you here?'

'Well – Jacqui, do you still consider yourself as being on our payroll?'

'Your – payroll?'

'It was quite a large sum of money I gave you. Neither your fault nor ours that Walther was recalled, but—'

'Haven't had your money's *worth* yet?'

'Another part of the deal was that when the chips were down we'd confirm you'd been working for us, were not the collaborationist a lot of people would otherwise take you for.'

'People like me, behind our backs they're calling us *horizontales* now.'

'I was going to say, what in fact they must *still* take you for, Jacqui. And soon not muttering it behind your back – screaming it in your face.' She nodded towards the door: 'Which naturally enough you've thought about – hence the new door, eh? Listen, you asked how did I know where to find you – but you know we have ways and means. Found you here as easily as I found you in Rouen. But for Gerhardt that answer plainly wouldn't do, so – oh, let him think I got the address from your *salon*?'

'From whom exactly?'

'Well – whoever you've got working for you there.'

'I have a manager, a Portuguese boy—'

'He'll do. I telephoned and asked for you, you were in Paris he said, and I got the address and a telephone number out of him.' She added, 'Best to say I tried the telephone but couldn't get through.'

'You'd have had a job persuading him. I gave very clear instructions—'

'I convinced him it was to save your life. Which in fact may not be far off the truth. Will you meet me tomorrow?'

'Tomorrow. Saturday. I don't know—'

'Jacqui – it could be only a matter of days before Paris blows up in our faces. In *your* case, if you're still here you know what that could mean. They won't only be calling you names, Jacqui.'

'You're proposing, then—'

'Offering you protection. I've no money for you this time, but if you help me we'll stand by you. Gerhardt will be on his way home to Berlin before the Allies arrive, won't he?'

'I—' Looking down at her clasped hands. She'd coloured – darkened – slightly. 'I don't know. It's *real* between him and me, you know. The *real thing*, as they call it?'

'I'm glad for you. Fact remains, you'll be on your own then, with a million *résistants* out there baying for collabo blood. And in Rouen the same. Jacqui – no misunderstanding now: what I'm promising is that *if you help me*, we'll stand by you. As I promised before – remember? But that *is* an absolute condition.'

'Help you in what way?'

'Go into that tomorrow – with more time. Look – shall we meet for lunch? Where? I have to come all the way from Vincennes, so—'

'Right here would be safer than any restaurant – for the sake of privacy as well as – all that other . . . Besides, I know quite a lot of people here now, French *and* German, and if Gerhardt heard of it – since I wouldn't have told him I was meeting anyone—'

'Like the one with the squeaky voice?'

'What?'

'I met him down there. He'd been visiting you – told me so. My only concern is that if I came here and he happened to blow in, then we couldn't talk – and time's crucial, I can't waste it.'

'You may be jumping to a wrong conclusion. He's chasing me, I don't even *like* him. I *should* tell Gerhardt, I suppose, but—'

'Tomorrow, Jacqui, I'll be all ears. See, if we met at a restaurant or café we might have just bumped into each other in the street. Then you could tell him I'm here, your old friend, and it's above board if we need to meet after that – here, or anywhere. But tomorrow, Jacqui, say twelve-thirty – where?'

'Ile de la Cité – know where that is?'

'Just about. Does Gerhardt work on Saturdays, by the way?'

'He does indeed. Nights are about all we have together. Not always *them*, even. But listen – the western end of Ile de la Cité – cross by the Pont Neuf – there's a restaurant called Paul. Twelve-thirty? Let's hope they have something we can eat, there's not much in Paris now. Do you have a telephone at Vincennes – if I had to put you off or—'

'No. Just *don't*. If you want help from *us*, Jacqui—'

'Well – just one thing to bear in mind, please. I won't do the dirty on Gerhardt – ever!'

'Nobody's asking you to.' She was on her feet. 'May I use your bathroom?'

Chapter 6

All the way from Rue de Passy she could see her destination. Montmartre, Sacré Coeur on its eminence being visible from just about anywhere in Paris, and Passy itself being high in any case, Passy and Auteuil both. In the foreground, below her, she had a slanting bird's-eye view of the sunlit Seine, close-ups of it then after a free-wheeling, cooling swoop down to the Avenue de Tokio. Children and young people were bathing in the river on its other side, the Quai d'Orsay; it would still be hot there, while on this bank shadows were already lengthening – her own shadow at one stage, with the sun lowering itself somewhere behind her. What she didn't know – one of the things she didn't know – was that there would be traffic snarl-ups at practically every intersection after this – due apparently to the French police having come out on strike. Might even have guessed this from the fact that such direction of traffic as there was was being conducted by *Feldgendarmes* – rear-echelon Boches with red and green signal discs on batons – but as a newcomer she only took it as it was: OK, so they have Boches directing traffic . . . She did know Paris to some extent – its general shape and the locations of landmarks such as l'Arc de Triomphe, Invalides, Tour d'Eiffel over there, l'Opéra, Louvre, Notre-Dame – remembering it all surprisingly well from visits here with her father before his death in 1930, and the memories refreshed of course by recent study of the map which Hyatt had provided. Only the gleaming width of the

Palais de Chaillot, on her left as she'd swept down to the river, was unfamiliar – but still triggered a memory: in the late thirties it had replaced an eyesore known as the Palais du Trocadero, which she remembered her father showing to her, remarking, 'Isn't that absolutely hideous?'

Up Avenue Montaigne now anyway, into the Champs Elysées for a while, then across Place de la Concorde into Rue Royale. La Madeleine then and l'Opéra, by which time traffic conditions had become noticeably bad. She was attributing it to the inoperative Métro having driven everyone above ground, until a fellow cyclist waving his fists in the air began screaming abuse of the absent gendarmes, then expressed astonishment that she hadn't known they were on strike. Striking against what or in favour of what; and what might be happening to the prisoners in French police cells, most of them only minor law-breakers but on whom the Boches drew to fill their quotas of hostages, many of whom ended up being shot. She'd not had time to put any such questions though before the traffic began to move again and she and her informant were separated; she keeping an eye on Sacré Coeur as a seaman might on a lighthouse. From Boulevard de Clichy, once she got that far, visual memory of the map would come into play again: Boulevard Rochechouart and then Rue de Clignancourt – more or less circling the base of the Montmartre hill.

Another halt. Any vehicle with a swastika on it was given priority, of course, and on the major crossings there were a lot of them – halts seemingly interminable and the *Feldgendarmes* no help at all. Boches already pulling out? It was better after that, anyway – having crossed the main stream of it, she guessed. This was Rue de Clichy. Rue, not boulevard. Must have gone slightly wrong, back there, but still pointing in more or less the right direction. Turning right somewhere up ahead here ought to put one back on track.

She hoped to God she'd be able to waylay Georges Dénault this evening. Might be a lot to ask, since according to Hyatt he was a figure of some prominence in the Resistance underworld and in present circumstances would surely have his hands full. A police strike wouldn't be some isolated factor, must be a symptom of political upheaval. How would the Boches *allow* the forces of law and order to go on strike? Unless they themselves were on the run? In which case, what might Clausen do with Rouquet and Léonie – if they were still alive? It was distinctly possible that they might not be. But also what might happen to Jacqui, when the lid blew off? Jacqui being all one had, so to speak – therefore precious, despite that unpromising 'Won't do the dirty on Gerhardt' line.

A programme of sorts was clarifying now: (a) locate those two; (b) either through Georges Dénault and his Resistance colleagues, or through Jacqui and some kind of bargain with Clausen – for Jacqui's deliverance *from* the Resistance – get them out and into hiding.

To the right here now. Boulevard heaven-knew-what. Didn't matter: Sacré Coeur was up there where it belonged, resplendent with the lowering sun gilding its white stone, glittering like fire on its dome. Rosie asking herself – in reference to that 'programme' – *bargain*, with the SD?

Au Chien Bleu faced on to a winding cobbled alleyway behind the Rue de Clignancourt. The blue dog itself, sitting up in a begging attitude, was a wrought-iron blue-painted sign at first-floor level; the railing for bicycles to be chained to was also painted blue. She took her suitcase off the carrier and brought it in with her.

Silence, after the door had thumped shut behind her. They'd have been talking amongst themselves, obviously; were now silent, staring, one of them actually open-mouthed. Unused to strangers – especially perhaps female ones. She was glad of her old raincoat suddenly. Camouflage: armour, even. Surveying the faces at that table, she was hoping that none of these would turn out to be Georges

Dénault. The stove – cooking-stove – was right here beside her, against the front wall; and a woman in an apron, bare arms as thick as a wrestler's only shorter, was coming this way from the back. There was a bar in the far right corner, a long table along each side-wall and a shorter one in the rear. There was an oil-lamp on the bar – and a man behind it wearing a cap like a jockey's – the staring male customers were around the table on the left, and there were oil-lamps on both tables but only that one was lit. Doubtless what the woman had been doing – she was dropping a smoking screw of paper into her iron stove now. She had a face like an outsize walnut, grey hair in a bun, a cigarette stuck to her lower lip waggling as she demanded, 'What can I do for you, Miss?' The man at the bar remarking with a wink at others, 'Moving in with us, by the looks of it.'

Her suitcase, he – *they*, now, were looking at. She explained to the woman, 'Didn't want to leave it on the bike. What I'd like is something to eat and drink. Whatever you've got.'

'Isn't much. Soup, if you like. Bread's stale, but—'

'Is there a sink or something I could wash in?'

'*Toilette* through there.' Indicating a door in the corner across from the bar. 'Come far, have you?'

All still listening, all staring. The three at the table looked like labourers: railwaymen, they might be. Dénault, Hyatt had said, worked at the Gare de l'Est, which wasn't far away. Gare du Nord was even closer. She didn't think any of those could be Dénault, but it seemed likely they'd know him. Frequenting this place, surely. She answered the woman's question: 'Long way, yes. I'm looking for my child – little girl – and her grandmother. I missed them first at Nantes and then at Dijon – far enough, uh? Haven't seen an old woman and a little girl around, I suppose?'

'Not lately – that I've noticed.' Glancing round, getting no response. None of them was saying a word or even changing expression.

Rosie shrugged: 'Have to go on looking, then.'

'In Montmartre especially?'

She put the case down on the bench on this side of the unoccupied table. OK, so her voice wasn't the kind they were used to, but at least she looked poor. Telling the woman, 'The old girl – my late husband's mother – used to speak of it. I guessed she might have come here. She had a relation – cousin, nephew, I don't remember – by name Georges Dénault. Wouldn't have heard of him, would you?'

Two other men came in, edged past her to the bar, nodding to the others. She heard the barman tell them, 'She's looking for Georges Dénault.'

'You don't say.'

'Whatever did become of Georges, I wonder?'

Lower-voiced then, talking amongst themselves . . .

'Want to take your coat off, dear?'

'Uh-huh. Thanks all the same.'

'Don't find it hot in here? Especially coming from outside? My old stove, see – and no through flow of air. In winter there's nothing like it, they pack in here like sardines, but—'

'Am I right in guessing some of you do know this Dénault?'

'Might. *Might.*' She'd taken the lid off the pot – casserole, whatever – that was on the stove, was stirring it with a ladle. 'Might be in later, come to that. What's *truly* your business with him?'

'Don't you believe what I said?'

Sideways glance, sly expression and no comment. Rosie asked her, 'Would you like a chicken?'

'Live or dead?'

'It's in the basket on my bike – all day in the hot sun, and to be honest I'm not sure how fresh it was when I got it. Ought to be cooked right away, if it's ever going to be.'

'Might have a look at it, then.' She called to the barman. 'Patrice – bike outside, in the basket!'

'There's half a cabbage with it.'

'All this just to encounter Georges Dénault?'

'There's no connection. But I *would* like to see him, certainly.'

In some general movement – the barman going outside and the newly arrived customers joining their friends at the table – the woman murmured, 'Political, is it?'

'How d'you mean?'

'Old woman and a child. Yeah. Hang around this sort of place, wouldn't they? Then it's Georges Dénault – and seeing how things are in Paris just at this moment—'

'Police on strike, I gather.'

'Have been since Tuesday.'

'Striking for or against anything in particular?'

'Sucking up to *us*. Tell us they're their own masters, not the Boches' poodles.'

'So who's guarding all their prisoners?'

'No one. They let 'em out.'

'All of them?'

'On bloody strike, what else'd they do? That your interest, is it?'

'Having only just arrived, I'm *interested* in all of it.'

'Hey – you took your time.' Addressing the barman as he came back with the chicken and the cabbage. 'Let me see.'

'It's all right. Bit gamey . . .'

She woke – hours later – to the sound of a bottle clinking on the rim of a glass, a deep male voice and the woman's soft murmur in occasional response. Her name was Adrienne, she'd told Rosie, but they all called her Adée in a way which in the French pronunciation might have been written as AD. That clink again, his rumble and her quiet, 'Not for me, not this time of night.' Then his long sigh and, 'Ah. Superb . . . Listen, they told me she brought you a chicken. I can smell it, too. Can't be *all* bad, eh?'

'The girl, you mean. By no means. The bird was on its way, though. I gave it a wipe with vinegar before it went in the pan. She had some, while she could keep her eyes open. Worn out, poor kid, hungry as a wolf.'

She'd slept – after they'd all gone – on this bench between the table and the wall, where earlier some of the other men had been sitting. *Much* earlier: the green glow from her watch – which had once been Marilyn's – told her it was 2.20 am. Saturday now, the 19th. Odour of beer, cigarettes, and . . . cabbage. When they'd all left – a whole crowd of them by then, but slipping out in twos and threes to sneak off to wherever they were having some meeting – it hadn't been much before 10 o'clock. Dénault had been supposed to meet them here, she'd gathered, for a private conference in advance of the meeting itself, and some of them had been getting a bit edgy at his non-arrival. There'd been mentions of the curfew, which of course had been in force by then, all of them thus making themselves liable to arrest as soon as they stepped outside – if there'd been anyone on the streets to do it, seeing as the police would not be. But the *Milice,* of course . . . Finally one of them, a thin, bald man in a striped shirt and black waistcoat, had said, 'Better start, lads. Like as not he'll join us there,' and they'd begun to drift away, a few at a time. Rosie had been conscious of a certain level of anxiety which had affected her as well, had also made her realise that Dénault was important to all these others, probably *would* be worth having on one's side. After the last of them had gone – that had been the barman, Patrice – Adée had told her as she locked the door, 'Up to you whether you want to wait, but he may come later. That is, if he decides it's worth the risk.'

'Risk?'

'Coming by a roundabout way to meet you, child. They'll have told him you were here. If it's only that he was delayed – when it's over he *might* come by.' She'd shrugged. 'In case you're more important than you look.'

'Thanks.'

'Pray he's all right, that's all.' She had a bowl of water

behind the bar, in which she'd begun washing glasses. Shrugging again: a facial shrug, screwing-up of the facial creases. 'Not an *easy* time, this.'

'What sort of risk though – curfew?'

'Few days back, they took a shot at him. So tonight, see, knowing the route he'd take, coming here *or* to the meeting—'

'*They* took a shot?'

'Communists. There've been a lot of killings. Easy as pie, blame it on the Boches or *Milice*, or Rue Lauriston. They've murdered several who were of value to us. All right, *they* haven't got off scot-free entirely—'

'They want leading Gaullists out of the way so they can take over before the Allies arrive – is that it?'

According to Hyatt and Willoughby, that was it. Adée confirmed it. 'They'd have us all in the streets on barricades *now*, if they had their way. Then de Gaulle doesn't get a look in; by the time he gets here Paris is *their* city. Then – who knows . . .' She was putting the last of the glasses in a wooden rack to drip-dry. Drying her hands then on her apron. 'What I was saying, in any case you could stay here – sleep, spend the night – or as much of it as may be necessary—'

'That good a chance he'll come, you think?'

Adée nodded. 'I'd say so. And I'll stay with you. The house is only three doors away, but he wouldn't go there, he'd try here and if it was all locked up—'

'You're very kind.'

'If you're here for something that does matter—'

'I am. It does.'

It was 2.40 am now; with all that in the back of her mind as she woke, realising that what had seemed like a long shot had come off. Conscious too that she was in a fair degree of agony – from two days' pedalling and several hours flat on this hard bench. It helped to convince her she wasn't dreaming: only *just* awake though, up on one elbow, other hand on the pistol inside Léonie's bag. Blinking at the faint emanation of light as well as those smells – an amalgam, including that from an oil-lamp that was on the floor behind the bar – and studying the bulky shadow this side of it. Big man. Wide, anyway, maybe not especially tall. If he was to match Hyatt's description he'd need to have red hair and a limp; without either light or movement of that kind she could only allow him the benefit of the doubt on either count.

He was facing her now, she realised. Had turned, with his broad back to the bar. Pinpoint glow of a cigarette, whiff of cognac in its smoke.

'Awake, are we?'

'More or less. You Georges Dénault?'

'If I had a notion of what interest we shared, perhaps . . .'

'Of course.' Hyatt's introductory exchange, he wanted. She told him, '*Je viens de la part d'Albert, m'sieur*.'

'Be damned.' Patting himself on the forehead then: 'Memory, memory . . . Oh, yes – Albert: that would be Albert the husband of—'

'Solange, who is one of my dearest friends.'

'Well.' A rumble of amusement. 'D'you know, it's the first time I've found use for that rigmarole? We can consider ourselves introduced, anyway.' He was at the table, looming with the aura of light behind him, now putting his glass down and hooking back the end of the bench with his boot. 'Question is, are you here to help us, or wanting *our* help?'

'The latter, I'm afraid.'

'Well. Don't have to be afraid. I'd accept it if you were offering it – *have* done, on occasion. I forget the guy's name now – not that it matters. Probably wasn't his own in any case. What name do *you* go by?'

'Jeanne-Marie Lefèvre. I'm supposed to be searching for my little girl, Juliette . . .' She gave him *that* rigmarole. 'Provides me with reason to nose around, you see.'

'Want a cigarette?'

'No – thanks. Trying not to.'

'Nose around for what or whom?'

'This is the crux of it. For two agents of SOE. The Gestapo caught them and brought them to Paris about a week ago. I need to locate them and somehow get them out. *Somehow* – and where from, God knows. Rue des Saussaies would be the obvious place, but things are different now – so I'm told. One is an Englishman, age about 35, was our *Chef de Réseau* in Nancy, and the other's a girl of about 23, Léonie Garnier, who was his pianist. Petite, dark-haired. He's tallish, slim, brown hair. I happen to know them both but the main thing – London's concern – is they've spent the past two years arranging paradrops to *résistants* and Maquis in that very large area – Nancy, Metz, Saarbrücken, Strasbourg—'

'Tomorrow's battlefield.'

'Exactly.'

'Well – Jeanne-Marie – I wouldn't want to dwell on this, but if the Gestapo have had them a week and have that kind of incentive, they'll have been tearing them to pieces, won't they?'

She'd nodded. 'Makes it *very* urgent.'

'One has even to admit the possibility that they may have broken them already.'

'*Possibility*, but—'

'All right. We assume they are exceptional people and that they're still here. I'd only mention that just about all Gestapo detainees have been shipped off to the camps in the past fortnight. Including a number from Rue des Saussaies. But I'd guess that's still the most likely place. They'd only have needed to keep a couple of cells and two or three of those pigs to – do what they do. We could have a look – for regular comings and goings of individuals, that sort of thing. They have a *Milice* guard on the place now. Used to bring prisoners up from Fresnes, but—'

'They wouldn't waste that travelling time now, would they? I know the routine – they had me in Fresnes, brought me in that van thing to Rue des Saussaies for interrogation

– and a whipping. But it's, what, twenty kilometres each way?'

'About that.'

He'd lowered his bulk to the bench opposite her by this time, and Adée had joined them, facing her through a couple of feet of almost total darkness. Dénault growling, 'Not so many have come through *that* and lived.' There was actually a hint of pre-dawn radiance from outside, she realised, might have been more if it hadn't been for the narrowness of the street. Or maybe moonlight – same applied, if the moon was almost down. No oil-lamp was burning in here now. She told them, 'I was lucky enough to faint, but I'm still striped from it. They put me back into storage for a while, then on to a train for Ravensbrück.'

'You a ghost, then?'

'The others who were with us must have got there, so they're dead, but I and another girl managed to – leave the train. Sorry, I'm wasting time.'

'It helps to know you. One . . . respects—'

'Oh' – Adée's murmur – 'does one *not*.'

Dénault said, 'Fresnes is empty now. Most of *them* were herded into cattle-trucks. You know the police are on strike? So *their* prisoners were lucky. Tuesday, that was. You want the general situation, how it is here?'

'If you can be bothered – don't want to get some rest?'

He was lighting another cigarette from the stub of that one. Assuring her then, 'I'll rest, don't worry . . . Well – Monday, about two and a half thousand prisoners were entrained for the camps. Although we heard the SD let another couple of thousand go free in the last two, three days. Because they're getting out themselves, would be the reason, non-combatant units all pulling out. Those prisoners – you caught your breath when I said how many – they'd be from the dungeons of Montrouge, Romainville, Vincennes, Valérian. Where incidentally they're still shooting hostages. Valérian and Vincennes for sure, every day, if you're within a few kilometres you hear the volleys. Of course there's Drancy too – that swine of a commandant, Brunner, even *he*'s left now. He sent off a whole trainload of Jews, fifteen hundred of them – oh, a week ago – and he himself left on Wednesday with all his Gestapo guards and another fifty-one Jews. Maybe sick ones they'd intended to leave behind, someone told me. So Drancy's empty now, gates standing open. But Thursday – day before yesterday, Saturday now – Thursday was the biggest exodus of bloody Fritzes. Every train packed, and the streets solid with their transport. I saw it from Gare de l'Est and Gare du Nord, and later on the Champs Elysées and thereabouts – chaotic absolutely, every through-road and all the boulevards jam-packed: trucks, cars, vans, ambulances, horse-artillery even. And crowds gathering around the requisitioned hotels adding to the congestion – looking for hand-outs, especially food.'

Rosie said, 'Traffic was heavy enough today – I mean yesterday.'

'Nothing like Thursday. And to complete the picture – the surface of it anyway – that night there was a wholesale departure of collaborators and ultra-collabs. They were assembling in Rue des Pyramides – because that's where the PPF offices are situated, and they'd organised transport, *Wehrmacht* cars and trucks to take the rats away in. Know what PPF is?'

'Partie Populaire Française. Fascists, pro-Nazis.'

'Yes. Scum. Doriot's lot, and Darnand's. Amongst them the intellectuals, so-called. My God, *that* crowd! All with their little suitcases and picnic baskets. Editors and broadcasters, scribblers of all kinds, politicians including some from Vichy. Laval left the day before, incidentally. He'd come up from Vichy and they put him in l'Hôtel Matignan. There were SS protecting them all, unfortunately, nothing we could do about it – might have been a jolly little party otherwise. Some of our lads have sacked the PPF offices since then – and the offices of *La Gerbe* and some others; but *what* a lost opportunity! You see, the Boche embassy's been handing out German passports to all comers, in recent days.'

'*Have* they . . .'

Thinking of Jacqui. Whether Clausen might have got her a passport: as presumably he could have. Or whether he might have a wife in Germany; and if so, whether Jacqui'd know it. Dénault was saying, '*Miliciens* were busy saving their hides too, Thursday night. Truckload after truckload. What the Boches will do with them in Germany, God knows.' He'd shifted on the bench, yawning: 'Getting light, out there. Jeanne-Marie – are you leaving it to me to find out where your friends are being held – or *were* being held?'

'Think you could?'

'I could put some lads on to it. Without telling them too much. Nothing guaranteed, mind. Some have contacts among the Boches: although one wouldn't want rumours reaching the wrong ears. But if we get anything – if either you or I have reason to get in touch – Adée's 'phone here, leave a message with her? All right, Adée?'

'Why not?'

Back to Rosie. 'You don't have any other lead on these people? Tell me their names again?'

'Guillaume Rouquet and Léonie Garnier. Those are their field names, of course. But yes, I do – didn't want to interrupt what you've been telling me, that's all. Here it is. A woman by name of Jacqueline Clermont worked for us as an informer in Rouen a year ago. I knew her then – recruited her, in fact, which is why they've given me this job now. She's here in Paris shacked-up with an SD man who calls himself a sergeant but is probably something more – I can't explain that, but his name's Gerhardt Clausen. He has, or had, a big reputation for catching agents like me. He's dangerous, and clever, and Jacqui's lover. She *says* she's crazy about him, it's the real thing, all that. I visited her – in their apartment, top floor of a house in Rue de Passy – on my way here yesterday. Clausen wasn't there. But *he* has charge of these two prisoners – this was reliable information received in London – and the hope is that through her I might find out where they are. She says she won't let Clausen down, but still agreed to meet me for lunch today at a restaurant on the Ile de la Cité. In return for her help – of what kind, I haven't told her yet – I'm offering her our protection, certification that she's been working for us.'

'To whatever extent *that* may influence anyone.'

'I'm promising it. And if I do get her help I'd ask you to back me up on it. I may say that in Rouen she did keep her end of the bargain.'

'See how it goes, then.'

'Meet here tomorrow evening?'

'Oh, I don't know. I suppose – if there's no set time, and you wouldn't mind waiting around. That's an amazingly close contact you have – I'd certainly like to hear how it develops.'

'Could I wait in your house, Adée?'

'Yes.' Adée nodded. 'I'd send round to tell you he was here.'

'So that's it – for the time being. I'm more than grateful to you both.'

Dénault spread his hands. 'You understand I promise nothing. I'd guess you're more likely than I am to strike lucky. I'll do what I can, but—'

'I know. But if I do get to know where they are—'

'You'd want help from us then.'

'Yes. Perhaps at very short notice. Like meeting you this evening, and—'

'D'accord.'

Stubbing out the cigarette, repeating, *'D'accord.'* Adée asked him, 'How was the meeting?'

'Much as expected. The Reds repeating "*Now* to the Barricades!" and "No Liberation without Insurrection!" We – our leadership – insist that doing so prematurely'd cost maybe two hundred thousand lives. What do we want here

– another Warsaw? This was a CNR meeting, you understand.' Interpreting that to Rosie: '*Conseil National de la Résistance*. Includes all sorts. And the Reds admit that in the whole of Paris they have only six hundred weapons. Against sixteen thousand well-armed Boches with light tanks – and supported if they want by squadrons of Stukas from within a few minutes' flying time of the centre. Anyway, we had our own meeting after that one. Messages have been sent to the Americans, begging them to come in before the bloodbath starts. The Reds of course don't give a damn for that. But we've a trick or two up our sleeves. Although God knows, we need arms too. Mind you, there again, seems we may have found a source.'

Pushing himself up. 'Jeanne-Marie, you were right, I do need to snatch a couple of hours' sleep.'

He did have a limp. Red hair – maybe, but the light wasn't good enough yet. Plaid shirt with a scarf at the neck, donkey-jacket. Forty-five, maybe: voice and manner suggested that sort of age. Adée locked the door behind them, Rosie left her bike where it was but brought the basket with her, and he came with them along the alley. It was only yards to Adée's house, and his route took him that way. There was already a hum of distant traffic, but nothing moving here; they'd stopped to listen, heard not another footfall. Rosie said quietly, 'It's heartbreaking you're not well armed. We've spent years setting up paradrops here, there and everywhere. I've taken part myself a dozen times, seen the stuff trucked away—'

'The Boches have dug up a lot of it. Informers, mostly. Plenty of *them* ought to be shivering in their boots right now. But others of course under torture, out of their poor minds. This your place, Adée?'

'*That* half of it.'

Rosie had stopped: remembering something important she'd meant to ask. Shaming in fact that it should have slipped her mind until now. 'Georges—'

He straightened from kissing Adée good-night. 'Huh?'

'Tell me if this rings any bell with you. When I called by to see Jacqueline—'

'In Rue de Passy?'

'Correct. There was a man who'd been visiting her. He had a grey Citroen Light Fifteen, and two thugs with him who'd been waiting in it. Bodyguards, could have been. He, though – tall, smartly dressed, mid-thirties maybe, and the extraordinary thing, his voice: as high-pitched as a girl's!'

'Lafont. "Monsieur Henri", they call the swine.'

Staring at him . . .

'Christ. Of *course*!'

He'd turned away to spit: a streak of silver across the cobbles. Shake of the head then. 'She keeps nice company, your Mademoiselle Jacqueline.'

Chapter 7

Less than a kilometre from the Etoile, an alarm rang mercilessly in a darkened bedroom and a woman groaned, her voice thick with sleep, 'Even weekends now. *Really*, Henri—'

'You sound like a wife.' He'd only murmured it. Adding, reaching long-armed to shut off the noise, 'Not only the *week* that's ending. A whole damned era. I think you should get out of Paris.'

'Not even daylight, and I get my marching orders?'

'Saving-your-life orders. Weren't you listening to what the *Standartenführer* was saying last night?' Lafont was out of the bed: long-limbed, broad-shouldered. Telling her, 'You were at your best last night. Beautiful, amusing and – altogether a splendid evening. I congratulate you.'

'And my reward is to be dismissed?'

'Unless you want to – shall we say – entertain the mob. I won't be here much longer, my people will disperse and this place will be empty. The riff-raff might even break in and smash it up – they've been doing so elsewhere. Why not go down to the country, stay with some of your less boring friends?'

'They mightn't want me. All joining the Resistance – or looking for Jews to shelter in their houses. But at a pinch I *might*: there's certainly one door I could get a foot in . . .'

He hadn't stayed to hear it; the bathroom door had slammed. She sat up, seeing that daylight *had* arrived, was actually quite bright in a gap between the curtains. And there was already traffic in the streets. Could be, she thought, that he was right: she *did* remember that ghastly *Standartenführer* droning on, not exactly adding to the general gaiety . . . Maybe one should have got out weeks ago. Although when one had been living like a queen, despite being only a pseudo-countess – and there'd always been the hope that if it did come to the worst he'd take one with him . . .

'Oh, come along now!' He was back, towelling himself. 'Rouse out some coffee, will you?'

'If I must.' Swinging her legs off the bed. Naked, as he was. In the early days – ten or twelve months ago, say – she actually *had* thought he'd take her with him, if ever it came to anything like this – and if she'd felt so inclined. As she would have – *then*. Now, the German citizenship they'd conferred on him seemed a lot less attractive. She reached for her negligée. 'Where are you off to, anyway?'

'Rue de la Pompe. They'll be waiting for me.'

'Still using that place, then.'

'For the moment.'

'*Here*, that stuff's finished, eh?'

Staring at her: his chin up, eyes hard. 'What?'

'I only said—'

'See about the coffee, will you?'

Shrugging, she pushed her toes into slippers, crossed to the bell-pull and gave it a tug, tightened the flimsy gown around her as she went out on to the landing. Thankful at least that the cells, former servants' bedrooms, were empty now; she'd always had a creepy feeling about that top floor, and at having his private army of gestapists in the house. Worst of all, the use they put the cellar to. He might still be using the cells and cellar in the house next door, which he'd taken over – oh, before *her* time. The red-headed marquise had reigned here then and it had been on her insistence, aimed at clearing that sort of unpleasantness out of *this* house. As apparently it had done – for a while . . .

The horse woman. She'd also persuaded him to buy the racing stables which he'd now got rid of. Horses – women – new toys never lasted long with him. Perhaps one should have understood the short-term nature of it all. But the way one had been then, and – admit it, in similar circumstances might well be again – one had dared to presume that in one's own case it would be different, would not only endure but go from strength to strength.

One certainly had not envisaged disaster of this magnitude. She didn't believe he had either.

'Ah, Brançion.'

'Madame la comtesse, bonjour!'

Averting his eyes. The negligée was tight around her; she was conscious of the swell of her breasts and the protuberance of nipples. So *let* him avert his eyes . . .

'Breakfast in the small salon in five minutes, Brançion. Coffee and croissants. Oh, and melon.'

'As madame desires.' An anxious look then – his eyes on hers and no lower – and speaking very softly. 'They're worrying, madame. Certain things that have been said – last night for instance – I'm sorry, but some voices—'

'Later, Brançion.' She'd turned away. 'See to the breakfast now.'

She wondered where Henri would go, when he left Paris. It wasn't the sort of question anyone in her right mind would *ask* him.

When he came out of the house, pausing on the steps to flick away a cigarette, Chauvier was polishing the car's windscreen and Montand was brushing out the inside. Two other men dressed similarly – leather jackets, green army trousers – who'd been loafing out front, were now opening the gates. Chauvier jerking the driver's door open and getting rid of the chamois leather, Montand holding a rear door open.

'Where to, boss?'

'Rue de la Pompe, first.'

Out of this courtyard and to the left, then a right into Rue Boissière, up to Place Victor Hugo, left into the avenue of the same name. Half a kilometre, roughly – and not a word; when he didn't speak they knew better than to speak to him – to a hairpin right turn into the upper part of Rue de la Pompe. Then it was only one block away: pausing for a *gazo* dustcart to putter by before nosing over and into a forecourt on that side of the road. A black van was parked there – a Renault – and an exceptionally ugly man in a fawn-coloured lightweight suit came from it to meet Lafont as he got out.

'All well, Victor?'

'They're ready for you. Paul's with 'em, Jubert boys are on guard, I've others in the van if they should be needed. Told 'em they could sleep it off. It was a great night in Le Chapiteau, I tell you!'

'Enjoy it while you can. None of us will much longer.' He had the Jubert brothers in sight simultaneously for a moment, one peering from the front door and the other re-entering at the side. Identical twins, and both carrying Schmeissers. He nodded to the one in the hall as they went in, asking Victor – Victor Bernin – as they passed on through, 'Any progress, Paul say?'

'Fuck-all. Ask me, boss, the guy's dead meat or near it, we'd do better to work on *her*.'

'I *am* working on her, Vic!' His voice had shot up higher. 'Christ, what d'you *think* I'm bloody doing?'

'Yeah, but—'

'What's wanted here isn't dead bodies – although you're right, likely we'll have *one* soon enough. Mind you, don't want *him* dead yet, if we can help it—'

'Boss – she's seen it all, knows what's coming like. When it's *her* turn—'

'She wouldn't stand a tenth of what he's taken. Wouldn't crack, either, just curl up and die. Then we *wouldn't* get whatever's in their heads. All right, forget *him* – in *her* head.'

He'd stopped, thinking about it: with a hand on the wall, leaning on it. 'All right, time's passing and she's holding out – longer'n I'd reckoned. For such a delicate little bitch—'

'She's *that* all right. Look, when he's snuffed it, if by then she hasn't—'

'I'll work on her myself then.' Pushing himself off the wall. 'Come on.'

The door to the cellar was halfway along a central passage leading to the back of the house. Smallish, heavy door, winding stone stairs, candles and oil-lamps and a smell of drains. At the bottom a male figure was standing waiting for him: broad, with a wide white face under a thatch of black hair. Young – eighteen or so. Looking down at him from above, what you'd notice would be his bull-like solidity; the surprise in store, when you got down to that level, was that he was barely five feet tall.

'All right, Paul?'

Paul Clavié, Lafont's nephew. He had a club in his hand. It might have been a hockey-stick with the curved end sawn off. Pointing it at the girl whom he'd strapped into a heavy chair, her ankles secured to its legs and her wrists and elbows tied behind its back so that her shoulders were forced back although her head hung forward, chin on her breastbone, a tangle of dark hair curtaining forehead and eyes. She could have been dead, held there only by the straps. Clavié told his uncle, 'She spat at me.'

Lafont like a tall crow, staring down at him. Round, fierce eyes and the jutting beak. Carrion-crow, dressed as always to the nines. 'So?'

A shrug, mildly challenging. 'I slapped her. I was bringing her rations – in the cell – bitch spat at me!'

'Slapped her, or hit her with that thing?'

'With *this*.' His bunched fist. 'Knocked her down, but—'

'She unconscious, or asleep?'

'Nah. Playing possum.'

'What about him?' Pointing with his head but still looking

down at the girl, moving the matted hair off her face with a forefinger. Her eyes stayed shut. There was heavy bruising on the near side of her face and blood-smears from a grazed cheekbone: she was wearing a torn shirt and a skirt that had worked up above her knees – which were also grazed and bruised. Clavié answering that last question with, 'All I can say is he's breathing. Wouldn't eat, only drank some water.'

'Has the use of his arms now, has he?'

'Nah. On his knees like a dog, sucking at it. Same as she has to.'

'Why would she—'

'Not untying her hands, am I!'

Rouquet was naked. Striped and patched with lash-marks, broken flesh and dry or drying blood, strung up by his wrists from an iron hook. His toes were in contact with the cement floor and for the moment he had his weight on them; as long as he was conscious and could manage it, he would have.

Lafont glanced back at the others. 'If he drank, he must want to stay alive. Extraordinary. How long has he been on the hook?'

'Ten minutes, quarter-hour. Juberts gave me a hand up with him.'

'Get my whip.'

'Right—'

'Wait.' Removing his jacket. 'Hang this up. *Carefully*, Paul.' Turning back to the girl, then. 'Did you hear, Yvette? See, you're going to have to spectate again now. Paul will keep your eyes open for you. Remember – you've only to say you'll co-operate, and he'll be moved to a bed with a doctor to attend him and you to nurse him. He won't stand much more of this – up to you whether he lives or dies.'

'He won't tell you anything. No matter what you do. Why not let him rest?'

'Hey – communicating, finally!'

'*Please*, let him rest?'

'Well, I *would* if you or he'd see a bit of sense. Otherwise when he's dead – well, have to work on you. Much nicer if you persuade him to start answering the questions. I don't *want* to hurt you, Yvette. Couldn't you really *try* persuading him? Really turn it on? With you, see, killing won't be on the menu. Come to think of it, might entrust you to Vic here. You know Vic – *this* fellow?'

Bernin – Vic – stooped with his face in close-up to hers, while Lafont from behind used his middle fingers to pull her eyelids up. Bernin's features and expression unquestionably bestial. Whispering – she'd smell his breath, feel his spittle – 'I'm hoping he *don't* tell 'em anything, kid. Great times coming for you and me then, uh?'

Clavié handed Lafont his whip. Black leather, with a stock about two feet long, lash about another six. Fondling it, drawing it through the fingers of the other hand as if the feel of it gave him pleasure.

Moving forward then.

'Now. *You!*'

He'd kicked at Rouquet's feet and the body had jerked – swung, weight suddenly on the racked arms, toes scrabbling to relieve that agony but not making it. Lafont's shrill squawk: 'Going to *talk*? Answer the questions I showed you, eh? Just for Yvette's sake, maybe?' Léonie's head back and eyes open under Clavié's fingertips; Bernin growling, 'She's watching the bloody ceiling, boy, shove her head *forward*!' Adding, 'Cut her fucking eyelids off, comes to *my* turn.' Lafont had stepped back from his suspended target, flipping the whip's lash out that way just once, measuring the distance and shrieking, 'Ready? No last words? First *and* last, eh? Still time, but – no? All *right* then—'

Chapter 8

The way she was *trying* to make herself look at it was that this was only her second day in Paris – first full day, at that – and she'd already (a) made contact with Jacqui and would be seeing her again in a couple of hours' time, (b) established a working relationship with Georges Dénault and would be seeing him again this evening. Those were the facts: whereas the way one *felt*—

Jinking left, to avoid an old man on a tricycle. Those had been rifle or pistol shots. Hostage-shooting from the Vincennes castle? No – too far, those had been much closer, and scattered shots, none of the discipline of a firing-squad. Earlier, there *had* been more distant bursts of rifle-fire which might well have been from Vincennes: but what *this* might be . . .

The old man with his beret and white beard was now stuck on the wrong side of the road: a *gazo* lorry had only just managed to avoid him and there was a lot of shouting going on. But also pedestrians being drawn down that way: some standing, staring, shielding their eyes against the sun while engaged in loud discussion of it, others trotting off in that direction – from which there was yet more shooting. Sub-machine-gun: Schmeisser maybe – short burst, pause, longer burst, and shouting drowned out by a car-horn either stuck or with a thumb jammed on it. Rosie freewheeling down that way and listening for more. Coming – had come – from somewhere to the south from here, distance perhaps a kilometre or so: or less, since she could already see traffic piling up. And wanted a sight of – of whatever . . .

She swung to the right. Had been on the Boulevard de Magenta with Gare de l'Est somewhere on her left, was peeling off now into what turned out to be Boulevard de Strasbourg. Then left, into Rue du Château, which seemed to run parallel to Magenta – more or less – and might get around that hold-up, which surely must be caused by that – disturbance . . . Another option now – a road that must cross Magenta as well as this narrower street. Holding on, anyway. Having heard no more shots. And to the right now, into Rue de Langry. Must be within a long stone's throw of the Place de la République, she guessed – re-envisaging the map, essentials that she'd memorised. A problem down there, she remembered, was that the same line of boulevard running more or less east and west changed its name about every 500 yards. OK, so boulevards plural, but all end-to-end, all effectively one and the same. Whatever it was, this fracas, she had to be close to it now. Whizzing on down and edging kerbward, where people were running, shouting to each other. The focal point, she guessed, was going to be the intersection of Rue de Langry and the stretch of boulevard that called itself St Martin. An end to guesswork then, she could see it – two Boche trucks looking as if they'd collided, and other vehicles parked around them, three, surrounding them at different angles. The trucks' doors that were in her range of vision were open, and from the nearer one a soldier hung out head-down, helmet hanging by its strap, blood puddling the road. Tailboards were down, men inside were passing out rifles and ammunition-boxes which others – Frenchmen – were loading into the *gazos*.

Dénault's growl, in recent memory: *Although God knows we need arms . . .*

Getting them, too. Or those might be Reds. She was close enough now to be at risk of finding herself in trouble when any live Boches finally turned up, close enough also to see two other dead ones in the road. One *gazo*, a light-coloured van, was moving off – along Boulevard St Martin – and a man in a vest and surprisingly a striped apron – butcher, fishmonger, from les Halles? – was slamming up the tail-board of a pick-up truck. Nobody was going anywhere near the dead Boches; despite a lot having run away there were quite a few just standing, gawping – as she was too, she realised; might be wiser to make herself scarce; any minute there'd be troops all over this district, wouldn't be exuding charm either – especially not after finding those dead ones. Thinking of Léonie and Rouquet again, of the fact that if one was taken as a hostage one would be of absolutely no damn use to them at all. Little enough *now*. Turning the bike around, to start back up Rue Langry; deciding it would be advisable not to be on any route that might have taken one through that intersection: they'd want witnesses, descriptions of individuals and vehicles, and wouldn't care how they got them. Back to Boulevard Strasbourg therefore, and south on that: it would take her into Boulevard Sebastopol, and on that she'd get right down to the Seine. Having come originally from Vincennes, of course: *slightly* roundabout route, just coming the way she knew.

It was a lovely morning, although there'd been some rain during the night apparently. She'd slept on a pallet on the floor of the front room in the little house Adée shared with an elderly female relative, and for breakfast they'd had ersatz coffee and amazingly fresh bread and dripping. The night had left her voraciously hungry again – as well as aching in every joint and muscle – but she'd been careful not to take advantage of Adée's generosity, especially as she'd be having – she hoped – a decent lunch.

More than Léonie would be getting, she thought. *If* she was alive. Might have been alive yesterday, might *not* be by this time tomorrow. And you could bet would not be eating *any* sort of lunch; the rest of it didn't bear thinking about. All right, so this was one's first full day in Paris, and one had taken a step or two – one hoped – in the right direction; but what if Jacqui backed out and Dénault failed to come up with anything?

The man with the high voice had been in her thoughts a lot, ever since she'd woken. Last night she hadn't been able to question Dénault about him, he'd been in a hurry to get away, had told her angrily, 'Tonight. Talk *tonight*!' Close to the end of his tether, seemingly. The fact was, she'd known of Henri Lafont and the 'Gestapo of Rue Lauriston' from way back – lectures in her training days and occasional references to him since then, the particular angle that concerned SOE having always been the French gestapists' infiltration of Resistance groups. Hadn't thought of them in connection with this business, though, and there hadn't been a mention of them in the two and a half days of briefing at Fawley Court. But – with everything here in a state of flux, SD and Gestapo pulling out – and the Rue Lauriston gang, she remembered having been told, having cells of their own . . .

Connection between Lafont and Clausen?

If there was a possibility those two were being held in 93 Rue Lauriston, and indications being that whoever was holding them must have had them more than a week now – ten days, maybe . . . SOE's expectation of agents who were caught was that they should hold out under interrogation for at least *two* days, forty-eight hours, in order to give fellow-agents that much time in which to disappear; whether or not one would be able to achieve that had always been one of the prime anxieties.

But *ten* days . . .

At the intersection of Boulevards Sebastopol and St Denis there was another hold-up, *Feldgendarmes* stopping everything from crossing until several troop-carriers and an armoured car had passed – westbound, coming *from* the arms hijack. Helmeted SS troopers staring grimly at the crowds: looking, she thought, for blood. They'd spill some too – hostage blood, probably a lot of it. They'd still have a few hundred hostages stashed away, she guessed – traffic offenders, curfew breakers, black-marketeers. Or people who'd done absolutely nothing. Like oneself – innocent young woman cyclist remounting as the traffic began to move again.

From that intersection to the river was about a mile, with the spires of Notre-Dame as a leading mark almost dead ahead. Then Quai de Mégisserie, and no more than 500 yards to Pont Neuf and over it to the island.

The Restaurant Paul was on the Place Dauphine, close to the narrowing western end. There was already a crowd of customers at and around the outside tables; many were barristers, male and female, in black gowns with white bibs. The Palais de Justice was only a short stroll from here. She spent a few minutes finding some railings and chaining her bicycle, also taking off the old raincoat – leaving it on the bike's carrier, where it should be safe enough in these highly respectable surroundings – and by that time very few tables down there were still unoccupied. If any. Not a single uniform amongst all that lot: the impression was of business as usual, a lot of comfortably-off people enjoying themselves. No sign of Nazi occupation, let alone of coming insurrection.

Why Jacqui had chosen this place, maybe. *If* she was coming. Twelve noon now, half an hour to go. In such surroundings, the beautiful and ancient heart of a lovely city, and its inhabitants so apparently unconcerned, laughing and chattering, it *might* be easy for her to turn a blind eye to the danger she was in. Pretend it's not there, and it won't be? But – strolling eastward along the *quai*, passing the Palais de Justice – she remembered Dénault's account of collabs (and 'ultras', meaning ultra-collabs, effectively the most virulent French Nazis) all mustering in the Rue des Pyramides on Thursday night, and his regret that there'd been SS around, that wistful *otherwise we might have had a really jolly little party* – meaning, jolly little *massacre* . . .

The SS wouldn't be there for ever, she thought.

Ahead of her now, in what was roughly the centre of the island, that solid-looking building of which she had an end-on view – with a forecourt the size of a parade ground behind tall railings – that was the Préfecture de Police. And beyond it – looking slantwise across that stone frontage – the Cathedral of Notre-Dame. But there was a whole mass of people, she realised – on the *quai* and clustering along those railings. Noisy, milling around excitedly, not just Saturday midday promenaders . . . Anyway – time to turn and go back, she thought, put herself where she'd see Jacqui when/if she did turn up. Primarily, whether she'd be alone or brought by car – and if the latter, whether by Clausen or—

The flag being hoisted over the police headquarters was the Tricolor. She'd paused – seeing and hearing the crowd's suddenly increased excitement – and was caught up in it now: gazing up as hundreds of others were doing, at the flag of France. At any time since 1940 when the swastika had replaced it, displaying it would have resulted in immediate, summary executions. Tricolor climbing the mast jerkily: was at the top now, flapping in the breeze. The crowd cheering and clapping – had gathered to see this, must have had notice that it was going to happen. Pointing up at it, waving to it, blowing kisses to it: cheering, slapping each other on the back, shaking hands, kissing, whooping. While inside the railing a mob of men in shirtsleeves were surrounding one who was standing up on something – joined by two others now – on the back of a truck, must be . . .

The striking policemen. None in uniform, but taking over their own headquarters. And not a Boche in sight. That was a situation which might change dramatically at any moment, she realised: envisaging the arrival of truckloads of them – armoured cars, tanks, machine-guns. Instead – gradually, at first, a few voices barely audible but the sound swelling fast as others – within a few seconds the whole crowd – joined in, bawling out the Marseillaise. Inside there, the gendarmes too were singing. Faces upturned to the flag, expressions – well, some grave, but mostly wild with joy. Rosie trying to sing with them – to her own surprise crying too, which made it difficult. A stout woman threw her arms around her, kissed her, screamed in her ear, *'Courage, petite!'* Rosie kissed her back, laughing as well as crying, and noticed an old man standing ramrod stiff, saluting, and tears coursing down *his* cheeks. *Having* to get back to the Place Dauphine now though: and asking herself *en route* – getting her feet back on the ground, as it were – what good any amount of flag-waving and singing of anthems could do for Léonie and Rouquet.

That was all *she* had to think about. Wasn't here to get emotional over the imminent liberation of France, was here to save two lives. Moving as that undoubtedly had been.

They were eating inside the restaurant. Jacqui had booked an inside table, and the ones outside were all taken anyway. She'd arrived on foot, alone, from the direction of the Quai d'Horloge. She was looking marvellous in an off-white cotton dress, sleeveless because she'd taken the jacket off, hung it over the back of the chair together with her handbag, which made Rosie's – Léonie's – look like something that should have been thrown away years ago. Two male lawyers at a nearby table were giving Jacqui a lot of attention. Rosie got some too, but Jacqui really was quite strikingly alluring. Rosie, in a lilac-coloured skirt and top which she'd owned pre-war but had thought was still quite smart – it was the only smart*ish* thing she'd brought with her – felt like some poor acquaintance out of an altogether different social *milieu*.

At least, though, not like a collab or high-ranking Boche's mistress. *Miaow* . . . Asking Jacqui quietly, 'Did you know the Préfecture has a tricolor flying over it?'

A nod. 'Heard some people talking about it, on my way here. Then all that singing and cheering. Watching, were you?'

'Yes. The Germans won't let it stay there, will they? Any minute there'll be – well, God knows . . .'

'From what I hear, they're trying to keep it all low-key.'

'Who are?'

'Germans. They don't want to provoke the rising that's obsessing *you*. Or was doing so yesterday. The last thing they want is to have to order troops and tanks into the streets.'

'But there *will* be a rising, Jacqui.'

'Here's our soup.' They were silent while it was served – a vegetable broth of some kind. Jacqui had ordered wine too, a carafe of Pelure d'Oignon which she'd told them to put on ice if they had any, and after the soup they were having what the restaurateur called *chevreuil* – venison – but which Jacqui said would probably be goat. The waiter had left them now.

Rosie told Jacqui quietly, 'To imagine that there might not be would be putting your head in the sand. I saw two truck-loads of rifles and other stuff being hijacked this morning. Trucks had collided – maybe through one of the drivers being shot or something. By the time I was close enough to see what was going on the drivers and some others were dead in the road – looked dead anyway, and there'd been shooting, I'd heard it from some way off – and *résistants* were transferring the loads to other vehicles. What would they want guns for, if not to use them?'

'How would they have known the trucks had rifles in them in the first place?'

'Some insider tipping them off?'

'What is it you want of me, anyway?'

'Your help – in return for which—'

'You'll protect me.' Glancing round, and a gesture with one hand. 'From all *this*.'

'Shall we be serious, Jacqui?'

'What *exactly* do you want?'

'I'd like you to back me up – as Jeanne-Marie Lefèvre with

whom you made friends in Rouen a year ago, and whom you ran into again this morning – where, by the way?'

'Wherever you like!'

'Somewhere Gerhardt would know you *might* have gone to shop?'

'Rue Froidevaux, then. Near the Montparnasse cemetery – off Boulevard Raspail. I go to a dressmaker there sometimes.'

'Well, fine. I *could* have been trolling around there, for the old woman and my child. Cheap hotels and rooming houses around there, aren't there?' It was where Ben had lived when he'd been struggling to become a painter, just before the war: keeping his head above water by washing dishes in the big hotels. 'Subject of my background, Jacqui – you'd have asked me this – to start with I could have hung around in Rouen a few weeks longer than I did; *he* wouldn't have known; he was leaving that weekend, wasn't he? But eventually I had to admit you were right, I couldn't make any sort of living flogging scent – so I gave that up and went back to nursing. I'd done some training, never completed it for various reasons. Then I found the old woman had moved from the farm where I'd left them into Nantes itself, and more recently from Nantes to Dijon – all that. You wouldn't remember every detail, it's not all that riveting.'

'You want me to back you up, you say. But in what way, and what for?'

'Well – if I should meet Gerhardt, for instance.'

'Do you expect to?'

'I'd *like* to. Didn't we more or less agree this, Jacqui – meeting by chance so we can then see more of each other – not as if I'd deliberately sought you out? So then naturally I'd meet him as well – if you were so kind as to invite me?'

'With what object?'

'Actually, that's a bit vague. But not to steal him from you.'

'*What* a relief!'

'I thought it might be. But seriously, not with any intention of damaging his interests, either. In your own words, not in any way to do the dirty on him.'

'You hope to get information of some kind, obviously.'

The soup-bowls had been removed. Rosie said, 'Nothing to his detriment. Or yours, of course. For instance, you can be sure I wouldn't say anything that might suggest you'd ever worked for us.' She saw *that* register: followed up with, 'But it did occur to me – tomorrow being Sunday—'

'That I'd ask you for lunch.'

'Oh. *Lunch* . . . Well – would you?'

The waiter was smiling at *their* smiles. Serving the *chevreuil* from a small casserole; there was some kind of sauce with it, and mashed swede. A much younger waiter, a lad of about fifteen, poured the wine – which *was* cold. When they were left alone again Rosie said, 'You mentioned that you get good rations from some German source, Jacqui. I'd very much like to lunch with you at your flat. Let this be *my* lunch, therefore.'

'It's not cheap here.'

'Never mind that. But listen – is there any risk, if I did come, of that Lafont creature barging in?'

'You know his name, then. Yesterday you didn't.'

'I've remembered. There and then I thought he might be some high-up *Milicien*. But his bodyguards wouldn't have been in mufti, would they, even though *he* was? Anyway, I realised – I did know about him and his organisation. Operating from Rue Lauriston, and – frankly, not nice at all. A partner by name of Bonny – and an office lined with steel? He was a petty criminal, wasn't he, the SD or the *Abwehr* took him on and he recruited his gang of thugs from that same source – prisons?'

'Quite a lot, you know.'

'We got to know of him because he was considered a danger to us and to Resistance groups.'

'And to Jews. Especially rich ones. He had a huge

commercial racket going. *They* went to the camps, and a large cut of whatever he could prise out of them went into his pockets. He has a very high style of life and – I told you – a whole succession of women.' She murmured, 'A marquise, even, and other – oh, high society.'

'That amazes me.'

'Well. Power, and lots of money, the very best of everything. Scent of danger too – I suppose . . .'

'Is he a friend of Gerhardt's?'

'No, not at all.'

'But they work together?'

'They *know* each other, their paths cross, but—'

'He wouldn't turn up at your place if – well, if he saw Gerhardt's car outside, for instance?'

Jacqui sipped some of the odd-coloured wine. She shook her dark head. 'I told you, I am *not* conducting an affair—'

'But he's chasing you and Gerhardt doesn't know it.'

'I don't *think* Gerhardt suspects it. He'd have no reason to be concerned at all. And I don't want – trouble, especially at this juncture. On the other hand he is *very* perceptive, and one doesn't always know what he's thinking.'

'Wouldn't it be as well to tell him, rather than have him find out? Since in any case you're innocent of any—'

'Is it Lafont you're after?'

'*After?*'

'Come on, Jeanne-Marie. This isn't just a social get-together, is it?'

'I happened to be accosted by that man when I came to visit you. Since then I've remembered what we were told about him, but when I came to see you I'd forgotten his existence. So – no, I'm not *after* him, just wary of him.'

'Could I persuade you to tell me what you *are* after?'

'Yes. There's something I believe your Gerhardt might help me with. I want you to introduce me as your former acquaintance from Rouen, so that – well, in the hope I might establish enough of a *rapport* with him to be able to discuss it. It seems to me that if he accepted me as your friend – and with the balancing consideration that I could help *you*, Jacqui—'

'To put that over, you'd have to admit who you really are.'

'Oh. Well . . .' A shake of the head. She'd known this was going to be difficult. But also that it was what she was here for, she simply had to get on with it. Would almost certainly have to face Clausen himself – unless of course Dénault came up with the goods this evening. Meanwhile, why should it be easy or even half easy? Léonie wasn't sitting in any restaurant, sipping wine . . . 'Perhaps not *exactly* who or what I am. I'm well aware that he's SD – and getting myself arrested wouldn't do either me or anyone else, including *you*, any good at all. But I might admit to having some personal involvement with—'

She'd checked, thinking about it. Then: 'Jacqui, I'll tell you. Friends who might be in SD or Gestapo custody. Two people for whom I have – a warm regard.' She gestured . . . 'I suppose I've said too much now. Putting *you* in a difficult position. The fact is, *I'm* in quite a hole. So – may I ask you to respect that confidence? It's an explanation for you alone, I'm not asking you to do or say anything at all—'

'Just have you to lunch.'

'That's all.' *Then* she'd have to take the bull by the horns, all right. Hoping to God there'd still be some point in it, that they were still alive and had not been either broken or shipped east. She drank some of the now somewhat less cold but still refreshing, clean-tasting wine. 'Is Gerhardt a kind man, Jacqui?'

'In himself, he is. And certainly to me.'

'Does he feel as strongly for you as you do for him?'

A flush – whether of embarrassment or annoyance. Then: 'I believe he does.'

'Is it possible he'll take you back to Germany with him?'

'Possible but unlikely. There's a complication – of the obvious kind—'

'I only asked because I was told the German embassy's issuing passports to – what's the word they use, I don't speak German – *Vertrauen*, is it?'

'I am not pro-Nazi, Rosalie.'

'Jeanne-Marie – please. No, I didn't think you were. Oddly enough. The word I was trying to remember means "trusted ones" – how I imagine *they'd* regard you if he did ask for a passport for you.'

'You say "oddly enough", but the simple truth is I'm pro Gerhardt Clausen and I'm pro *me*, Gerhardt's business is his own, my business is *him* . . . Listen – talking about *you* for a change – would your papers stand up to close examination?'

'Yes, I think so. Why, if you have friends to lunch, does he ask to see their papers – at the door, or before the soup, or—'

'The German embassy closed yesterday, incidentally.'

'Oh.'

Jacqui put down her knife and fork and reached for the carafe, topped up both their glasses with the little that was left. Forgetting, perhaps, that Rosie was the hostess now. Adding, 'Gerhardt mentioned it last night. Both of us knowing how that affected us, why he was telling me. How it is, that's all. Except that in the longer term—'

'He's married, I suppose.'

'Yes.' Taking a sip. 'And it's been no secret at any stage, I've always known it.'

'In the longer term, you began to say – might sort itself out?'

'Might.' She crossed two fingers. '*Much* longer term. If one could really see that far ahead – as sometimes one dreams one can. Or know how people will be, after such a length of time and God knows what upheavals. Yes, one *hopes* . . .' She changed the subject: '*You* have a man, you told me. A fiancé – who's in your Navy? But that wedding ring—'

'Not his. Not yet. But – yes.'

'I'm glad – for you, but also that you'll understand *me*.'

'Understand you very well.' Not adding, this time, 'oddly enough': accepting what she was saying about herself and Clausen despite knowing very well that she'd had – well, more than just a few men. Hans Walther the rocket-site engineer for one, numerous others when she'd been working for a woman then known as 'La Chatte', a double agent who'd overplayed her hand and was currently in Wormwood Scrubs. When working for her Jacqui had become known as 'La Minette' – the kitten. Rosie asked her – in the hope of slipping this one past her guard – 'What sort of work is Gerhardt doing now, in Paris?'

A frown: 'I don't know anything about his work, we don't discuss it. As I warned you—'

'Only wondering whether he's still laying traps for – you know, people like me. That evening in Rouen when I was in your flat and he blew in, I can tell you I was shaking in my shoes. Got away with it that time because – well, he was obviously crazy for you, hadn't seen you for a long time, and—'

'That's *exactly* how it was.' A smile in her eyes, remembering. 'But in fact, why should he have suspected you of anything, at that stage?'

'God knows. The way they work, you could just as well ask why should he *not* have. Just as now I'm wondering whether going to lunch with you might be – insane.'

'Depends what you're really up to, I suppose. But – it's your risk, don't look to *me* for—'

'No.' The risk had to be accepted, too; she had no alternative. 'Come about midday, shall I?'

'All right.'

'A second thought, though. The business of having run into each other just by chance . . . Thing is, since your man and Lafont see each other from time to time – might do today, tomorrow, even?'

'For all *I* know—'

'Lafont might have mentioned having seen me at your place? If he'd only been calling by on the off-chance of finding Gerhardt at home?'

'I don't know why he'd bother.'

'But he *might*. And that's too much of a risk – for you to have kept it from him, lied about it. So tell him I was there, and we arranged to meet today. I had the address from your Portuguese – went to see you at the salon, heard customers sneering about you and your German lover—'

'*Were* they?'

'Certainly. Gave me the willies. I was worried for you before, but the way things are *now*—'

'It might make better sense if you had any practical way of helping. Unless you're ready to admit what you are?'

'Hardly. But I do have the beginnings of an idea – and I'll work on it. We can say you didn't want even to discuss it except in Gerhardt's presence. It means getting you out of Paris – before *he* leaves, so you're not left here on your own. D'you see?'

'I *would* want him to hear it.'

'There you are, then. The truth, nothing but the truth. Tomorrow, Jacqui.'

Chapter 9

Saturday afternoon now. During the forenoon a seaplane had appeared from seaward and circled around over this end of the fjord, Ben and the others holding their breath and suspending the operation of dumping the *Ekhorn*'s drums of petrol over the side. The seaplane, 3-engined, did a couple of circles and then flew away up-fjord, eastward, and they'd heard it again ten minutes later to the south of them, flying south-westward probably to search down-coast – Frojen, Norddals Fjord and half a dozen others between this one and the biggest of the lot which was Sogne Fjord, 5 miles across and 100 deep and with a dozen offshoots, most of them pretty big just on their own. *That* lot would take a bit of searching. Here in the mouth of Nordfjord MGB *600* was in what was really no more than a fissure in the rock – actually a narrowing gap between two rocks: she had anchors down at both ends, a tent of camouflage netting over her, two fathoms of water under her keel and room for the *Ekhorn* to lie astern of her – if by some miracle Iversen did show up.

It wasn't likely; hence the decision to dump these drums. They'd be easily recoverable and of great value to some later clandestine visitor, were certainly much better stashed here than taken back to Lerwick. Other cargo – weaponry and explosives, etc. – might have to be taken back. Hughes was impatient to be off: obviously not now, in daylight, but in the first period of darkness after Vidlin returned with the escapers. He – Vidlin – had set off in his 16-foot dinghy – clinker-built, pointed at both ends, from a Norwegian point of view the real McCoy, even with an old fish-head or two lying around, and well-used gear, splintery oars and so forth – he'd rowed himself away up-fjord soon after piloting them in here yesterday just after dawn.

If the *Ekhorn* had been going to show up, she'd have done so during the night. From about midnight onwards, had been Ben's guess: allowing Iversen time to enter the fjord slowly i.e. quietly, and penetrate this far in darkness or semi-darkness. One hadn't expected that he'd make it; but if he'd been going to, that would have been the timing.

Vidlin, asked by Mike Hughes how long he expected to be away – collecting the agents/escapers and getting them back here – had shrugged, glanced at Ben as if surely *he*'d understand this, and told the skipper, 'One day, two day. Three, maybe.' Pointing in various directions then: 'Is here – here – here. Ten kilometre, twenty. Who know?'

Hughes had said, 'Damn sure *I* don't.'

'I think he means he knows where his contact is but not where they're keeping the other drongoes.'

The double-ender with its odour of fish and litter of old gear had been in the water and riding alongside by then, it was fully daylight – high cloud, and cool for the time of year – and Vidlin had been breakfasting on eggs, bacon and corned beef before leaving. Daylight was fine by him, he had papers that would pass muster, probably *would* put his lines over and catch a few fish somewhere along the way. He'd gulped down the rest of his coffee, and got up. 'I go. Saying goodbye.'

The tail-end of a rocky holm hid this slot from the main-stream of the fjord. He'd raised a hand in farewell as he disappeared behind it, and Ball muttered pessimistically, 'Let's hope we see him back this side of Christmas.'

They'd got the last of the petrol drums over the side before lunch – one drum at a time, using the davits of *600*'s own

10-foot dinghy, and the drums all linked by manilla rope from the end of which a grass line ran up to a buoy – small, inconspicuous buoy, disguised in a wrapping of seaweed. Meanwhile the rest of the crew had been cleaning up the ship, overhauling and greasing guns and doing whatever needed doing around the engines. Lunch was corned beef and pickles. Ben and Mike Hughes had theirs in the bridge, where the camouflage netting had small apertures from which to see out in various directions, although with that rock islet blocking any view of the fjord you'd see aircraft but not much else. From this height you might see some of that trawler's upperworks – bridge and funnel – if it passed close enough, but not if it stayed out in the middle. The fjord was about two and a half miles wide at this point – but with a mass of holms and skerries in it, about as much rock as open water. Eastward – up-fjord – mountains stood massive against the lightly clouded sky; there was high ground behind the southern shore too.

Hughes finished his corned beef and mug of coffee, gave himself a cigarette and offered Ben one. 'Don't know about anyone else, but I'm going to crash my swede.'

'Good idea. Ball and I'll stand watch and watch, if you like.'

'Count me in on it – and young Cummings – far less strenuous.'

'Right . . .'

Nothing to do but wait, in any case. Nothing one could usefully do anyway, if disaster struck – for instance, a scenario such as aircraft over and circling, then the trawler presenting itself in the gap there with its four-point-one. All right, so *600* would give it a good pasting with her own not inconsiderable armament; in fact you'd shatter the bastard, and keeping a lookout would have been worthwhile because you'd have let rip pretty well as soon as he poked his snout in. But in the longer term – well, it wasn't likely you'd get out of here. Not very far out, anyway.

* * *

The *Ekhorn* arrived as he'd guessed she might have done the night before, half an hour after midnight. Ben had been asleep in the wardroom and the young sub-lieutenant, Cummings, had sent a man down to wake them all, seamen-gunners meanwhile rushing up from the for'ard and after messdecks. Cummings had been keeping watch on the bridge and heard the *Ekhorn*'s engines; by the time the guns were manned and officers in the bridge, she was a low, black moving shadow in the gap at the end of that rock barrier. Engines slow-revving, a sound like some sea-monster coughing, in danger of bringing up its lungs.

Vaguely familiar, at that.

'Searchlight on him, sir?'

'No. Wait . . .'

The intruder's engines had stopped, and straining his eyes through night-glasses Ben realised a second before anyone else did that it definitely *was* the *Ekhorn*. He'd thought it might be – against all the actual or apparent odds. Several others had by now sprung to the same conclusion, there was a cheer or two and by this time the launch was inside the screening rocks, engines still muttering but probably going astern to take the way off her. Stopped, now. Hughes used the port-side Aldis lamp to show Iversen his way in and a minute later was using a megaphone – not the loud-hailer, which would have been louder than was necessary in this quiet night – hailing Nils Iversen, and some moments later getting a shout of, 'Nils Iversen bad hurt. Here is Petter Jarl. We berth on you?'

'Wait, please.' Muttering, 'Want him in stern-first . . .'

Ben offered, 'I'll transfer and—'

'No. *I* will. Ball—'

The boats touched, port bow to port bow. Hughes jumped over – which Ben with his damaged knee might have made a mess of – had Jarl re-start his engines and turn her, bring her in stern-first then to berth on *600*'s port side, where Ball with a couple of seamen secured him.

Iversen was semi-conscious – or in and out of consciousness, apparently. One of his crewmen had been killed, and they were the only casualties although the launch had been knocked about a bit – sections of gunwale, coaming, sternpost and other timbers shot away, wheelhouse holed and most of the glass in it smashed. Nothing in any way crippling or that a shipwright couldn't fix easily enough. The crippling loss was Nils Iversen. Ball took CPO Ambrose and another PO over with a stretcher and a medical kit including morphine, and the Norwegian was manoeuvred very carefully over to *600* and down to the bunk in Hughes' cabin. Ben, being spare, kept out of the way at this stage, but heard the story presently in the wardroom where young Jarl, shaking with nerves, gulped neat whisky while he told it. Fortunately his English wasn't bad.

On Thursday night, finding themselves alone, Iversen had had no doubt they'd fallen astern of station, so increased speed to catch up; but failing after a reasonable period of time to re-establish contact had eventually stopped to listen for *600*'s engines, heard what at first puzzled them but turned out to be a seaplane circling. The pilot must have spotted *Ekhorn*'s wake: from a height of only a few hundred feet it probably *would* have been visible, vertically downwards, a spreading white track on slate-coloured sea, even through that fog. Iversen had immediately altered course away from the nearer land, heading as if to pass outside Stadtlandet in order not to compromise the whole operation – including the escapists on shore, and this gunboat – which he would have risked doing if he'd led the Germans to Nordfjord or its vicinity. Meanwhile the seaplane had completed its circle, dropping even lower and then attacking from astern with machine-guns. Iversen left it to Jarl to con the boat from inside its wheelhouse while he and a man by the name of Sundvik manned the two Lewis guns in the open stern. Iversen was hit quite badly in the first attack; Sundvik shot dead in the second; another crewman took

Sundvik's place. Jarl had gone to help his skipper but had been told to get back to his own job – in any case it was only a scratch. The hell it was – and he was hit again in at least one other pass. The seaplane came in five or six times, and on the last run they thought they'd hit it, which could have been why it broke off the action and flew away north-eastward. Iversen had been hit in the face, chest, and left arm and shoulder. He'd been unconscious for some periods, then awake and obviously in agony. No, they'd had no morphine. In a lucid period and speaking out of the undamaged side of his mouth, he'd ordered Jarl to turn inshore and get into hiding before daylight and/or the 'plane or another one came to pick them up again – which meant *now*, double quick – and in the event they'd lain up in a bay south-east of Stadtlandet, amongst rocks and under their camouflage netting. Ben fetched the chart and Jarl showed them the place: 'Here. See – Hafvruskalle,' Iversen had told him during one conscious spell. 'Nightfall, go Nordfjord.' Several times during the day they'd seen seaplanes searching, mainly off Stadtlandet – 'And beyond – maybe think we go Alesund' – and had also seen an armed trawler, almost certainly the one *600* had been very lucky not to run into. As a result of all this, as dusk approached Iversen had changed his mind, told Jarl to wait another whole day, *then* see about getting into Nordfjord.

Ball had said, 'Suppose we didn't hear any of that because we'd got going again before it started? And I did think I'd heard an aircraft some time before that – you did too, sir—'

'And it didn't find them – or *us* – at that time. Making a sweep seaward, perhaps, caught 'em on its way back – by which time there'd have been a few miles between us.'

Jarl was in a considerable state of anxiety. He looked about seventeen. Iversen had told Hughes in Lerwick that he knew the boy's father and that he was a good lad, lacking only experience which he, Iversen, was seeing that he got. Jarl mumbling now, 'I don't know what now we do. Don't know *what.*' Demanding of Hughes – as if *he* could do more than guess – 'Skipper goin' die, uh?'

'Please God *not*, but—'

'Goin' die, sure.'

No one who'd seen him could have doubted it: it was surprising he'd hung on this long. His face – jaw – was an awful mess. At about 2.00 in the morning Ben and Hughes were in the little cabin with him when he came round: there'd been a shudder through his whole body, lips drawing back on that side over clenched teeth, left eye a bloodshot slit – the other one, with most of the right side of his face, was covered in black and scarlet bandaging – breath dragging in and forcing out in hard gasps, the visible eye by then actually bulging; Ben chuntering urgent nonsense to him about getting him out of this, back to Shetland and into hospital, while Hughes administered more morphine which after a while took effect and put him out again. He was *not* going to live: you wouldn't have wished it on him, either. Ben said, after he'd lost consciousness, 'Deserves a medal anyway. Leading 'em away from us – and *staying* out there—'

'I agree. I'll try to get him one.'

'It'd be posthumous – like Rosie's.'

'Rosie – that girl you were nuts about?'

'She's getting a George Cross. Remember you allowed her the use of this cabin – to l'Abervrac'h and back, one time?'

'Dare say I would have. But a GC, huh! *Posthumous?* Ben – I didn't know, I'm—'

'Tell you about her, shall I?'

Chapter 10

She'd had supper in the Dog, as the locals called it, hoping Dénault might turn up early – which he did not – and Adée had taken her to the house to wait, put her feet up and sleep. 'You look played-out, girl.'

'If he comes, though—'

'I'll come or I'll send Patrice.' The barman, who when she'd sat down to her supper had asked her, 'Heard what's flying on the Préfecture?'

'Better than that, I saw it hoisted, joined in the singing.'

Adée put in, 'She cried, she was telling me.'

'Adée, that was in confidence!'

'Shows your heart's in the right place, that's all.' Nodding towards Patrice: 'For *him* to know it. The cretin had doubts of you. He's—'

'Only as one should have. A time like this, stranger walking in.' He'd bowed, sweeping off the jockey-cap – revealing an advanced state of baldness. 'My apologies. You identified yourself to the satisfaction of Georges, one knows.' Replacing the cap, which was half blue, half orange. 'Didn't find your little girl yet?'

'No.' Thinking not of the fictional Juliette but of Léonie; and of Léonie, she'd come to realise, more than of Rouquet. Through naturally identifying with her, she supposed – having *been* there, or somewhere like it, knowing how it would be – had been – for a female almost the same age. Whereas Rouquet – Derek – was older, and male, and a very experienced agent who'd been chief of other SOE groups before this last one, had had years in which to condition himself mentally and physically for – the ultimate.

Plausible anyway, that he would have. Although how *anyone* could condition themselves to it . . . No, it didn't wash. What *did* was simply that Léonie was so very young: self-possessed admittedly, but – *little*, vulnerable.

But that again was only how one saw her, thought of her, it didn't necessarily tell you how she'd stand up to it or for how long. Nobody could be expected to hold out indefinitely. The only mercy was that after a certain length of time you'd end up dead, not only be finished with it but have triumphed.

How it seemed to others, anyway. In citations and so forth.

Adée had brought her along to the house; explaining that the old cousin although amiable enough was slightly gaga and might have refused to let her in. And that Patrice was related to them both, being a cousin of Adée's late husband. She'd added, 'He works with Georges.'

'Going by last night, so must a whole crowd of them.'

'Yes. There are some he values more than others, naturally.'

'One thing, Adée – I've given your telephone number to the person I lunched with today. I had to, really – for emergencies – but I made it a condition that it was for herself alone. If she did call to leave a message for me, she'd give you her name as Jacqui.'

'Does Georges know of her?'

'Only what I told him and you last night.'

'The one who lives with some specimen of SD?'

'Not quite as bad as that sounds though. She doesn't know anything about his work, doesn't discuss anything of that kind – *this* kind – with him. All you'd need do is take the message. I'm just a lodger, you wouldn't know my business. Except – if you like – that I'm looking for my child. I mean if you were asked by anyone at all . . .'

After Rosie had paid the restaurant bill, Jacqui had made

the point that if Clausen should happen to be working tomorrow, not coming back to lunch, it would be pointless for Rosie to come either. Better to postpone it to the evening, or some other time.

She'd hesitated: sickened by the thought of postponement, further delay, inaction; also in regard to the 'phone number, concerned that anyone could see it wasn't a Vincennes number. The answer was simple, though – to be ready to give up that fiction. She'd have moved, that was all. There had to be hundreds of rooming houses in this 18th *Arrondissement*. She'd told Jacqui it was a telephone in a café-bar not far from her lodgings, that the proprietress and the barman knew her as Jeanne-Marie Lefèvre and would pass on any message. She'd torn off a corner of the lunchtime bill, copied the number on to it and asked Jacqui to keep it to herself.

Adée had said she could use her bed, get an hour or two's *real* rest, but the old cousin had already turned in, the front room consequently wasn't in use and she thought it better to be down there, handy to the door and the street when they came for her. She'd spread the pallet again therefore, slept on it fully dressed without even a sheet over her. It was a warm little house and they didn't open the windows much – which was why it was also stuffy and smelt of old women and old clothes.

She'd dreamt of Ben, and been woken out of it by Patrice's insistent knocking; with Ben still in her mind but no recollection of what he and she had been doing, or where. The day would come, though – bloody *would* – when the two of them would be shot of everything except each other and however they mutually decided to spend the rest of their lives.

Dénault had brought with him the slightly older man who last night had taken the decision not to wait any longer for him. They were both drinking beer and were in much the same clothes they'd worn the night before: this one for instance, whom Dénault introduced as Martin Leblanc – a schoolmaster, apparently – in a blue-and-white striped shirt, dark blue tie, and the same black waistcoat. Blue-black jaw – hadn't shaved today. There were two other men whom she recognised but they were on the point of leaving, perhaps on account of her arrival; they greeted her with handshakes, the older of them then murmuring to Dénault, 'Until shortly, Georges.'

'One hour. You'll collect Bernard on your way by?'

'Yes.' To Leblanc then: 'But you're not coming?'

Rosie thinking, *One hour, then he's off.* She had the feeling he wasn't giving much attention to *her* business. If for instance she'd found out from Jacqui where they were being held, she'd have been counting on action now, tonight: and he, presumably, would have pleaded this prior engagement.

She had *not* obtained that information, though, so what the hell? Obviously he hadn't got anything for her, either. Unless it was what they were off to *now*?

Fat chance. He'd have been bursting to tell her, wouldn't he?

'Jeanne-Marie . . .'

Adée, giving her a mug of 'coffee'. Patrice was collecting empty mugs from around the room, and Dénault coming back from shutting the door behind those others.

'Well, Jeanne-Marie.' A large hand on her shoulder, and a smile which to her seemed patronising, big cheese sparing a moment from *important* matters. 'What's new?'

'I was hoping you'd tell *me*.'

'Well, unfortunately—'

'Sit down, girl': Adée.

Rosie sat – slopping her drink slightly. 'Damn . . .'

'You neither, eh? Your meeting with the woman who—'

'I had a wild hope ten seconds ago that whatever you're doing tonight might be connected with it.'

'I'm sorry. But Martin here will be on his way presently to meet someone who *might* have information . . .'

Rumbling on, about the someone who might. Or, she thought, might *not*. Might *well* not. While those two might well be dead, or on the point of dying, or alive but had been tortured into spilling all the beans; while she, Rosie, would be lunching tomorrow with the man who'd done it to them, heard their screams and watched their writhings – prompting from time to time, as *her* Gestapo man Prinz had: 'All right, the names and locations first. Go ahead. Then we'll have a nice cup of tea together, isn't that what you'd like?' She could hear him, as she must have done about a million times in the past twelve months, those echoes in her skull: but hearing Dénault telling Leblanc now, 'So just in case, Martin – Jeanne-Marie, correct me if I have any of this wrong – the man's name is Rouquet, Guillaume Rouquet, middling tall, brown-haired—'

'And a narrow, bony face. English, but his French is as fluent as your own. Léonie is French – petite, dark-haired, very pale skin, age about twenty-three. He's forty, forty-five maybe.' Looking meanly at Dénault: 'Starting from scratch, are we, but leaving it to him because you've more pressing things to do?'

'Not exactly – not from scratch, and I *have* initiated some enquiries – regrettably without result as yet – and I'm not leaving it to Martin, no, only ensuring that when he meets this individual tonight he'll ask the right questions.' He paused, lighting a cigarette. 'Also because the professor knows all our business, you see, he'd step into my shoes if necessary – *and* do a better job than I do.' Addressing him, then: 'First thing, Martin, is to find where they're being held and by whom, the second to decide how best to get them out. Most likely places of detention being of course Rue des Saussaies, and not Avenue Foch, that's empty now, but conceivably Rue Lauriston or Rue de la Pompe.'

These people were immersed in preparations for an insurrection, Rosie thought, probably didn't give what Ben would call a tinker's fart for whatever might be happening to *any*

British agents. Any moment now Dénault would admit to Leblanc that for all anyone knew, those two were already dead or on their way east; there was barely a chance they were still in Paris and alive. Which of course might be true; but if he said it, it would amount to telling him not to waste too much time on this . . . She put her mug down, said to Dénault, 'As you say, Rue Lauriston. Lafont. Last night you didn't have time to discuss it, but the point is I met Lafont – by pure chance – yesterday afternoon.' She told Leblanc, 'I'll explain. You haven't heard this, and it could be relevant.'

'Unfortunately,' – Dénault – 'we don't have all that much time even now. But—'

'You and Martin are not going in the same direction now, you said, perhaps *he* has time?'

'All right, but—'

'Listen – please. There's a young Frenchwoman by name of Jacqueline Clermont whom a year ago I recruited as an informant. She had valuable connections in an area of great importance, and she played her part well, gave us value for – for money and support. But that's over and she's now in Paris, living with an officer of the SD called Gerhardt Clausen. They have the top floor of a house in Rue de Passy and Clausen, wherever he operates, has responsibility for the custody and interrogation of the people I'm looking for. That much is fact, the information was passed to London and was part of my briefing a few days ago. So I've been in touch with her, we lunched together today, and she's agreed to back me up as just a friend she happened to run into – that is, when I lunch with her *and him* in their flat tomorrow.'

'God Almighty . . .'

She looked at Dénault, 'It's important enough to take the risk, that's all.' Back to Leblanc: 'She'll help me to this extent, but she won't inform on him – says she doesn't know anything about his work in any case. All I can do is try to be accepted on that basis and *maybe* find out what he's doing and where.'

'But Lafont comes into it?'

'He may do. On my way into Paris yesterday I located the house on Rue de Passy, and he – Lafont – was just leaving. I'd no idea who it was but I described him to Georges last night and he said immediately: Lafont. And I've heard of him, of course, it just hadn't occurred to me, there and then. But today I elicited from Jacqui that he and Clausen aren't exactly friends but that – quote – their paths cross. And he's chasing *her*—'

'Lafont, chasing Clausen's—'

'Exactly. In which case his business with Clausen—'

'Holding your friends, on behalf of Gestapo or SD.'

She nodded. 'Since the Boches are closing down here and there. Wouldn't it make sense?'

'For your friends' sake one might hope not.'

'Yes. One's heard—'

'They're murderers and rapists.' The schoolmaster added, 'He'd have been dealt with long ago if he wasn't always surrounded by bodyguards.' He looked at Dénault: 'It makes sense, what she's guessing.'

'So – her friends could be in 93 Rue Lauriston, or 3b Place des Etats-Unis—'

'Didn't we hear they'd moved out of there?'

'—or Rue de la Pompe. If *that's* still in use.'

Leblanc said he'd find out. Rosie asked Dénault, 'Couldn't you break into all three places?'

'Not impossible. Depending of course on what else is happening.'

'I'm suggesting, do that before anything else and irrespective of whatever the hell else—'

'Could get them killed, you know.'

'Think they'd be safer just left there?'

'Of course *not*. And if you accept that risk – yes, we could smash our way in simply for what those houses are, not on the face of it expecting to find—'

'*Will* you do it?'

'We'd need a strong team, and well armed. The Lauriston gang have *everything* – sub-machine-guns, grenades, fast cars—'

'Another thing I saw this morning was what might have been your people – or perhaps Reds – making off with rifles and ammunition from two Boche trucks that had crashed. There were about four dead ones.'

'Dead what?'

'Boches!'

'Where? When?'

'The *carrefour* Rue Langry/Boulevard St Martin. This morning about eleven-thirty.'

'*That*.' A nod to Leblanc. He was on his feet: stooping then to tell her in a stage whisper close to her ear, 'Tonight we hope to do even better.' Straightening, and reaching to shake hands. 'Which is why I can't stay now. Look, we'll meet here in the morning . . . Patrice – ready?'

'As always, chief. How many of us will there be?'

'Thirty, maybe forty – from the five groups. Six of *us*, including you and me.' He turned back to Rosie: 'Jeanne-Marie, I'm sorry this business of yours is taking time, and you're naturally anxious—'

'That's putting it *very* mildly.'

'One understands.' All of them were looking at her as if they really did; and Patrice looking at her mouth – which she found annoying. Adée moved up beside her, put a hot, heavy arm round her shoulders. 'Poor Jeanne-Marie!'

'No. Poor Léonie and poor Rouquet.'

'But we'll meet here in the morning to decide about those addresses.' Leblanc, nodding reassuringly to Rosie, added to Dénault, 'Which if you make a good job of it tonight—'

'It'll make a difference. *Then*, no matter what else is going on. Start *our* ball rolling, you might say.'

'What time in the morning, though? I have to be in Rue de Passy by about noon.'

'Ten o'clock here, then?'

'Make it nine?'

'Nine-thirty.' Denault shrugged. 'And there goes my Sunday lie-in. What we do for our beloved allies!' Dénault winked at Adée. 'Especially pretty ones . . .'

'Four kilometres?'

'About that. It's not a place I'd have picked, mind you. Given them enough trouble around there already.' Dénault had unchained his bicycle, was waiting for Patrice to do the same. They were at the side of the Hospital Lariboisière, close to the Gare du Nord, the building shadowing them from the setting last-quarter moon. Too many bikes tethered outside a café-bar at a time like this might well attract the kind of attention you didn't want. Visitors to places of refreshment had to get away home eventually, and when a curfew was in force – how, without infringing it? Whereas a hospital – or indeed a brothel . . . Dénault added, 'Sod them, anyway. And if we get what we've been promised . . . Come *on*, man—'

'Padlock's rusted.' Patrice got up, pocketing the lock and chain. 'You lead?'

'Sure. Stay well behind me, so we don't both ride into trouble. And because I've gone round a corner doesn't mean it's safe for you to whizz round after me – take care, eh?'

'Doubt we'd meet trouble.'

'Famous last words. Know where it is now, do you?'

'North of the cemetery. Rue St Fargeau . . . Yes, I do, but—'

'Close to the far end of it, over the Avenue Gambetta. A working garage – repairs, *gazo* conversions. Fécontel's to have one of his people looking out for us, we ride in and they shut the door again. All right, here we go.'

East – Boulevard de la Chapelle – then south-east, Dénault pausing at every blind corner, usually in shadow. Patrice keeping 30–50 metres behind him. Swinging to the right *without* pausing at the La Fayette/Jean Jaures junction, into Avenue Secretan: it was all wide open, that crossing, moonlit as well, no cover; if you were spotted by *Milice* or *Schutzpolizei* you'd stoop low and race, simply trust to luck.

Over it now, anyway – in Avenue Secretan. Ahead, Dénault weaving somewhat drunkenly as he turned to look back. Patrice muttering, 'Don't worry about *me*, just keep going' – at that moment hearing a car behind him – not *gazo*, petrol engine. Up at the crossroads somewhere, no sight of it or shred of light, in a quick glance back; telling himself it might *not* be coming down this way.

Dénault had swung off to the right. Patrice put his back into it, maximum effort, pedalling like crazy to get to that turn-off *before*—

Streak of light from a masked headlight behind there, at the crossing. He wondered, *Fall off, act plastered?* On the assumption that neither *Milice* nor SD would take much interest in a *drunken* curfew-breaker. Unless they were out trawling for replacement hostages. But have to smell of drink, which despite being a barman he did not – not tonight, anyway. He'd reached the fork, was careering into it. That blackness a few hundred metres ahead had been the *Buttes Chaumont*, a steep wooded rise, which meant that this curl of road had to be – oh, Avenue Simon Bolivar? The car's engine was loud behind him – shifting gear. To make the same turn? Spotted him, in pursuit now? There was no sight of Dénault in front; no cover either – not a corner, tree or parked vehicle, entrance with a wall, or—

It had passed the turning, and gone on – straight on down Avenue Secretan. Either had not seen him, or had more urgent business. Patrice braking, guessing that if he didn't slow up he might shoot out at the bottom of the next wide bend just as the car passed at that lower junction, this end of the *Buttes*. Although Dénault – well ahead of him, presumably – which would mean *he* must have put on a hell of a spurt – might have a better chance of doing precisely that.

'Hey! Patrice!'

Speak of the devil. Riding sedately out of this intersection – a slightly smaller road, whatever the hell it was. And the sound of the car passing the other end of it, its junction with the lower end of Secretan, at just this moment. Gone then, and the sound fading.

'All right?'

'*Now*, it's all right!'

'What was it, did you see?'

Dénault was so thickset that approaching head-on as he was you didn't notice the bike, only the squarish mass of him above it. Patrice had stopped, one foot on the kerb. Telling him no, he'd no idea; some Boche general, been dipping his wick, maybe. Was this the Avenue Bolivar though?

'Exactly. At the bottom we go over the *carrefour* into Rue des Pyrenées. Five hundred metres then and Saint Fargeau's on the left, and after about another five hundred—'

'OK.'

They'd be getting – had been promised – several hundred Schmeisser machine-pistols tonight, also a large quantity of 9-millimetre.

Dénault had stopped to wait for him on the Rue St Fargeau between Avenue Gambetta and Boulevard Mortier.

'It's up there.'

The approach was by way of a concrete strip with a warehouse on one side and a 10-foot brick wall on the other. At the back of the warehouse it led to a cindered parking area with some wrecked-looking *gazos* here and there and a single-storey garage frontage at the back. *The* garage. As their bicycles scrunched off concrete on to cinders, a torch flashed once, over there. It was very dark but one's eyes had become used to that – the moon being down now, and of course no street-lighting. To keep its lights on and the Métro running Paris needed 10,000 tons of coal a day, and wasn't getting *any*. Dénault dismounted, began to push his bike towards the garage, calling into the silence, 'Georges Dénault and Patrice Macombre.'

The torch came on again, licked across timber double doors – closed – and lingered on a small personnel door set in the left-hand one. This was clearly for their guidance, the torch-man calling to those inside, 'Dénault and another. Open up!' It was opened, and another torch shone into Dénault's face and then Patrice's as they wheeled their bikes in, Dénault grumbling, 'Trying to blind me? Oh – you, Alain.'

'No problems?'

'None at all. Are my people here?' Shaking hands. 'This is Patrice Macombre. Alain Fécantel.' The place was crowded but reasonably quiet, men standing around chatting, smoking, exercising patience: there was an aroma of oil and cigarette smoke. Dénault adding, 'The way we came, nothing's moving.'

'Boches are patrolling the main through-roads. *Milice* don't seem to be out at all.'

'A lot of 'em left town Thursday night. But they're still in and out of Rue Monceau, I heard. And the Auteuil synagogue they're using for a barracks. What time's this fellow due?'

'Twelve to twelve-thirty.'

'But that's *now*!'

'Yes. You were a little late, Georges.'

'What sort of guy is he?'

'Typical black-marketeer. Name of Maurard. The guns and ammo just happened to fall into his hands, he says.'

'What about payment?'

'He's accepting a promissory note. Parodi's backing it so he can't doubt it's good. My idea's to stash most of the stuff here and move it out load by load Monday. Your one-fifth to Gare de l'Est – that still OK?'

'So all we do tonight is unload the man's transport?'

'And divide it. Jabot and Ruard are taking theirs, they've *gazos* out there.'

'I thought those were wrecks!'

'It's a risk, moving the stuff at night. But that's what they want, so—'

'Hey . . .'

A thump – a bang on the small door. In here, sudden and total silence. Then the voice from outside – not loud but carrying, in the hollow stillness: 'A truck's backing up now!'

You could hear it: a big petrol engine. Some of these crooks really took the biscuit – you could bet your last *sou* it would be a 'borrowed' *Wehrmacht* truck, would have stood virtually no risk of being stopped. Dénault had just put a cigarette in his mouth and would by now have lit it, instead was returning it to the pack. Muttering to Patrice as the other man left them, 'Fucker's on time, what's more. Too good to be true, huh?'

'Hello there, Georges!'

'Who's that?'

'Paul – also Marcel and Bernard.'

'Where's Tallandier?'

'He's here somewhere. Hi, Patrice. Make mine a double, eh?'

Chuckles, handshakes, pats on shoulders, cigarette stubs being dropped and trodden on. Sound of a heavy vehicle braking out there, and the torch-man's call of, 'Open up, lads!'

'Yeah. Let's get on with it . . .'

They were working on the doors, which began scraping open. Still only the one torch – no, two, but both of them dim, in need of new batteries. Dénault muttering, 'Need more light . . .'

They got it. Brilliant, from the open back of the truck. Guns too, the kind they'd come here for, Schmeisser machine-pistols in the hands of maybe a dozen SS men, some jumping down but others staying up there with the stubby blue-black barrels of the Schmeissers glinting in the spill of light from those blinding, shifting beams and trained on the mob inside here. A German voice then yelling in accented French, 'Stay where you are – hands up! Move, you're dead! *You*—'

A short burst: and the man who'd been outside and had backed into the garage with his torch, guiding the truck's driver, and who must have made some move – maybe to get out past it – was down on his knees on the concrete, arms clutched around his belly; there'd been ricochets, steel-cased slugs singing away to smash out through the tin roof. The officer jumped down and finished off the torch-man with a single shot in the back of his head. Facing them again in the outspill of the lights that were intermittently blinding everyone; two other Germans had jumped down, those still up there watching keenly over the helmeted heads, machine-pistols as well as the light-beams shifting this way and that. The officer again: 'Any of you carrying arms, drop them! Use only one hand. *Now!* So . . . One man at a time – starting there; *you* – forward! Any still carrying a weapon will be shot, so – *drop* them! All right – hands up! Higher! *Und* – *forward*! No – in file, in *file*!' A few gutturals then to those up behind him on the truck, and a sack was dumped over, crashed down on the concrete – heavy, metallic, a weight of chain.

Chapter 11

By 9.30, when the men were due, Adée and Rosie had washed the tables and swept the Dog's floor; Adée had also riddled the cinders out of her stove and topped it up, and given the *toilette* a once-over, while Rosie took on the easier job of polishing and stacking glasses – Adée pointing out that Patrice having got away with it last night would be expecting to do it when he came on duty at 11 o'clock.

'Won't be coming with Georges, then?'

'Doubt it. He's a lazy devil.' She had the door open to the street, to air the place. 'And Georges is late, of course, but that's his habit. Don't worry, he'll turn up with some cast-iron excuse . . . Morning, Susanne!'

A fat girl who'd been passing – people were walking or cycling past all the time – had stopped, just about filling the doorway. 'Adée . . . Did you hear, they're flying the tricolor over l'Hôtel de Ville as well as the Préfecture now?'

'Who are?'

'Why, the *Résistance*, surely! What's more, they say there are barricades—'

'Only in some side-streets here and there.' Martin Leblanc, with a hand on the girl's elbow, squeezing himself in past her. 'Not on any of the boulevards or main streets. The Boches are still patrolling those, and they look as if they mean business.' He patted the girl's arm: 'Run along, you'll be late.'

'Oh, I've been to *early* Mass, m'sieur!'

'Run along anyway, there's a good lass.' He came on in,

glancing back to make sure she'd gone. Then: 'Georges not been in touch?'

'No.' Adée shrugged. 'But when *was* he on time?'

'Morning, Jeanne-Marie.'

'M'sieur le professeur . . .'

He looked ill, she thought. Had shaved, and nicked himself in two places; his rather close-together eyes looked weary and had dark pouches under them, and his skin was yellower than she remembered it. Daylight, of course: but still . . . She asked him, 'Did you by any chance – you know, Georges said you were meeting someone—'

'No luck, I'm sorry to say. Something may come of it – at least the word's out in that quarter now. But as of this moment, no.' He was wearing a pullover instead of the black waistcoat, and a collarless grey shirt under it. Teacher's Sunday gear . . . Asking Adée, 'Want the door left open, do you?'

'For air, yes – and for Georges, damn it . . .'

'Any chance of coffee?' Sliding himself on to the bench behind the left-hand table. 'I've had nothing since I was here last night. *Hell* of a night, and now it's worse. I'd better break it to you – not that one can be *certain*—'

'One can be muttering gibberish, by the sound of it.' Adée, on her way to the stove, shrugging and raising her eyebrows at Rosie; Rosie at the other table now, facing the distinctly rough-looking schoolmaster across the room. He'd looked less rough *un*shaven. Giving himself a cigarette but pausing, holding the packet up: 'Anyone?'

'No, thank you. What are you telling us?'

'Had a *nuit blanche*, he said. Don't make it more serious than that.' She was very anxious, though, Rosie saw, clearly didn't *want* to hear whatever bad news he'd brought. He warned Rosie: 'If it's what it looks like it's more than just "serious".' His match flared: then, expelling smoke in a sudden gasp. 'Nothing would delight me more than to have Georges walk in that door, but—'

'Why shouldn't he?'

'Adée, the facts are these. Listen. I pray that I'm wrong, jumping to conclusions.' The cigarette smelt like smouldering horse-hair. 'Please, God—'

'Please, Martin—'

'First – no, not first, but I'll start with this – at about six I had a telephone call from Henriette Fécantel, whose husband was running the show last night. It was with him – Alain Fécantel – the crook with the load of Schmeissers got in touch, you see.'

'Go on.'

'He's not home. Alain is not at home. Wasn't then and *still* isn't. Well, twenty minutes ago he wasn't. I checked again before I left. He'd guaranteed he'd be home before sunrise, and he's a man who makes a plan then sticks to it.'

'Well – if he *can*, but—'

'No, wait. Henriette sent her boy round to her friend Antoinette Jabot – and Marc Jabot hadn't got back either. They wouldn't have been together, but the fact is they're both missing. And there's another – I forget his name, one of Alain's younger follows—'

'So they've been held up somewhere!'

'Now we have Georges and Patrice also missing. Incidentally, I tried Georges' number and had no reply. He could have been on his way to you; until I got here I didn't know for sure. No, wait, Adée, there's more – the worst of it, in fact, I'm trying to break this to you gently—'

'Do you know the garage – where it is?'

'I do, and I thought of that, of course, but' – blinking at the rectangle of morning light and the people, shadows and reflections making their brief appearances across it – 'I think it might be foolish to show one's face around there. The Boches aren't stupid; and – see, if a trap works once—'

'Trap?'

'Yes. Listen. Before any of that I had a visit from – you wouldn't know him, his name's Mishon. In regard to *your* business, Jeanne-Marie, Georges and I arranged for certain addresses to be watched for comings and goings, and Mishon was alternating with another man in Rue des Saussaies. From a scrap of garden on the other side from number eleven and further along – nearer the Montalivet corner than—'

'Here you are, your coffee.' Adée grim-faced, not looking at either of them. 'Jeanne-Marie, want some?'

She didn't. Watching Martin sip at his and flinch from the heat but persevere, really needing it: putting the mug down then and drawing deeply on his cigarette, telling them through the smoke, 'At about one o'clock two SS trucks arrived at number eleven and a whole crowd of prisoners was herded into the building. Mishon was as close as he could get and watching for it because there'd been activity by *Miliciens* just before – the gates opened, torches flashing and so forth – but he heard more than he saw, because the disembarkation was inside the courtyard, and only by torch-light of course. But there was a Gestapo car as well, one of those Citroens.'

'You said a whole crowd . . .'

'He guessed a couple of dozen. Started off saying maybe fifty, then no, not that many. You can imagine, in the dark and they'd have been on the qui vive, and he's got to take care they don't spot *him*. It's about right though, from what Georges said was being arranged – thirty or more, he expected. Anyway, when the trucks had driven away and it had gone quiet, Mishon got on his bike and he was waiting for me when I got home. About three, that was. I'd been at these meetings. He was worried, had he done the right thing – deserting his post, he called it. Old soldier – sixty if he's a day.'

'So Georges and Patrice, you think—'

'I've told you what I know.' Sucking loudly at the hot liquid, then continuing, 'What's *your* guess? I'll tell you, anyway, we have to face this – far from that prospect of acquiring Schmeissers, putting ourselves in a strong position for whatever's coming now' – shake of the head – 'instead, disaster. From *your* point of view as well, Jeanne-Marie, I'm not forgetting that. But across the board, disastrous. Our chief and five others, maybe the best we had – not to mention the other groups: Fécantel's, Jabot's. Ruard's—'

'Is there no chance you're wrong?'

'No. *I* was trying to convince myself. On my way here, telling myself Georges would be here large as life, explaining how they'd had to lie low in the garage because of Boches in the vicinity, or – whatever else.' Another jerk of the balding head. 'No. One *knew* it, too.' Insisting to Adée – quietly, intently – 'And we must now face it as it is – that they'll either kill them or release them. These aren't the sort of prisoners they'd work on – not for long – they don't have the kind of information Jeanne-Marie's friends have. But, Jeanne-Marie, you know the inside of number eleven, Georges mentioned to me that you were a prisoner there?'

She'd nodded. 'They put one in cells in the basement – the cellars. From the *rez-de-chaussée* there are winding stone stairs leading down. One passed armed sentries, then came to a locked iron door with a grille in it, then more concrete passage to another locked door. A guard drove one along with the butt of his rifle, you know, one wasn't given time to stop and look around exactly – but then there was a smelly, concrete – vault, you might call it. You'd get a lot of people in there, all right, maybe that's where they'd put them. But beyond it are doors to inner cells. Mine had one barred window high up, nothing else. For interrogations they took one upstairs . . . Are you thinking of breaking in?'

'No. *Thought* of it, but – we'd get ourselves killed, get them killed too. Whereas if we just wait . . . I know what I said, but – a while ago they did release a whole lot of prisoners; and what would they achieve by killing these? Or for that matter from knocking them about – even if they knew anything the Boches don't already know.'

'Your guess is they'll interrogate them, get nothing, let them go.'

'I'd say there's a good chance they will. Especially as they seem to be taking a soft line now. The tricolor, for instance – and doing nothing. Incredible, isn't it?'

'Ignoring the one on the Préfecture, I was told yesterday, because they don't want to provoke a rising and have to send troops and tanks into the streets.'

'So by the same principle, why would they murder those – what, thirty-five . . . Was it the SD man's woman told you this?'

'Yes. Not that I was questioning her – the flag was there. I'd mentioned it, was all. Look, I'm sorry, Martin – I mean, to be any sort of burden to you now. You have a hundred things to cope with. I have only the one, well, fixation. And now since you've had this setback—'

'For Georges and Patrice, *quite* a setback!'

'I know, Adée – and believe me—'

'As far as your task is concerned,' – Leblanc again – '*you're* set back, huh?'

'But I'm meeting this SD man today—'

'The SD *thing*.' Adée looked at Leblanc. 'Who might have taken part in last night's business.'

'If he did, it's not likely he'd be talking about it. But naturally, if he *did*—'

'Might I offer some advice?' Leblanc was lighting another cigarette. 'I'm sure you know your business, Jeanne-Marie, you wouldn't be here if you didn't – and all *I* know is *résistance* business. But it seems to me you need to be very, very careful. This situation now – well, look at it – the Boches permitting us to display the flag of France, but at the same time sending a supposed black-marketeer to Alain Fécantel – knowing Alain for what he is and where to find him, knowing also our desperate need of weapons and using that as a bait we couldn't refuse—'

'But they *are* getting out of Paris. Aren't they? Not all at once, but—'

'They're patrolling the boulevards. *Holding* Paris. A lot of non-combatants – clerks, specialists and technicians – have been cleared out. But last night's operation – they weren't backing-off on *that*. See what I mean, Jeanne-Marie?'

'It's a point – and thank you – but I can't just sit on my hands and do nothing, when—'

'Don't underestimate this man. If he's SD he's a trained interrogator. Smiling to himself, waiting for you. D'you trust the woman?'

'I think so. Yes. For the same reason she won't inform on *him* – in a way.'

'I'm sure *you* know what you mean.'

'Hard to explain. How she *is*, that's all.'

'I shouldn't be lecturing you, I know.' Thin smile, and a shrug: 'Force of habit – my apologies. But – to approach such a man with questions, if you *were* thinking of—'

'No. No questions – other than trivialities. One can *show interest*, of course.'

There was an occasional outbreak of small-arms fire that didn't come from the directions of either the Château de Vincennes or Mont Valérien, where most of the daily hostage-executions were carried out. Maybe they didn't do it on Sundays anyway. But these occasional fusillades, Leblanc had said, would be from the barricades with which communist elements of the FFI were reported to have been blocking some back-streets, giving the impression of Resistance-controlled neighbourhoods. There'd been talk of it last night apparently at meetings all over Paris, including two which Leblanc had attended in the hours around midnight, representing Dénault and his Gaullist FFI group, and supporting arguments against premature action in the streets. Arms raids in several locations, including one on the Hotchkiss factory and of course Fécantel's at that garage, were scheduled to take place during the weekend, and the Gaullist preference was to wait until they had those weapons in their hands, at least a chance of standing up to the enormously better-armed and organised

16,500 remaining Boches. It was also a matter of playing for time, for representatives who – touch wood – would by now be on their way to Eisenhower's headquarters to plead for immediate intervention.

Leblanc had people out now, rounding up other members of Dénault's group. Later the Blue Dog would be packed, for alternatives to be discussed and decisions taken in the light of the night's disaster. The schoolmaster had told her, 'As Adée will confirm, I'm our group's leader now – temporarily, at any rate. And I have it *here*' – tapping his forehead – 'I'm a planner, I can see ahead a little – but I don't have Georges' personality, that forceful leadership. I'll do my best, that's all – and pray we have him back with us very soon.'

Rosie rode south by way of Boulevard Magenta and Rue du Temple, with the Tour St Jacques as her leading mark, wanting to see for herself the tricolor on l'Hôtel de Ville. And there it was: she could tell Jacqui she'd seen it. L'Hôtel itself was said to be full of FFI who'd taken possession of it at first light. She heard rifle-fire again then – from the left bank and some distance off – vicinity of the Panthéon maybe, or the Sorbonne. Leblanc had dismissed all of that as 'Playing soldiers. Barricades that'd hardly stop a bicycle, let alone a tank.' But to assert their own questionable authority they'd shoot over people's heads, he'd said, make them stop and identify themselves, and insist to all and sundry, 'If you're not for us, you're against us!' and '*A chacun son Boche!*'

In contrast to which boys and girls were splashing in the river, under this blaze of sunshine and cloudless sky. In her thoughts as she rode north-westward Rosie contrasted this gentle, pretty scene with how it would be for Georges and the rest of them in that cellar. There'd been a bell to ring, she remembered, when one wanted to go to the lavatory, and as long as it wasn't between 8 pm and 8 am a burly Gestapo female would eventually turn up and take one to it. But with more than thirty of them . . . Better not to think about it, even. Pedalling west with the sparkling river on her left, having passed the Louvre – this now was the Quai du Louvre, with the Tuileries up ahead and the sun on the river, shrill cries of the bathers; swinging over and closing in to the right-hand kerb then as an armoured troop-carrier trundled by, overtaking her. Gone: with its load of goons in helmets. Place de la Concorde now: and the bridge, and yet more swimmers and sun-bathers. Rue des Saussaies would be – what, a kilometre from here, roughly due north? Perhaps less: 750 metres, say. Cycling due west now with the Invalides off to her left, its dome golden in the sun, and beyond it the gaunt vertical of the Eiffel Tower.

Maybe they *would* let them go – Georges and company. If they did, when she next saw Georges he might be able to tell her whether there'd been any other prisoners in that building.

Jacqui answered the ring of the doorbell within seconds, must have been waiting for it. *Would* have been: one had to realise, she'd be nervous too.

She didn't look in the least bit nervous. She was wearing what in England before the war had been known as 'beach pyjamas', floppy cotton trousers and a hip-length top – vine-leaf pattern, brilliant green. Glossy dark hair swept back and shoulder-length, wide eyes lightly shadowed, small jade earrings. Rosie, in the outfit she'd had on at lunch the day before, felt even dowdier than she had then.

Jacqui drew her inside. 'Hurrah, you made it!'

'You're *stupendous*, Jacqui.'

'I told him.' A whisper, as they kissed. 'And that I persuaded you to come, because you're someone I can count on.' Voice up again: 'You're looking marvellous too, I may say!'

Playing her part, all right. While Rosie made *her* effort – feeling idiotic as well as scared – an idiot for coming here, taking on the 'trained interrogator', and scared because – because she *was*, while at the same time being very much aware that it was essential not to look or sound as if she might be. Nervous, and/or shy – fine, no problem, but *never* scared. That was *her* play-acting, and so often had been: while Jacqui might have been overdoing it a little – gushing, rather. Mightn't Clausen, who'd no doubt be in earshot of this, pick up the falsity? Anyway they were inside by this time, the new-looking door had clicked shut and Rosie was saying, 'Marvellous, my foot. Scruffy little country cousin just come to visit, more like it.' Glancing round: '*What* a nice flat.'

'We were lucky – Gerhardt took it over from a friend who was leaving. Come on through. I don't think he's finished changing, hasn't been back long. He's kept so busy – up half the night, and then—'

'This is a *lovely* room!'

'It's not bad, is it? And – here, come and see . . .'

French doors led out on to a balcony, on which a glass-topped table was set for lunch but still left plenty of room. Wicker chairs with bright cushions – all very pretty. And a fine view to the west and north-west – ignoring the immediate foreground, a street lined with houses and further up-slope a wide intersection – that was the way she'd come, on Friday. Two days ago was all; it felt like at least a week. Jacqui pointing: 'Lucky those houses are in a dip so one looks right over them. To the left up there are the gardens – Ranelagh, named after some English place, I'm told – and the rest of it, all that forestry up behind—'

'Bois de Boulogne. Lovely walks, right on your doorstep.'

'Two thousand acres, yes, but unfortunately full of soldiers just now. They rest them there under canvas, whole regiments in transit – from Normandy, Gerhardt says, resting-up before continuing – oh, to wherever, don't ask *me* . . .'

'I won't, I promise. One thing I do hope, Jacqui, is we're not going to talk about the damn war!'

'Is there anything *else* to talk about?'

Clausen, behind them, joining them on the balcony. Rosie glancing round, startled – which was all right, why *not* be?

The timing in fact had been fortuitous: it couldn't have been accidental that he'd crossed the room – parquet floor, uncarpeted – as quietly as he had; if she'd been saying anything she shouldn't have, he'd have heard it. And one might have, *might* have thought that out here a conversation would have been safe enough. There were lessons in that too – not least, that he'd suspected they might have had confidences to exchange? Looking at him now rather shyly, answering that question with, 'I'm sure there must be. Could talk about Jacqui for instance – who's even more beautiful than she was a year ago. Isn't she incredible?'

'Well, yes, I have to admit . . .' His French was only slightly German-accented. Tallish – in a silk shirt, cravat, off-white cotton trousers, loafers with tassels on them. Could have been a character in a Noël Coward play: and yet was still Germanic.

Through being conscious of his own membership of the Master Race, in the company of Jacqui and herself?

Membership of the SD, at that. *Shaking hands* with him, for Christ's sake – Jacqui having introduced them. He *was* good-looking – as she remembered from a year ago. Late thirties, with a summer tan and dark hair greying at the temples. He looked good standing beside Jacqui, and vice-versa. But like a couple in some advertisement, she thought. Or – again – the Noël Coward play . . . Hearing him say to Jacqui, 'I do remember now.' Meaning that he remembered *her*. Releasing Rosie's hand: 'We met in Rouen, of course. When Jacqui mentioned it I didn't immediately recall—'

'No reason you should have. Five minutes or so – as I remember it – and you only had a day or two, you'd been away and—'

'I am impressed by *your* memory, Jeanne-Marie. Is it all right to call you by your first name? Jacqui's been going on about you and your anxiety on her account, and that's how she refers to you in telling me about it.'

'Quite all right. Yes, I *am* concerned for her.'

'As I am myself – very much so—'

'Jeanne-Marie: an apéritif of some kind?'

'Oh. Perhaps – fruit juice?'

'Or a glass of wine? Gerhardt has a Riesling from Alsace which I personally—'

'*Well*—'

'I'll get it. For you too, Gerhardt?'

He'd nodded. 'Please.' Pulling back a chair for Rosie, then. 'Do sit down. You must need to – all the way from Vincennes by bicycle?'

Where they were putting her, she'd have a view of that panorama of woodland. Jacqui would be on her right, Clausen was already on her left. Asking her did she smoke, would she like to: no, she told him, she wouldn't, French cigarettes were awful now as well as rationed and expensive, she was within an ace of giving up completely. 'But you were saying – about our shared concern for Jacqui . . . I suppose sooner or later you *will* be leaving Paris – France, even – and it's not possible to take her with you?'

'No.' A frown, and a gesture of helplessness. 'I should like to very much indeed, but—'

Jacqui returning. He'd flipped open a pewter cigarette-case. 'The French ones aren't fit to smoke, I agree. As it happens, these are German – Jacqui smokes them—'

'Don't I just! Light one for me, *chéri*? But now here we are, Jeanne-Marie.' Bottle and three tall green glasses on a tray. 'It's not as cold as it should be, but—'

'Without electricity there's little one can do about that, unfortunately.' Clausen stood up, to pour the Riesling. 'Mind you, its absence gives rise to greater inconveniences than having to drink a wine that's not as well chilled as it might be – uh?'

Rosie nodded. 'Hospitals, for instance.'

'Indeed. You were a nurse, Jacqui mentioned.' Sitting again, and lighting two cigarettes. 'So glad you were able to come today, Jeanne-Marie . . . Where did you do that – the nursing?'

'In more than one hospital. Most recently at Nantes. And as a trainee at first, which was mostly scrubbing floors and so forth, here in Paris. But I'm not really cut out for it, I'm afraid. When I met you in Rouen of course I was trying to sell perfume – and Jacqui was *so* kind to me . . .'

'That job didn't last long, I understand.'

'You're right, it didn't.'

'And you have a child – little girl – for whom you're searching now in Paris?'

'She's with her grandmother – my late husband's mother. The old woman must be crackers, but I do know she'll be looking after her. Trying to steal her from me, I suppose. It's a long, boring story – via Nantes to Dijon, then here – no, Rouen first—'

'To find Jacqui, eh?'

'Partly. But I was seeing another friend there too.'

'And in Jacqui's *salon* they gave you this address?'

'Yes. Eventually.'

'That Portuguese she's taken on?'

Rosie looked at Jacqui. 'I believe I'm being interrogated.'

'I beg your pardon.' Stiff-faced, formal. *German*. 'Such was not my intention – only it is surprising—'

'*I'm* surprised that such details should be of interest. I got the address – here I *am*!'

'The surprise to us both arises from the fact that he was told not to release such information. So much for *him*.' To Jacqui: 'But it might not be easy to replace him. And as things are now he might be better on your side than as your enemy. Perhaps just caution him?' Back to Rosie: 'You told Jacqui some customers were gossiping about her relationship with me?'

'Yes. Not that your name was mentioned. Only – you know – catty remarks. Which in the long run it struck me could be lethal.'

'And that's what brought you here. For which we're both grateful. Not that we aren't in any case well aware of that danger. May I ask you – with apologies in advance – one *more* question?'

'Go ahead.' She nodded to Jacqui. 'This *is* a good wine. From Alsace, you said.'

'Which is currently German again but may very well revert to French occupation before much longer.'

'You think you'll soon be right out of France?'

'Out of Alsace too – if you'll allow me my own historical perspective. But – almost certainly. They won't stop *before* the Rhine, that's for sure. And now we're talking about the war, which you particularly requested we should not?'

'*I* thought the subject was wine.'

'So it was. Yes, all the Alsace whites I like very much. But my question – a serious one, Jeanne-Marie – is about Jacqui again. You're worried for her, and so am I. She, on the surface anyway, less so. Is that also *your* impression?'

'Talking about me like this – as if I weren't even here—'

'The motive behind her display of sang-froid being, of course' – continuing to Rosie – 'to make it easier for *me*, although the predicament is very much her own. I tell you, Jeanne-Marie, I love this woman very much indeed.'

'I understand it's mutual.'

'I too. I have had some evidence of it, even.' Joke: thin smile to label it as such. Rosie wondering how Jacqui could stand him, let alone be in love with him. Even that 'love this woman very much indeed' had had a coldly formal ring to it. *False* ring. Adding now, 'Should be straightforward therefore, but unfortunately that's not the case – on account of complicating factors of which I believe you know. Hence this question now: you intimated to Jacqui yesterday that you have a practical suggestion – what we could do, what *she* could?'

'Well.' She took another sip, and put her glass down. 'No great brainwave, I'm afraid. Rather obvious. Simply that she should get out of Paris and stay out until things have settled down.'

'Until the Resistance has finished taking its revenge, you mean.'

The riposte in her mind was *that might take a bloody century*. She didn't say it. Instead, 'Stay away from Rouen too. That would be as bad – having heard those women. They'll be denouncing people to prove *they* weren't collaborators. But there's this farm not far from Nantes, where my child and the old woman were. A quiet, hard-working couple, getting on in years, with a house larger than they need. I could take Jacqui there and introduce her as a friend who's been ill, needs peace and quiet.' Looking at Jacqui: 'Peace and quiet's about all there is; you'd be bored out of your mind, I warn you. But – second thought – might let it be known that you were a *résistante*.' A nod towards Clausen. 'Might have been in *his* hands?'

'In my – hands . . .'

Staring at her, hard-eyed. Inducing in Rosie a not totally unfamiliar tightening of the nerves. But one was *here*, and hadn't contrived to get this close to him merely to indulge in small talk, couldn't expect to be smiled at *all* the time. Bull by the horns, therefore: 'Aren't you in the SD – don't you have prisoners, interrogate them – torture even, send them to concentration camps, and so on?'

'*She*' – a head-movement towards Jacqui – 'tell you this?'

'It's common knowledge, what SD do. Even in Rouen I knew that was what you were – Jacqui'd have told me *that* much, obviously.'

'Well . . . For your information, Jeanne-Marie, I *have* conducted interrogations – yes, many times. But where your imagination may run beyond that, and off the rails a little – torture, deportation—'

'No.' Jacqui, quietly: 'He could *not*—'

'*He* might not, but having established a prisoner's guilt it would follow, wouldn't it?'

Blinking at her, thinking about it. Deciding to ignore it then, telling her, 'What I am, Jeanne-Marie, is an intelligence officer. As such I've many times identified and arrested, or caused to be arrested, enemies of the Reich. You might say that's been my speciality – detective work. Now, most of my time's spent sifting, collating and summarising intelligence, compiling daily and weekly reports for my Berlin head office and for OKW – the General Staff, that is. I tell you this in confidence, obviously, but – *not* so terrible – uh?'

'Intelligence to do with the Resistance, by any chance?'

'Why ask me that?'

'Well – for Jacqui: and this *is* perhaps a brainwave. Why not draw up a report on *her*? It'd be absolutely authentic, wouldn't it – you'd make it so – and she'd have it leaked to her somehow, could use it as proof she's only been with you in order to work *against* you. Passing on your secrets – who's going to be arrested next, that sort of thing? You've caught her out and she has to run for it. You wouldn't file the report, perhaps, because of the nature of your relationship. Might even go so far as to suppress it – *warn* her?'

'I believe I'd shoot myself.'

'Alternatively – as a loyal German officer – or sergeant, is it—'

'I am an officer. Using the rank of sergeant and dressing as a civilian is a special dispensation from my superiors, facilitating my work in certain ways.'

'Right. As a loyal German officer, then – the report exists, say, it's on your desk, you might be in two minds about it but – do you have staff, some of them French?'

'Most of our clerical employees are French.'

'One of them secretly working for the Resistance is how Jacqui might get to hear of it. How she'd have got hold of other material too. Anyway, she's tipped off. What then? Well, if she doesn't immediately disappear you *would* confront her with it – arrest her, I suppose – have to, wouldn't you, no matter how agonising that might be for you? But then – well, how long have *you* got? Mightn't you be recalled to Germany at any moment?'

'I might. Yes.' He'd reached over to put a hand on Jacqui's: a gesture that might have made him seem more human being than secret policeman. To Jacqui, it might have done, but to Rosie it seemed wooden – a stage-direction followed unconvincingly. Shaking his head: 'One doesn't know. No one does. There is a considerable degree of administrative confusion – in the circumstances perhaps inevitable. That's what's at the back of all this, isn't it?'

'But – two things . . . One: if you were going to do this, or something like it, it might be best to draft the report right away – have it ready. And two: Jacqui getting wind of it wouldn't hang around, would she – knowing she faces arrest, being locked up and then God knows what? Locked up where and by whom, incidentally?'

'What d'you mean?'

'Well – Gestapo, or—'

'Why should that detail concern us – concern *you* – in any way at all?'

It was the sort of question, she realised – seeing Jacqui's look of surprise, alarm even, as well as the sharpness of *his* reaction – that she should *not* have asked.

Chapter 12

She'd recovered from that blunder, she thought. Having come close to cooking her own goose or at least warning him off with the direct question she'd promised herself (and assured Martin Leblanc this morning) she *wouldn't* ask. The parallel between the fiction she'd been proposing and the position of Léonie and Rouquet being so close, the question had virtually asked itself – and might have paid off if one had taken a few seconds to weigh it up, gone for it less directly. She'd actually got out of it quite well, she thought, pointing out (a) that Jacqui's story needed all the background it could get, since it might have to stand up to close scrutiny by FFI or other post-Occupation investigative authority, and (b) that Clausen's withdrawal from Paris being for all he knew imminent, he might well have baulked at the prospect of leaving her in, say, Gestapo hands: so what alternative might he have had – in her account of it, the way she'd tell it – other than either dithering, thus allowing time for the leak and her escape, or himself tipping her off, letting her go and *then* on the face of it discovering what she'd been up to?

He'd stayed silent: watching her, presumably thinking it out, unmoving while Jacqui decided abruptly to get lunch and declined Rosie's offer of help. Rosie recalling Leblanc's *Don't underestimate this man . . .* Adding then as her own unhurried afterthought, 'What you'd have told your own superiors would have been your own business, you'd know how to address that. You'd be gone and so would all your records; all anyone here would have to go on would be what Jacqui told them. *That*'s what would have to be realistic enough to hold water. Don't you agree?'

He hadn't come out of his own deliberations until Jacqui had gone inside.

'You've come up with a good idea, Jeanne-Marie, but we'd spoil it by allowing it to become too complicated. In principle, it's excellent. I'm delighted Jacqui asked you here – and grateful that you sought her out in the first place . . . Speaking of which, when you called here on Friday Jacqui tells me you met Henri Lafont downstairs?'

'He approached me, yes.'

'You didn't know who he was?'

'Not at the time. I asked Jacqui.'

'Oh, yes. He told me he'd met you, too. That was before Jacqui told me you'd been here – or that he had.'

Rosie shrugged. 'A weird character, I thought. That high voice – and to start with, a threatening manner. Is he a friend of yours?'

'We have some professional interests in common, that's all. He'd come by in the hope of catching me, he mentioned.' Watching her, dwelling on a pause as if inviting comment. Rosie thinking, *He'd have known you weren't in. No car down there – known it for certain. And not being an idiot, you're at least as aware of that as I am . . .* Remembering Jacqui's chatter an hour ago: *He's kept so busy, up half the night . . .* A statement in which she, Rosie, had shown no interest: just as she wasn't reacting now to whatever Clausen was trying to convey or probe for. He was changing the subject anyway: 'As I say, I'm grateful for your excellent suggestion. Regarding detail, I'll sleep on it. A possibility one must of course allow for is some French member of my office staff volunteering evidence to any subsequent inquiry, challenging Jacqui's story.'

'How might you deal with that?'

'Brief Jacqui on how to challenge any of *them*. I'd have spoken to her of my suspicions of X, Y or Z. I'll give her some notes to memorise . . . You really mean it, though, you'd go down to Nantes with her, stay there with her?'

'I don't see why I shouldn't. One difficulty may be this business of finding my daughter, but—'

'Here we are, at last!'

Jacqui, with a loaded tray – an entrée of stuffed aubergines. Rosie still thinking of her and of the freak with the girlish voice: wondering whether she might be two-timing her beloved Gerhardt. As Gerhardt *might*, she thought, suspect? Knowing as one did quite a lot about Jacqui's past, and guessing that Clausen might know even more, might also have in mind that leopards were at least reputed not to change their spots?

This one might have, though. Although in circumstances such as she was facing now – and needing Clausen as her protector—

'How lovely, Jacqui!'

'Please take lots.'

'You might be sorry you said that. How on earth d'you manage – so quickly, so little effort?'

'I had a girl in this morning, for a few hours. And we cook on gas – the same cylinders they use to drive the buses – which aren't running now in any case . . . But certainly we do live well.'

'Do indeed.' Clausen: he'd opened a second bottle of the Riesling. It had already had a relaxing effect on him, Rosie had noticed. 'In fact it's breaking a lot of hearts to leave this city. I'm giving away no secrets, admitting that. Our women are especially sad about it – understandably enough – but for all of us, in fact—'

'What women are those?'

'Our own – who work with us here. Basically two kinds. You don't speak any German?'

'None.'

'Well, there are the *Edeltrippen* – which literally means "noble typists" – girls of good education and background who mainly work in our offices but will also – oh, sew on buttons, *anything* – and they have a great social life, I can tell you. As well as the shopping, which at the rate of exchange that *we* enjoy—' He shrugged. 'Best not to rub that in, perhaps. But in Germany right now, life's not so comfortable – especially with the bombing, not much fun at all. What I was saying though – another German word for you – there are also what we call the *Blitzmädchen*. War Maidens, eh? They work for our forces – in canteens and so forth, telephone exchanges—'

'And more personal services?'

Jacqui laughing: 'Really, Jeanne-Marie—'

'I meant the "noble" ones. He said they'd do *anything*.'

'Bring *tarts* to *Paris*?'

'I suppose not.'

'The brothel-keepers will be sorry to see us go, I can tell you. D'you know how many are reserved solely for the *Wehrmacht*?'

Jacqui began again on the same note. 'Really, Gerhardt—'

'I'll tell you anyway. Out of the one hundred and twenty which are registered, forty are reserved for soldiers, four for officers and one for generals.'

Rosie said, 'A bit limiting for the generals.'

'It must be,' Clausen agreed. 'One might even refuse promotion to general's rank when the time came.'

'One *serious* question – if it's not a secret—'

'If it is, I'll tell you.'

'The tricolor on the police headquarters – I saw it yesterday when I went to meet Jacqui – and now there's one on l'Hôtel de Ville as well. You're *allowing* this?'

'Surprises you? Yes, I suppose it would.' Putting down his fork. 'The answer is that the military commander of Greater Paris, General Dietrich von Choltitz – a fine soldier, I may say – is not anxious to destroy Paris unless he's forced to. Those two buildings are of no military importance, nor is he interested in a few roughnecks throwing their weight about in the back alleys. As long as he can keep open the roads that matter – those through Paris and encircling it – and the bridges, of course – thus allowing for orderly withdrawal, or fighting withdrawal if necessary – it's all that concerns him. I might add that all the bridges and certain other structures are being wired for demolition in any case.'

'Although you just said—'

'It's officially still a secret: but the Resistance know it. Just as they know we have a number of fortified defensive points – blockhouses, which we call *Stützpunkte* – thirty-two of them commanding what *are* strategic points.' He stood up, continued while removing the first-course plates – Jacqui replacing them with others – 'The head of the Paris FFI – Parodi, a young man who calls himself a general, is allegedly the representative of de Gaulle – was quite by chance arrested at a checkpoint yesterday and taken to be interviewed by von Choltitz at the Hôtel Maurice. They talked, and von Choltitz then released him. Yes – imagine it. Well – to anyone who knows that man's military background, it's astonishing. But you see – what I'm telling you is actually no secret. You could say it's as good as finished here.'

'The occupation of Paris, you mean?'

'To all intents and purposes, you could say so. Oh, there'll be some fighting, more killing – and for those of us who are ordered to remain, of course—'

'Might you be?'

'I would not have thought so, but actually until one receives one's orders—'

'You can't tell. I see. But as regards Jacqui's future—'

'I wouldn't want her to stay here even if it looked as if *I* were going to. No – I'll rough out some sort of dossier in the morning, bring it home and talk it over with you tomorrow night perhaps, *chérie*.' An arm round her shoulders, a quick hug. 'It's a very good idea, isn't it?'

'Quick as that.' Jacqui had pecked him on the cheek. 'Decision taken, we're for the rural peace and quiet, Jeanne-Marie. Seriously, we're both *very* grateful to you. Here now – *Noix de Veau*.'

'Incredible!'

'Oh, the Master Race lives well. How will it be on your farm?'

'Well, we won't starve, but—'

'How will we get there?'

'When the time comes' – Clausen was offering *sauté* potatoes – 'we'll settle that and other details. More importantly here and now, Jeanne-Marie, is how soon *you*'ll be ready to leave Paris. To give up on the search for your daughter, to put it bluntly.'

'I'm *not* giving up. But how long would you guess we *might* have? A week?'

'Maybe that long.' Pausing, he and Jacqui exchanging a thoughtful look: Rosie recognising that even if she *was* playing fast and loose – or contemplating it – neither of them was going to find the separation easy. Thinking fleetingly then of herself and Ben, who'd already been separated for what felt like an eternity – *felt* like it but could not, touch wood, last *much* longer now . . . Clausen saying, 'How I should have put it, perhaps, is whether when the time comes for Jacqui to leave you'll be ready to go with her, irrespective of having found your child. Otherwise – well, locating the farm, and her introduction to the people – and in any case you'd be company for each other. The journey itself may not be at all easy, you realise?'

'I know. Yes. Ideally of course I'd bring them along too. Juliette, anyway, the old woman can go hang. Can we leave it as a decision to be made when the time comes? I *won't* let you down—'

'You're living now at Vincennes?'

'Have been, but I'm moving. The telephone number I gave you, Jacqui, is a café-bar in Montmartre where I've been basing myself in daytime – and that stands. I'll be in lodgings quite close to it. Vincennes is *so* far out.'

'By bicycle, I'd say it would be.'

'Further still to Nantes, mind you.'

'Oh, *very* funny—'

'I don't mean it as a joke, entirely.' She looked at Clausen. 'Transport may not be easy, I guess. In fact getting through at all – as you said . . . Very likely be chaotic on the roads.'

'On *bicycles* – with an old woman and a small child?'

'Well, no, of course—'

Clausen said, 'I'll requisition a *gazo* for you. With spare gas cylinders. Easier from your point of view than wood or charcoal. That can be done tomorrow too. I'll have one of my staff bring it here and park it at the back. He won't bother you, *chérie*, he'll just leave it.'

'French staff, or German?'

'Oh, French. Why?'

'Mightn't he chauffeur us to Nantes? If you paid him well enough?' Jacqui clapped her hands: 'Listen! He might play a rôle in the charade – in the plot with me stealing information?'

'No. Too complicating. The fewer people who know anything at all, the better.'

Rosie nodded. 'I agree.'

'I suppose you're right. What a *mess* it's going to be. *Résistants* and pseudo-*résistants* – that's me, of course – denunciations, no one believing anyone else . . . I'll *hate* it, leaving you!'

'I wish to God I could take you with me.' Shaking his head. 'If I could have that one wish granted . . .' Swirling wine around his glass, tossing it back . . .

'You see' – Jacqui, to Rosie – 'how it is with us.' A shrug then: 'Although, *chéri* – although we know it can't be – can't *now*, that is – we also know that *some* time, even if it's *years*—'

'*Will* I'm afraid be years.' Putting down his knife and fork;

the others had already finished. 'But the future's a blind alley.' To Rosie then: 'Here and now, all we can be certain of is that we have now a rather excellent cream cheese, then for dessert Fraises des Bois in red wine. As one might say, living for the moment, uh?'

The cheese was Fontainebleau, and the little wine-soaked strawberries were delicious. Rosie then accepted a German cigarette as well as coffee – *real* coffee – and a glass of Cognac. 'How I'll stay on my bicycle after all this, God knows . . . Gerhardt – the French staff you mentioned – when you leave, won't *they* be in danger from the Resistance?'

'Those who stay, yes. They know it, of course, they'll have made their own arrangements. Others will come with us.'

'To Germany?'

'By no means all of them, though. As perhaps you realise, we employ literally thousands one way and another. The rest will' – pausing, lighting a cigar –' will disappear, become *résistants* – whatever.'

'What about the man with the high voice?'

'Lafont.'

Jacqui grimaced: 'Who cares?'

'Well – you have a point,' Rosie agreed. 'I thought he was – sinister, in the extreme. But still – interesting, from this distance and in a repulsive sort of way. You said he has a lot of women friends – and lives grandly on money stolen from Jews he's sent to the camps?'

'Jews and others.' Clausen lit his own fresh cigarette. 'But your question, what will happen to them when we leave – for Lafont himself, that's no problem. Two years ago he was granted German citizenship and the rank of captain in the SS. Reward for services rendered – in the course of which he's enriched himself very considerably. As well I must admit as destroying countless *résistant* groups. If it hadn't been for the Gestapo of Rue Lauriston, the Resistance today would be a very much more formidable force than it is.'

'Did he start life as a policeman?'

'Far from it. Actually his story's an amazing one.'

'I'm sure Jeanne-Marie would like to hear it, Gerhardt.'

'Not from *me,* though.'

'Not?'

Rosie said, 'Never mind.' A smile at Jacqui: 'You can tell me, when we're alone in the depths of the countryside with damn-all else to talk about.'

'Gerhardt – after all, what harm?'

'Oh, no *harm* at all. In fact I suppose – if it would entertain you—'

'I'm sure it would!'

'The main facts, anyway – as well, mind you, as *I* know them. But if you should meet him again—'

'God forbid!'

'—just don't tell him *I* told you any of this . . . Policeman – no, that he was *not*. He was a child of the slums who became a petty crook, and my people – that's to say the *Abwehr*, which I was in before I transferred to SD, and the two were merged in any case, eight or nine months ago – *Abwehr* recruited him from a prison cell. Fresnes, as it happens. This was – oh, soon after the Armistice, when the Gestapo took it over. His name then was Chamberlin, he changed it to Lafont. Recruited his people in that same way – they're all criminals, to begin with all men he'd known before as fellow-criminals. Even now there's not one who doesn't have a prison record. To start with he set up an agency locating and seizing assets of all kinds for the Reich government. Everything from gold and bearer bonds to cattle. Then he became a gestapist – and very highly thought of – by catching and breaking down a Resistance leader who was our own Gestapo's most wanted man. Name of Lambrecht – head of the Resistance in Belgium, and by that time with active cells all over – France, Holland, everywhere. Lafont found him living under cover in Toulouse, personally broke into his bedroom and knocked him out, flung him into the boot of a car and drove to Bordeaux where he'd arranged to have the use of a Gestapo cellar – in which he and half a dozen of his gang worked on Lambrecht for two days and nights without a break. Finally, as I said, broke him. Lafont himself uses a whip – but clubs, boots, chains, whatever. Imagine it – and that voice shrieking all the time in his ears – two days and nights . . . Anyway, Lambrecht broke, and the result was more than six hundred arrests all over Europe. I heard there were even some in Germany. It was a major *coup* – triumph for Lafont, of course. He took on a man by name of Bonny – Pierre Bonny – who'd been an inspector in the Sûreté; a crooked one, before the war they threw him off the force – Lafont took him on as his adjutant. Administrator, keeps the books and so on. I'm not sure Lafont can read or write.'

'Extraordinary your people recruiting him in the first place.'

'Those are the facts of it, anyway. He's an extremely powerful man now, and on the best of terms with everyone who matters. The chiefs of Gestapo, for instance – in particular Carl Boemelbourg – ever hear of him?'

'Should one have?' Blank look, despite the bell that was ringing in her skull. Jacqui murmuring to her, 'Boemelbourg is *pédéraste* number one. Lafont, they say, used to send him flowers and boys.'

'But *all* the top people here – generals, politicians, newspaper editors, actresses, writers, leading lights of Paris society, Vichy ministers – Laval especially – all treat him with respect and accept his famously lavish hospitality. "Monsieur Henri", they call him.'

'And *still* the whip?'

'Oh, yes. Still the whip.' A shrug. 'So one hears.'

It was past 4 o'clock when she left them. Jacqui came down to see her off; Clausen had a telephone call to make. He'd given her their number here, suggesting that all communications in either direction should be via Jacqui and by the sound of them purely social. He'd copied the Blue Dog's number into a notebook.

'This is in Montmartre, you say. You're moving from Vincennes right away?'

'To somewhere near it. On my way this morning I left my things there. There are dozens of rooming houses close by.'

On his feet and with the lunch-party concluded, Clausen's manner was brisk, even impatient. The telephone call which he'd told Jacqui he had to make, for instance – Rosie had the impression he wanted her out of the way before he made it. He'd be working out details for Jacqui's dossier this evening, he'd said, and making a draft of it in the morning; also seeing about a *gazo* . . . 'When the time comes, you'll come *here* – correct?'

'But not in the next few days – unless I find Juliette. If or when I do, I'll let Jacqui know.'

'It's hardly likely, is it? In just days, and a city the size of this one.'

'You could add that they might not even be here. I'm very much aware of it. Three days *isn't* much, I know, but – give me that long anyway?'

Three days in which to find Guillaume and Léonie. If the summons came before that, she would *not* move. Instead, disappear. Move away from the Dog – since they had its number and would be able to pinpoint it quickly enough. Leblanc would help; or Dénault, if they released that crowd. One would be relying on them now entirely. On Leblanc, anyway.

Not having had the guts to push it with bloody Clausen.

Why *not*, though? If the worst came to the worst – no leads or results despite the ringing bell – which was only a clue of sorts, seemed to her at this moment convincing enough but in the longer run might not pay off – if for instance Leblanc and company couldn't handle it. But with Clausen breaking his own rules already – not finding it easy but *having* to, for Jacqui – for himself, in fact, besotted with her as he was, which in itself was a handy ring in the bull's snout – hell, why not use it? When one got his call or Jacqui's, instead of, 'All right, I'll come right away', tell them, 'There are two others I want with us: won't move without them'; faced with that, and with his beloved's means of escape all set up, feeling perhaps a bit windy about it all, wouldn't he go the extra distance?

If they were still alive . . .

She asked Jacqui – outside, down on the forecourt, unlocking her bike – 'You mentioned when I arrived that Gerhardt had been up all night.'

'Did I?' A shrug. 'He certainly was late. *And* had to go in again this morning. Well – short-handed as they are now—'

'Had to go in where, this morning?'

'To his office. In the Propaganda Division in the Avenue des Champs-Elysées – number 52. Propaganda *Abteilung*, they call it.'

'Just offices?'

'Rather grand ones. But yes, what else? Oh, he also has facilities at l'Hôtel Continental – in Rue de Castiglione. That's all SS and SD, but for his own work with the staff he spoke of—'

'Yes. Right.' Straightening, dropping the chain and padlock into a pocket of her raincoat. 'Remember I told you yesterday, Jacqui, that there were two people who I've reason to think may be in SD custody?'

'What I remember best is telling you I know nothing about any of that stuff. How can you allow yourself to be seen in public in that garment?'

'You're just envious! Would you think it's possible that if they'd been in Gerhardt's charge he might have handed them over to Lafont?'

A moment's silence. Then: 'As I said only a moment ago, I don't know *anything* like that. But I doubt it: doubt it in fact very much. Now *please*—'

'I must be off, mustn't I?' Leaning over the bike to exchange kisses. 'Thank you for a delicious lunch, Jacqui – and I do like your Gerhardt.'

The hell I do . . .

Bell still ringing, anyway. That stuff about Gestapo chief Carl Boemelbourg, who according to information received by SOE and/or SIS – Pierre Cazalet's report, as quoted by Hyatt a week ago at Fawley Court – had delegated Léonie and Rouquet's interrogation to Clausen, but was also a crony of Lafont's. Riding out between the tall iron gates, looking back to wave goodbye, putting as much as there was together, logic – instinct, anyway – did seem to point to Lafont.

In which case, God help them.

Chapter 13

At the Dog, Adée was cleaning fish into a bucket and an elderly couple were drinking ersatz coffee. Adée's seamed face twisting into a smile as she murmured, 'Didn't arrest you, then.'

'Far from it.' Rosie exchanging 'good evening's with the old ones; turning back then to Adée. 'Gave me a magnificent lunch and a lot to drink.' Dropping her voice still lower: 'Any news of Georges and Patrice?'

'None. Martin Leblanc left soon after you did, and I've not seen him since.'

'D'you expect him this evening?'

'When I see him, is all. He's up to his eyes in it. No shooting out there now, uh?'

Rosie hadn't heard any on her way over from Passy. *Had* seen bathers in the Seine as well as rod-and-line fishermen, and a lot of Parisians sauntering along pavements and crowding café terraces. Adée said, 'There's talk of some kind of truce between FFI and the Boches. Some who were in here at lunchtime spoke of it. Reds don't want it, of course. If it's anything more than rumour anyway. They're still patrolling the main streets, I hear. *Your* day, though – you had a boozy lunch – and that's all, didn't find out where—'

'Not with certainty. But – some pointers.'

'You'll talk to *him*, then.'

Waiting for Leblanc then, while hours ticked by. A new barman/assistant arrived at about 6, by which time there were a dozen customers – beer-drinkers, Rosie guessed all railwaymen. Adée introduced the new one as Nico Plevin: he was in his late teens, she guessed, with fair hair and a spotty face on which he might have been trying to grow a beard. Customers came and went, some having whispered exchanges with Adée – about Leblanc, or leaving messages for him. She decided that unless when the schoolmaster arrived he had news for her or reacted positively to what she had to tell him, she definitely would try to see Clausen again and put her cards on the table. No – not *try* – get on to Jacqui and arrange it. Otherwise – what, just sit around and wait, with mental images of Léonie being flogged by that shrieking sadist?

Rouquet, bad enough. But Léonie . . .

But where did Clausen fit in?

Probably less as interrogator than Intelligence Officer, who'd assess whatever came out of it – if/when either or both of them did talk. Both he and Lafont having had their orders from Boemelbourg: Lafont to break them down, Clausen to apply his analytical skills to what spilt out – essentially, Resistance and Maquis locations and identities, planned deployments, methods of operation, weaponry and other equipment details, and arms dumps of course – in what had been Rouquet's diocese. Lorraine to the Rhine, effectively. Clausen could have been put on to this without having any general responsibility for the prisoners. Lafont might well have been given *carte blanche* in that respect. Very *likely* he would have, and very *un*likely that Boemelbourg would have gone into any such detail with his friend Cazalet. Much more likely an offhand, 'Oh, I'm leaving it to this fellow Clausen . . .'

Leblanc walked in just after 10 pm. Every time the street door had opened she'd had a moment's hope, although just minutes ago she'd told herself to forget it, he wasn't coming, she'd see him in the morning – *maybe* . . .

Sitting still now though, exercising patience: watching him and Adée embrace, Leblanc shaking his head to something Adée had asked him as they separated. Rosie taking note of his look of exhaustion, then seeing Adée's head-movement in *her* direction, Leblanc beginning to turn this way but immediately surrounded by others who'd been waiting. Adée extricated herself from the mêlée, and came over.

'He'll be with you shortly. I'm getting him a brandy, you want one?'

'How about I pay for three?'

Leblanc sipped at his second glass. She'd told him about her lunch and her deductions about Lafont, and he'd agreed it made sense or seemed to. He'd had no news of Georges or Patrice or any of that lot. Gestapo officers had come and gone from Rue des Saussaies throughout the day, and the outside of the place was guarded by *Milice* who if they saw anyone loitering around tended to become aggressive.

'We're watching 'em anyway. Not as we were doing until last night – that's too dangerous now, maybe impossible – but frequent checks: passers-by, delivery vans, so forth. If your theory's correct, of course, the only places that count from your angle are Rue Lauriston and Rue de la Pompe. Wouldn't bother about the house in Place des Etats-Unis, I'm assured it's empty. Avenue Foch eighty-two to eighty-six, same applies.'

'Couldn't we do something about those houses right away?'

'You suggested it to Georges, I remember. But the answer's still no, not—'

'*Why* not?'

'—not right away, is what I'm saying. You look tired, Jeanne-Marie.'

'So do you. Why *not* right away?'

'Because – first – we're in the process of getting ourselves equipped – armed. Two operations have been moderately successful – but not all *that* productive – while a third, Tuesday night, is much more promising, might well solve all our problems. For operations of this kind, you see, as well as weapons we need people who know how to use them. *Especially* for the Tuesday job. You don't need to know what it is, but the man I've persuaded to lead it will be coming from the Préfecture – along with a bunch of others he'll have picked himself. Policemen, yes – or will be when they put their uniforms on again. This is what I've been at pretty well all day. Believe me, it's a necessary preliminary to taking the kind of action you want.'

'Had Georges not set up anything of that kind?'

'He thought he had, but – no. Dedication and fighting-spirit's one thing, professionalism's another.' A shrug. 'Listen to who's talking. Rank amateur. But if we pull that one off—'

'*If*.' She leaned closer. Whispering . . . 'And Tuesday night. That would mean – if as you say you get it right – then not before Wednesday. Wednesday *night*, of course. While these two – God's sake, even if they're alive *now*—'

'I do understand that situation and your anxiety, Jeanne-Marie. But please try to see how I'm placed too. All right, Georges was under an obligation to help you, I've inherited that obligation, naturally I accept it. Also however I've inherited leadership of this group; there's reason to believe matters may be coming to a head in the next few days, I've *got* to have these people equipped and able to play their part.'

'Couldn't make the big effort tonight?'

'No. Not tomorrow either. We couldn't, it's out of the question. Believe me, physically impossible; and even if it were not – see, we've had one failure already, we can't' – shaking his head – 'Jeanne-Marie, I'm *sorry*, but – look, I'll tell you. Not where, but *what*.' Glancing around, then whispering, 'A *Milice* armoury. Everything we need is there. Also one thing we could do without – well-armed *Miliciens* protecting it and what's more on the alert, on account of other things that have been going on. Not easy, eh? No. But the man organising it is a former senior NCO with battle experience from 1940, a police weapons instructor since then, leading men he's personally selected – armed with Schmeissers and the long-handled grenades, and knowing exactly what they're doing.'

'Should have a chance, then.'

'But couldn't any sooner, for the simple reason he's occupied elsewhere.' Leblanc put a hand on one of hers. 'Wednesday, Jeanne-Marie. If it's a success tomorrow night I'll have him here Wednesday and we'll make plans. All right?'

'Plans for that same night?'

'If he agrees – yes.'

'Meaning even *that*'s not certain!'

'How long did *you* spend in Gestapo hands?'

'This is quite different – doing nothing, while *they*—'

'Jeanne-Marie, this may sound to you ridiculous, but I'd suggest you put it out of mind – at least, out of your imagination – until we *can* do something about it. Well, I'm sorry – lecturing again. But I'm talking facts, reality. Georges might have said yes, we'll do it right away – but where is he now? Where's Fécontel? Eh? What use is *that*?'

'Writing them off, are we?'

'Facing facts, is all. What can be done, and what can't. Jeanne-Marie, how will you spend tomorrow?'

'Biting my nails down to their quicks. How else?'

'An alternative might be to take a ride on your bike around these various addresses. So when we're talking with my military friend you'd have a picture of it.'

'*Not* a bad idea . . .'

'Keep you busy, too. But don't be tempted to hang around in Rue des Saussaies.' Yawning, and checking the time. 'Just ride through, above all don't make a study of number eleven.'

'D'you treat *all* your pupils as if they were born yesterday?'

'Speaking of pupils – that one there, now.' Pointing with his head at Nico, the new barman. 'His problem was always a reluctance to pay attention. He'd sit dreaming, one had to hit him over the head quite often. But why not take him with you – if Adée permits it? I'm sure you know Paris well enough, but he'd still be a help, he's never been outside it. He's a *résistant*, of course – and a bit of cover for you, as well as company – boy and girl on a day out, uh?'

'My kid brother . . .'

'If you like. But you don't look so old, you know. Got a man of your own, have you' – down to a murmur again – 'over there?'

She'd nodded. 'When this is over we'll be getting married.'

'*Lucky* man! Soldier, is he?'

'Sailor. Motor gunboats. He's been wounded in action twice.'

'Deserves you, then.' Raising his voice: 'Hey, Nico, here a minute?'

The boy joined them, Leblanc made the suggestion and he jumped at it: smiling shyly at Rosie, then explaining, 'Well, to get out into the sun and fresh air, a few hours . . .' Starting in mid-morning, then, subject to Adée's agreement, and giving Rosie a sight of Rue des Saussaies, the more extensive SD headquarters in Avenue Foch, also Rue Lauriston and Rue de la Pompe. Leblanc asked him whether he knew the Café Mas on Place des Ternes; it was much used by Lafont's gang, he said, and there was a waiter by name of Charles Lerique to whom Nico might give Martin Leblanc's regards and enquire after the man's son Marcel, another former pupil. Lerique sometimes had items of interest to pass on; if it was possible to have any private conversation with him, Nico might say Martin Leblanc wondered how things were going, whether they were still getting a lot of business from one particular group of customers.

'With what object, to ask this?'

'He might tell you if he'd had wind of any move afoot. More of them than before, or fewer. It's less than two kilometres from there to Lauriston or to La Pompe, after all, waiters do have ears and that one's heart is in the right place – or used to be.'

'All right.'

'But only if it's safe. And don't push it, let him tell you if he *wants* to, and don't utter a word if there are any of those animals around.'

'All right.'

Leblanc told Rosie, 'I used to teach him history. Or *try* to.' A shrug. 'Now we're helping to make it, eh?'

'How did you get to know about that café?'

'I've been associated with this Dénault crowd for some time. Three and a half years. And I suppose because I'm slightly more literate than most I drifted into being you might say the information/intelligence advisor, and . . . well, at one time we were working on the idea of planting a bomb on that terrace. Another group approached us on the subject – to kill Lafont himself was the idea, they felt they owed him nothing less – which was the truth and still is, in fact even more so; but we dropped it eventually because his comings and goings were so irregular and there was no way of ensuring innocent people weren't killed. Listen, I'll give you two telephone numbers at which you might get me if you needed to. If you got news of your friends, for instance. Two other numbers besides Adée's here, that is. D'you have a good memory?'

'Usually.' She nodded. 'If you'd write them down. I'll memorise them, then tear it up.' Groping in Léonie's bag for paper and pencil. Leblanc adding, 'And now I'm off for a few hours' sleep. Might not see you *before* Wednesday, by the way. I'll let Adée know what time.'

'Wednesday morning, though?'

'I expect so.' He was jotting the numbers down. 'Unless – again – a message with Adée—'

'Don't even *think* of putting it off!'

'Let's hope we don't have to. Look at this, though.' Showing her, under cover of the table's edge, an arm-band, white with black lettering, the slogan in French 'Live Free or Die' – *Vivre Libre ou Mourir*. 'For when we go into action. Like it?'

'Carrying it around with you?'

'Showed it to some of them at the Préfecture. When the time comes there'll be thousands of these on the streets. Tuesday, though, Fernagut and his team will be wearing red ones. Commies will have done it, see?'

'Any special reason?'

'This half-baked truce. Reds don't want it, and the Boches know that. We, on the other hand—'

'You're observing it?'

'*Using* it, say.' Folding the band back into his pocket. 'Take care tomorrow, eh?'

She went to sleep quickly, and dreamed of Ben. Joan Stack was all over him, half naked; he was fending her off, shouting, 'Could be she *isn't* dead! Could be those drongoes got it wrong!' Rosie chipping in then, telling him what SOE in Baker Street hadn't had time to tell him: 'They *did* have it wrong! Lise heard shots and assumed they'd killed me – and they thought they had, left me for dead – I *was* bloody dying – *damn* you, you bitch!' Trying to drag the woman off him, but before she could get a grip on the sweat-slippery body she – *it*, La Stack – was on her feet and swaying around in a slinky low-cut dress in the arms of a man whose name Ben had mentioned but Rosie didn't remember; they were in a hotel of somewhat dubious repute in the Sussex downland, she'd come down from London to meet Ben for this dinner-dance and to spend the night with him in a four-poster – Ben's gunboat being based at Newhaven then, in easy reach of this place, and his commanding officer – fellow-Australian, by name Bob Stack – had married Lady Joan, who'd been Ben's bit of stuff before that and was now cheating on her husband with this rather supercilious character whose name in the dream escaped her. Rosie telling Ben, 'She'll always cheat with *someone*. If I *was* dead and you were daft enough to marry her she'd cheat on *you*. It's how she's *wired*, my darling!'

'What if *I* get dead?'

Ben's Aussie voice – sudden and clear, its tone quite level, as if postulating an easily envisaged scenario. Rosie startled by it, moving her arms over the tumbled blankets and meeting nothing else – bedclothes in this state because in some vaguely remembered dream she'd been grappling with La Stack. Out of that now anyway: it *had* been only a dream. But what he'd just come up with – so close, so *real* – lying motionless in the dark, musty closeness, straining her ears for a sound of breathing other than her own – for his stronger, harder breaths. Then *wide* awake – but still with a need as it were to exorcise the lingering illusion: her own voice out loud in the darkness telling him, 'I'll be back in England before you will, probably. Welcome *you* home.'

In the morning, she and the boy checked what would be their itinerary on the map before starting out. He'd arrived at the Dog at breakfast-time to help Adée with the various chores; Adée had told him to be back by mid-afternoon, she'd handle the lunchtime customers on her own.

'Rue des Saussaies then, Nico.'

A nod. 'Left out of Place Pigalle into Rue Pigalle.'

'Test your history. Who was Pigalle?'

'A sculptor?'

'You did learn a few things from him, then.'

'He's a good teacher.'

'I believe you.' They'd unchained their bikes. 'Nico, you lead, eh? If you see me in any trouble – being stopped to show papers, anything like that – don't turn back and involve yourself, take the next right turn and wait for me to join you.'

'Any reason you might be stopped?'

'No, but they're unpredictable, aren't they? If I see it happening to you I'll keep going, pass you if they'll let me, make a right turn and wait for *you*. All right?'

'Sure, but—'

'Best to have a plan, that's all.'

The only real danger if she *was* stopped and searched would be the pistol in what had been Léonie's bag. With papers as good as Jeanne-Marie Lefèvre's there was no reason one should be searched, but with *résistants* more or less in the open now – back-street barricades, seizures of weaponry, all that – there might be spot-check searches.

From Rue de Clignancourt, right into Boulevard de Rochechouart and then 500–600 metres to Place Pigalle. Left there, into the road of the same name. It was a beautiful morning, the sun already hot and the traffic on the streets more or less normal. Nico riding about 30 yards ahead, glancing back from time to time: from here it was about a kilometre south-westward and down-slope, easy going into the Place de la Trinité, with the skyline ahead a frieze of towers and spires, familiar silhouettes against the blue, still slightly hazy background. Nico had looked back again and she'd waved to him: as always there were a lot of cyclists on the road, and in her drab raincoat she didn't exactly stand out from the crowd. It might look a bit silly on such a sunny day, she realised; even Adée who wasn't exactly a smart dresser had looked at it in surprise.

Nico swinging right: Rosie following a few seconds later. Place de la Trinité. Leaving the church on their left, then trickling southward into Rue de Mogador: about 500 metres of that, but having to pause where it crossed Rue de Provence. Running up alongside Nico: 'Hello, little brother.'

'See *that* load of crap now . . .'

A truckload of *Miliciens*: the open-topped vehicle barrelling down and swinging right into Boulevard Haussmann. The boy muttering, 'Where're *they* going, I wonder?'

'Not our way, is it?'

Shake of the head: 'We go straight over. Rue Tronchet down to La Madeleine, *then* right.'

'Oh yes . . .'

'Now. Come on.'

Over, and south along Tronchet into Place de la Madeleine, Nico ahead of her again and with a couple of *gazos* in between. All the way down – best part of a kilometre – and to the right then, around the top end of the Place; she was close behind him again by that time. Into Rue Royale, then right – St Honoré. Traffic was thicker here, and it was a considerable advantage to have a guide, not to have to rack one's brains, take chances and make mistakes. Simple enough on this stretch, as it happened – west along Rue St Honoré into Place Beauvau, which the map had shown her was at the south-west end of Rue des Saussaies. As they'd planned it, they'd turn right into Saussaies and ride right through to its top end – which was the *Place* des Saussaies – then carry on westward towards l'Etoile.

But they'd be doing no such thing.

Not without being shot. Nico had looked back, waved and pointed ahead across the square, and she saw the reason for that now: Boche soldiers in grey-green uniforms and helmets, with slung rifles and grenades – the type Leblanc had mentioned, long wooden handles on them – hanging from their belts; they were guarding a barrier made of X-shaped supports, each pair linked by a single horizontal pole and festooned with barbed wire. Nico continuing westward across the Place and into *that* road, turning to the right 30–40 metres further on.

He'd stopped not far from the corner, waiting for her to join him.

She said, 'Top end will be shut off too, won't it?'

He nodded. 'And both the side-streets leading in. *Would* be, anyway I saw more Boches at the corner of Rue Montalivet.'

'I wonder what for.'

'Expecting an attack on number eleven? Thinking we might try to get 'em out?'

'Could be.' She shrugged. 'Might go on and see Lauriston and the others – come back this way later?'

A nod. 'Might have lifted it by then.' He nodded again: spotty face pink and damp-looking. 'So – *that* way, down to Avenue des Champs-Elysées at the Rondpoint, to the right there, say a kilometre and a half – less – to l'Etoile, buzz most of the way around it and turn west into Rue Lauriston. Easy as pie. Then up to Rue de la Pompe – and right on into Avenue Foch, OK?'

'I'll just follow my leader.'

'Then Café Mas. From l'Etoile, Place des Ternes is – oh, five or ten minutes up l'Avenue de Wagram. By then we'll be ready for a beer, uh?'

No. 93 Rue Lauriston was a well-kept, grey-faced, noticeably large house in an obviously expensive district. Four storeys tall, with a wide railed forecourt and – Leblanc had mentioned – a central garden, Spanish patio-style. Front door and steps leading down into the forecourt, though: presumably you could get in and out by way of the garden – she'd had a glimpse of that gated access – the gate undoubtedly kept locked and chained – but having to be quick to take in the rest of it, even just free-wheeling by fairly slowly. Noting the line of fourth-floor windows which had been servants' rooms and Lafont was said to have converted into cells: there'd be contrastingly spacious, luxurious apartments on other floors. In even greater contrast of course, the cellars: from which one shied away even in imagination. The house next door, she'd been told, had been taken over as additional prisoner accommodation.

Out of her sight back there now anyway; and she'd seen no movement or sign of human presence. Gates shut, and apparently unguarded. Might have turned back for a longer, closer look: did think of it – of crossing the road and joining the eastbound traffic; but she had a reasonably good impression of no. 93 in any case – like a slightly out-of-focus snapshot in her memory, and really there wasn't so much one *could* see.

Thinking again though of those top-floor rooms, and the cellar, the route down to it – a servants' staircase at the back of the house, she guessed – and Lafont waiting down there with his whip.

Clausen knowing all about it?

Surely. As he'd also have known of hundreds of others, probably. Despite his disclaimer yesterday, 'I *have* conducted interrogations . . . but where your imagination may run beyond that . . .'

As if there'd ever been an SD interrogation – of an uncooperative prisoner – *without* torture, or at least threat of death, or without the prisoner being handed over *for* torture or execution. Clausen a Pontius Pilate, hand on heart: 'Me, do anything like *that*?'

For Jacqui's benefit, she guessed. Enabling Jacqui to continue thinking of him as a *kind* man.

Or at least professing to. She'd said, when Rosie had asked whether he was kind, 'In himself, he is.' Meaning – if it meant anything at all – 'to *me*, he is'. Allowing for there being areas and circumstances in which he might be extremely *un*kind, but which didn't concern her, from which therefore she remained aloof?

'I don't know *anything*!'

So much nicer not to . . .

Up Rue Boissière to Place Victor Hugo: recognising that at the lunch yesterday she'd come close to being fooled into accepting Clausen's vision of himself as an Intelligence Officer pure and simple, nothing to do with whips or cellars or cattle-trucks to Büchenwald . . . Around this road-junction, though, and out of it westward. A few hundred metres, then a sharp turn to the right. Rue de la Pompe. Nico signalling to her that he was slowing – stopping – on this side, 20 metres ahead. Dismounting as she braked in behind him and dismounted too.

'Brake's jamming on the front wheel. That's my story. See the house right opposite?'

'Is that it?'

'Is indeed. This'll give you a minute or two, but don't look *too* hard.'

A thickset, maybe shaven-headed man came to the closed gateway and stared across at them. There was other traffic passing, but not much. She propped her bike against the kerb and stooped close to Nico to see what he was doing.

'We're being looked at.'

'Yeah. And there's a Renault van parked in there – petrol, not *gazo*. Bonny-Lafont vehicle, therefore. See what you need to see, don't take too long at it.'

She straightened, checking the time on what had been Marilyn Stuart's watch. Shrugging, her body-language indicating to the watcher that this delay was unwelcome. He was still there, still watching. The house was cream-coloured, with grey surrounds to its windows and a slate roof instead of tiles: other respects in which it differed from 93 Rue Lauriston were a narrower frontage, only four instead of eight small windows on that top floor – only *three* floors, in fact.

Facing away from the man at the iron gates, she murmured, 'When you're ready, Nico.'

'Yeah. *Should* be OK.' He'd straightened, and she turned quickly as if relieved that he'd fixed it. Both preparing to mount then, Rosie pushing Léonie's bag back behind her hip and letting him start first: Nico peering down at his front wheel, pumping the brake on and off as he got going, calling back to her after a few yards, 'OK. Come on.' With so much foliage on the inside of those railings you couldn't see much at ground-floor level – other than the van, a black Renault, parked on the driveway inside the gates, and the upper parts of windows, entrance door dead centre. The man was watching them leave: open-neck khaki shirt, greenish army trousers pushed into knee-high boots, pudgy face. Not shaven-headed – that must have been an effect of sunlight, he had shiny, slicked-back brownish hair. Not one of the two she'd seen before – who might have recognised her, which might *not* have been so good . . .

Riding on, following Nico, conscious of escaping a two-fold danger – to themselves, conceivably, but also to the prisoners inside – if their gaolers suspected outside interest in them. They *were* in there – in those top rooms. It might have been only that man's watchful, threatening presence that had told her so, but that *was* the place, she *knew* it.

Chapter 14

She was excited at having located them, although the rest of the trip was an anticlimax: 82 to 86 Avenue Foch, former SD headquarters obviously now untenanted, and at the Café Mas, where they had bread and goat-cheese with their beers, the waitress told them that Monday was Charles Lerique's day off and he'd as like as not have gone fishing. There'd been no one there who looked anything like a gangster or gestapist. Then on the way back to Montmartre they found Rue des Saussaies still cordoned off.

Leblanc had to be told about that, anyway. Might know already – most likely would – but she wanted to tell him about Rue de la Pompe as well. Having admittedly no real evidence to offer, only her personal conviction – intuition, one might call it – but since he'd accepted that they were almost certainly in one or other of the Bonny-Lafont houses, he surely wouldn't mind being told he could forget Rue Lauriston and concentrate on that one.

Her business, anyway. She was so to speak the client.

Back at the Dog, putting the chains on their bikes, she thanked Nico for his help. He smiled, countered with, 'Thank you for the lunch.' Then: 'Did you see all you wanted?'

'More than I expected.'

'Solved the problem?'

'I think so. Yes.'

'Rue de la Pompe, eh?'

'Is that your impression too?'

He nodded. '*Something* there, all right.'

'So it's *not* just me.' She patted his arm. 'Thank you again, Nico.'

There were no customers inside, but there had been; Adée was washing up.

'Hah.' A glance at the clock. 'I get my slave back.' A nod to Nico; then to Rosie, 'Any use, was it?'

'Yes – I think so. Use your 'phone?'

The first of Leblanc's numbers rang unanswered, and at the second a woman offered to give him a message if he came in later. She didn't sound like a wife; in fact Rosie didn't even know that he had one. She left no message, anyway; hung up, told Adée, 'No luck. Would that have been his wife I spoke to?'

'Who knows? But whoever, you could have asked for him to call back.'

'I might not be here. And not knowing who that was—'

'Give *me* a message for him, then if he does call – huh?'

'Thanks, but I'll try again later. Rather like to talk to him myself.'

'So what'll you do now? Go to the house, take a nap?'

'Might take a walk. How would I get up to Sacré Coeur, for instance?'

'Well, I'll show you. Nico, you'll hold the fort, uh? Yes, that's a good idea. Quite a climb, mind you – no electricity, funicular's not working of course.'

Adée went out into the alley with her, ostensibly to point her in the right direction. Advising her meanwhile, 'From the Sacré Coeur terrace you have all of Paris to the south, but if you have strength left you can go in and climb to the top of the dome – see even further, and in all directions . . . Don't mind going by yourself?'

'Should I?'

'I could spare Nico for another hour or even two hours, you see.'

'Thank you *very* much, but—'

'There's all sorts around, you know. With the gendarmes on strike, uh? When I'm on my own, I can tell you, I keep that door locked!'

'It wasn't locked just now.'

'Maybe not, just that one time. But you be careful.'

'I will.' She smiled. 'I *can* look after myself, Adée.'

'Oh, I'm sure, but—'

'Anyway—'

'May I ask you something?' Guarded look around and behind them. 'Is it true you're English?'

So that was why she'd wanted to have her to herself. Rosie asked her, 'Did Leblanc tell you so?'

'No, Georges. In great confidence, naturally. He was explaining – after you'd blown in, complete stranger asking for him by name—'

'Did he tell anyone else, or only you?'

'Well – Patrice was with us.' The old woman's damp hand clutching Rosie's elbow, as if steering her around the curve of the alleyway, 'Georges told me don't breathe a word. Don't worry. Neither he nor Patrice would *ever*—'

'I'm sure not.'

Patrice and Georges being in 11 Rue des Saussaies now. Home of the whips, straps, chains, rubber truncheons and pliers. That game of theirs in which they brought you to within seconds of drowning in a bath of cold water, repeating the same action over and over again: on your back in the tub, your head pushed under and held there. Head up then: 'Talk? No?' Under again. In Rouen, that was one of the games they'd played. Another was where they made you kneel on the sharp edge of a shovel's blade and a heavyweight assistant stood on the handle end so that the blade pushed up into the sinew below the kneecap. And of course the *pièce de résistance*, the pliers. For men it was often the testicles they went for, one had heard.

She said again, 'I'm sure not.'

'You can count on it. But – that's the truth, is it, you *are*?'

She nodded. Horse having bolted, stable door wide open. 'I have an English mother and I've lived in England since I was twelve, when my father died. But I was born and brought up in France – he was French, and if I'd had any say in it I'd have stayed here.'

'But one can understand, your mother being alone then—'

'I don't mean there's anything about England I don't like. It's just that I had a happy childhood and I adored my father. But I'm used to England now – I *am* English, yes. I have an uncle I'm very fond of, and cousins . . .' Ahead, a rectangular slab of sunlight was the alley's emergence into Rue de Clignancourt. 'Adée, don't tell another soul I'm English. Please, absolutely no one? Georges should have kept his trap shut.'

'Ah, poor Georges . . .'

She found the steps at the head of Rue de Steinkerque, off Rochechouart, and climbed. She'd been up here with her father, she remembered – mainly for the view, which Ben too had mentioned in dissertations on his Parisian days. She took Adée's advice, first checking out the southerly aspect from the terrace, then going inside and climbing to the top of the dome from where she tried to pick out Rue de la Pompe. But – 5 or 6 kilometres away, she guessed, that straight-line view: even if one had had a telescope . . . *Visualising* the house, though, and those two inside it; and in frustrating contrast, herself like some gawping tourist. The sense of impatience was going to be worse tonight – knowing precisely *where* now, and having to just sit around . . .

She came down from the dome and crossed over to the church of St Pierre de Montmartre, only a few yards away and not only older than Sacré Coeur but one of the most ancient churches in Paris. Her father had brought her here too. She couldn't remember the particular features he'd wanted her to see, but had an idea that there were parts of some even older church incorporated in the structure. She hadn't the expertise to find them, though, and was disinclined to ask; it had something to do with her father – or rather with his absence: she didn't want the information from any lesser person. On impulse, on her way out, she slid into a pew and knelt to pray; not that in recent times she'd been all that convinced of the efficacy of prayer, but in a place of such antiquity where over the centuries millions must have cried for help of one kind or another – and feeling she needed any that might be on offer. Less for herself – as she'd told Adée, *she* could look after that – than for Léonie and Rouquet, Georges and company, and finally – additionally – for Ben. Whatever *he* was up to. *Please, bring him safe home?*

Adding in her mind as she left the old church. *And let me be there too, and with him for ever after?*

Surprised at herself: yielding to that impulse which at any rate to *her* was indicative of some sense of insecurity – when no obvious threat existed . . . And twenty minutes later, rubber-necking around the Place du Tertre – which to all intents and purposes was a village square still, with shady trees in the middle, small beamed house-fronts and café-bars all around – she was still . . . well, *on edge*, for no good reason: reminding herself that if it was *security* she wanted she could have stayed in Sevenoaks as a shift-working wireless-operator – which was what she had been before her husband Johnny had been killed and she'd volunteered for training as an agent.

And met Ben. Then not seen him for a year and a half, and run into him again – thank God.

Frustration accounted for most of this. Impatience. She needed to snap out of it, take a grip. *He*'d have told her that.

'Yes, Miss?'

'D'you have apricot?'

The girl took a bottle of it from the shelf behind her; there were several vacant tables out there, and one of them was actually in the shade. Rosie paid and took the drink out with her; that table was still unoccupied.

A fat man in a badly fitting suit and a greasy-looking soft hat stopped – at the sight of her, it seemed – and stared. Rosie sipping at her juice, ignoring him, watching sparrows pecking around for crumbs. The man shrugged, half-smiling at her, and shuffled inside. She considered leaving the drink and moving on, disappearing before he came out: it was the smirk that bothered her, for some reason. Recollection of Adée's warning too, of course; but she was hot and thirsty and her legs were tired, and she had time to kill, and – the hell with him, she *could* look after herself.

A minute or two later, hearing him coming back out – hearing and sensing it – she sat still, waiting for him to join her. Which he did – setting a half-litre of pale, fizzy beer down on her table, and pulling back one of the other chairs.

'Permettez?'

'No. There are other tables, look.'

He sat down. Small piggy eyes, and a pencil-thin moustache under a wide, flat nose. If she got up and moved to another table it wouldn't get rid of him, he'd follow. Anyway, what harm – apart from nuisance? If she did need help there were people at nearby tables, and a constant stream of passers-by.

Thinking about needing help again, for Pete's sake . . .

He drank some beer, put the glass down, asked her, 'Day off from work?'

'Please leave me alone!'

'Cigarette?'

'No, thank you.'

She'd have loved one. He murmured, *'Résistante?'*

'What are you – an informer?'

'You insult me, mam'selle!'

'That might be difficult. Just go away, will you?'

'All right. All *right.*' A finger pointing: 'How much money d'you have in that?'

In Léonie's bag. She had the strap over her shoulder and her hand on the bag itself where it hung beside her chair.

She pulled it on to her lap now. The people who'd been at the nearest table had chosen this moment at which to leave; the pair beyond them, she saw, had gone as well. She could see the foursome who'd been at this nearer one moving off across the square, through the area of shade on that side of the trees. He was leaning closer: 'Show me. Turn it out. Otherwise – see this?'

Glitter of a knife in that pudgy-looking hand. He was close enough by now to grab or slash or both. Probably both. He was flabby, sure, but he'd have the weight to smother her and wrench the bag away. He'd want her money first, then any other valuables, she guessed. Rings, her watch, ration cards – especially clothing coupons. She supposed the old raincoat made her look down-at-heel, an easy mark. That, and being about a third his size: and the fact – which she realised too, suddenly – that nine people out of ten weren't likely to take the slightest bloody notice, or involve themselves in this kind of thing. All it might achieve if she screamed for help – well, it would virtually oblige him to go for her with the knife – clasp-knife, blade about 4 inches long.

There were several things she could have done. She decided on the easiest. Sliding her right hand into the bag, not in any way surreptitiously, letting him see her do it. Resignedly: 'Money you want, is it?'

'And quick. Gimme your purse.'

'Or how about this?'

The Beretta – in her hand, at the table's edge. She'd racked a shell into its breech in the course of bringing it up and he'd have heard that, would know this was for real, the short barrel aimed at the bridge of his nose from a distance of about 18 inches. He'd flung himself back, jarring the table and slopping both drinks. Mouth open, small eyes stretched wide, fixed not on her but on the stubby little gun. She *would* have shot him if his reaction had been to go for her instead of recoiling as he had, and she'd have got away with it all right, she thought, nobody *would* have interfered – one glance back with the gun still in her hand as she walked away was all it would have taken. She told him evenly, 'Fold the knife and put it on the table.' Watching him do it – fumbling, shaking. 'Now take your glass inside, stand at the counter and don't turn. Go *now*. Don't think I wouldn't shoot – it would give me pleasure. Stay in there at least ten minutes – because if I see you again—'

He'd gone. She finished the fruit juice before she left.

At the Dog, Adée and Nico were already busy, Adée at her stove and Nico around the bar. Adée called to her, 'Did you get up there all right?'

'Sure did. *What* a view! What's your news?'

'Mine – none, but Nico has a message for you.'

'Right.' There were only four or five customers at this stage. She went to the bar, where Nico was pouring beers; he nodded to her. 'I'll be right with you. Get you something?'

'Any Cognac today?'

'Cognac, this early?'

After that, she thought, she might have a 'coffee' and take a long time over it. She was a lot less on edge now, but it *was* still early and it was going to be a long evening, maybe a sleepless night in anticipation of tomorrow. Excitement at the prospect of finally *doing* something . . .

Nico brought her glass of brandy, and sat down beside her.

'I've put it on the slate. Run all the way up there, did you?'

'Of course. And down again. Adée said you had some message.'

'Martin Leblanc on the 'phone. Said he'd guessed it might be you that called. I told him about Rue des Saussaies being shut off – he knew it, didn't know what for – and how you and I both reckoned Rue de la Pompe was the right address.

I said it like that, quick, but he caught on, said, "Good, tell her we'll talk about it when we meet."'

'So that's fine, isn't it? Thank you . . . Oh, Nico, this any use to you?'

The clasp-knife. He was delighted, and she was glad to have found a good home for it.

Adée had made a fish pie for supper and Rosie had hers early, guessing it wouldn't last long. The Dog was about half full by then, some of them people she'd seen there before – that first night, when they'd been off to some meeting and Dénault hadn't shown up. She hadn't known any of their names then – only Adée had trusted her at first sight – but she had several of them tagged now. Sougy, Dehais, Clavel, Laplanche, Godin. None of them seemed to know what Leblanc was up to, only that he had *something* going on. Adée had speculated, 'Chasing girls, I dare say. You know schoolmasters.'

He did have a wife, apparently – presumably the woman Rosie had spoken to. Adée had said, 'We don't hear much about her – nor about his children, but there are some. He's a man keeps himself to himself, you know?' Even she perhaps didn't know about the *Milice* armoury: and there was no reason she should have. A question in Rosie's mind was whether he, Leblanc, would be taking part in the operation; having stressed the value of the other man's military training, and having none himself – as far as she knew. Perhaps he'd have felt that as group leader he had some obligation to go along.

After supper she borrowed a pack of cards from Adée and played patience. Other card games were in progress, and a noisy game of dominoes. She wasn't drinking anything, only waiting for time to pass, customers to push off. As it was, they were risking the penalties of infringing curfew. So was she, for that matter – but with only a few yards to go – and the police on strike, which was why they were all ignoring it, she supposed . . . She didn't want to go to the house before Adée packed up; she was physically tired but guessed that if she turned in early and was woken after only an hour or so she mightn't sleep again.

Starting another game. The air was heavy with smoke under the low, stained ceiling, and it was very noisy; when from time to time Nico joined her they had to shout in each other's ears. The domino players were a major source of it, roaring like bulls – especially the very large one, Clavel, who was like that even before he'd had anything to drink. Nico was leaning that way now, to see what was happening with the dominoes, the game by the sound of it approaching climax. Rosie in contrast putting her cards down swiftly and silently, anticipating that this time it *would* come out; but still not exactly concentrating on it. A depressing thought at about this time was that although in the three days she'd been here she'd actually covered quite a lot of ground, it was a fact that one week ago from tonight had been her first night at Fawley Court, and even *then* Rouquet and Léonie must have been in Gestapo, SD or Bonny-Lafont custody for several days.

Ten days now at *least*, therefore.

The patience game had stalled. Might force another 'coffee' down, she thought. And if any of these characters thought of offering her a cigarette – since she didn't have any of her own . . .

The street door exploded inwards. Noise, games and jollity all shock-blasted into silence: lamp-lit apparitions through the haze were uniformed Boches crowding in. Not in fact all that many; it had only *seemed*, in that first second . . . They were SS, anyway. Three of them – no, four. And a civilian – bulky man in a hat and coat – a Frenchman, shouting for silence, which there *had* been but only momentarily, hadn't lasted. That one had heeled the door shut behind him and the SS – with Schmeissers – had spread themselves across that end of the room, one of them pushing Adée away from her stove. There'd been shouts and protests, including angry shrieks from her, amounting in aggregate to a secondary explosion, a lot of them on their feet and the bench on the far side of the other table crashing over; the SS simply watching, waiting, only their guns' barrels moving, covering everyone – waiting for any *real* trouble.

Rosie meanwhile guessing they'd come for *her*: courtesy of Georges and/or Patrice.

Going quiet again: mutters and growls replacing shouts. Eyes on the levelled Schmeissers too. They'd got that bench the right way up again, but on that side of the room were mostly still on their feet: looking if not at the guns at the Frenchman who with his hat tilted back and both hands in his coat pockets was just standing, looking around. While he was there in front of them the SS couldn't easily have opened fire; so with luck it was *not* to be a massacre of suspected *résistants*. Clavel – the half-drunk man-mountain – was still poised like a statue, inclined across the table with one great paw still raised, a domino piece between finger and thumb and his mouth open as if checked suddenly in full bellow. As he *would* have been: it was only seconds since the irruption. An oil-lamp on the table beside him was smoking darkly; becoming aware of it, he'd grimaced and pulled back, was subsiding slowly on to the bench.

Nico was looking at Rosie: looking scared. She smiled at him, shrugging slightly. Adée began, 'M'sieur, this is *my* café, my customers are entitled surely—'

'You don't care about curfew?'

'So who's on the street?'

'Not *yet* they aren't. Anyway, shut your face.' He'd seen Rosie and as it were gone on point, wasn't looking anywhere else now. Georges or Patrice might have tried to strike a bargain, she guessed – Patrice, more likely. Give away a British agent, retain at least *some* fingernails and say a working testicle. But this was *her* party now, for sure, hers and the Frenchman's; he'd stopped with his open hand extended towards her over the heads of Sougy and Laplanche – whose eyes like Nico's were fixed on her, Sougy's pink-rimmed in his unshaven face and Laplanche's simply bulging.

'Papers!'

'Mine?' She glanced around as if for explanations: then back at him. 'Why, what—'

'Papers!'

'Very well.' Reaching for her folded raincoat. 'They're perfectly in order. Just a minute – you'll see . . .'

One of the SS came forward to stand beside the civilian with his Schmeisser covering her. Her bag – Léonie's – containing the pistol which she didn't want them to find, was on the bench on her right-hand side, close against her, and in turning the other way to get at the raincoat and unbutton its inside pocket she managed to push the bag closer to Nico. She was half-standing – now *right* up – had room, just, between bench and table – had that pocket open and was pulling the papers out; the gestapist reached to snatch them from her and she dumped herself down again, this time pushing the bag off the bench, meeting Nico's shocked eyes and shaking her head slightly – a twitch, no more, intended as an instruction to leave it, *not* politely and unhelpfully pick it up for her.

'You are Jeanne-Marie Lefèvre?'

'As you can see.' She had her back to Nico now. 'As *anyone* can see!'

'You're wanted for questioning. You'll come with us now.' A nod to the SS man beside him, who passed his Schmeisser to another of them and produced a pair of handcuffs. Gesturing to Rosie to come out from behind the table. Adée's voice again. 'If the young lady's papers are in order, as I'm sure they *must* be—'

'Ta gueule!' A glance round, and a quieter order: 'She opens it again, hit her.' He'd snatched the coat from Rosie, checked its side pockets and shaken it, tossed it back to her. She began to edge out sideways but paused while Nico – rather

gallantly, she thought – held it so she could get her arms into the sleeves. She thanked him. The Frenchman could only be a gestapist, she thought, one of the thousands who worked for the *Geheime Staatspolizei*. If he'd been one of the Bonny-Lafont lot he'd have had his own people with him, not SS. The trooper had grabbed her right arm, snapped a handcuff on that wrist and the other now on his own left one. Taking his Schmeisser back then, cradling it in his right arm. Rosie demanding of the Frenchman: '*Why* are you arresting me?'

'As if you didn't know!' To the others then, with a jerk of the head, 'Let's go.' One held the door open, one went out into the alleyway and this one followed, dragging her behind him: if she'd tried to hold back it would have hurt. No point in *inviting* pain – which was coming anyway. Or resisting in any way, for that matter. None of the Germans had said a single word. Had no French, maybe. Although this one had seemed to understand it. Rosie was close to Adée for a second, muttered, 'Don't worry, I've done nothing, they'll release me when they realise.' Then as she was jerked forward, almost off her feet, 'Tell him to go ahead without me.'

'Out!'

Stumbling, again almost falling; then they were all outside and surrounding her, boots loud on the cobbles, the Frenchman bringing up the rear. If Leblanc got that message he *might* go ahead and raid the Rue de la Pompe house. Nico would tell him how certain she'd been that that was the place: he *would,* surely. As long as Leblanc's business tonight went well: which please God . . .

End of the alleyway – Rue de Clignancourt. On the far side of the road a black or grey Citroen and a *Wehrmacht* half-ton truck were being guarded by four more SS. Making a squad of eight – crack troops in steel helmets and with automatic weapons, all for *her*? In anticipation of trouble from *résistants,* she supposed. Taking no chances . . . The gestapist was telling the man who was linked to her, 'In the back with her. No – in *mine.* Rest of 'em in the truck and follow, stay close.'

She was pushed in and made to slide over from the pavement side, while the Frenchman got in behind the wheel. Doors slamming, engines starting. Off the kerb then and away, quite slowly along to the corner and right into the Boulevard de Rochechouart. Picking up speed then. Dark streets and only a shred of moon, reek of cigarettes – but not French ones, she noticed, wishing someone would give *her* one. Left into Rue Pigalle. A familiar route, this far, and with no other traffic whatsoever, driving fast. There'd be Boche patrols out though, bound to be. She thought, *Let's have a crash. At the next corner let's have a lovely smash-up!* The hat in front of her tilted as the driver half-turned his head: 'Listen. You said to that old woman, tell him go ahead without you. Tell who to go ahead with what?'

'Entirely private business. In any case you must have misheard me slightly.'

'In what way?'

'It doesn't matter.'

'You'll tell us anyway. Save yourself a lot of suffering if you just answer questions as they're asked.'

'I've nothing *to* answer. What I said to my friend in the Blue Dog – I've done nothing wrong, as soon as that's established I'll be back. Look, I'll want my papers back too, so—'

'Forged papers. Forged in London, eh? And you feel safe' – they were passing the Opéra, Rue de Richelieu ahead, and doing about seventy-five – 'feel safe because you think the Americans will soon be here. Well, maybe, but by that time you *won't* be, you'll be on your way east. To Ravensbrück, I expect.'

'And where will *you* be scuttling off to?'

Shouldn't have asked that. And he's probably right, it *will* be Ravensbrück. Second time round, they might actually get me there. Can't have *all* the luck. The gestapist was assuring her that she certainly would *not* be here for the Americans or her own people to find: she could count on that, it was policy now to ship captured agents east, to be disposed of. Rosie believed him: also that being 'disposed of' was what it *would* amount to. In fact always had. Only now they had a deadline, would be in a hurry. But – Rouquet and Léonie, same thing? In which case what was in Rue de la Pompe – if anything, any*one*? This rescue attempt pointless from the start, for all anyone had known? Well, they *had* known: she remembered Hyatt saying, 'Does give us *some* chance – we hope . . .' And that was it – as long as there was any hope at all, you had to try. Thinking then of Lise – *that* Ravensbrück trip, the interruption to their journey east when Lise had done exactly what Rosie had told her, with admirable promptitude – Rosie making her own run for it and being shot, Lise diving under the stopped train and rolling down the bank into the river Meurthe, in leg-irons which might have drowned her – and no fingernails at all on her left hand, by that time. But ultimately surviving, getting home with the information they'd *had* to get out somehow.

And that had been a *hell* of a long shot. So – cross your fingers . . .

Out of l'Avenue de l'Opéra into Rue Rivoli, westward, towards Place de la Concorde and the Champs Elysées. Taking her where – Rue des Saussaies? *Could* be: if he turned up Rue Royale, for instance, then into Rue St Honoré. Longish way round, for sure. But if not Rue des Saussaies, where? Seeing that the *Sicherheitsdienst* headquarters in Avenue Foch had shut up shop. Please, *not* a Lafont establishment. The address one hadn't bothered with, for instance – Place des Etats-Unis. Could be: if Leblanc had been misinformed . . .

'Where are we going?'

'*You* – Ravensbrück!'

The smart answer seemed to have amused him. She said, 'By then *I'll* have something to laugh about – the thought of you dangling from a lamp-post. Isn't that what the Resistance are saying they'll do with traitors?'

'Traitor? I'm a Doriotist – and, let me tell you, *proud*—'

'Doriot's done a bunk, I heard.' Doriot, head of the *Parti Populaire Française,* who'd seen his own destiny as Führer of an independent French Nazi state. She added, 'Most of his close supporters have too. As you'd know.' She was improvising slightly, but it was close enough to what Georges Dénault had told her last Friday night or the early hours of Saturday; Doriot had run for it and so had his friend Darnand – former French Army war hero turned rabidly anti-Semitic thug, chief of the *Milice* and proud bearer of the rank of *Sturmbannführer* in the Waffen SS. The car was slowing, its driver growling, 'The fact the so-called Allies may be in Paris soon doesn't mean Germany's lost the war. Don't think *that,* for one moment. In any case *you* won't see the end of it.'

Breaking off then: winding his window down and spitting out the stub of his cigarette. They were in the Champs Elysées – but not continuing west, instead turning up towards those fine old buildings behind gardens and chestnut trees. And waking up to it then: to the fact that she was being brought to *Clausen.* Jacqui's voice in memory, rather surprisingly answering her question as to where he had his office, telling her offhandedly, 'L'Avenue Champs Elysées – Propaganda *Abteilung,* they call it.'

Chapter 15

Nils Iversen died in the early hours of Sunday and that night the Norwegians had buried him and the other one – Sundvik – canvas-wrapped and weighted, in deep water on the outside of this slope of rock. Pending the return of Sven Vidlin there was no certainty about leaving the *Ekhorn* here, some doubt therefore as to how long MGB *600* might have to stay if she was to escort the Norwegian back to Shetland. Petter Jarl wasn't competent to conduct the survey as planned by Iversen, so that had to be called off, obviously: Iversen hadn't had the foresight to allow for the contingency of his own death.

Ben had offered to transfer to the *Ekhorn* for the trip back – not as CO, which might have ruffled some Norwegian feathers, but as navigator and in the hope of *not* getting separated from each other as they had on the way over – and Hughes had agreed it might be a good solution. He wanted his passengers, though – agents and escapers whom with luck Vidlin would be bringing; there was also the cargo of weaponry in *600*'s forepeak, which he'd have transferred to the *Ekhorn* if she'd been staying in the fjords but might now have to take back to Shetland.

During Sunday and again on Monday there'd been air patrols – seaplanes, again. As likely as not patrol boats too, which one didn't see. It wasn't easy to just sit and do nothing, but Hughes was insisting that not a face or movement should be shown outside the netting. The first day had been all right – having just got here, and having the petrol to dump – but Saturday had been tedious, Sunday rather more so. That evening – *last* evening, this was Monday now – there'd been the committal of Iversen and Sundvik, also the retrieval of about half the petrol – enough to top up the *Ekhorn*'s tanks. Ben thought he'd have done that in daylight – could have done so safely enough, keeping under the nets and with a constant lookout skyward, as they'd done when they'd been dumping it – but Hughes was becoming more and more cautious as time went on. Ben supposed he was right, in principle: it would only take one careless move, and one pair of German or quisling eyes just happening to spot it.

Anyway – Monday night now – getting towards midnight. Four whole days gone. Main purpose of the operation blown – by Iversen getting himself knocked off, poor fellow – and the only achievements so far being to have dropped a load of 100-octane over the side and then hauled a lot of it up again. Idle thoughts while playing liar dice with Hughes and Cummings in *600*'s wardroom; both thoughts and game then interrupted by Nick Ball sending down word that they had visitors – a pulling-boat, might be Vidlin . . .

Lightning evacuation – to the upper deck forward, to look out from under the netting. Ball was already there, and a dozen sailors who'd come up through the forehatch. Hughes barking, 'Gangway, please!' – stooping double under the netting, getting around the two-pounder mounting and then over anchor gear – and already hearing oars thumping in rowlocks.

'Challenge him, Number One!'

Ball yelled, 'Jens Vidlin?'

'Ja, *Vidlin*!'

The boat had four people in it. Within minutes it was alongside, cam netting lifted to accommodate it and passengers being helped up over the side. An excited exchange between Vidlin and some Norwegians from the *Ekhorn* – delight at *Ekhorn* having after all survived, shock and sorrow at Iversen's and Sundvik's deaths – Iversen's particularly of course, since he'd been crucial to the operation, *the* crucial element, in fact. A torrent of Norwegian anyway; and out of it suddenly Mike Hughes' rather high-pitched, 'I'll be *damned*!' and – incredibly – a girl's laugh. Then her voice in Norwegian-accented English: 'A shock for you – should I apologise? But I just hear what they say – Nils Iversen, that's *terrible* . . .'

Her name was Anna Berge, and she was wearing – well, a wedding ring, Ben noticed, also baggy trousers with plimsolls and a sweater, despite which she looked – again, incredibly – like Marlene Dietrich on one of her better days. Actually, *terrific*. Blonde hair rather long, now she'd removed her oilskin cap and let it all fall loose. Hughes asking her a few minutes later, over coffee in the wardroom – the other two Norwegians she and Vidlin had brought with them were berthing in the *Ekhorn* for the time being – 'You're the agent here, then – of SIS?'

'My father, hereabouts, is coordinator of resistance. I was in Oslo – doing those things, yes, also teaching – but the Germans trapped my husband, and—'

Pausing, looking not at any of them now but only into her coffee mug. Ben recognising and sympathising with an aversion to talking about it much, at any rate to strangers – something like that – and cutting it short by murmuring, 'I'm sorry.'

'Yes.' Looking at him, then, and brightening. 'Although I can say *I* was very lucky. And my father was alone here, so I came to join him. I don't think they're looking for me – they can't be, didn't know my . . . background. I have to tell you, though' – telling Hughes – 'these two who escaped from Ulven prison camp not long ago, my father's gone for them, but how *long*' – shaking her blonde head – 'because they were being moved from place to place, you see—'

'Roughly how long – would you guess?'

'A few days.' Sipping coffee. 'Maybe a week. If he should have to – you know, hole-up some place – Gestapo are searching, you see – they don't like it, people escape before they can murder them. *Could* be a week.'

'I suppose we could wait that long.' Hughes had said that to Ben; explained then to the girl, 'There's a slight problem with the *Ekhorn* – can't really leave her on her own. The boy Iversen brought along as – well, his back-up – he's a nice lad, but—'

'Sven was telling me. Might the answer be for Sven to go with him? Then you *could* leave – and they follow with the others when we have them?'

'Well—'

Ben told her, 'We'd more or less decided *I*'d move over. And I think Mike here needs Sven to get him out of this place. Which I could *not* do. Whereas in the *Ekhorn* there's at least one man with local knowledge – who brought her in, guided Jarl in. Nils was unconscious a lot of the time. But I'm a navigator, you see, so once we're out of pilotage water I can be with Jarl in that capacity but – you know, keep an eye on things in general.'

Hughes confirmed to Vidlin, 'I would be happier to have you stay with me.'

There were exchanges in Norwegian then, which Anna interpreted eventually as, 'He says OK with him.'

'He's a very good fellow, tell him.' She did so, Vidlin stood up and bowed, and they all laughed. Hughes told her, 'There's another thing. I have a cargo of Sten guns, ammunition and explosives – with fuse and detonators, all that. Oh, and R-type mines. Under the plan as it was I'd have transferred it all into *Ekhorn* before Nils pushed off – since he'd have been going up-fjord, wouldn't he? You'd need at least three or four trips in Sven's boat, though.'

'I think we should move the *Ekhorn* in any case. After – that is, if you sail tomorrow night—'

'Move her higher up the fjord?'

'Close to where I'm living with my father. With the camouflage she'll be as safe there as here. Safer – they've learned that you prefer the mouths of fjords, don't like to go far up. And if that's agreed, if you like – this was to Ben – 'I can be your pilot. I grew up around here, all the time in boats.'

He smiled at her. 'Be great.'

He thought, *Be bloody marvellous* . . .

Hughes was saying, 'That's it, then. Tomorrow we'll tranship the cargo into *Ekhorn*. And you, Anna – if you and Ben are going to shift her up-fjord as soon as I shove off – soon as it's dark tomorrow – *today* now – about eleven, eleven-thirty say—'

'If you've a hole for me somewhere to curl up, I'll stay with you. You could put Sven's boat back on board then, if you wanted to.'

'You can use my cabin. It's small, but—'

'Oh, how *kind*!'

Some smile, she had. Truly did. Like the sun coming out. And imagine – outdoor girl, with a brain in her head and the guts to be coping with this sort of life, and – crikey, looking like *that* . . .

Chapter 16

'What do you have to do with propaganda? And *these* things – what *for*?' Lifting her handcuffed wrists towards him, jangling the chain. She'd allowed herself to sound slightly hysterical: up to this point having kept her mouth shut, only letting him see bewilderment and shock; but she was alone with him now, in this large room with its high ceiling and ornate chimney-piece, disparate assembly of furniture. The SS goon had been dismissed and the Frenchman, addressed by Clausen as Dubarque, had deferentially placed her papers as well as the handcuffs' key on the desk in front of Clausen.

Modern desk – plain and solid, incongruously so. The oval table in the middle of the room was probably Louis-Seize – rosewood, she thought – with chairs around it of similar vintage and elegance. The carpet was not only huge but beautiful, and there was a crystal chandelier above the table. Not lit: light came from oil-lamps on a timber filing-cabinet near the door, on the mantel and on Clausen's desk.

No pictures on the walls. You could see where they *had* been. Crated-up and removed to Berlin, she guessed. She was taking overt interest in the room and its furnishings while getting her wits together and assessing *him* – attitude and intentions. Jacqui's lover, or SD hatchet-man? Rolled-up shirtsleeves, loosened tie, shirt open at the neck; he was smoking a cigar as he glanced through her papers. Hadn't looked up yet; his only reaction to her outburst had been to growl, 'Sit down. Wait.' Looking up now though, putting the papers aside – grim-faced, no genial-host act this evening – telling her, 'You're here to answer my questions, not to ask your own. The answer to your first one however is – nothing. My kind of work benefits from peace and quiet, and these rooms were available. As it happens, most of the building's empty now. So—'

An inch of ash fell off his cigar; he blew it away. She broke in, 'Are you going to tell me why I've been dragged here?'

'As I said – to answer questions – which I'll preface with a warning: you may imagine that my having entertained you to lunch and discussed Jacqueline's predicament with you might put you at some advantage. It does not. It was Jacqui who invited you – on the face of it, in point of fact you pushed her into doing so. Like many others she's facing problems, which you and she discussed and in respect of which you made certain proposals. Resulting from . . . from certain peculiarities in the way you went about it, I've spent the last forty-eight hours checking on your background; and this is the outcome of it.'

'What am I supposed to have done?'

'I may as well add that my inquiries – to Berlin, by telephone – were started on Saturday evening after Jacqueline told me she'd seen you – twice – and you were coming next day. By *that* time – Sunday midday, when we had the pleasure of your company – answers had begun to come in, and now, of course' – he patted the file – 'it's all here. More than enough, I may say. And I must point out to you that my having requested the information and being supplied with it is itself now on the record; which means I have no latitude in how I deal with you, I can only go by the book. D'you understand?'

'Your superiors know you've got me here, do they?'

'As I said, *I* ask the questions!'

'Perhaps I might ask this one, though – if I'm to be "disposed of", what happens to Jacqui when you leave?'

'I think I can ensure her safety. Yes – I *can*. Your idea was a good one.'

'You'll do it that way, then. Except for the farm, of course.'

'Of course.'

'Are you confident that the FFI will swallow the story – mightn't know enough about her to dismiss it as a hoax?'

'As long as we can see to it that *you* have no further communication with them – yes.'

'You think I'd rat on her?'

'I can ensure you're not in a position to. I don't have to – trust, or risk . . .'

'So on no account can I expect to be released.'

He dropped the stub of his cigar into a brass shellcase ashtray, and tapped the file. 'In view of what's in this, I doubt I could justify a decision to release you. In fact even to *hold* you – as an alternative to putting you on a train to Germany.'

'Hold me where?'

Shake of the head. 'Your proper destination – on the basis of what is *known* – that's to say, no interrogation being actually required—'

'No torture. Just dear old Ravensbrück.'

'You were on your way there not long ago, weren't you? You're an extremely *resourceful* agent, I grant you that. But I can guarantee you won't escape a second time – *if* that's the decision I'm forced to make.'

'Entirely up to you, is it?'

'Yes. As matters stand, at this time. Incidentally, do you think you were wise to return to France with the field-name you were using a year ago – which you must have known would be on your file?'

'There'd have been problems if I'd turned up with any other. To Jacqui especially – or in Rouen, Estelle. The name they both knew me by – thought I *was*.'

'Certainly made it easy for me. The very first inquiry to records in Berlin – at once, the connection's made!'

'You'd have traced me anyway.'

'Not as easily or instantly. But' – hands flat on the desk – 'you understand your position now.'

'As you've explained it – yes.'

'Beyond that, however, another aspect is that in your background – in here' – the file – 'some of it is, anyway – there are areas in which I have personal interest. A lot might hang on your giving full and truthful answers to some further questions. All right, you could refuse – you're in it up to the neck, so—'

'Ravensbrück.'

'Well – I *have* explained—'

'While maintaining that this isn't an interrogation, that you don't need one.'

'I beg your pardon?'

'Threat of death as alternative to torture.'

'No. These questions are – supplementary. Your record as it stands would justify several death sentences.'

'Difficult to carry out more than one, though.' She shrugged. 'Must be galling.'

'Your flippancy is – really, out of place. Ravensbrück is hardly a joke. Be quiet now and listen.' He pulled the file closer, extracted a sheet of foolscap. 'These are my own notes – memoranda. All right – Jacqui introduced you to me in her apartment in Rouen, late July last year. I was there only briefly. I'd come to see *her*, had no interest in you, in fact I had no duties in Rouen then, was only packing up. But I remember her telling me that you were trying to sell perfume on behalf of Maison Cazalet and having a hard time of it; she was trying to give you a start but was not optimistic for your chances. She was sorry for you, you were a sweet girl, short of money, widowed, had a child you couldn't afford to have with you – et cetera. That's how it was when I left Rouen – on recall to Berlin, as it happens. But it's on the record that this same sweet girl with all her problems was arrested a few days later near Bellencombre, at a Lysander rendezvous, spent a day or two under interrogation but then in somewhat peculiar circumstances escaped – I have my own theory about that—'

'So do I. Tell you, if you like.'

'It's not important. Oh, *having* escaped, you killed a man, a captain in the SS – which makes for one death sentence. I only call it unimportant in relation to what I'm putting to you now. The essence is that you were – and are – an agent of SOE, and you'd made yourself known to Jacqui because she was at that time the paramour of the German officer organising construction of rocket sites in the Pas de Calais. This accurate, so far?'

'I was trying to make friends with Jacqui for that reason, yes.'

'Did she know that was what you were after?'

'Of course not. My aim was to establish a close friendship, and then try to recruit her. I didn't get that far, though, didn't have time. I'd arranged for an agent code-named Romeo to be picked up by Lysander – oh, and for a couple of *parachutages* – but I'd only been there – what, a week or ten days maybe – and of course Jacqui was away every weekend in Amiens. I hadn't had anything like enough time before I was arrested. And tortured, by the way.'

A silence. Staring at each other. Rosie knowing she had to put Jacqui in the clear: otherwise she'd be on the skids and bang would go whatever leverage she, Rosie, might still have. *Might*. Also by now might not. *Cling to it, though . . .*

'You're telling me that Jacqui had no reason to suspect you were a British agent?'

'I certainly gave her no reason to suspect I might be. I'm not a complete idiot, and even then I wasn't inexperienced as an agent. One doesn't approach someone one barely knows – and who has links to Germans, for God's sake!'

'But you would have at some later stage.'

'When I knew her better, and if by that time I thought I could take the chance – yes.'

'So when you arrived on our doorstep last Friday, from wherever – Rouen, did you say?'

'Yes. I'd gone there hoping to see her, was told she was in Paris and got her address.'

'Which wasn't easy to believe. The young man had sworn on his mother's grave he wouldn't give the address to anyone. His job depended on it, and he's well paid, so—'

'He didn't give it to me.'

'Estelle, then?'

'Can this be off the record?' He nodded. She thought it was probably off any *official* record anyway. This was Clausen's personal investigation of his lover's probity, politics, loyalty to *him*. She admitted, 'I took her to supper, and persuaded her. Told her Jacqui was in danger from the Resistance and all that – and if I got to her I could save her life.'

'Estelle is a dimwit, of course.'

'She's very fond of Jacqui. What I told her was the truth, in any case. Don't you accept it? Incidentally, I promised that no one would know she'd told me. I told you and Jacqui I'd got it from – Joao, is his name? – for that reason, and because anyway I didn't like him.'

'All right. Recapitulating now, though: you went to Rouen last year with the intention of subverting Jacqui, but you were arrested before you were ready to make your move. Consequently she could not have been responsible for leaks of intelligence concerning the rocket sites.'

'I didn't say *that*. If there were leaks – well, I know nothing about any, I wasn't there.'

'So you think Jacqui *might* have—'

'Might – I suppose. But so might anyone. *You* might have, the colonel of engineers might have. Or *nobody* might have – I wasn't in any position—'

'But you *did*' – selecting another document from the file – 'did persuade *résistants* in that and surrounding areas to investigate any construction work that might be for rocket sites, and report on it.'

She nodded, smiling ruefully at her own poor memory and/or at the conclusion he might draw.

'So?'

'I was dealing with those country people mainly over *parachutages*. Getting their requirements and passing those to London, and in some cases setting up the drops at very short notice. In the course of all that I did, certainly, ask for their help in our rocket researches too.'

'To whom would they have passed any such information?'

'To me, of course!'

'But in your absence?'

'I had every intention of staying in touch with all of them. I wasn't *expecting* to be arrested – if that's what you're—'

'Surely an experienced agent – such as you admit you were – is conscious every minute of the day and night that such a thing may occur, and especially on such an important issue would have made alternative arrangements?'

'I wonder if I could get you to understand – well, two things. One, I had a good cover-story and papers to match. I didn't know that the creature representing himself as my *Chef de Réseau* was actually an officer of the SS, that the man he was impersonating had been tortured to death in Lyon, this impostor passing on anything I told him to – to your people, I suppose. Or Gestapo – there was a change-over in progress at just that time – in Rouen, I mean. The other thing is that my job would have been taken over – eventually – by whoever they sent out from London to replace me, and he or she would quickly have re-established contact with those people.'

'Whereas if you'd been able to recruit Jacqui, she might have acted as your post office?'

'You mean those sons of the soil might have trekked in from the wilds, visiting the beautiful Jacqueline Clermont in her *salon*?'

'Or sent wives or daughters?'

'Well – one hadn't thought of any such thing. Christ, I hadn't got around to approaching her about her colonel, even!'

'I was only speculating. SOE do make use of such "post offices", don't they?'

'Some might. I never have. Aren't you going a bit far now – in this effort to work up some utterly spurious case against poor Jacqui?'

'Very much the opposite. To establish *absolutely* the opposite.'

'But *you* introduced her to the colonel in Amiens, acting – excuse me, I don't know how else to put this – as her pimp?'

'I *beg* your pardon?'

'Well – I'll beg yours, if you like, but *didn't* you introduce them?'

'Not in the manner or with the intention—'

'You did introduce them though. Jacqui mentioned it. I've often wondered about that. Seeing that you and she were already in a close relationship?'

'She came for a weekend with me in Amiens, when he was setting up his headquarters there. There was a celebratory party – all the high-ups, including a few of my people of course, also Gestapo, an Army commander, and – well, I attended, having done a lot of spade-work on the security aspect, and Jacqueline came with me.'

'But left with *him*?'

'Effectively – you might say that was how it turned out, yes. But this has no relevance—'

'Was she supposed to keep tabs on Walther, for the information of the Gestapo or *Sicherheitsdienst*? Did *they* tell you to be a good boy, stand aside and let it rip?'

'That's a completely unfounded – and insulting—'

'New man – *technical* man, not a real soldier – and an absolutely vital, top-secret project – something that's going to win the war for you, even – wouldn't your top brass be tickled pink to have a head on that pillow, so to speak?'

Staring at her: but more surprised than resentful. Might have hit the nail on the head, she thought. Explaining, 'That was guesswork based on the fact that I can't see why else you'd have passed her on to him. You were crazy about her, and she was certainly in love with you. Is now, was *then* –

I *knew* it then, from the way she talked about you. She didn't care much for the colonel.' Rosie smiled, lifting her shoulders: 'Heavens. Year-old mystery solved!'

'Aren't you being a little incautious?'

'It's you who keep bringing Jacqui into it. You raised the subject of Amiens too. In your mind, Jacqui's at the centre of all this, isn't she? Whatever you say, you *do* seem to distrust her. May I make one more point?'

He raised an eyebrow. 'Well?'

'The Rouen and Amiens business. I've often thought that if I *had* had longer, however carefully I'd played my cards she'd have turned me down flat because of her feelings for you. And it strikes me now that if there's any truth in the scenario I just dreamed up – her spying on the colonel, on Gestapo orders – how could she *possibly* have undertaken to do the same thing for SOE?'

Spreading her hands, as well as she could manage it in the handcuffs. 'What do you think she is? Mata Hari?'

He was watching her: his hands shifting too, clasping each other on the blotter in front of him. A shrug: 'If there *were* any validity to your rather colourful imaginings—'

'If I'd put my proposal to her, she'd have gone straight to her Gestapo controller, wouldn't she? And if by then I hadn't *already* been arrested—'

'All right.' A gesture almost of surrender. 'I'm prepared to accept that she was not recruited by you.' He added, 'In fact I agree that if you'd tried to recruit her she'd have turned you down. So – moving now to the next stage – why go to so much trouble to seek her out again?'

It was the question that really mattered – to which all that earlier stuff had been building up, and to which she didn't have any ready answer.

Had to produce one, though. Looking at him in what she hoped he'd take for feigned surprise: 'I'd have thought that being such a hotshot investigator you'd have guessed that right away.'

His telephone had jangled. His eyes stayed on her as he pulled it closer and lifted the earpiece from its hook.

'Clausen.'

Listening. Frowning then. Her German was so limited as to be almost non-existent, but the next few words, in a tone of irritation, must have been something like, 'All right, I'll wait, if it's not too long.' As far as she was concerned it could take as long as it liked. The problem being that knowing as much about her as he did, he was *not* going to believe she was risking her neck to save Jacqueline Clermont from the rough justice of *Forces Françaises de l'Intérieur* purely on the strength of having found her helpful and companionable in Rouen a year ago. One needed some credible and potentially *achievable* objective.

Either to recruit her for something, or to pick her brains. More likely though – because of her closeness to Clausen, to use her to pick *his*.

The truth, in fact. But adapted to fit some other line of inquiry . . .

He'd snapped into the 'phone, '*Ja, Clausen!*'

Switching into French then: 'Yes. I *am* working late. So—'

Listening. Nodding repetitively then, as if bored by whatever information he was getting. 'All thirty-four. Very well. Thank you. I appreciate that you were obliged to inform me – although it's not *my* operation; I've had no part in it.'

She could hear the quick gabble of French from the other end, but not well enough to make anything of it. It was a shorter speech this time – and Clausen reacted to it more positively. 'Yes, you *could* – as it happens. Yes, virtually at once. Tell them, please, *one*. Female. In' – checking his watch – 'an hour, say . . . Well, too bad, have to wait up, won't they?' A snort of amusement. '*Ja*. A big help – thank you.'

He'd hung up, pushed the 'phone away.

'You thought I'd have guessed *what*?'

'Well.' She shrugged, with a clink of the handcuffs. Seeing it now, or beginning to. Thank God. Or *please*, God. She tried,

'What motive *could* I have had, other than to get close to *you*?'

'In that case you've achieved your aim.' No smile. Probably thinking he had her on toast now, which logically might not be good for Jacqui either: then there'd be no *question* of any smiles – or for that matter of avoiding Ravensbrück. Sardonic tone: 'Would you say it's been worthwhile?'

'Not yet.' She thought of adding, 'Well, I had a good lunch out of it', but decided not to rely too heavily on his sense of humour. Instead: 'In fact – *no*. It was a long-odds gamble, in any case. But I was back in England, after a rather long deployment – some of which you know about—'

'Stick to the immediate present, your aim here *now*.'

'All right. Agents have disappeared – SOE agents. Arrested, obviously, but then – *disposed of*, and in a number of cases we don't know where or how – crucially, whether they're alive or dead. You'd have all those answers, we thought, anyway most of them, and you were of interest because we knew you had Jacqui with you, somewhere here in Paris. Also that once you've *left* Paris, which of course one realised might be quite soon—'

'Two questions: first, how did you know Jacqui was with me? Second, what advantage did you see in it for yourselves?'

'*How* – were told so by SIS. How they got to know, I can't tell you. A report from one of their agents, surely. What advantage – we'd hoped to recruit her earlier on, as I've been telling you, and – well, it had seemed worth trying *then*, hadn't been put to the test and here was fresh motivation – to get not at the colonel of engineers but at Gerhardt Clausen, *Sicherheitsdienst* genius at the very centre of counter-espionage. And since Jacqui and I had got on rather well—'

'So the idea was—' He'd checked himself. 'No. Ridiculous. You thought you'd persuade *her* to get the information out of me.'

'That was one possibility. The other was that with things breaking up here – plus your concern for her – there might be some chance of a deal. It was a matter of seeing how the land lay, then playing it off the cuff.'

'Which is what you're doing now?'

'Now, I've been answering your questions – in the hope of not being sent to the slaughterhouse.'

'As to that, we've some way to go yet, I think. But to regress yet again – when it was decided a year or more ago that Jacqui should be approached – what reason did your controllers have for believing she might betray us?'

'Excuse me. She's French. A French person who might be persuaded to work for the freedom of France is not *betraying* anyone.'

'Answer the question.'

'No clear or positive reason that I remember. But *you'll* remember that earlier in her career Jacqui – known to some of us then as La Minette – worked for an independent intelligence gatherer we called La Chatte?'

'La Chatte who was trapped by a colleague of mine by name of Bleicher.'

'Trapped and turned – although she was never an agent of ours, worked only for herself, for money. She had contacts with SOE but no more than she had with you.'

'And she's in gaol in England now?'

Rosie nodded. 'She was counting on being taken on by SOE, then acting as a double agent, with you people – *Abwehr* – pulling the strings and dishing out the Deutschmarks. Anyway – Jacqui was her employee. In fact – perhaps I shouldn't mention this, but you must know it, in any case it's water under the bridge now – La Chatte used her solely to entertain men. And by the time we were thinking about her, she'd dropped out of sight – her employer having been taken out of circulation, she'd become a hairdresser, and – SIS got wind of this – was spotted weekending in Amiens with the colonel.'

'Short answer therefore, it was because of her previous association with La Chatte. The rest doesn't matter. But – all right, back to the current situation now. Your idea was that through her you'd get information out of me on what had happened to your missing agents. Or she would, on your behalf. *Have* you made your long-delayed approach to her on that?'

'No. I was harping on the danger she'll be in when you pull out. You know all that, though. I'd heard those awful women gossiping in the *salon*, and—'

'You persuaded her first to meet you at a restaurant, then to invite you to lunch with us. Believing I'd tell you or her what you want to know?'

'When I hinted at – I don't recall exactly, I asked some question relating to your work – first she said she knew nothing at all about what you did, then came back on it quite fiercely, told me she'd never let you down. Wait – exact words were she'd "never do the dirty on Gerhardt".'

'Must have been quite a leading question?'

'I *thought* I was being careful.'

'So . . .' Fingertips massaging his temples . . . 'When you called at the house – Lafont was there. You met outside . . .'

'He was leaving, yes. Look, do I *have* to wear these things?' Holding her cuffed wrists up where he could see them. 'Am I such a danger to you?'

'Potentially so, yes. Of *course* you have to wear them. If it weren't that a lot of this interview is of a confidential nature I'd have an armed subordinate behind that chair as well. You're a British agent, your record includes murder, there's a death sentence on you and you've been on our "Wanted" lists for some considerable time. Frankly I wouldn't want to raise your hopes in any way at all. We can talk like this because we have a common interest in Jacqueline – but in the longer term—'

'We have a common interest in Jacqui's *safety* – but if you were to send me to Ravensbrück—'

'Why did she agree to have lunch with you the next day?'

'I persuaded her. I wanted to talk, there and then. I'd come by bike all the way from Rouen – and you might have arrived home at any minute—'

'But you were keen to meet me?'

'Not on the stairs, me going down and you coming up, feeling and looking like God knows what. In any case I wanted to sound her out first.'

'Which in the event didn't get you far – except for the invitation to lunch with us. What persuaded her to go that far?'

'Have you thought of asking *her*?'

'Answer the question!'

'You *know* the bloody answer! To talk with you both about getting her out of Paris!'

'Weren't you discussing that anyway?'

'No practical details, no. She didn't want to go into it without your being there too. A good reason for having me to lunch, I'd have thought.'

'If she knew nothing of your true motive, maybe.'

'God's sake, she *did* know nothing!'

'Accepted without question that simply out of the goodness of your heart, you'd come like some guardian angel—'

'Be as sarcastic as you like, the fact is we do get on. Yes, I've been trading on that, *using* it, but I do quite genuinely—'

'On Friday, was it agreed she wouldn't tell me you'd been there, or that you were meeting next day?'

'Yes. I thought it would be better if you didn't know I'd come to Paris looking for her. If we'd met – on Saturday by chance, lunched together, talked about how things might be for her when you left – then she'd have asked me to lunch with you in order to continue that discussion. But it occurred to me – actually in the restaurant on Saturday – that having met Lafont there, if he'd seen you and mentioned it, and she hadn't—'

'Yes. Wise, but too late. She told me on Saturday evening.

She'd forgotten to mention it the night before, she said. Or that morning – despite having it in mind that she was meeting you, which I must say I found difficult to swallow – so much so that I came back here that same night and . . . initiated my inquiries.'

He thought he'd got her on this point, she realised. His aim in fact being less to get *her* – he'd already got her – than through her to double-check on Jacqui, with whom he was undoubtedly in love but would cut off his nose to spite his face to know for certain that she was or wasn't, had or *never* had been making a fool of him.

Reasonable, she thought. In his shoes, *she'd* want to know. Her own blunder too: should have let Jacqui tell him on Friday night that she'd been there.

She offered – into a few moments' silence – 'I can explain some of it. *I* suggested keeping it to herself, but her main reason for going along with that was that I was telling her she ought to get away before *you* leave – and, you see, her reluctance even to discuss it, go behind your back, a part of *that* – this is what I *think*, she didn't actually say it – is that if she made too much of – well, being left in the lurch, you might think she was trying to blackmail you into taking her with you. Which she knows you *can't* do. It's – an impression I had, that's all.'

'All right. But you said her *main* reason. Is there another?'

In for a penny . . . She sighed, letting him see she'd much sooner not tell him this. Shrugging: 'The other reason is Lafont.'

'What about him?'

'After I'd met him out there I was thinking – there was something odd – oh, there *is*, of course, but – odder still after I'd told him I was there to visit Jacqueline Clermont. Something – secretive but also boastful. I did guess what it might be – and I asked her and it's a fact, he's chasing her. Not getting anywhere – she's in love with you and dislikes him. She hasn't told you, although she'd like to, because she doesn't want to cause what might be very serious ructions between you and him – apart from the fact that if you're suddenly recalled to Germany, leaving her here – *he'd* still be here, wouldn't he, ruling the roost? One way and another, anyway, she's not finding any of it very easy.'

'She wouldn't. No.' A gesture . . . 'As to Lafont – I knew it. But I trust her, you see. Although that may surprise you.'

'What surprises me most is that we're having this conversation at all.'

'But why she couldn't tell me . . .'

'How she *is*, Gerhardt. And so many uncertainties. Not knowing how she'll cope – or whether she'll ever see you again – whether after some space of time and completely changed circumstances you'll even *want*—'

'For your private and personal information, I not only want, I *intend* – subject to remaining alive—'

'You're married, of course.'

'That's one impediment, but – not insurmountable. The other is the war: damn near finished here, but won't be over for *me* for – for quite some time, at least.'

'I dare say not.' Fleeting thought of Ben . . . Clausen with an elbow on the desk, chin in hand, looking at her sombrely while he thought about it. Nodding and sitting back then.

'It's a bit woolly, what you've been telling me, but it holds together and it's not untypical of Jacqui.'

Reaching into the cigar-box, picking one up, looking at it for a moment, dropping it back in. 'I believe that by and large you've been telling me the truth. "By and large" because it must be in the front of your mind – *should* be – that to be put on a train to Germany is very much on the cards for you; also that what scores points is often less the truth itself than a general *ring* of truth, its details may be obfuscated. An example of this is what you were telling me half an hour ago – that you're here with the aim of tracing agents. Any old agents, more or less?'

'Well. Not exactly.'

'Ah.' Raised eyebrows, and heightened interest. 'The *whole* truth coming now?'

'Why not?'

Because she wasn't getting anywhere this way – beyond reassuring him of Jacqui's devotion to him. Whereas if she could persuade him to strike a deal and then trust him to keep his word, as distinct from congratulating himself on having wrapped up this little investigation – another feather in his cap – and packing her off to Ravensbrück . . . Léonie as well maybe, Rouquet more likely to Büchenwald or Natzweiler – *if* either of them were (a) still alive and (b) still here in Paris. She began – like diving from a height into water that might have rocks just below the surface – 'I could do better than the farm at St Saven – Nantes – for Jacqui. I could take her to England. That is, if she and I are both alive and free when the Allies get here. In England I or others might keep an eye on her until – well, if you meant what you said just now, *eventually* you'd be in a position to send for her, or fetch her?'

Watching her while it sank in. Questioning and evaluating it, obviously. A frown then: 'In return for what, this unprecedented offer?'

'Two agents who were caught about a fortnight ago. I'd want to take them back with me too. With us, I should say. A man and a girl – he's Guillaume Rouquet and she's Léonie Garnier.'

'*That* pair.' A shrug. 'I know *of* them of course, but . . .'

He pulled a drawer open, took out some files like the one already on the desk. Glancing at the labels on their front covers. He kept two, put the others back, slid the drawer shut.

'You have their names wrong. Field-names, no doubt. In fact he's – Derek Courtland, and she's Yvette di Melilli. French-Italian, by the sound of her. So happens, I've never set eyes on either of them.' Eyes back on *her*, then. 'Quite exceptionally important to you, they must be . . .'

Chapter 17

Rue des Saussaies. It was no surprise. There'd been a hint of it earlier, and she'd heard the SS man to whom she'd again been handcuffed give the order to the one who drove. Clausen had sent for them, giving brusque orders in German over the telephone, and she'd made nothing of that; he'd transmogrified into the stony-faced interrogator again by then – *ex*-interrogator, disinterested in her now the interview had been concluded, case wrapped up. She'd tried a sally or two and got nowhere, might as well have been talking to herself. Even in regard to Jacqui, who having featured so largely in their exchanges didn't come into it now and – she supposed – didn't have to. He'd got everything he wanted – *truly* had, she realised soon enough, having wishfully thought at first that maybe this was just an act. It hadn't been: he'd barely glanced up when the SS had come to take her off his hands.

She'd wondered whether the road-blocks would still be there, but they weren't, the truck hadn't even slowed: swinging to the right out of Place Beauvau, *then* slowing in its approach to number eleven. She'd been guessing at the route they'd been following – going by the turns and visualising the map: Avenue Marigny into Place Beauvau, she'd imagined. She'd been on the floor of the truck with her right arm raised uncomfortably, joined at the wrist to her SS companion's; there'd been another of them beside him and two facing them. Plus the two in front, making six; two of the original eight must have been sent off to get their heads down. The last time she'd travelled on the floor of a truck like this one had been after the *débâcle* at Ardouval near Bellencombre, the Lysander rendezvous which Clausen had mentioned. That truck journey had been all the way from Ardouval back into Rouen, and to pass the time they'd given her a few kicks.

Slowing. One wheel clipping the kerb as they turned into the courtyard and the two nearer the tailboard crouched over it, preparing to let it down.

Might run into Georges, Patrice and company?

She thought probably not. In that telephone call in which Clausen had shown little interest at first – and to which she hadn't paid very close attention because she'd been at a point of crisis in fielding his questions – the number 34 had been mentioned, which was approximately the number of Georges' group, whom they'd been holding here. This hadn't occurred to her until the next bit. Clausen saying yes, he'd have one female for them in about an hour; her guess being then that 34 prisoners had been moved out, so they had room for *her*.

Obligatory report to him, she guessed. To whom it might concern. An earlier inquiry maybe, if he'd been wondering where to put her. But by 'moved out', meaning released?

Hardly, at this time of night. Send 34 men out into the streets with the curfew in force?

Being consigned to 11 Rue des Saussaies would normally have been a depressing and frightening prospect. But as the alternative to being put straight on to a train for Ravensbrück – or Fürstenburg, which was the station for Ravensbrück – which she *might* have been, in which case they'd have dumped her under guard at Gare de l'Est. Where Georges had worked . . .

'Raus!'

Yanking her out, the iron bracelet biting into her wrist. Stumbling: one of them grabbing her arm, holding her up.

A torch shone in her face. There were *Miliciens* all over the place, uniformly attired in breeches and boots, khaki shirts with black ties, black berets, pistols in holsters on their belts. Darnand's devotees – one of their better-known slogans being *Against Jewish Leprosy and for French Purity!* French *purity*, for God's sake. Come-uppances by the bucketful were long overdue, she thought: seeing their youthful faces and the hatred in them as they glared back at *her*. Her people, these – her father's people: *French* . . .

This woman wasn't, though. If it *was* a woman – as the bulge of breasts did indicate. Bulge of biceps too, and black hairs on her chin. What looked like a policeman's truncheon hung from her belt. Thick trousered legs apart, thumbs hooked over the belt – waiting just inside, in the entrance hall – the SS man hurrying Rosie in with him and this creature looking her up and down contemptuously: Rosie in her old raincoat, hair unkempt, on her feet the felt slippers she'd been wearing in the Dog for comfort. The SS escort had taken the handcuff off her; he gave the woman a card on which Clausen had scribbled some notes – essentially, she guessed, her name and the charge against her.

Or – *Don't bother to keep this one alive*?

'Jeanne-Marie Lefèvre . . .'

She nodded. She would also have admitted to being Suzanne Tanguy or Justine Quérier: submission and compliance being the thing in this place. She'd seen the woman before, she realised: on her previous visit – June, if that was when it had been. Recently as *that*? She'd thought of her, she remembered, as 'the weight-lifter'. Another one – taller, scraggier – was coming now from the direction of where Rosie remembered the stairs were, remembered being dragged up them to an office where she'd been left for a long time strapped to a chair before being interrogated and, being non-compliant in the provision of answers to the man's questions, whipped.

A couple of months ago, was all.

The new one, who had one of the smallest heads Rosie had ever seen on a grown person, asked a question in German, to which the muscular one replied, 'Englander' and added some further piece of information, after which the tall one said to Rosie in passable French, 'Won't have you with us long, then.'

'Why d'you say that?'

'Death sentences are not carried out in this building, that's why.' The weight-lifter cut in: 'Down there. *Move* it!' Rosie knew the way, shuffled in her slippers towards the head of the basement steps; the one with the head like a chicken's calling after her, 'You'll love it down there, I bet!' It was a joke, apparently – and even at the top of the downward curve of steps it was obvious what she thought was funny. The stink. Sharply, eye-wateringly ammoniac. Having to continue down into it though, step by step, with heavy grunting breaths from the thickset one who was following close behind with a torch-beam lighting the way ahead. Passing a level bit where on Rosie's last visit there'd been a guard with a machine-pistol – as well as a man behind her with a rifle, who'd used its stock to drive her along in front of him. In relation to which the cosh on this woman's belt wasn't there only for decoration either, one knew she'd use it if she felt so inclined or if one gave her any lip or opposed her in any way. While if she, Rosie, was the only prisoner here, with *Miliciens* outside and only these two Gestapo creatures on the inside – *and* their knowing she was for the chop in any case . . .

She thought she might be, too. That Clausen had simply tricked her into telling him what she'd come for, and that was that – her card was marked. He'd told her he hadn't ever set eyes on Léonie/Yvette or Rouquet/Derek Courtland; perhaps he wouldn't have to set eyes on *her* again either.

The cement floor of the big cellar was slippery with urine. And not *only* urine. Her felt slippers would be soaking it up. She half-turned, gesturing around with one hand in the torch-light: 'Why – like this?'

You didn't want to breathe. Didn't expect an answer either, at least not a civil one, but surprisingly did get one – in clumsy, heavily accented French: 'Pigs. Many, many. *Toilettes* blocked also. Men – *résistants. Pigs!*'

One of the words she happened to know . . .

'Have you released them now?'

'Huh?'

'The pigs – *résistants* – you've let them go?'

'Let go?' A burst of laughter. '*Ja* – let go!' That was a *real* joke: she'd laughed again. They'd passed through the cellar now, were at the iron gate that led to an area off which there were individual cells. It wasn't locked – had no one on that side of it of course – and Rosie pushed it open. The woman telling her in that tortured French of hers, 'Not let go – never. Not for *you* go!' Staring at her fixedly with the torch-beam in her face: Rosie having stopped and turned to face her, awaiting instructions as to which of the cells was hers: 'You – here – before – uh?'

She nodded. 'Two months ago.'

Otherwise – if she'd denied it, and there was some record in which the creature could have looked it up, she'd maybe have earned a beating. The woman asked, still with the torch on her – 'So – was let *you* go?'

Meaning presumably *Did we let you go?* Rosie shook her head. 'Uh-huh.'

'Huh.' A nod: as if that said it all, proved her point, everything was as it should be. Muttering to herself in German as she dragged the left-hand cell door open and shone her torch inside: swinging it back on Rosie then – stopping her in the doorway, Rosie having tried to move in quickly past her, to give her no excuse to *throw* her in: or – whatever else . . . She'd noticed with some relief that the cement floor looked dry, had a slope to it – she'd forgotten that – that the iron bed was as she remembered it but the foul-looking straw pallet was maybe a stage or two worse. There was a bare bulb – unlit of course – in a wire cage on the ceiling. The Gestapo woman's stocky figure filled the doorway now, shutting out that glimpse of luxury; short, thick arm coming up, thick, short-fingered hand patting Rosie's cheek: 'Pretty. *Very* pretty!'

She'd pulled back, physically unable to stand there and accept it: but aware that too violent a reaction, *positive* resistance, would only make it worse.

'*Ach! Ça!*'

Her watch. Actually Marilyn's watch. She'd been surprised that Dubarque or the SS hadn't taken it when they'd roughly searched her in the anteroom to Clausen's office. Reacting to that gesture of affection, admiration or lust, she'd jerked her hand up to her face and the raincoat's sleeve must have fallen back, uncovering it – and this creature wanted it, had the torch on it. Rosie took it off, held it out to her: next moment had been sent spinning into the cell, the door clumping shut behind her. Total darkness . . .

She'd kept the raincoat on. Had deliberated whether to do that or spread it like a ground-sheet on the mattress – or rather pallet. Had decided that keeping it on would be best: she'd *had* to lie down, even though the pallet was damp, stained and smelly, and having it on and wrapped tightly round her with the collar turned up did ensure that much protection; whereas if she'd lain on it and moved around much in her sleep it might have slid out from under her or become rucked up. There'd be lice in the straw, she guessed. Not wanting to have her hair in contact with the pallet – *especially* not wanting that – she lay on her back with her hands linked under the back of her head. Nothing like adequate protection, but some. After a while the position imposed a certain strain, but it was really the only way to lie and she made herself put up with it. She'd sleep all right, she thought: it had been a long, tiring day. The bike tour with Nico, the climb to Sacré Coeur and the incident in the Place du Tertre, long evening in the Dog and to cap it all the exhausting two-hour session with Clausen: only when it finished had she realised *how* exhausting that had been.

Exhaustion might have been a major factor, she thought, in her state of depression and uncertainty as to what was going to happen next. Whether this *was* the end, at any rate in *his* intention was the end – end of *her* – allowing him to keep his brilliant reputation untarnished, while getting rid of her as an unwanted and possibly dangerous loose cannon in the next week or few days while he was making his plans for Jacqui. If indeed he *was* making plans for her – at any rate plans that were as clearly in her interests as she believed.

If she did, as devoutly as she'd let it seem. In the restaurant on Saturday there'd been some hesitance when Rosie had questioned how strongly *he* felt about *her*: then as to whether he might take her back to Germany with him she'd said, 'Possible but unlikely' – suggesting it might be on the cards, although when they'd been together next day it had been clear that it was not.

Proving what? Well – only that there were doubts where one would not have expected any. Doubts heightened now through his not having jumped at the offer she'd made him – virtually a guarantee of Jacqui's safety.

If he was as concerned for her as he said he was, wouldn't he have fairly *leapt* at it?

Faint greyish light was spreading across the concrete ceiling. She remembered from last time a small, barred window high up in her cell's end wall – that one. If this was the same cell, which it might be, the grating on the outside would be at about ground level, must provide some small circulation of air in here which in the big cellar there would not be. Thinking of Georges, Patrice and thirty-two others in there: standing or squatting room only, probably called out one by one for interrogation. Then with that process completed, passed on to – execution, or a cattle-truck eastward from Gare de l'Est? The former, probably: at Montrouge, Mont St Valérian or the castle at Vincennes, the centres of hostage-slaughter. Simply to get rid of them would be the thing.

Some *truce*, she thought. In pitch darkness and the latrine stench and one's own condition generally, one saw it as nothing but stark reality, how it *was* . . .

She could make out that ventilator now, just – the small rectangle of grey and the dark pattern of the bars. Dawn light – on Tuesday August 22nd: tonight, Leblanc and/or his ex-military colleague would be attacking the *Milice* armoury. Which, please God, would be successful. Then Wednesday, when she didn't turn up to meet him at the Dog—

But they'd know, of course, would have heard well before then from Adée. And might decide to go ahead without her?

That thought about Clausen again: if he'd had any real interest in her offer to take Jacqui to England, *wouldn't* he have enthused about it, there and then?

He'd shown interest, but in a detached sort of way, not as one would have expected, more as if his *real* interest had been in the fact of her having made the offer, and her own motivation – why those two, Léonie and Rouquet, so especially? In reply to which – questions, comments starting with *Quite exceptionally important to you, they must be* – she'd said nothing about their special knowledge of FFI and/or Maquis dispositions in Alsace-Lorraine – in case that *hadn't* registered, despite Cazalet's report to SIS; she'd only told him that Yvette and Derek were friends of hers, that she owed them for help they'd given her at some earlier time, was in any case personally concerned for them, and *she* had persuaded the hierarchy in London to let her have a go – banking on her friendship with Jacqui and the generally confused state of affairs, approaching climax, here in Paris.

'You mean try to help them escape somehow?'

'Delay their being sent east. Yes. And what I'm asking you now – the deal I'm offering—'

'Yes. Yes, of course . . .'

Straight-faced, but she thought maybe laughing at her. Half-smiling anyway – rather smug self-satisfaction, in retrospect, as he'd replaced those two files in the drawer, glanced at the clock and double-checked on his own watch; that hand then moving on to rest for a moment beside the telephone, its fingers drumming . . . 'So that's about it, eh? Unless there's anything else you'd like to tell me?'

He'd been clever on Sunday, she thought. Having had answers from Berlin that morning and knowing already that she was an agent of SOE, but giving her no reason to suspect he knew it. On his guard to the extent that he would have been anyway, even without that knowledge – being what he was, and she to all intents and purposes a stranger – but *acting* it cleverly, entertaining her with tag-ends of what might have been privileged information – in fact wasn't, but might have lulled her into thinking he was accepting her as Jacqui's friend in whom he could to that extent confide. The stuff about General Choltitz for instance, and the Lafont background – admitting his personal dislike of 'Monsieur Henri', all that.

Actually she couldn't imagine him and Lafont as buddies. Especially with the Jacqui complication. Which rather strangely he'd shrugged off. Assumed the leopard *had* changed its spots? That she'd changed them for *him*, no doubt: the lover she'd always wanted and never found. Except she *had* – and switched to the colonel of engineers. But maybe had very little choice, especially as he must have connived in it. She'd told Rosie on Saturday, *I'm pro Gerhardt Clausen and pro me: his business is his own, my business is him.* She'd have fed *him* that line. Might even have meant it. But if all that *was* mutually on the up-and-up – here we go again – *wouldn't* he have grabbed with both hands at the offer of sanctuary in England for her?

Theory-time. Exercise the imagination time. Think up some explanation that might improve morale, give grounds for *hope*. Lying still in the lavatorial-scented darkness, watching the slow spread of the coming day up there, guessing at the time – perhaps 4 am, 4.30. – and wishing that creature hadn't taken her watch – which was luminous, would have been something of a companion, ticking away and glowing green . . . Clausen, though – a cold fish, by the nature of his job, must live to a large extent inside his own skull—

Hang on . . .

One possible answer coming through. Whether it might be that – well, his side of the deal would mean producing Léonie/Yvette and Derek – obviously. What if he wasn't certain he'd be able to, if he might have to look into ways and means before he could take it any further? He'd said – surprisingly – 'I never set eyes on either of them' – which did suggest that Boemelbourg's intentions might either have been misreported or overtaken by events.

Conceivable?

No. Didn't match his manner in the closing stages, that slightly contemptuous, 'Anything else you'd like to tell me?' All that fitted any of it – words, tone of voice, switching-off of interest – was that he'd got all he wanted out of her and would be taking care of Jacqui in some way he'd work out for himself.

She was woken by the scrape of the key in the lock of her cell door, then the squeak of its hinges as it was pulled open. She knew immediately where she was and all the circumstances of her being there; in the three or four seconds it took for the door to open she was wondering – guessing – Gestapo woman – Clausen – SS coming for her?

The first guess had been right. The tall, chicken-headed one: electric torch in one hand, tin mug in the other. Something else in that hand too, pressed against the mug. A bun? Oh – lump of bread – of a kind she remembered – technically speaking *black* bread, actually grey, with a musty taste and odour. Pinhead had put it and the mug on a shelf at that door end of the cell.

'Breakfast.'

'Thank you. May I ask, what is the time?'

'Gone eight. Want visit *toilette*?'

'Yes – please . . .'

Torch-beam travelling around, touching here and there. In fact one could have seen one's way around without it now, by the seepage of light from the barred aperture high in the end wall. Pinhead had the torch in her left hand, and having the other one free now had jerked a stick or something from her belt. Riding-crop. Bone handle, silver band: Rosie saw it in close-up as she edged out past her. 'Thank you.'

You had to be polite to them. Stupid not to be. All you got, if you weren't, was beaten: and – as she'd thought before – if the whole place was empty, the freaks not answerable to anyone . . .

'To your left!'

'I know. Thank you.'

The *toilette* was as appalling as she'd expected. By anything like normal standards, wasn't usable. One tried not to breathe. The woman waited with the torch shining in, her shape framed in the doorway like some great bird, possibly prehistoric. Tall, small-headed, straight-sided, exceptionally long feet.

'Quick, you!'

Wasn't taking any longer than she had to. Wasn't exactly longing to get back to her cell either, although of the two – yes, that was preferable. But only performing the essentials while breathing as shallowly as possible and taking – well, great care: needing the light from the torch in that respect, while avoiding that unwavering stare. Eyes like some sort of bird's too: they'd look at *anything* without blinking. Rosie asked her as they passed through that end of the big urine-stinking cellar again, 'This place was full until last night, did your colleague say?'

'*Résistants*. Criminals.'

'Big crowd of them?'

'It was *full*, God's sake—'

'She doesn't speak much French, does she, wasn't easy to

understand. I think she said they moved them to some other prison.'

Turning right where the barred door stood open: dampness squeezing through the slippers and up between her toes. At the door of her own cell now though, on dryish cement again; glancing round. 'A different prison?'

'*In.*' A poke with the crop; then as she moved on in: 'Gestapo of Rue Lauriston taking them. What's it matter to you?'

'Well. Wondering how long *I'll* be here.'

'Not long. Tell you that – because we leaving too.' A catarrhal snort. 'You to your *peloton d'exécution*, we home Bavaria. Eat breakfast, maybe last you get.' Backing out, the torchlight withdrawing with her and cut off with the thud of the door, leaving Rosie to grope for the lump of coarse bread and the tin mug – which contained about a third of a pint of some sort of gruel, thin and lukewarm but still better than nothing.

Peloton d'exécution in that context meaning a firing-squad, presumably.

All day now, she supposed. Her eyes were accustoming themselves to the semi-darkness again. She wished to God she still had her watch.

All day. Dozing a little and trying to dream of Ben. Thinking for maybe the four-hundred-and-ninetieth time about how it would be when the war was finished, these bastards back in their own country, *not* bloody goose-stepping all over Europe and England too as they'd planned and had expected. Ben had told her about that, having seen a translation of captured printed orders which had been issued to the German 9th and 16th Armies for the invasion and occupation of Great Britain, including mention of an SS extermination outfit which would have had its headquarters in London and gas-chamber units, *Einsatzgruppen,* in specified locations across the country. There'd been details such as setting one up at the southern end of the Forth Bridge, unless the bridge had been destroyed in the course of the invasion, in which case another would be needed to the north of it. Ben had pointed out, over drinks in a bar-restaurant called the Wellington, in Knightsbridge, 'Won't happen now because whether or not they know it we've got 'em licked. But for instance – every male between seventeen and forty-five to be sent to slave labour over there. How about that? I tell you – you marvellous, *marvellous* object, you – any time between now and eternity I set eyes on one I'll have in mind how it would have gone if they'd had *us* licked!'

It was about then that she'd said, '*Do* let's move to Australia, when it's over?'

He'd talked about it before, as something they might do together. There'd been some Australian government scheme announced, an offer to ex-servicemen of grants of land which if the grantee had cleared of scrub within a certain time he'd then be entitled to another vast adjoining slab of territory: end up (he'd told her) with a spread about the size of – hell, Kent or Sussex. He'd been attracted to the idea, only doubtful as to how she'd take to what would be a rough life, comparative isolation and so forth. She'd told him she thought she'd take to it like a duck to water – above all, of course, with *him*.

But with his gammy leg now? Clearing hundreds of square miles of bush – and being stuck with it then no matter how the old leg reacted?

Well – if he was fit to have been sent back to sea now, maybe . . .

She spent a lot of the time pacing up and down her cell, also did press-ups and sit-ups and running-on-the-spot. Pinhead came about twelve hours after her morning visit, bringing a supper that was every bit as good as breakfast, and allowed her another outing to the *toilette*.

Midnight, roughly. In fact it must have been at about this stage that she'd lost her sense of time – effectively, lost a whole day. Whether either Pinhead or the gorilla had missed a visit or even two, or whether she'd gone through it as an automaton, like sleep-walking – weird enough, but actually the more likely, since otherwise she'd surely have been even hungrier than she was, missing two of those great meals – anyway, she came to realise afterwards that she must have been thinking of this being Tuesday night when actually it was Wednesday. Wondering about Leblanc and – what was his name, the ex-soldier – Leblanc *had* mentioned it . . . No doubt of it though, she'd been thinking about them as if it was tonight they'd be raiding the *Milice* armoury, *tomorrow* night maybe attacking the Rue de la Pompe house.

Fernagut was the man's name. Not bad, Rosie – seeing that Leblanc only mentioned it that one time. But how would they go about it, she wondered. More exercise for the brain – for the imagination anyway. A strongish force, ten or twenty men, say – well-armed, if last night's raid on the armoury had been successful. If it hadn't, she guessed, they'd be sitting tight. But assuming they'd got the Schmeissers and grenades – smash in, using all they had, or break in softly-softly like burglars?

Visualising it: remembering that road and the cream-coloured house, only having to picture it now in darkness. There might be just a sliver of moon but maybe not, maybe not risen yet, she thought. Might even be moonless – *would* be, somewhere about now: it had been full on the night before the attack on the factory in St Valéry, and that had been – the ninth of this month. In which case the dark period would start tomorrow night, you'd need to allow for *some* moon now – worse luck. Whether in any case it would light the front of the house – the ground inside that shrubbery behind the railings . . . You wouldn't get in that far unseen anyway – there'd surely be a guard or two. Approach *might* be possible from the back, although the gestapists would have taken care of that as well – if they'd even considered the possibility of being attacked. Anyway – if one had had to plan it oneself, here and now, on as little as one knew or could guess: OK, a truckload of at least a dozen men, say. With automatic weapons, obviously. In by the gate which if it wasn't open you'd either smash through with the truck or have a couple of them drop off to open it – giving them covering fire from the truck if necessary – then rush either the front door and/or windows or the side or back door – or all of them if there were enough of you – smashing in with axes or sledge-hammers, but anyway making it so fast and furious they wouldn't get time to kill their prisoners.

From a front bedroom window in number 107 Nico watched the house, which from this angle when the small remnants of a moon showed as it was doing intermittently through slow-moving cloud – there'd been rain earlier, might well be more coming – was in dark silhouette against it, the house's moon-shadow reaching all the way to the gravelled entrance drive and the gate across it. The gate was shut, as it had been when Nico had stopped to fix his brakes on Monday. It was 12.20 now: Thursday. Zero-hour 12.30, in ten minutes. No guard on the gate anyway, as there had been then. There'd been one individual moving around, but Nico hadn't seen him in the past half-hour. It would be *very* convenient if they'd withdrawn him, called him inside to join a card-game or something. Nico was standing well back from the sash window, but had it open so he could hear as well as see; old Vignot had opened it for him hours ago, in daylight, everything natural and above-board, a window opened on a hot afternoon by the owner of the house, no one across the road there sharp-eyed or bright enough to notice that it had still been open at nightfall. It was draughty in the house since the wind had got up, and the old boy had groused a bit about it. But he was a good sort, they'd been lucky with him. How it had come about was that Nico had said, when Leblanc and Fernagut had been conferring in the Dog this morning, 'If we had access to one of the places opposite, wouldn't be so bad. See what comes and goes, get an idea of the numbers we'll be up against?'

'Boy's damn right.' Fernagut, former sergeant-major. Nico turning pink with pleasure as Fernagut told Leblanc, 'We'd find one we could use, too, bet your life. With a choice of say these five, that'd be close enough?' They had a map spread on the table. Fernagut continuing, 'Since every son of a bitch in Paris is calling himself a *résistant* now – needing only one out of five?'

Vignot's had been the third they'd tried – Fernagut himself and Nico with him, the old soldier simultaneously making his own recce of the surroundings. Ostensibly, if challenged, he was in the business of buying antique furniture at knock-down prices. At the first house the woman was stone-deaf and wouldn't let them in, and it mightn't have been too healthy having to bawl your head off on a doorstep right opposite the Bonny-Lafont establishment; at the second no one came to the door, and at the third they'd found old Vignot, a dapper octogenarian who'd had some managerial position at Longchamp, loathed the occupants of that house as much as he detested Boches and had expressed delight at being allowed to help.

He was on the stairs now, in easy calling distance from Nico's position in the bedroom, had his telephone with him at the full length of its flex from where it was plugged in, in the hall. He also had a torch and the 'phone number of a house two blocks away where Fernagut was waiting inside and a truck with fifteen men in it was parked with its *gazo* engine chugging in an alleyway beside it. In any emergency Nico would call Fernagut, otherwise Fernagut would call and check before he got going at 25 minutes past the hour.

Getting close to that time now. Vignot calling, 'Still all quiet, lad?'

'Yes. How long now?'

'Three minutes. I *suppose* you'll—'

'Hang on.'

Lights – powerful torches. The guard had had one when he'd been there, and there'd been light visible in some windows from time to time, but most of the blinds were drawn – and nobody had come out with torches as they were doing now. Rumble of artillery then, on the wind from the south-west. Nico and his host had been listening to it earlier and speculating about the hoped-for arrival of the Americans. He wasn't listening to it now though – instead, to the sound of some heavy vehicle approaching from the direction of Avenue Foch.

Definitely coming this way. A petrol engine.

'Monsieur Vignot – call him up please, say wait, don't move!'

'Oh, my . . .'

You could see the truck now – flicking masked headlights approaching from the right. Not necesarily coming here – *there* – but with virtually no other traffic in the past couple of hours, and a lot of activity over there now – men, torches, voices, a whole crowd of them milling round suddenly: and they were opening the gate . . .

Evacuating?

'Tell him something's definitely happening, don't move!'

Vignot had Fernagut on the line: 'He says to wait, monsieur, not to move. Apparently there is – activity, of some kind.'

The gate was open and one of them was out on the pavement signalling to the approaching truck. Big, a three-tonner, dark-coloured: turning in off the road, lumbering up through the open gateway and the crowd inside there surging towards it. Those with torches, as Nico made it out, were herding others – who had their hands up. The truck's tail-gate crashed down, forming a ramp up which the prisoners were now being driven. He caught glimpses of Schmeissers, heard shouts and derisive laughter. He called to Vignot: 'I'm coming. Tell him I'm coming, I'll explain . . .'

Chapter 18

Clausen got home to the flat just before midnight, which was bad enough but less so than it had been on Monday or Tuesday, when she'd waited up for him until well into the small hours – early hours of this morning, in fact. Not that she blamed him for it – with so many of them already gone, his work-load obviously was tremendous, had been building up steadily in the last fortnight or so; and tonight at least she'd known he was going to be late, he'd managed to telephone her earlier. Often he couldn't – private calls being difficult, depending on where he was and who was with him.

Anyway, here he was now. For the moment at least, all well.

'You must be whacked.'

'Probably less so than you. Sitting around waiting . . .'

'Haven't had your marching orders yet, anyway?'

Asking this while taking a bottle of Cognac and two glasses out to the table on the balcony. He'd said if he went straight to bed he wouldn't sleep, needed time to relax with her for a while, and talk: there was still ground to cover. He'd had supper in the mess in l'Hôtel Continental – from where he'd made his call – and it had been a hurried, working meal – talking shop, of course. Answering her question now with a headshake: 'Not yet. If I had been, you'd know, wouldn't need to be asking me.'

'But they might have given you some – indication—'

'The first thing I'd do' – holding her again, talking into

her hair – 'I'd come out here at once to tell you, discuss it with you, finalise plans for *your* move. That is, if we haven't got you away first – which I'd prefer, is what I'm aiming for.' A tighter hug, a long kiss . . . 'Believe me. No matter what order I received, or from whom—'

'Of course I believe you. It's just that' – he'd released her and she flopped down, leaving it to him to pour the brandy – 'as you say – waiting around, no idea what's going on or how *long* . . .'

'I know how it must be for you. Busy or not, you're in my head pretty well all the time.'

Sliver of a moon up there, in and out of cloud. This side of the house was sheltered from the wind and the air was warm despite earlier rain. The view in fact was beautiful – even over rooftops and climney-pots, shifting patterns of light and shadow and the shine of still-wet slate; and, of course, the dark mass of the Bois de Boulogne behind all that.

He'd poured the Cognac; paused with the bottle in his hand, listening to the distant rumble of artillery. 'Hear it?'

'Been hearing it off and on all evening. How far away, d'you think?'

'God knows.' Raising his glass to her. 'Far enough that it needn't spoil our sleep.'

'Closer than last night, though.'

'Doesn't necessarily make it an advance on Paris. Indications are still that they'll bypass us here. Paris is not essential to them. What they want – in fact must have – are the ports. They may leave us to stew for – oh, another week, even.'

'Or a day or two?'

'Days, plural, in any case. The direction of their advance – American and British and a so-called Free French division – is eastward and north-eastward. Paris would only bog them down. But yes, all right, time is limited – especially as far as *I'm* concerned, finalising details in regard to you and getting you on your way. But you don't need to worry. Well – I say *not worry* – I mean over detail, which I really do have well in hand; but in saying this I'm not for a moment – oh, trying to make less of – of the heartbreak we're facing, you and I. I was going to say the *tragedy* but that's too strong, isn't it, the word implies a permanence which in our case does *not* apply – we both know this, uh? – *believe* in it?'

'Of course.' Gazing at him: 'I do, and I don't doubt you for a moment, my darling. Despite your French going funny sometimes.' Smiling at him: knowing he'd never found it easy expressing any depth of feeling in her language, despite his fluency in it otherwise. Maybe even in German he'd be like this. All she knew – or cared – was that the feelings he expressed so stiltedly were genuine, that as long as she wanted to – needed to – she could rely on him.

He'd leaned over to kiss her. 'Whatever's in store for us we'll get through all right. But listen – detail now. Tomorrow I'll be bringing back with me some extracts from the dossier I'm compiling. You need to know the basics of it so as to have a matching account which you can trot out when you have to. You could vary it or elaborate as you wish, as it may suit you, there's nothing to say we mightn't have some of the detail wrong. In fact an error or a blank area here or there is – characteristic, actually makes it more realistic. But for instance, the names of individuals with whom you were working, to whom you were passing your items of information: these come from other records, and the people concerned are either dead or would find it contrary to their own interests to contradict any of it.'

'Clearing themselves by accepting that they were somehow involved with me.'

'As you say.' He added, 'A point about the dossier, incidentally, is that you won't know everything that's in it, but the bits I'll show you will then be in your memory and match it closely enough to be virtually indisputable. You'll have had a tip-off that we're on to you, and – panic, some escape route alerted, and you've vanished. Leaving me in an embarrassing position obviously – it being no secret that I've been romantically involved with you, despite which I've been doing my duty following up these allegations – on top of which your abrupt departure will have absolutely stunned me. Then *I'll* be gone – maybe—'

'Maybe?'

'Unless I'm to be one of those who stays. In which case if I didn't escape independently I'd become a prisoner-of-war in due course. This is pure speculation, and strictly between ourselves, but since all my working experience in the SD has been in France, and France now so to speak goes off the map—'

'Or so to speak comes back *on* the map?'

'There speaks the secret *résistante.*' He leaned over to light her cigarette. 'The *gazo* is here, I'm told.'

'Oh, *is* it?'

'Round at the back. We'll have a look at it in the morning. But incidentally there's another possibility now, something quite new, which at the moment I'd sooner *not* discuss with you, but – could be – marvellous, if—'

'In what way?'

He shook his head. 'Tomorrow, *chérie*. I *hope*. I don't want to raise hopes before I'm certain.'

'All right. But – no word from Jeanne-Marie?'

'I wouldn't have, would I? She's to contact *you*, remember? Oh, if or when she's found the child. Otherwise she'll be waiting to hear from us – from *you* – again. So tomorrow, with the dossier complete – and maybe this other business by then clarified—'

'Changing the subject' – reaching to him, to stroke his hand – 'while it's in my mind, don't you think I should have a page of the dossier – some proof it exists? I know, you'll bring extracts, but – a piece of it in its final shape that I can keep? Otherwise maybe it doesn't come to light and I've no evidence at all – I'm investigated as a collaborator, I say,

"Oh, I was working for the British" – hell, protestations alone as self-defence—'

'Yes.' He'd nodded while she was speaking. 'You're right.' Pointing his cigar at her: 'You're *absolutely* right. In fact *I* should have thought of this. With the tip-off that's put you on the run you've also been given this piece of paper – which will have scared you stiff – but you've hung on to it, and it would lead very conveniently to a search for the rest – which it would exactly match of course: could be a missing page . . .'

Jacqui sent smoke pluming into the moonlight. 'Seems I have to do all the thinking around here.'

'You do it brilliantly, too. Although that point would have occurred to me, I think – when we're going through the stuff tomorrow.'

'Today, you mean.'

'Ah. Of course. Perhaps more tired than I'd realised . . .'

'So why not leave the damn cigar and come to bed?'

Looking at her. Hand moving to find the ashtray, drop the quarter-smoked cigar into it. Eyes moving, examining her face . . . 'From the most desirable girl in France – such an unsolicited invitation – my God, how can we still be sitting here?'

'I *was* beginning to wonder . . .'

Would the Boches here surrender, she wondered? In which case, had she and Clausen made love for the last time? He was deeply asleep, she still wide awake listening to the distant rolling thunder of artillery. Bypassing Paris, he'd said – bypassing pretty damn closely by the sound of it, she thought! Leaving the city and its environs surrounded, anyway – maybe then cutting the roads and rail-lines leading east? Wouldn't they *have* to surrender, then? She'd have asked him, but he was on his back and snoring, her body sprawled half over him, his arms loosely around her. Straining her ears to hear the guns again. They seemed to have gone quiet. Why would one want to hear that far-off rumbling anyway, she wondered – while still listening intently for its resumption – when a much closer, startlingly loud racket broke out of – Christ, it could have been right out there in the street!

Machine-guns?

'That's right *here*!'

She'd said it aloud – or shouted it – *squawked*, as it echoed in her own ears now. Might have been dropping off, *dreaming* about listening to the distant barrage, blurting that out as she was jolted awake with a picture in her mind of gun-muzzles spurting flame – which *certainly* she could only have dreamt of. Hadn't dreamt *this*, though – what sounded like screams – men screaming, amongst that gunfire. A pause, then more of it, bursts of high-pitched metallic reverberations from God knew where, but *close*. Machine-guns, or machine-pistols. Gerhardt had launched himself off the bed growling angry-sounding German: he'd rushed out as he was, stark naked. More of the shooting – short bursts, also single shots – and shouting, like a crowd at a prize-fight but with that screaming in it; like pigs being killed, she thought – having lived on a farm at one time, years ago. Remembering it as she wrapped a negligée around herself and hurried to join him on the balcony.

Nothing, now. Had suddenly all ceased; you were back in the quiet night, and the moon was showing.

'Where, and – what, any—'

'In the Bois, somewhere. Nothing to see – obviously, wouldn't be. Two kilometres, I'd guess. Two to three. That'd make it – oh, Pre Catalan, Bout des Lacs – thereabouts.'

'Sounded so *close*!'

'That's close enough – for sound, at night.'

'I was listening to those other guns.' She had her arms around him: the negligée open, pressing herself against him from behind. 'I was hardly even breathing, trying not to disturb you. Listen, why don't you *always* go round like this?'

'Where would I put my sergeant's stripes? No, now look, I—'

'Right *here* of course!'

'*No.*' Moving her away. 'I must telephone. Maybe a patrol got ambushed. Sounded like – massacre, or—'

'Won't have to go out, will you?'

'No.' He'd gone inside. Calling back to her, 'I hope not.' She heard him snatch the receiver off its hook.

Rosie had slept, but she thought not for very long: there was no sign of dawn smearing the darkness overhead, as yet. She'd been thinking of what might be Fernagut's tactics in the Rue de la Pompe, she remembered. Keeping the brain working, and keeping it off depressing, frightening supposition as to what she was in for now, this coming day. Wednesday. Saying to Ben in her imagination – thinking again of his reference to what the Boches had 'put her through' – 'Didn't quite see it through, though, didn't manage it, did they? Will now, probably; I think this Clausen's going for the limit. Doesn't want Jacqui kept safe for him in England, must have his own plans for her, damn him. Or none . . . Worst of it is they know now what a slippery customer I am, so they'll make bloody sure of me!'

Ben would be thinking they'd *already* made sure of it. In a way, one could be glad of that – that he'd have got over the very worst of it, shed his tears and – knowing him – pulled himself together. As long as some message from Marilyn hadn't reached him during the past week – while *en route* to Norway, or on the Norwegian coast, wherever – telling him that the reports of one's death had been greatly exaggerated and that she sent her love. Please God might Marilyn have had the sense to leave things as they were, *not* jump the gun: or have been unable to communicate with him, say.

But damn it – the allegation that she was alive would still get to him on his way back. Or when he *was* back. She could just hear his howls of premature delight.

Wouldn't be fair to him. Really, wouldn't.

Please, *not*?

So *you* make sure of it. Stay alive – silly bitch – rather than lie here as good as giving up the ghost before anyone's said you've got to!

Escape?

Oh, fat chance . . .

A shot at it for his sake, though? Christ, for your *own* sake too, you idiot! You have some small stake in the matter, don't you?

Well. Only need a magic wand – then action on the lines of 'with one bound she was free'. Almost giggling in the dark: not quite, helplessness wasn't anything to laugh at, not when the inadequacy was your own. By 'inadequacy', meaning panic. The sense of helplessness – reality of it – was actually suffocating, claustrophobic. 'Almost giggling' thus a symptom of hysteria?

Thinking of magic wands, though – pictures in mind of the wands dangling from those Gestapo females' leather belts. Riding-crop on Pinhead's, truncheon on the weight-lifter's. That was who'd be bringing one's next sumptuous repast and escorting one to the delights of the *toilette*. Pinhead's day off, no doubt, the other one's turn of duty. Might call that one '*It*'. The truncheon would be the only weapon between the two of them: on top of which *It* would have been having regular meals, fresh air and so forth; looked like a rhinoceros anyway, wouldn't be anything like easy meat. In fact, far from it. You'd go for her eyes and throat, naturally – as taught at Arisaig in Scotland during that rather tough part of the SOE training course – but it *might* be rather like going for the eyes and throat of a medium-sized rhino.

This iron bed, she thought suddenly, might come apart quite easily. The horizontal framework supporting the mattress would be secured at each end by two bolts, two in the vertical head section and two at the foot end. If one could unscrew the nuts on those bolts – if there *were* nuts on them – at the foot end which, since it was lower than the other, would be less unwieldy. As she envisaged it, she'd be standing well back from the door – having rehearsed it, got the distance and angle right – with the iron framework up over her head; all right, you'd have it resting back against the wall, might have some time to wait – then when *It* came through the door, let her have it.

Then what?

Take the truncheon, make sure *It* was out for a good long count, and lock *It* in the cell. Having taken any other keys or weapons, obviously. Up the spiral stairs and through to the outer door. Looking out for *Miliciens* – outside, for sure, but even inside, maybe. Not likely to be more than one or two, she guessed – night shift, and only one prisoner in the whole place . . . Take *It*'s shoes, by the way, if they were wearable: and once up at ground level – well, a toss-up absolutely, but – having reached the street, say – get to a telephone and call Leblanc.

No need to look further ahead than that, she thought. Might work, might not. Might get shot: or beaten to death by *It*. What the hell – might stay here, not lift a finger and get shot anyway. In any case, better make sure of being ready: start right away, see if dismantling the bed was feasible – which it bloody well *had* to be – then get in some practice. If *It* came at 8 or thereabouts – as she should – you'd have several hours in hand. Having detached that end of the bed there'd be a slope on it of course, foot-end resting on the concrete, but you could still lie on it – rest, conserve whatever strength remained.

Not a lot, she thought. It wasn't a body-building diet, exactly, and conditions generally weren't conducive to vim and vigour. But rest was rest – even on this foul pallet, from which after this length of time one was foul oneself, the back of the raincoat damp and maybe the pullover and shirt damp*ish* inside it.

Anyway – get cracking. Feeling for the foot-end of the pallet and pulling it up, rolling it back. Not difficult: but when she thought that was far enough and let go, it flopped slowly back again. Have to sit or kneel on the wire mesh of the bed with one's back or a shoulder holding the thing back out of the way, while finding the bolts – or wing-nuts, whatever . . .

Didn't work.

Awkward position, and didn't have room. Best to get the pallet right out of the way – pull this end off the bed, swivel the horrible thing cross-wise.

It snagged. Sodden material ripping on something – wire – underneath. So stop again, and free it. Dragging the pallet up as far as the point where broken mesh had dug itself in, then feeling under there for which way to shift it to unsnag it. Even this wasn't as easy as it might have been, but she managed it eventually and slid it off the bed.

That had been the *easy* part. She was feeling for the bolts now: bolts with nuts on them, she imagined. Might be wing-nuts . . .

They were ordinary hexagonal ones. Wing-nuts had been a bit much to hope for, she'd known it. As if they'd have chosen to make it easy for people in her position who didn't carry spanners around with them. She wrapped her hand around this one and exerted all the strength she had: aware within a couple of seconds that it was rock-solid – or rather iron-solid – had been put on by someone with a spanner and muscles like *It*'s.

There were three such nuts and bolts, one at each side and one in the middle. All three would have to be removed, of course. She'd located the other two after giving up on the first one and groping along the iron flange – with no confidence at all about being able to shift any of them.

Still no grey up there. No hurry at all therefore, really could take one's time. Telling herself this in order to calm down, lower the pulse-rate. Pause, reflect. To be stopped in one's tracks by just three nuts and bolts, for God's sake, was ridiculous. But not having iron fists . . .

A slipper for a wrap-around hand-protector, maybe. Its soddenness might actually help. Gritting her teeth, straining at it. On her knees, working at this first one again. Slipper compressed tightly around the sharpish, palm-bruising nut, left hand reinforcing the other – *trying* to. Leaning over the job, getting all the muscle she had into it: grunting with the effort.

Damn. For a second or two she'd thought she had it moving, but that had been the slipper slipping. Face it – was not feasible. And nothing else in the cell was movable, in any way usable. In fact there wasn't anything. Sitting back on her heels, massaging that hand, recognising that even if she'd had *days* in which to work on this she wouldn't manage it.

Other end?

No reason it should be any different, but it might be. Might even find there were no nuts at all, or that they were loose. Nuts in fact weren't essential; the weight of the horizontal framework, let alone a body on it, would hold it all together. Stupid therefore not at least to find out.

It would take a bit of handling, as a weapon. Bigger – taller – probably half as heavy again as the other. You'd *need* to be a weight-lifter. Manage somehow, that was all – *if* one could get it off.

One couldn't. Hadn't taken long to find that out. Three large nuts as immovable as if they'd been welded to their bolts and to the flange.

So that was that. Nice idea, but – shaking her head in the blackness, getting the pallet back on the bed, telling herself she couldn't give up, just had to find some other way.

Weaponless?

Sitting, with her head in her hands. *Not* taking long, deep breaths the way she usually did to slow her pulse-rate: down here, deep breathing didn't have much going for it. Hadn't been anything like as foul as this at the time of her previous visit. Georges' crowd, of course. Probably not their fault, the way they'd been kept, herded in. Although they'd had access to the *toilette*, for sure.

But – yes, weaponless. Hit her hard enough and suddenly enough, taking her by surprise as she blundered in – with her hands full, or anyway one hand full: oh, a torch in the other one, of course. Hit her maybe as she turned to put the mug on that shelf.

Shelf?

No. Forget it. It was screwed to the wall, and one had no screwdriver. Might wrench it off – but it would be fairly light, probably just boxwood, even if swung edgeways wouldn't have anything like the flattening effect the iron framework would have had.

Wrench it off the wall, split it somehow, make a dagger of it?

No. So-called dagger would break on contact, you'd have wasted time and chances of success. Weaponless was the answer. Rest now, conserve remaining strength. Be ready for it – a few hours after the first show of light up there – allow the door to open, then hit her like a – well, flat out, going for the eyes and throat, knee-jab in the gut. She'd have thumped back against the wall or door-jamb, having to protect her eyes or fight you off before she could get the truncheon up, have room to use it. She'd jab at you with the torch, maybe. Go for the truncheon though before she's recovered from shock and whatever initial damage – claws, teeth, the mug's rim driven hard into her face . . .

Rest, meanwhile. Feet up, Rosie, lie back, relax. Think about it, how you'll do it – then when the time comes, not think at *all*, just go for it, bloody *fly* at it, maybe screaming, going for the eyes and throat.

She'd woken with a jerk: then immediate, crushing recognition of having blown her chances. Cell door already opening, a vertical crack of light widening: door right back then and torch-beams lacerating the darkness, centring on her, blinding her – torch-beams plural, in the hands of *men* – Germans – SS – crowding in, heavy boots on concrete. *Dreaming* this? She was up on her elbows, creature of the darkness part-blinded—

'Up with you! *Up!*'

It, wielding torch and truncheon. Should have been some kind of hate-crazed animal at *It*'s throat by now, thumbs gouging into its eyes – with its head back then as it would have been, throat exposed: and for want of a knife, *teeth* . . . Couldn't have slept more than a minute: *couldn't*. On the other hand, since *It* had come several hours early and accompanied, she – would-be wild-cat Rosie – hadn't blown anything, had only been pre-empted.

Wouldn't it have been Pinhead's turn anyway? Mind and memory had to be off their bloody hinges!

'What's happening?'

'Come for you, bitch, is what!' Pointing with the truncheon: 'Want your wrists, don't he! Come, English slut – *wrists!*'

She was telling her companions in German then what she'd just said. Smirking, proud of it – choice of abusive terms, linguistic skill. Rosie had been sitting up, one of them had jerked her to her feet while another slammed the handcuffs on, squeezed them tight. Helmet-jerk and a snapped order – '*Raus!*' Meaning 'Out!', one of the very few words in German that she recognised. Torch-beams not only on her but wandering around poking at this and that – floor, walls, that shelf, the useless overhead bulb; illuminating also machine-pistols, shiny boots, SS uniforms. Three of them, plus *It*. Torches centring on her again as she moved towards the open door and they backed out of the cell ahead of her, unpleasant faces showing distaste – as if they thought *she*'d created the atmosphere down here. *It* was already out there, waiting to precede them to the barred door which led into the urine-stinking cellar. Lucky to have eyes now in that pudding face – would never know what it had missed. Wednesday, Rosie reminded herself, wishing the handcuffs weren't so tight: Wednesday August the 23rd. Come-uppance day, the day she'd go to where Ben thought she was already. In not much of a state to make that transition, either: whether angels with harps or devils with red-hot tridents, they'd be holding their noses when *she* floated in, she guessed. Not all that amusing, in fact pretty weak, but one had to think of *something* other than what was actually happening here and now and before long would be culminating somewhere else. All right, so think of Ben, talk to him, maybe he'll hear you in his dreams the way you thought you heard *him* the other night. For one's own sake anyway, the *escape* of talking to him. Ben, my darling, this is where it finishes, really has to, nothing I can do about it. Had a crazy plan in mind, would have been *very* satisfying if it had come off – I'd have loved to have told you about it one day, in some London pub maybe or better still in bed – but the sods forestalled me, I never got to try it. Had this coming, dare say, had a good run for my money and I suppose taken a lot of amazingly good luck for granted. It's all right, anyway, nothing's hurting yet and maybe won't, there'll be no torture because there's nothing they want to know that I haven't told them. Well, not much. What that smarmy bastard Clausen didn't have the *nous* to ask me I wouldn't have told him anyway – so maybe it's as well he didn't. Oh, Ben, what a bloody waste of all the lovely years we thought we had ahead of us; hey, *damn* it – the Boche behind her had poked her in the back with the barrel of his Schmeisser: she was climbing the spiral of stone stairs up which she'd envisaged herself creeping like a tiger or leopard leaving its kill – with that truncheon in her hand ready for re-use. *It* unconscious and maybe blinded, maybe dead or bleeding to death in the locked cell back there – instead of heaving her squat bulk up step by step with the jerky motion of a semi-cripple, truncheon swinging on a thong from the thick wrist of a stubby arm with which she was steadying herself against the right-hand wall as she climbed, torch in the other hand lighting the stairs ahead. Rosie with her arms in front of her of course, wrists linked close together; meek and mild and dirty, not thinking about escape now, knowing she didn't have a chance: deflated, depressed and frightened – which as always was the one thing absolutely *not* to show. Across the short landing where in some earlier age they'd had a Gestapo guard posted; climbing again now, wondering whether Clausen would put in an appearance at the execution – which she supposed would take place at one of the forts or at the Vincennes castle. At dawn, perhaps? She doubted if he'd show his face, though. For one thing, he never had anything to do with such nastiness, he'd maintained – only consigned his victims to it – and for another, if he didn't *have* to get up early, why should he? He'd be tucked up with Jacqui in their flat, making the most of his remaining days and/or nights with her, and probably not saying a word about how he'd settled Jeanne-Marie's hash for her. Jeanne-Marie would simply have failed to get in touch with them as she'd said she would: then *he*'d be taking off, and as for Jacqui – who gave a damn?

Actually, *she* did. Rather liked her. Wouldn't have left her on the loose around Ben for long, but otherwise – yes, *did*. Tart, for sure, but . . . weren't there worse things?

Clausen might have some regrets at leaving her to face the music. *Might*: one still had one's doubts on that score. While as for Léonie – Yvette – and Derek—

Haven't done *them* much good.

There was another SS trooper at the top, leaning there with a Schmeisser in his hands. Exchanges in German now between him and the one behind her. Then they were off the stairs and through the arch-topped doorway into the vestibule where you turned right to get to the front – this end of it anyway, it was a very large building and there were probably several entrances – or left to reach the stairs, *that* staircase. Turning right now, of course, the one behind having grabbed her arm and swung her that way, given her a shove. He might be the one who'd brought her to Clausen on Monday night, or might not: they looked so much alike, and emitted precisely the same sounds when communicating with each other; she couldn't see any of them as individuals, barely in fact as humans. *Could* see them as Clausen's close associates though – SD being the security service of the SS, there wasn't much of a dividing line. SS of course ran the extermination camps, herded Jews to gas-ovens, fired the volleys that sent men, women and children tumbling into pits.

Jacqui know anything about such things, she wondered?

She thought there was a chance they wouldn't send her to Ravensbrück now, road and rail movements being as difficult as they must be by this time. In that respect, she thought, maybe my luck's still in. Looking round for wood to touch – but that one had grasped her arm again, was leading her out into cool night air and she was gulping it, happily surprised, even exhilarated by it – and ignoring the way the gravel hurt her feet. She'd left the slippers down there: the one she'd used to cushion her grip on that nut had been in tatters anyway. So, barefoot, what the hell, it wouldn't be for long anyway; unless her destination *should* be Ravensbrück. Meanwhile – breathing clean air, looking up at cloudy sky; there was a light breeze from – oh, south, south-west. Moon very low, wasn't much of it anyway. Behind her, one of them was thanking *It* for its kind assistance – some such courtesy. Rosie still looking up at the sky and taking deep breaths when her escort halted her at the rear end of another of those small trucks, the kind in which they'd brought her here, and another of them climbed up into it and then hauled *her* up, dumped her at the forward end of the left-hand bench and parked himself beside her. The rest embarking then: one facing her, another pulling up the tailgate and securing it, the fourth getting in up front.

Rosie leaning forward, manacled forearms on her knees, so as to face the open rear: the night air still a blessing, despite wafts of cigarette smoke as all three of them lit up.

Question was – as the truck's engine fired and it started across the forecourt – taking her where?

Not that it made all that much difference. Only please God might it *not* be Gare de l'Est.

Chapter 19

Out of Rue des Saussaies south-westward: it was an encouraging indication but not conclusive. Although prospects were further improved then by turning from there into Avenue de Marigny, which was not the way you'd send anyone who wanted to get to the Gare de l'Est. Unless this driver wanted to keep to certain major thoroughfares – like turning left at the bottom into the Champs-Elysées, then up Rue Royale and so on. Could be simply a route he preferred or knew best. The hell with it anyway, with it and with them too. She leaned back, shut her eyes. Being surrounded by them and at their mercy as well as foul and very hungry reminded her of how she'd felt for poor old Gulliver when he'd been in the land of the creatures who'd pelted him with their excrement. She didn't remember what they were called, and these didn't go that far – or hadn't yet – but they were as far removed from one's own concepts of humanity and normality as those had been from Gulliver's. Yahoos, they were called, she remembered. She'd opened her eyes in thinking of them, was looking at as much as was visible to her of the one *en face,* whose knee-caps were only a few inches from her own. His face was too small, under the width of his helmet: thin and pointed like a rat's. Long, thin nose *very* rodent-like: if it had quivered, you'd hardly have been surprised. He was looking back at her now, she realised: she could make out the gleam of rat's eyes. With her own only partly open and her head tilted back against the canvas, she'd thought he wouldn't know he was under observation, but in that moment he'd winked at her: she'd seen it because at the same time he'd been drawing hard at the last inch of his cigarette – illuminating amongst other features the tip of the ratty nose.

She'd shut her eyes. Thinking *Don't believe it . . .*

In the state she was in? Like something recently dragged out of a sewer? Pale, sweaty, dirty, stinking?

One sewer rat's greeting to another, maybe?

Or even – serious consideration of this now – an expression of sympathy, a wordless *Never mind, stick it out*?

Even some Yahoos might have sensibilities?

The truck swung right: into the Avenue des Champs-Elysées. Heading west now. She'd reopened her eyes and was leaning forward to see out past the man on her right; and that *was* where they were. A mile or so astern in a haze of moonlight – indistinguishable, you knew what was contained in that haze, was all – was the Place de la Concorde and the monumental gateway to the Tuileries; while the way this truck was going – if it held on the same way – well, half a kilometre say to the Rondpoint, then another one and a half to the Etoile.

Rue de la Pompe, then? Rue Lauriston?

Rat-face had dropped his cigarette-stub on the floor of the truck and put his heel on it. The movement had caused her to glance at him, but with no moonlight getting in he was only a toadstool-like shape hunched in the darkness and smelling of cigarettes. Probably had *not* winked, she thought. How would one have seen it, in the momentarily brightened glow of a cigarette-stub? Trick of one spark of light, plus somewhat dopey imagination – not a vestige of *rapport* of any kind. One thing you could be damn sure of was that they weren't going to let one escape. It would be why they'd put her on the inside with rat's eyes on her at point-blank range and the other two between her and the tailgate. If one *did* take a loony chance on it – sudden dash, dive over the tailboard – well, *sounded* loony, but with no street lighting and so little moon – if one made it that far alive and without limbs broken—

They had torches, for God's sake, and Schmeissers.

Not going to try it, Ben, old darling. Would have had a chance with that Gestapo woman in the cell, I think, but here there'd be none at all.

She leaned back again, shut her eyes: *All right, I'm dead already, aren't I? For all you know, I am. And as it's turned out – well, what's the difference? If a chance did come up, mind you . . .*

You'd only have to hide out for a few days. The Allies weren't going to leave Paris to rot and starve for ever. Leblanc was out there somewhere in any case. And in the present chaotic state of things . . .

She wondered whether Leblanc and/or Fernagut and company had been successful in their raid on the armoury, and whether if they had they'd go for the Rue de la Pompe this next night.

Rondpoint: trundling round it. Avenue Matignan slanting away north-eastward. Victor Emanuel a dark slot leading due north. As well to keep oneself orientated as far as possible, through rearward glimpses of where one *had* been. Brief view then in something like close-up of one of those Boche troop-carrying vehicles with helmeted soldiery in it – *on* it – machine-guns on swivel mountings at each end. Some kind of searchlight or floodlight that you were in for a moment and then out of and still dazzled. So much for ideas of escape, for heaven's sake. Out of the Rondpoint now anyway, and still heading west. From here to the Etoile – yes, about one and a half. A year ago she'd done most of this stretch on foot, she remembered. Carrying a suitcase and her radio, at that. She'd come up out of the Métro at Concorde and walked from there, on her way to call on Pierre Cazalet in Rue de la Boétie. Had thought doing it *à pied* might be safer, having suspected she might have a tail. Had forgotten just how far it was – could have stayed in the Métro another couple of stages, and very soon wished she had.

Doing it in style now, she teased herself. Personal transport, and armed escort. Not to the Rue Boétie, admittedly.

Where, though?

'Want to smoke?'

Guttural French – from the one on her right, who'd turned her way slightly to make the offer: switching a torch on to show her a packet of German cigarettes, the kind Clausen smoked.

'Thank you very much.'

Having to move both hands, of course, but he pushed them away, put a cigarette between her lips, and the man opposite – Rat-face – leaned forward with a match flaring between cupped hands. Rosie inclined herself that way, and when it was lit brought her hands up again so she could take it out of her mouth long enough to thank them both. She was both surprised and genuinely grateful: leaning back, inhaling greedily, realising how much she'd needed this and telling them after a moment – whether or not they'd understand her – 'It's very, very good. Thank you.'

'English?'

The one beside her had asked it. Someone must have told him – told them. She nodded: 'Half English, half French.'

'Uh?'

'Mama English, Papa French.'

Grunts of comprehension; and conversational efforts seemingly concluded. It *was* a good smoke, though. And why bother with giving up the habit if you didn't have such a great stretch of life ahead of you in any case? About a kilometre to go, she guessed, to the Etoile. Wondering whether to ask them where were they taking her. Whether they'd understand the question, or resent it, or even know the answer. And whether she needed to know, whether the rest of the trip mightn't be less uncomfortable *without* knowing. Since the answer might well be Rue Lauriston or Rue de la

Pompe. Clausen did have dealings with Lafont, he'd admitted it, and that might include handing prisoners over to him when he'd finished with them.

But what *for*?

Well – disposal. Clearing the decks, prior to evacuation. If they couldn't ship one east, didn't have anywhere to lock one up, didn't in any case want to leave evidence lying around?

She thought the truck might be doing about 40 kph. One kilometre in a minute and a half, say. But having no watch – not having thought to ask that Gestapo thing to give it back to her. Fat chance anyway, she'd as like as not have responded with her truncheon. The truck was slowing, she realised: doubtless the Etoile coming up. Might learn something – for better or for worse – from which way one branched off now. Circling the great arch with its currently not visible swastika banner hanging from it – an insult and provocation to the entire French nation; continuing straight on would mean following the Avenue de la Grande Armée – to God only knew where – well, Neuilly, of course – and the one after that would be Avenue Foch, off which after a certain distance a left fork would take one into Rue de la Pompe. Or, carrying on round past Foch, Avenue Victor Hugo, and then – before Kleber – Rue Lauriston.

Turning off *now*, though. Avenue Foch was her guess. Destination therefore Rue de la Pompe? Accepting it as probable, although the prospect chilled her. If she was right, the turn into it would come in a bit less than a kilometre. She'd come on this route but in the opposite direction – out of Pompe into Foch and thence to the Etoile – with Nico on Monday. Straining her memory – there was another broad avenue intersecting with Foch at right angles: not as wide or as grand as Foch but still a big one. Poincaré? She thought so. This *was* Avenue Foch – no doubt of it, from the rear view she had now: and the left fork into Rue de la Pompe led out of that Poincaré intersection. Truck still picking up speed, having slowed so much in getting round l'Etoile. Allow one minute, she told herself, and you'll either fork left or you won't.

Please, let's *not*?

Eyes shut, counting seconds. Remembering Lafont and his unpleasantly high voice and what Clausen had said about him at lunch on Sunday. But would the boss of the Lauriston Gestapo be up and about at whatever time it was now – 3 am, say, something of that sort?

Maybe. These weren't *normal* times.

Should be at the intersection by now. Getting ready for it: telling herself, *If that's what it's to be, too bad. Not a thing you can do about it. Only grit your teeth and – oh, pray to God it's over quickly. And if it isn't, if they make you wait for it, lose yourself in thoughts of Ben, and the lovely times with him . . .*

Ben as refuge. The best she knew, had ever known.

She was surprised they hadn't made the turn by now. Counting too fast – or miscalculated the distance, maybe. It surely did have to be Rue de la Pompe. Having come this far and straight as a die, so to speak, and being the worst prospect of all, therefore the one you had to accept as the most likely . . .

It did make unpleasant sense, transfer from SD to Bonny-Lafont for the purpose of being got rid of. Ravensbrück no-go on account of transport problems, the SD complex on Avenue Foch having shut down, Rue des Saussaies the same now – and Fresnes emptied of all *its* prisoners, hadn't Georges told her? Disposal of prisoners would be a major problem. 'Disposal of' being a phrase that had cropped up recently in some conversation, she thought, not just in her own thinking as it was doing again now. One was, admittedly, to some extent confused – frightened as well as empty-feeling, nowhere near the pink of condition either mentally or physically. Best to keep that in mind, perhaps, allow for it, discount at least some of this sense of – *inevitability* . . . Drawing on the last of her cigarette, deciding it might be safe by now to assume that her destination was *not* the Rue de la Pompe house . . .

So what happens at the western end of this magnificent Avenue Foch? Come on – *think.*

Why – Porte-Dauphine, of course!

Large *carrefour*, also a Métro station and one of the entrances to the Bois de Boulogne. She'd been there with her father, she remembered. One marvellous summer afternoon when she'd been about – oh, ten, perhaps. They'd left the Métro at Porte-Dauphine and taken a *fiacre* to the lakes where they'd hired a boat for the afternoon, landing on some of the islands, taking snapshots of each other and eating chocolate ice-cream. Happy memories – the boating, choc-ices, Papa's invariable *tendresse* and sense of fun. She couldn't get any more out of this cigarette without burning her lips. She took it gingerly – of necessity with both hands up – dropped it on the bed of the truck and asked Rat-face – who was watching her practically all the time – 'Monsieur?' Pointing down at the glowing stub: 'Would you be so kind?'

He looked puzzled. She lifted a bare foot into his field of view: 'I can't, you see. Please – so not to start a fire?'

He grunted, minimally shifted one boot; glancing at the man beside her, cocking an eyebrow, while this one leaned over, peered down at her feet. A mutter in German: *Keine* something. She explained. 'Wasn't expecting to be arrested. Had slippers on, and they gave me no time to—'

'Uh?'

'Doesn't matter.' But on the spur of the moment – having broken the ice, maybe, and enunciating the words slowly and clearly: 'Where are we going?'

They were looking at each other, then – the three of them. Exchanging views or comments in that hideous tongue. Arguing as to whether she should be told or not? But she guessed it then – recalling that the road entering the Bois at Porte-Dauphine was called Route de Suresnes and that having passed the lakes and through the full depth of the

Bois it led to the village of Suresnes, which was only a stone's throw from Mont Valérien, the fort where they incarcerated hostages and at intervals shot them in reprisal for the anti-German activities of others.

Could be where they'd taken Georges and company?

She tried it on Rat-face: 'Mont Valérien?'

Another exchange of glances. She was being a bore to them, she supposed. They'd be puzzled too: she'd asked the question almost happily – in finding a solution that did not involve Lafont. Those two were looking puzzled, although ignoring her and her question, but Rat-face had decided to make a joke of it – putting an imaginary rifle to his shoulder, aiming it at her head and pulling a trigger, shouting 'Boom!' A shout of laughter then – his own – while the one beside her growled at him as at a misbehaving child. The other one lighting a cigarette, taking no notice; Rat-face now waving his hands as if wiping stuff off a blackboard, and explaining – even apologising – something like, 'Sorry, just my little joke . . .'

After what must have been about twenty minutes – quarter-hour maybe – they'd taken a right turn. Presumably were *not* going to Suresnes. Or this might be a short cut the driver knew of. *Or*, her own recollection of the topography might be wrong. Childhood memories often were; and in studying the maps at Fawley Court the Bois hadn't seemed to call for any particular attention. Mental processes wandering somewhat anyway: for instance, remembering how less than half an hour ago she'd grabbed quite cheerfully at the thought of a firing-squad awaiting her at Mont Valérien – as an alternative to being delivered to Lafont, which for several miles back there had had her sweating – well, thinking *straight* now, she thought – the best option in present circumstances would obviously be delay, stay of execution – to be still alive when the Yanks rolled in. Too much to hope for? Perhaps. Depending on how long these people took, how much of a rush they felt they were in. Whoever *they* might be – SD, SS, Gestapo, Bonny-Lafont. One was an object being disposed of, that was all. A *thinking* object: which of course was part of the reason one did *have* to be got rid of. Leaning forward, in that position with her forearms on her knees, her eyes on the rectangle of dark night astern: it was greying a little, she thought. The moon had set, though – either *had* set or was close to doing so, so low that you weren't seeing any of it through the trees. Wednesday, this was. *Last* Wednesday had been her last full day of briefing at Fawley Court. Thinking back to it over the interval of just seven days was like remembering a different person, or at least one in a completely different mental state. That degree of *optimism*, for God's sake. Shaking her head then, thinking less optimism than a combination of drive and hope and impatience to be getting on with it – get those two out, as they'd done their successful best to get *her* out. All right, to start with she'd been averse to the idea of going back, had resented Hyatt's even proposing it: but a lot of that had been her own sense of let-down – no Marilyn, no Ben. Within a few hours of getting down to brass tacks she'd been in a far more positive frame of mind. In particular, obsessed by the absolute imperative of keeping Léonie out of bloody Ravensbrück. Remembering every detail of the train journey when she and Lise had escaped and the others hadn't – Edna, Maureen, Daphne, hadn't – and visualising Léonie in their situation. How could one *not* have told Hyatt yes, yes, of *course* . . .

So you were still of that mind. With less hope, certainly, *much* less hope – in fact damn *little* – unless Leblanc—

The truck was on a left-hand bend and by the sound of it not on tarmac now. Definitely not, in fact, that was dirt and gravel rattling under its wide mudguards.

Going *where the hell*?

She felt as if she'd been dozing. The truck was slowing, anyway. The man next to her moving – crabbing towards the rear. The other one too – gymnastically, on his feet and hanging on to the canopy's supporting framework at the back, most of him still inside but his head up over the top to look forward. They were both in that position – and the truck slowing even more – while Rat-face watched *her*, had shifted the Schmeisser on to his lap, she noticed. Brakes on hard then and the truck tilting, skidding to a halt in the loose surface of the track with its right-hand wheels up on some sort of banking . . . The driver was getting out – slam of his door – and the two at the rear jumping down, leaving the tailboard up. Rat-face with the Schmeisser actually in his hands now. Expecting her to make a break for it? If that was something that seemed likely to them, one might reasonably expect the worst. A shout in German somewhere outside there was answered by the acknowledgement '*Jawohl!*' She'd begun to move – as much as anything to see what might happen – and Rat-face had gestured to her to stay put. That seemed somehow to clinch it – solution to the disposal problem; they were going to shoot her, here in the woods. A torch-beam probing in over the tailboard focused on her for a few seconds: and one of them out there was peeing. Not all they'd stopped for, surely. *She* wouldn't have minded one: wouldn't have minded a cigarette either, was thinking of asking Rat-face if he'd spare another – but he was preoccupied suddenly, listening – one of them muttering something to his companions and then starting up the road, calling something that sounded like, 'I come, *Herr Major*!'

If there was a *Herr Major* around, she guessed, Ratty wouldn't give her a cigarette. Fraternising with prisoners *verboten*, one might guess. Having to keep it all light and easy in one's mind – all the more so if one *was* within minutes of being shot. But he obviously wouldn't let her into the bushes for a pee either. Be dying with a full bladder: *not* very dignified or decent, letting it all go as the bullets whacked home. Voices of Germans in conversation were returning now anyway: one questioning, the other giving brief, soldierly answers. The driver, she guessed – he'd have been the one peeing, heard the officer call to them and hurried to meet him, was now coming back here with him . . .

But she *knew* the other voice.

Even speaking German. Was pretty sure she did, anyway. Yes – she did. Had been mistaken in an earlier presumption that he'd be unwilling to get out of the nice warm bed he shared with Jacqui.

Passing, boots scuffing gravelly dirt, coming to the truck's rear end. A torch flared, illuminating her. Then another. And they were letting the tailboard down.

'Come on out, Jeanne-Marie.'

It *was* him.

She didn't move: had her chained hands up to shield her eyes. The torch shifted and Clausen urged her, 'Come, please. There's nothing to be frightened of. I'll have those things off you in a minute.'

Things. Handcuffs? And – *nothing to be frightened of*?

One of them helped her down. The driver, she guessed. Short, thickset man. Clausen standing back, shining his torch on her bare feet, asking her in his lightly accented French, 'No shoes?'

'I was wearing old slippers when you had me arrested. In the cellar in Rue des Saussaies there's urine all over the floor and they were soaked. I'm in a foul state altogether, can't you smell me?'

'Since you mention it—'

'*Your* doing.'

'I regret that it was necessary—'

'Going to shoot me now?'

'—although of course I was not aware of the conditions as you describe them. In any case one would have had no choice. You were my prisoner, and had to be seen as such – also to *feel* you were, so that you'd behave accordingly . . .' Then: '*Shoot* you?'

Not aware of the conditions as you describe them . . . His accented French as it were reverberating through her slight dizziness – as coldly formal an explanation as if he'd put it together from some SD glossary of useful phrases. As far as he was concerned, he was in no way to blame. Was or was *not* about to shoot her or have her shot – she didn't know, although he'd *sounded* genuinely surprised at the suggestion that he might. Addressing the corporal now – the driver – who produced the handcuffs' key and after some further question and answer took one cuff off her wrist and clicked it on to Clausen's briefly extended left one. He was wearing an Army greatcoat over civilian trousers and a striped shirt, with a major's insignia on the coat's epaulettes. She shook the chain of the handcuffs: 'Thought you said taking these *off* me?'

'Soon – yes. It's necessary now, for the sake of appearances.' A movement of the head: 'Come with me, please.' There was a troop-carrier parked a few yards ahead, she saw; soldiers in helmets standing around it, others on top close to its machine-guns. Clausen turned back, gave this truck's driver an order; the man saluted and turned away. Dismissed, she guessed.

So this *was* as far as she was going.

Moving again now though, towed by the wrist: wondering what the *hell* . . . She began to ask him, but he cut her short with a mutter of rapid French: 'Not to converse now. It should appear that you're my prisoner.'

'What the hell else?'

'You're in fear of execution—'

'Damn right I am!'

'But I just *told* you—'

'Ach – *Herr Major* . . .'

A young officer – lieutenant, but not SS – had appeared from somewhere beyond the front end of this vehicle, asking him something in German. About *her*, she thought. Clausen had given him a brief answer – an affirmative. Telling her then, not in that quiet, private tone but loudly, authoritatively: 'You're here to see if you can identify any of these people.'

'What people? Where?'

'You'll see.' A nod and a jerk of the head to the younger man, who followed. She *thought* he was following them. Recognising Clausen's car then: there was a gap in the trees flanking the roadside at this point, and it was parked just beyond it – a dark-coloured Citroen fifteen. It could hardly have been anyone else's, and Clausen wouldn't have come on that other thing. The gap in the trees gave access to a clearing with beyond it, a long way down-slope, a shine of water. Back-end of the lakes, she supposed. Glancing round, seeing that the lieutenant was still there and had two soldiers with him – common-or-garden infantrymen, slung rifles in place of machine-pistols. Clausen said – quietly – 'You may find this – disturbing. You *will*. I'm sorry. I hope not unbearable. You see, there's no one else who could make the identification – at least, if my guess is right—'

'Talking about identifying *bodies*?'

'Thirty-five of them. I do regret inflicting such a task on you.' Showing her – in a sweep of the torch-beam angled downwards – 'See. These.'

A double row – or two ranks. From the road they'd been in dead ground, owing to the down-slope and the earth bank. Aiming his torch at the right-hand end of the nearer lot: 'We'll start there. If there are any you recognize—'

'Who are they, where'd they come from?'

'*Résistants* who were caught with a load of stolen Schmeisser machine-pistols a few nights ago.'

'And killed where? Here?'

'Yes. About three hours ago.'

'Were they in Rue des Saussaies before this?'

'At one time – yes.'

'Thirty-four of them then, not thirty-five.'

'Why do you say that?'

'It's what *you* said. In that telephone call when you were interrogating me.'

'Sharp ears and a good memory. Yes, you're right. But there are thirty-five here. An error in the message I received, perhaps. Or perhaps not. That's the point of this procedure. So – if you wouldn't mind?'

She could see tracks where the bodies had been dragged around, bloodied tracks over and through last season's fall of leaves and this summer's growth of bracken. The ground had been well trampled over, and there was a lot of blood.

'Did whoever killed them line them up like this?'

'No.' A gesture towards the lieutenant. 'His men did so – at my request.'

'Who killed them?'

'I can only tell you that from Rue des Saussaies they were transferred to Rue de la Pompe, to one of the houses used by the Gestapo of Rue Lauriston. I want you to understand, this was *not* in my area of responsibility, not in any way at all. It seems they were brought here – alive – a few hours ago.'

'Gestapo using Bonny-Lafont to get rid of them?'

'Well – we *are* facing certain problems—'

'Which justifies *this*?'

'*This* is entirely the responsibility of Lafont.'

'You mean *your* Gestapo would have expected Monsieur Henri with his kind heart and gentle ways to have provided them with comfy beds and three square meals a day?'

'We should get on with this now. You know what I think of Lafont. Please – we don't have all that much time.'

'One more question, though. What d'you imagine I could ever have had to do with any of them?'

'That we shall see. You have only to tell me if there are any you do recognise.'

'All right. But first take this off me, please?'

The handcuff. Clausen unlocked it – his own too – dropped them into his left-hand coat pocket and took a pistol out of the other one. A Luger, she noticed. There were lots of them about but they weren't standard equipment, hadn't been for years. She looked from it to him: 'This also for the sake of appearances?'

A nod. 'Exactly. Get on with it now.'

'I'll need a torch.'

'I will accompany you, with mine.'

Around the end of the nearer line of them, so as to see them – their faces – the right way up. Clausen came with her and stayed close, holding the light on each face in turn until she moved to the next. She was inspecting two at each move: one on her left, second on her right, then out around that one's feet and up between the next pair. In close-up there was a lot more blood than she'd expected; most of them were soaked in it. Georges was the fifth in the line; he'd been shot in the lower part of his face, most of his jaw shot away, and there were numerous bullet-holes in his chest. She didn't look at him for longer than at any of the others. Patrice, near the other end of the same line, had multiple wounds in his body but his face and head were intact. It had been done with machine-pistols, obviously. She was being careful where she put her feet and Clausen helped, lighting her way for her as she picked her way along. It did occur to her, especially when passing some of the smaller men, that she might purloin a pair of shoes, and she knew it was actually quite silly to be squeamish about it; they were dead, didn't *need* shoes now. Doing nothing about it though. Lacking the strength, maybe. Weakness coming in waves. Glancing at Clausen and the Luger as they moved to the second rank to start back the other way. Multiple-millimetre bullet-holes were standard in all of them, as was the blood and some faces drained as white as sheets of paper. There'd certainly been no economy of ammunition. In some cases there was scorching from what must have been ultra-close-range bursts of fire. Some of the faces might not have been recognisable even if she'd known them when they were alive. There was certainly one other that she'd seen before – in the Dog, obviously – but couldn't ever have put a name to. No reason to say, 'Oh yes, this one I knew', in any case – or to tell Clausen that those others' names had been Georges Dénault and Patrice Macombre. She couldn't guess why he'd even want to know their names, or that she'd known them.

Moving on. As it were brain-frozen, one stage removed from the sickening bestiality of it by exertion of self-discipline, self-control, the fact of *having* to get through it – almost in the way *they'd* had to: that at least as an example, while knowing also virtually beyond question that she'd be going through it over and over again in nightmares from which if she was *very* lucky she'd wake in Ben's arms, as she had often enough after waking *him* with her screams and thrashings-around.

Stepping carefully around a big, grey-headed man's blood-coated legs and boots. Clausen following, moving his torch-beam to the next one's face.

Clean face. Bruised and lacerated but no blood on it at all. Some bullet-holes in the shirt that was buttoned right up to the neck, but no blood there either. Blood*less*, entirely. Rosie stooping closer – crouching, beckoning for more light . . .

Derek Courtland. Field-name Guillaume Rouquet.

Chapter 20

She was in Clausen's Citroen: he'd carried her to it. She'd come round briefly *en route* and then passed out again. The first time, she actually had fainted – when on her knees beside Courtland's body, had simply toppled – but the second time round, while being carried had relapsed into unconsciousness and come out of that to find herself alone in the car, Clausen conferring with the infantry lieutenant in the roadway beside that other vehicle. While before *that* – memory was vivid and immediate – Courtland in close-up but like a wax effigy of himself, as bloodless as anything they had in Madame Tussaud's, she kneeling beside him, the tears once started seemingly unstoppable but silent; Clausen unaware of them, telling her, 'He died from being flogged. Probably two or three days ago. The body's rigid as well as emptied of blood. Are you *certain* it is Courtland?'

Seeing her move – having recovered consciousness again in the car – he'd come back to it, to her side, jerking the passenger door open, about to help her straighten herself up, which she could do for herself anyway. 'Better?'

She'd nodded. Then found her voice, and begun, 'But now what—'

'I'll take you to Jacqui and leave you with her, then go on to rendezvous with this detachment in Rue de la Pompe. In the *hope* of course, that the girl—'

'I'll come with you.'

'No – you're in no condition . . . And to go via Rue de

Passy – a few minutes only, small detour – you need food, a bath, a sleep . . .' He'd gone round to the other side, to get in behind the wheel, but she flopped over and held on to that left-hand door. 'Tell him we're going straight to Rue de la Pompe. Please. I'm all right now, I'll manage, let's not waste time?'

Standing, looking in at her. 'You are not *fit*, Jeanne-Marie—'

'All that matters is finding Yvette. For that I *am* fit. Let's go?'

She knew she sounded hysterical. Felt it, and must have looked it – looked like nothing on earth. He'd spread his arms helplessly: turned away, started back to the lieutenant who came to meet him. Rosie squirmed back to the passenger side. Weak as a rat – sick, famished, desperate. Didn't need to pee now: suspected she must have done that somewhere. Oh God, she *had* . . .

All that mattered was Yvette. Léonie. Although if Rouquet – Derek – had been dead two days . . . Trying to think straight and not panic – or pass out again. They wouldn't have dumped *her* body there. Would have counted on his going unnoticed, just one more amongst thirty-five to be scooped up and deposited – wherever, some common grave. Simply taken the opportunity to get rid of him, but wouldn't have expected one small *female* corpse to be similarly overlooked.

She might still be alive. Odds heavily against, but – *might* be. Scour every square foot of Rue de la bloody Pompe – failing that, Lauriston.

'It is a fact'— Clausen, sliding in – 'that without you, identification might not be positive. In the absence of Lafont and others—'

'You're assuming you'd only find her body – and that they'll have taken off?'

'Not *assuming*, exactly . . .' Wrenching the wheel over: it was a narrow track to turn in, and the banking didn't help, but he'd backed-up by a metre or so. The troop-carrier – troops now re-embarking – wasn't going to find it easy either.

Unless it was four-by-four, which it might be. Clausen finishing – 'but with this detachment of Ritter's – and they have guns on that vehicle—'

'*Wehrmacht* versus Bonny-Lafont?'

'*If* they refused to produce the girl or facilitate a search I'd have justification – yes. But one doesn't – *anticipate* such . . .' Reversing the wheel: almost there now, one more to-and-fro and they'd be pointing the right way. The troop-carrier was waiting for him to get clear and past it before it moved. He told her, 'There's tank action in progress in the south-west. Not far away at all, by the sound of it.'

'Think they're coming?'

'It sounds like it. Last night it was close enough, but – ten minutes ago, this began.' He had the car turned and moving, passing the troop-carrier with about an inch to spare. 'Jeanne-Marie – a question that's of great importance to me.'

'Well?'

'Jacqui. Your offer of sanctuary in England. I should explain: I couldn't make any immediate response, despite the fact – which you may not have found obvious – that I was – *amazed* by the proposal.'

'You managed to disguise your interest in it quite successfully, I must say.'

'Seemed almost too good to believe in. While also I had to ensure I'd be able to produce them. In any case, as an officer of the SD, and you being what *you* are – the concept of making such a bargain—'

'Now, anyway, there's only Yvette.'

'And if I find I can – and do – deliver her?'

'Then it's a deal.'

'Your people would allow it?'

'First thing they'd know of it is I'd have her there with me – *fait accompli*. But yes, they would, they'd have to.'

He'd been watching in his rear-view mirror; shifted gear now, accelerating. 'They're with us. But you see – moving Jacqui to some other location in France – better than nothing

– but they're going to be hunting down collabos, you know, it won't be a – a *casual* process.'

'What about the idea I gave you – her having spied on you on behalf of the Resistance?'

'Well – so far, so good.' Another gear-change. 'But a member of my staff, a Frenchman—'

'Dubarque?'

'No, not him. Another to whom I've given a great deal of responsibility, and who up to now has been loyal and outstandingly efficient. Now, you see, just about everyone's changing attitudes and allegiances; and this fellow knows what I'm trying to do for Jacqui. *Someone* else had to know – unfortunately.'

'And a denunciation might save *his* bacon?'

'Exactly. There's bound to be a lot of that sort of thing. You'll understand, therefore, the attraction of your offer – a *guarantee—*'

'In return for Yvette di Mellili – alive, of course.'

'But if they've killed her—'

'Then there's *no* deal.'

'Despite your alleged friendship with Jacqui?'

'You know what I am and *why* I made friends with her. As it happens I do like her, but that's – by the way. Any deal has two sides to it – as you'd be the first to insist if our positions were reversed. Even as it is, you kept me in that stinking hole for two nights and a day—'

'Three nights and two days, as it happens, but—'

'No. Monday was when—'

'And it's now Thursday. Go on with what you were saying?'

'Thursday?'

'What you were saying, Jeanne-Marie—'

'Yes – but if it's Thursday—'

Gazing at him. Then shrugging, accepting it. 'All right. Yes. My offer was to you, not Jacqui . . . You – SD – are one department of the *Reich*'s bloody Security, the *Geheime*

Staatspolizei's another, and linked closely to it is the Gestapo of Rue Lauriston. If Yvette's dead, you're her murderers – just as you're one of Derek Courtland's murderers. Expecting me to show *fondness*?'

He was watching the road ahead and from time to time glancing at the rear-view mirror. They were almost at Porte-Dauphine, she realised. Her brain seemed to be working fairly normally now – apart from having apparently gone haywire date-wise – and she felt that if she'd said OK, she'd take Jacqui back to England with her anyway, she'd have been prejudicing chances of getting Yvette out. Clausen had to know that Jacqui's future depended on Yvette's.

He'd shrugged, emerging from his own thoughts. 'It suits you to hold me responsible for the actions of Lafont.'

'You *are*. You were supposed to take charge of the interrogation of those two. I was surprised you didn't raise this when you were interrogating me on Monday night. I'd admitted using Jacqui in order to get to you – right?'

'So?'

'Didn't it occur to you to wonder what reason I – we, SOE say – how we happened to see *you* – a mere sergeant, incidentally – as the key to whatever was happening to them?'

'I didn't ask you that, did I . . .'

'Taking it for granted that anyone *would* see you as the kingpin?'

'*Touché*.' A shrug. 'May I ask the question now?'

'Carl Boemelbourg, no less, told a pederast friend of his that he was leaving you in charge. That person told another, who got the news to us. You should learn to look to the top of the heap for your Intelligence leaks, perhaps.'

'Thanks for the tip.'

'Tell *me* now. Since Boemelbourg did issue that instruction, how come it didn't happen?'

'The instruction – if he gave it – is news to me. Probably verbal and not recorded – nothing about it in the SD files that were passed to my department, which I was able to consult when you were with me. The fact is I was out of Paris – there was an investigation to be cleared up in Lyon – when those two were brought from Nancy to Avenue Foch, where initially they were held for several days.' Pointing ahead, at the broad avenue leading to the Etoile. 'Avenue Foch 82 to 86 – now, as I'm sure you know, defunct. Anyway the officer supervising the close-down had to move them somewhere, and made arrangements with Lafont – stressing the importance of information believed to be in their possession.' A glance at her: 'Information important enough to bring *you* here, eh?'

'I doubt Léonie would have much of it in her head.'

'Then why are you so desperate to find her?'

'I simply want her *out*.'

'*Why* would she not have this important information?'

'She is – was – a pianist. Transmitting whatever messages she's told to send, receiving what comes in. No need to memorise, even necessarily understand.'

'With some, it might be like that—'

'One doesn't *want* it in one's head. Unless one's operating solo – as I was, most of the time. Was Lafont told what questions to put to them?'

'There'd have been some test questions, but he was to reduce them to – a state of compliance, is a term they use for it.'

'Term *they* use?'

'All right – *we*.'

'A state to which he evidently did *not* reduce Derek Courtland.'

They were in Avenue Foch now, with the troop-carrier close behind. Clausen agreeing quietly, 'As you say.'

'Why would they have tried to hide him like that?'

'I suppose – having failed in that task, and having always prided himself on – delivering the goods . . . But also being on the point of pulling out?'

'You really do think—'

'You heard the guns.' Rearward jerk of a thumb. 'It's also

a fact that our defences are so thin they're practically non-existent. All the anti-aircraft batteries from central Paris for instance have been moved out for use against tanks. In essence therefore the Bonny-Lafonts can either do a disappearing act or get ready to be strung up on lamp-posts. To them of all people their fellow-French aren't likely to be kind.'

The house was in darkness and the gate across the driveway was standing open. Empty driveway, no transport in there or in the road here either. Clausen parked his Citroen short of the driveway entrance, he and Rosie watching then as the troop-carrier drew up half on the pavement in front of the house, the soldiers disembarking in a swift dark flood that melted into that lower darkness, the railed area of shrubbery. There were men still on top at the machine-guns; Rosie could see them from her wound-down window – head out in the cool dawn air, waiting for Clausen to move before she did. The machine-gunners would have a field of fire over the shrubbery, covering the front door and windows and maybe up the left-hand side there as well. There was a side door, she remembered.

The place had an empty look about it, though. If there'd been any guard on the outside he/they had to either be lying low or to have ducked inside. This open gateway, too . . .

Clausen said – with his door open, and half out – 'You'd better stay here. I'll send a message if anything . . .'

She was out – missing the rest of that. Hadn't felt too good at some stages along the way, but fresh air still helped. In streaky dawn light – a pale orange glow over central Paris, houses, trees and telegraph-poles jet-black against it – she saw that apart from the soldiers at those guns the street was empty. Rumble of gunfire continuing from the south-west. The soldiers who'd disembarked must have been inside the railings by this time, although she'd seen no such move; they'd be in the cover of the bushes, maybe around the sides as well. There was a pedestrian gate opposite the front door, but she thought most of them must have gone over the railings – all in one swift movement in the course of disembarking. Maybe straight over from the truck. Clausen had growled over his shoulder, 'Stay *there*, anyway', and gone in at a trot, in at the driveway and through the garden towards the house. Torch-beams showed here and there around it, and she heard a door burst open – minor explosion, a crash and the sound of splintering wood in the pervading quiet: all quiet again then, except for the background mutter of artillery. Twenty or thirty miles away? Then on her way along the front of the garden she heard not only that distant rumbling but from much nearer and more or less the opposite direction – central Paris, roughly – rifle shots. Quite a lot of it – definitely rifles, not automatic weapons, sometimes in flurries but mainly well separated: thickening then, as if that outbreak had spread rapidly elsewhere. *Résistants* in the streets again, she guessed. Anticipating the arrival of the Yanks? She was at the house now – where torchlight was showing at uncurtained windows. On the third floor even – within barely a minute of breaking in they seemed to be all over it.

Probably *was* empty. Gestapists on the run, saving their own foul skins. But in one of those top rooms, Léonie might be. Rosie went up the steps and in by the open front door into a fairly spacious hall – doors left and right also standing open, a rising curve of staircase, wide corridor leading away towards the back – to the dining-room, she guessed, doubtless also to kitchen, scullery, larder, butler's pantry, ironing-room, servants' hall, so forth; but first an inner hall, with what looked like a cellar door standing open. She'd been thinking of the top floor – prisoners' cells – also of finding a bathroom on her way up, but this one drew her, for some reason.

Knowing what they used cellars for, of course.

Reminiscent of 11 Rue des Saussaies: small, heavy door

and stone steps leading downward. Not as foul-smelling, but not pleasant either. An ingredient in the odour – as well as the smell of lamp-oil – which she didn't *want* to recognise.

Heavy timber chair with straps fixed to its arms and a coil of rope – washing-line cord – on its seat. She leaned on the back of it for a moment, taking a few breaths while the dizziness came and went. Still with her weight on it then, but able to take notice again, looking round. Seeing that the flicking, yellowish light came from an oil-lamp on an iron bracket a few feet away at about shoulder-height. It was smoking blackly, either running out of oil or burning dirty oil or needing its wick trimmed.

No wine-bins that she could see. But—

Centrally, directly above a patch of dark staining on the concrete, was an iron hook in the ceiling with a few feet of cord dangling from it. Same cord as the heap of it on the chair. Blood-stained, though. And the circular dark patch under it – she didn't need to examine it any more closely to understand what purpose the hook had served.

And *that*—

She stooped, picked it up. A club, of sorts. Clean at this end, blood-stained where it flattened, where she realised the curved end of this former hockey-stick had been sawn off. Bludgeon, was the word for it. Taking it closer to the sputtering oil-lamp, recognising dried blood and – long, dark hairs adhering. Remembering – visualising – Léonie's hair, the smooth, dark shine of it. She'd worn it pulled back into a pony-tail – at any rate when Rosie had stayed with her in her flat in Nancy above the hat-shop.

'Mam'selle . . .'

The lieutenant – Ritter – with a torch: telling her in passable French, 'There are no prisoners here, mam'selle. It is empty, the house. But – I like to show you, please—'

'Ah, Ritter.'

Clausen, clattering down. A hard look at Rosie, who

pointed at the hook, the blood-caked cord and the stained concrete under it. Watching him as he looked from there to the chair and to the bludgeon which she was still holding. She dropped it: didn't want to impart to him her own near-certainty that Léonie was dead.

'He wants to show me something, he says.' A nod to Ritter. 'So?'

'Excuse me, *Herr Major*.'

She followed him to the stairway and up it; Clausen following too, telling her, 'Rooms on the top floor have been in use as cells. But there's nothing to indicate – connect with – either of them. So—'

'What d'you think that hook was for? Or the chair with the straps?' Turning to face him at the top as he came up. In Rouen a year ago they'd had her strapped into a chair very much like that one: why, even the sight of it had made her head swim. Asking Clausen, 'Want me to *tell* you – what your friends and colleagues must have been doing down there?'

'No – thank you.'

'Mam'selle?'

Ritter – reminding her, waiting for her in the passageway leading to the front hall: saying again to Clausen – in French, out of politeness to *her* of course – 'Excuse me, sir . . .'

'I'm coming.' Joining him in the front room to the left, coming from this direction. She'd still have liked to find a bathroom, but had no pressing need for it now except for purposes of cleaning up – which would have to wait. Some of the soldiers were coming down the stairs: stopping near the foot of them to let her go past and into that room – sitting-room, whatever it was. There was an oak table in the centre with kitchen-type chairs grouped around it; some old newspapers and a saucer of cigarette-stubs – nothing else, and no pictures on the walls. Ritter crossed over to the fire-place – stone chimney-piece, wide timber mantelshelf, remains of a candle in the bottom of a jam-jar. Ritter pointing with his torch-beam at a pair of shoes which seemed to have been put there as ornaments. Women's shoes, but virtually a child's size – imitation patent leather with blunt toes and wooden soles. Clearly a French wartime product – and just about as clearly, on account of their exceptionally small size, Léonie's.

Trophy? Souvenir?

Clausen's voice from the doorway, addressing Ritter in French: 'The garden – shouldn't you be seeing what they're—'

'*Jawohl, Herr Major!*'

Rosie was sitting, had hooked one of the hard chairs to her and subsided on to it. Ritter had pushed the shoes into her hands on his way out. She felt bad again. Looking at Clausen: 'What was that about the garden?'

'Looking for newly turned earth. Just in case. No more than a possibility . . . What have you got there?'

'Her shoes. Léonie's. They were *there*, on display.'

It did *not* mean they'd killed her. At any rate, didn't prove they had. Did rather give that impression, though. They were, of course, quite literally beasts. Her hands were steady, she was surprised to note, she might have been all right even without sitting down. Except for the dizziness now and then. In fact shock, horror, became less shocking and/or horrific after a while, one came to take it in one's stride. Only one's sense of balance – and she supposed digestion – seemed to react, be affected. Digestive problem no doubt attributable to the Rue des Saussaies' chef's specials.

She got up: Clausen was beside her, looking at the shoes. 'Why, I wonder.'

'Bravado? Souvenir – then didn't bother, or have room—'

'Doesn't mean – necessarily – what it might seem to mean.'

'What about Rue Lauriston now?' He'd nodded: she followed up with, 'Are we on the same side still?'

'If you mean will I continue to *try* to help you find—'

'What I mean is can I count on it? Rue des Saussaies was – a surprise, you might say. To put it mildly. When you claim to be so desperate for my help, with Jacqui—'

'It was necessary, that's all – in the sight of others, and there being no alternative.'

'Tell me this, then. Re those "others" – how can you get away with this, vis-à-vis your own people? Your Hotel Continental buddies, for instance?'

A shrug. 'For one thing Rue Lauriston's all that's left, and it can't take us long. If they've pulled out of there as well – God knows, but the way it's going – down-town, snipers, and – actually, a lot of trouble, a lot of people are being killed, and' – pointing with his head, south-westward – 'the real thing about to hit us – within just hours, maybe. One might say there are no precedents – in my own case perhaps especially, since I'm—'

'What about Ritter and his detachment now?'

'He'll need to get back to his unit. I'll keep him as far as Lauriston – if he's willing. About Jacqui though' – nodding towards the shoes – 'if this one *is* dead—'

'Until it's proved otherwise I'm assuming she's still alive. So rather than waste more time, Rue Lauriston right away – get Ritter and let's go?'

'Another question is are *you* fit for any more?'

'I need to be there when you find her. Yes.'

'But then – no matter what – you'll stay with Jacqui. There'll be nowhere else to look, will there? If Lafont *has* left Paris, he'd most likely be making for Sigmaringen – in which case—'

'Sigmaringen?'

'In Germany – where they've all gone – Pétain, Laval, Darland, all the ultras who've run away. It's a castle, huge place on the Danube south of Stuttgart. Couldn't have taken her with him, wouldn't have left her here either – not alive. You may have to face this, Jeanne-Marie: she probably *saw* him murdering Courtland, and' – a shrug – 'with retribution perhaps not so distant—'

'Lauriston, then – let's go?'

They *might* still be there. 'They' meaning Lafont and including Léonie too – whether he'd be taking her or not, or leaving her – dead, presumably . . . Clausen had nodded, turned away. 'Meet me at the car. I'll see what Ritter's—'

'Herr Major!'

The man himself. Rosie thinking sickly, envisaging recently turned earth, *They've found her* . . . A stream of German, which Clausen cut short and then told her. 'Nothing in the garden, far as can be seen – in this light, mind you – but they've arrested some kid who was nosing around. Go to the car, will you?'

Having tortured Derek Courtland to death, *would* they have left Léonie alive? Was there a hope in hell they would have?

She didn't think so. Didn't think Clausen could believe there was, either.

Outside, the 'kid who was nosing around' had one of Ritter's men on each side of him, holding his arms. Clausen's torch shining in his face now, and Rosie – on her way to the car, hoping to God this wasn't going to delay them any more than they'd been delayed already, happening to glance that way.

'Nico!'

A gasp: 'Jeanne-Marie?'

'You know this boy?'

'Friend of mine. He was helping me to try to find them. Please, let him go!'

A gesture and a word: Nico then rubbing his arms, from where they'd gripped him. Clausen asked him, 'What are you here for?'

'We thought they might have her friends here.' Pausing, then asking Rosie, 'Tell him, shall I?'

'Yes, Nico, but be quick. They're trying to help find them too.'

'We – this lady's friends – were going to attack this place, try to rescue them. I was on lookout – over there – old gent's house. But this truck came – before my friends would've smashed in—'

'What time was that?'

'Oh – twelve-thirty—'

'*Résistants*, you're talking about?'

Looking at Rosie. She said, 'Just people who were helping me. Go on, Nico.'

'We know about the truck. Go on from there.'

'I told them over the 'phone, hang on, not to attack. There were some of them left here – standing around with guns, Schmeissers. I kept watching, heard shooting from that way, the Bois – and later the truck comes back. All of them singing – fascist songs about killing Jews and that.'

'How long ago was this?'

'About two hours. Then the ones they'd left here got in – with baggage, bundles—'

'No prisoner?'

'None I saw. I don't *think*—'

'After they'd gone again, did you go in and look around?'

'Yeah. Side door – *that* side—'

'True.' Ritter said in French, 'It was not locked – we found after we'd broken in at the back—'

'All right.' Clausen asked Nico, 'What did *you* find?'

'Nothing. Oh – pair of shoes, on a mantelpiece—'

'These.' Rosie showed them to him. 'They belonged to the young lady I'm looking for. The man who was with her is dead – Lafont murdered him – and she may be, too. Nico, this is Major Clausen of the SD, and – as I said – strange as it is, he's helping me. Martin Leblanc knows some of the background, so does Adée. You can tell them what I've said.' She asked Clausen, 'He can go, can he?'

A shrug. 'I've no reason to hold him.'

'Nico – we're going now to 93 Rue Lauriston. They may have her there, or they may have deserted that place too. From there, I'll be going to a house called Le Clos de Fretay – at the end of a cul-de-sac off Rue de Passy, north side, just a short way down from its intersection with Avenue Paul Doumer. An apartment on the top floor. Got that?'

'Yes, but what—'

'My things – suitcase and the bag. You'll need a few hours' sleep, I know, but when you can – *if* you possibly can—'

'No problem. Mind you, it's begun now – barricades, snipers – M'sieur Leblanc said on the telephone—'

'Think you can make it?'

'On the bike – detouring, like—'

'So grateful, Nico. Tell Martin all this, will you?'

'As well as I *can*.' He'd glanced down at her bare feet: trying not to show surprise. At Clausen then – and Ritter, and the soldiers who'd caught him. You could see him struggling with it: that these were on *her* side – although she looked as awful as if she'd been through God alone knew what – and were letting *him* go . . . Telling her quietly, as if he and she were alone here, 'We all thought you might be dead. Can you – *trust* these?'

'Oh, yes. At least – this far—'

'Adée'll be over the moon. M'sieur Leblanc too. Well, my bike's over there . . .'

Getting towards full daylight, in Rue Lauriston. Rosie in the Citroen with her window wound right down, watching as Clausen with two of Ritter's men as back-up first tried the front door and then hammered on it. Others had distributed themselves along the front, and Ritter had taken some of them through the gateway into the central garden. He'd shot the padlock off that gate; and she'd thought there might be a battle starting, then seen him kick it open and dash in with the rest following. Front door open too now: Clausen pushing in, pushing whoever had opened it in ahead of him, Ritter's men crowding in as well.

Might as well move too. He'd said to stay in the car, and for some reason this time she had. Thinking utterly depressing thoughts, and not expecting to find Léonie here or anywhere else alive. Might be somewhere in this place dead, or might not have been here at all. In which case – as Clausen had said, where else? Except in a hole in the Rue de la Pompe garden, or this one. Disposal of dead bodies shouldn't present the Lafont gang with any problems – unless they were really seriously on the run, lacking time and maybe now facilities? She got out, pushed the car door shut, went in across the forecourt looking up at the house's tall, grey façade. Windows uncurtained – or with curtains already drawn back to admit the early light. By whom? Well – *someone* had opened this door to Clausen; Ritter entering by way of the central garden must still have been outside at that stage.

He and his men were in there now, all right. Boots clumping around, voices calling in German to each other. And here – in the hallway, Clausen talking to a pale, balding, middle-aged male in a dark suit and high wing collar. He was visibly trembling: turning to look at her now – and a double-take, as Clausen glanced round and snapped, 'I said to wait in the car!'

'I quite often don't do what I'm told.'

Even when physically and mentally impaired: due very largely to *him*. They were searching the house, clattering from room to room, doors being wrenched open, slammed or flung back; Ritter on the first-floor landing, giving orders and acknowledging reports. The man in the suit had noticed her bare feet, was fairly goggling at her. Not just for that, of course, more that she'd look to him like an assassin, tramp, alley-cat . . . Asking Clausen, 'What's going on?'

'Place is empty except for this – butler. Brançion, you said your name—'

'Yes, *mein Herr*.' French – and obsequious – mumbling flabby-lipped to Clausen that Monsieur Lafont had taken his departure soon after dark, Madame la Comtesse yesterday in the morning.

'Who else with Lafont?'

'Oh – his nephew – M'sieur Clavié, that is – and M'sieur Engel—'

Rosie broke in: 'A prisoner with them?'

Mouth slightly agape, as if he'd never heard of prisoners. She could imagine him here in this wide, light hall with its duck-egg-blue paintwork, chandeliers glowing as he admitted – and took the caps, capes and hats of – Nazi high-ups and French traitors, bowing and scraping to them. *Decent* people in chains in other parts of the house; and in the cellars, God only knew what. In the cellars. God *shuddering* – and this Brançion knowing *exactly* what was going on. She raised her voice: 'Asked you a question, Brançion!'

'I'm sorry, mam'selle – no, not that I—'

'One in particular. Female – young – smaller than I am?'

Quiver of denial: looking at Clausen as if for help while having difficulty framing his own words. Clausen asked him, 'Are you saying there were never any prisoners here?'

'Not in recent months, sir.' The beginnings of a head-shake, but then a pause. Face gleaming with sweat, eyes watery, blinking rapidly. 'Oh. In the house next to this one, sir, number ninety-one. There, I *believe*—'

'Are now, or there were?'

'A girl?' Rosie, shouting: 'Young lady, as I described?'

'It's a – *possible*, mam'selle, *mein Herr* – but—'

'Come on, you smarmy *bastard*!'

'Sir – *mein Herr*—'

'Not worth keeping, is he?'

'No. You're right.' Clausen had the Luger in his hand. 'You're no use to us, Brançion.' He took a pace backwards as he cocked the gun. Ritter meanwhile on his way down, reporting that every room had been checked, there was a lot of stuff lying around, some of it valuable, and the fourth-floor rooms seemed to have been in use as ordinary bedrooms – beds with sheets and blankets still on them.

'All right, lieutenant. Take some of your men now to the house next door – *that* side – and search it. I'll join you there in a minute.' To Brançion: 'D'you have a key to that house?'

'Oh, yes.' Panting, running with sweat. 'Shall I—'

'Get it, give it to that officer.'

'Of course, of course!'

'Wait. Where are the other servants?'

'Oh – discharged, sir. Yesterday – M'sieur Bonny instructed me to pay them their wages, and—'

'Get that key. Yes, lieutenant?'

Ritter told him, 'The cellar, *Herr Major* – there's nothing in it except smashed bottles. Not one left intact, only heaps of broken glass, whole place swimming in wine, just taking a breath could make you drunk!'

'Half mad . . .'

'Didn't want anyone else to enjoy it, I suppose!'

Brançion was back with the key, gave it to Ritter, turned to Clausen then. 'Having had a moment to think about it, sir, I believe there *was* a female prisoner next door. I'd forgotten, it's been – turmoil, these few days. In any case I had nothing to do with ninety-one – or any prisoner *ever* – God's truth, sir, I swear it. In this case I only happened to overhear some reference, and—'

'Did they take her with them?'

'I think – they must have, mam'selle, but—'

'You'd have helped carry out the baggage, you'd have *known*!'

'Not from the other house, you see. If I might explain . . . There were several other associates of M'sieur Lafont's – in number 91, with the prisoner. Also of course M'sieur Bonny – but *he* always stayed in *this* house.'

'Where were they going?'

Clausen had asked simultaneously, 'In what vehicles?' Brançion evidently preferred this question to Rosie's, told him, 'Two Citroen motorcars and one Renault van, sir.' His glance flickered towards Rosie, from her then to the Luger in Clausen's fist. He was scared of it but more scared still, she thought, of *her*. She cut in again: 'Brançion – the major will agree, this is the last chance you get. *Where have they gone?'*

It was the only thing that mattered. If this sod had been telling the truth, not just trying to buy his life. Eyes on Clausen now: Clausen raising the pistol again, slowly. Brançion stammered, 'I can answer that, sir, but in no way that would help you. They've gone to the farm – M'sieur Lafont's. None of us were allowed to know where it is. He'd take Madame la Comtesse, or – a weekend, or—'

'Which direction out of Paris – and how far?'

'If I knew—'

'In travelling time, how far?'

'It was never possible to know, *mein Herr*. I swear it! This is the truth, Mam'selle – I'd tell you if I could, I *swear*—'

Chapter 21

The search of number 91 had been swift and perhaps somewhat perfunctory, after Brançion's statement about Lafont having taken a female prisoner with him. Hadn't bothered looking for recent digging in the garden either. Main reason being that if one accepted Brançion's statement, the farm became the focal point of interest now.

Maybe should *not* have taken the bastard's word for it, she thought. He might have dreamed that up simply to get rid of us. According to Ritter there'd been a lot of valuable-looking silver in the first-floor dining-room, for instance, and that might have been Brançion's reason for having stuck around after Lafont had taken off. Waiting for daylight, to start sorting and packing.

Why the curtains had been opened so early, as she'd noticed. Needing daylight to work by. It was light now, anyway, despite the overcast and drizzle. Warm, muggily humid, after at least seven days of baking sunshine. The thunder of artillery in the south-west was louder than it had been, and pretty well continuous. Sporadic rifle-fire from down-town too. She was mentally crossing her fingers for Nico on his bike in the middle of all that.

She said to Clausen, in his car, about a telephone call he was going to make – best hope, he thought, of getting the location of Lafont's farm – 'Could have done it from the house, if we'd thought of it.'

'Actually, could not. I had Ritter's men pull the wires out

in all three houses as soon as they got into them.' Smug glance at her as he swung the car out of Lauriston into Rue Boissière. 'So nobody – Brançion, in this last case – would be passing on any warnings that we're after him.'

Two or three kilometres to go, to Rue de Passy. The windscreen wipers were noisy; it was only drizzling now but there'd been a heavy shower while they'd been in number 93 and the roads were still awash. The telephone call Clausen was going to make as soon as they reached the flat would be to the Hotel Continental, to ask some SS colleague of his about the farm. If anyone knew where it was, Clausen thought, *he* would.

Or could find out – if it was on record anywhere.

'If he doesn't, and it's not – on *your* records, that is—'

'I don't know.' Shifting gear. 'And as for finding out – which I did say, I know – I'm afraid they've got rather a lot on their hands right now. So' – shake of the head – 'it's not something we can count on.'

'What about the countess Brançion mentioned?'

'I asked him about her. Left Paris, he said, forwarding address Montauban, somewhere. Which of course—'

'What about other women?'

'They'd be collabs, all of them. In any case not exactly my field of study. Only one I could name off-hand is the film star Corinne Luchaire; her father Jean Luchaire is – has been – publisher of *Nouveaux Temps*. They'll have taken flight with the rest of that crowd, you can be certain.'

'Nazis, but you sound contemptuous of them.'

'One respects one's enemies, perhaps, *makes use* of sycophants. But – the farm – I don't know.' Slowing for the turn into Avenue Kleber. 'Failing this one source—'

'So let's pray it comes up trumps. And *then* what? Might as well give thought to that – seeing as you weren't able to hang on to Ritter. What about the SS you sent to arrest me – or the ones you sent to get me out?'

'With *that* going on?' The street-fighting, he meant: a

gesture in that direction. 'Not a chance. This is a crisis now, Jeanne-Marie, not just street-gangs showing off to each other!'

'Gendarmes, then. Well – you know, that *is* an idea? If they saw a chance to arrest Lafont—'

A staff car came fast from the left out of Rue de Longchamp, skidding round in a scream of tyres into this Avenue Kleber, in the skid taking the right-hand turn so wide that although Clausen had braked and swung over he'd avoided a high-speed collision by no more than a metre. Swearing quietly, in German: Rosie had jammed herself back in her seat, ready for the impact which hadn't come. *All* one might have needed, at this stage . . . She glanced at him: he was keeping the speed down now anyway, with Place Trocadero just up ahead. She queried – making light of it – 'Desperate to get into the battle, d'you think – or out of town?'

'Perhaps he overslept. His last night in Paris. Finale of a liaison such as mine and Jacqui's.' Shake of the head: 'I'm not asking for commiseration, but last night may have been *my* last in this city. Half a night, at best. I knew it and she knew it. How it feels is – really indescribable, you know?'

'I know a lot about separation, if that's what you mean.'

'Separation of the kind that might turn out to be permanent?'

'Always that possibility, isn't there?'

'But I was going to say, when that imbecile tried to ram us – you were talking about troops, gendarmes, so forth – even if one had a whole battalion, with no idea where to deploy them – uh?' He'd slowed further, for the Trocadero – Place du Chaillot, formerly Palais du Trocadero, the architectural monstrosity for which Rosie's father had had such contempt – and she had her window down, listening again to the small-arms fire, which was fairly constant: from the Rive Gauche especially, she thought. Not only rifles, machine-gun fire as well now. She wound her window half up as they turned right into Avenue Paul Doumer: drizzle blowing in, as well as that stench of burning.

Worst of all, a growing sense of frustration. Clausen asking her, 'Did that boy have far to go?'

'Far enough. He knows every little back-street though, he'll be all right. Please God he will. Was there some big fire when I was in that place?'

'The Grand Palais, you must mean. We blew it up. Its basement housed the 8th *Arrondissement* gendarmerie, who'd ambushed a truck full of our soldiers and killed them all.'

'Well, good for them!'

'A somewhat provocative comment, Jeanne-Marie.'

She nodded, 'I'm serious, too. Maybe they *would* be keen to arrest Lafont. A real trophy for them. *Could* be our answer.'

'Having of course struck lucky in the first place.'

'Yes. I wish you *had* 'phoned from Rue Lauriston.'

If he did get the location of the farm, she thought, the thing would be to get on to Leblanc, explain it all and get him to bring his gendarmerie friends in on it.

Hell of a long shot, still. Even if Clausen was on the blower to l'Hôtel Continental in say ten minutes' time, and got the answer straight off the bat; and if she, Rosie, was able to get through to Leblanc say ten minutes after that, and *he* could get straight on to the ex-soldier – Fernagut, who'd have to agree and be able to move immediately . . . More than enough 'ifs' and suppositions even if Leblanc, Fernagut and company were *not* currently engaged in street-fighting, as they might well be.

Clausen had cleared his throat. 'Jeanne-Marie, listen now.' Quick change up, double-declutching, to pull out quickly around a *gazo* truck with a load of logs in it. 'We have to face this – that if Lafont was all that secretive about his farm, it's quite possible the man I'm telephoning won't be able to help. Lafont's every kind of swine but he's efficient, and if he set out to keep it secret—'

'We're finished and so is Yvette. Give up, leave her to whatever they have in their swinish minds for her.'

'Brutally – yes, if it turns out that way. And you see, we

can't – *I* can't – see, we're at a point of crisis, aren't we? I'm keenly aware of your anxiety, that the girl's life's at stake, all that; so that talking now of my *own* primary concern – Jacqui – must be – well, may seem selfish, to put it mildly . . . But what *can* I do except beg you to stay with her now and take her with you when you move out? On the practical side of it – no, listen, please, this has to be discussed – there's food in the apartment for – oh, a week or so. Tins, mostly. The Americans *must* be here within a week. Heaven's sake, a *day*, perhaps. I imagine you'd communicate with your own people through them, somehow? Might be British forces sent in too? I don't know – maybe they'll be pushing on eastward to secure the ports. But also, if the American arrival's delayed, you might get help from your Resistance friends? What I mean is that if there were any threat to her *from* the Resistance – FFI, whatever—'

'In a nutshell, you're thinking of leaving us.'

Eyes back on the road. It *was* what was in his mind, obviously. Continuing now, 'This is not an easy position to be in. In regard to Jacqui, I had anticipated getting her away – not with *you*, that bullshit of yours on Sunday didn't wash at all. The dossier idea was worth working on, but not the Nantes business . . . What I'm trying to explain is I'd been counting on getting her away before all this blew up – as it now has, and I've left it too late. For the last three days I've been thinking of those two – Courtland and the girl – as her passport to safety. *Your* idea. Set that up, I thought, and OK, Jacqui and I can kiss goodbye – I won't say happily, but at least I'll know she's *safe*.'

Half a kilometre from here to the junction with Rue de Passy, Rosie guessed. Re-hearing his last words and thinking *Jacqui safe but Yvette di Mellili very far from safe.* In fact either dead or damn soon will be. Clausen adding – in a tone of desperation she hadn't heard from him before – 'It's all come on so *fast*. Two days, as I say – not three, *two* – failing to contact Lafont, to locate him or get any response to messages. Bonny I did manage to speak to, but he's no damn use, only covering for Lafont. And last night that dreadful butchery, and – Courtland – and now the girl – and there goes Jacqui's passport to safety!'

'We *might* still find her. Yvette, I mean.'

'But might very well not, and if I don't – *we* don't – would you – just walk out, when the time comes?'

He was actually desperate, she realised. The tone of his voice: and now his driving, too. She could see the junction up ahead, and on the shine of wet road between here and there a few *gazos* and a horse and cart with what looked like a family's household belongings on it; getting past that now but having to swerve in again to avoid a van that was turning out of a side-road which the lumbering cart had hidden from view in the last few seconds. Clausen had started to pull in behind the van, then seen he'd be stuck, accelerated and swept past it – with other oncoming traffic as well as the cyclists making this move extremely dangerous. But had got away with it, somehow: and far from having learnt any lesson from it was staying out in the middle, ready for the hairpin left turn that was coming. Rosie averting her eyes, saying – what she'd been thinking about, as well as the fact that he was driving like a drunk – 'See what they say at the Continental. *If* they give you a lead to the farm—'

Dragging the wheel over: around the hairpin and on to the down-gradient of Rue de Passy, where if there'd been anything coming *up* – but actually turning his head to look at her while in the middle of it – 'Go on. You say if they do . . .'

Luckily there'd been nothing coming. And with only forty or fifty metres to go, he was easing up. She said, 'It's a question I'm putting to you. Your side of the deal, if we still have one. If they tell you where the farm is, will you stay with me – and any other help we can get, those friends of mine for instance? I asked this before, I know, but – *now*, could I count on—'

'In principle – and on the understanding that in return—'

'Right.'

Turning into the cul-de-sac with the tall gates at the end of it, and as usual one of them standing open. Through into the house's grounds quite slowly, and then stopping. Still grasping the wheel, and staring at her: sweat on his brow, eyes anxious. Rosie looking away then, at the stone nymphs. They looked better shiny-wet from the rain than they had when dry. She confirmed to him – or began to – 'If I have your promise on that—'

'Yes. Because I can see how I'd fix my end of it, with my own superiors. You are actually promising you'll stand by Jacqui even if the answer is no one's ever heard of Lafont's farm?'

'I'll look after her, yes.'

'It's still a deal, then. Thank you.'

Moving on again slowly, to park at that front corner of the house.

Jacqui in a pale green sleeveless cotton dress looked as if she were going to faint.

'What's *happened* to you?'

'Oh—'

'Three nights and two days in a Gestapo cell did most of it,' Clausen answered for her as he embraced Jacqui. 'What she needs is a bath, food, brandy maybe, rest, *more* food—'

'And a good answer from this man at l'Hôtel Continental.'

'Yes. I'll get on to them right away. Are the telephones still working, *chérie*?'

'I don't know. I haven't—' She'd put an arm round Rosie but pulled back, wrinkling her nose. 'Christ! That thing's for burning.' Meaning the raincoat. 'Just drop it here – please, don't bring it inside. Jeanne-Marie – bare feet, and carrying—'

'These aren't mine, I'll explain, but—' She'd checked the coat's pockets – they were empty, reminding her that

Dubarque had taken her papers and given them to Clausen – and let it fall, there on the landing. Maybe one wasn't going to need papers from here on anyway. Jacqui asked Clausen as she followed him and Rosie in then, 'What was it, that shooting?'

'A massacre by the Bonny-Lafonts of thirty-four *résistants* and one other. Gestapo had requested Bonny-Lafont to take them off their hands, Bonny-Lafont then decided to get rid of them any way they could. That was what we heard happening. But that extra one was my excuse to get Jeanne-Marie out of her cell for the purpose of identifying it. *Him*, I should say. Look, I'll make this call now. I'll explain, *chérie*, but for the moment – well, everything from here on hangs on it. Run a bath for her? Is the water hot?'

'Warm, anyway. I've been keeping the stove stoked-up for *you*. But Jeanne-Marie, what on *earth*—' Checking herself: maybe stuck for which of a dozen questions to ask first. Clausen had gone on through, presumably to their bedroom. Jacqui shrugging, giving up: 'All right – first things first. The bath. It's through here.'

'I know.'

'Of course, you were here. Sorry, I'm – gaga, slightly. Such relief, to have him back. And to see you, of course. But – food, now. To be quickest – cold roast pork?'

'Lovely. *Anything*.'

'Who arrested you – and why, what—'

'Gerhardt did. He'd discovered I was not what I seemed. That's to say I *am* not.' She'd winked at her: water gushing in, and she was about to step into it, to wash at least some of the grime off her feet while it was running cold – and talking above that noise, partly for Clausen to hear Jacqui being informed of something she supposedly hadn't known and which obviously must astonish her – if he could hear it, wasn't already on the telephone . . . 'He'll tell you. You'd better be ready to be shocked.' A whisper then: 'You're in the clear, don't worry. I was going to approach you for SOE purposes in Rouen, but never got round to it, I thought you'd turn me in. I was waiting to know you better before I risked it.'

'Whatever you are – or are not – I'll tell you this' – her voice rose – 'your clothes are *foul*!'

'There was urine all over the floor, and the mattress was – God, I can't tell you. I'm longing to wash my hair . . . This is getting warm, by the way.' She stepped out of the bath. 'Some other clothes are coming, thank God, by—'

'Well . . .' Jacqui put the plug in. 'I can rout out a few rags that mightn't be too bad on you.'

'—boy on a bicycle, bringing my things from Montmartre. But yes – great, thank you, he can't take less than an hour or two. Maybe just slippers and a dressing-gown meanwhile?'

'Hush – a moment . . .'

Clausen's voice out there: he was through to the Continental, by the sound of it. Rosie moved to the door, nearer to him and away from the sound of the running water.

Talking bloody German, of course. She beckoned Jacqui, whispered, 'Understand any of it?'

'Very little. No, not when they talk fast.' Voice up to normal again: 'Now you watch this' – the bath – 'and I'll make – sandwiches? Like – what, a brandy with them?'

'Sandwiches, lovely – but if you had coffee—'

'Easy. Two minutes . . .'

Clausen was only putting in brief contributions, mainly *Ja*'s, and grunts. A lot more was being said at the other end than at this one, obviously. At least he was through to someone telling him something he thought worth listening to. Maybe this man did know about the farm, was giving him directions to it. Bath water meanwhile not hot, but warm enough to relax in it while stuffing down whatever food they gave her. Like contemplating paradise – except for anxiety over what was or was not coming over that telephone.

Clausen was talking now. She heard – suddenly, unexpectedly – '*Ja*, Carl Boemelbourg . . .'

The bath was about half-full; she turned off the tap. Sniffed at the cake of soap: lavender. A lot better than her *present* scent. She heard him ring off.

Then: 'Jacqui?'

Prompt answer from the kitchen: 'Just one moment!' She was pretty good, Rosie thought. Really a minimum of questions, this far, and what had seemed like very quick understanding of the other business. She opened the bathroom door by a few inches, saw Clausen standing there looking undecided. Thinking she might have undressed, no doubt.

'Do they know where it is?'

'No. But he's going to look into it and ring back. The rest of all that, he was telling me there are *résistants* occupying certain buildings, and on rooftops with sniper rifles, especially around the strongpoints – *Stützpunkte*. Our tanks are in the streets – light tanks, which is all we have here. And – ah, *chérie—*'

'Coffee will be a while yet. Stove's not at its best. Only wood, of course, no coal. I'll give you some breakfast in a minute anyway. Was the call satisfactory? Jeanne-Marie – here we are, you can eat while you soak. Don't lock the door, I'll bring coffee when it's ready. And later I'll try to do something about your hair. I'll bring you a fresh towel too. What else – oh, shampoo. Here . . .'

'You're twice the girl I thought you were, Jacqui.'

'Aren't I a marvel? The sandwiches I'll put here, look. You can reach, eh? Plenty more when you want it. Otherwise—'

'I'm glad I promised Gerhardt I'd take you to England with me.'

'Oh, well . . .' Double-take, then. 'You promised him *what*?'

'Ask him. Get him to tell you the whole story. Including why he had me locked up in that filthy hole. I'm about to cram my mouth full – ask *him*, d'you mind?'

He and Jacqui had stayed inside, breakfasting together. The breeze was cool and the balcony where they usually had their meals was wet with drizzle, sky still overcast, only a vague brightness where the sun should have been. When the 'phone rang Rosie heard him answer it immediately, before even the second ring. She got out of the bath then; she'd been in it for about half an hour, eaten every crumb of the sandwiches, of course, drunk all the coffee, felt like a new woman – or the old one, more or less resuscitated.

Except for pictures in the mind – like that of freshly turned earth in the inner garden of number 93: and Brançion smirking to himself at having got rid of them so easily.

Clausen had spoken only a few words this time, and then hung up. Did *not* promise well. When she joined them – not quite dry but wrapped in a yellow towelling gown with her hair combed back, still damp – he pointed at a squat, dark bottle: 'It's marc – quite a good one. You'll need it.'

'Bad news, then.'

She'd known it was going to be, and could see it in his eyes, hear it in his tone. Jacqui was looking despondent too, despite the promise of refuge in England – which was tied up with the prospect of losing her lover, of course, she'd hardly be dancing with joy in front of him.

Rosie nodded to Clausen: 'I'd love a marc. Would have even if it had been *good* news.'

'I may as well tell you' – Clausen leaned over with the bottle – 'I had prepared the ground quite well so far as my own position is concerned. Telling them, incidentally, nothing much more than the truth. That Lafont had a prisoner, female, believed to be an agent of SOE and having information that might be of considerable military value. She should have been sent to me in the first place – as instructed by Carl Boemelbourg – but was transferred to Bonny-Lafont on the closure of Avenue Foch – in my absence – with a request that she be brought to a state of compliance. Now Lafont's made a run for it and it seems taken her with him, and even if he knew the questions he should be asking—'

'So your extended absence would have been justified. Your obvious duty in fact to go after him – her.'

'Exactly.' He'd poured himself another tot. 'If they'd been able to give me the location of this farm. But I mention it, Jeanne-Marie, to have you know I *would* have kept my side of the bargain. That call, as you'll have guessed, was to say no one knows anything about this farm.'

'There's no land registry now, I suppose?'

'If there is, Lafont wouldn't have bothered with it.'

'No.' She shrugged. 'I suppose not.'

They'd have killed her by now, she thought. Or would be continuing some process of killing her.

She asked Jacqui, '*Will* you come to England with me?'

A nod. 'I can't tell you how grateful or how – frankly – *astonished*—'

'Goes for both of us.' Clausen nodding, reaching to take Jacqui's hand. 'You save two lives, Jeanne-Marie, not just one.'

'But listen.' Jacqui gently took her hand back from him, put her head back, closed her eyes. 'Gerhardt, *chéri*, I'm going to shock you now. I know *exactly* where the farm is.'

Chapter 22

'Not sail tonight, Commander.'

A shake of the grey head. Einar Loen, Anna's father: a lean, fit-looking man in his middle fifties. He'd got back last night with the two escapers, a Petty Officer Olsen and Leading Telegraphist MacEvoy, who were now ensconced in the *Ekhorn*. Ben had come up to the house for a late breakfast – he'd been having all his meals up here; and from the living-room there was a fine view of the fjords – the main one and this smaller, banana-shaped one that ran off it southward and south-westward – and of the search activity that was in progress. There was certainly more of it than there had been in recent days, and Loen was guessing that maybe some tongue had been wagging, on the subject either of escapers or the agents who'd gone in MGB *600*, or indeed of the *Ekhorn* if someone had seen her on her way up-fjord on Tuesday night/Wednesday morning.

They definitely would not have *heard* her. It had been Anna's idea – to use the boat hitherto referred to as Vidlin's, with two strong Norwegians at the oars, towing *Ekhorn*. Anna as pilot had cox'd the boat; they'd left their former berth after *600* had sailed – at about 11.30 – tied up in the creek here just after 3 am and spent most of the day shifting the cargo of weaponry up to a timber outhouse and dumping other gear – nets, lobster-pots, cordage and the remains of an old pram dinghy – on top of it. The weaponry was for a resistance group based in Alesund, who'd be making arrangements to pick it up – but obviously not while all this searching and/or patrolling was going on. Seaplanes were coming over every hour or so, and that same armed trawler which had been fussing around yesterday was today at anchor on the far side of the main fjord, opposite its junction with this one.

Not exactly a comfortable situation. The *Ekhorn*'s berth was reasonably secure, though – as Anna had said it would be. Well inside the creek, which was overhung by spruce that ran thickly from a high crest right down to the water's edge, and with Leon's boat, a 50-foot Möre cutter – two-masted, big wheelhouse amidships – moored outside her, shutting off any view of her from the fjord.

Ben said, over breakfast, 'To be honest, I wouldn't mind *how* long we stuck around.' Looking at Anna as he said it. No sign of a maidenly blush, as convention might have demanded – her skin was too well tanned to show much of one in any case – but she got the message and it seemed not to displease her. She had lovely eyes. He added, 'Except we're a danger to you. From that point of view, sooner we're on the move the better.'

'I wouldn't worry. You're well hidden, down there.' She was pouring second mugs of tea. 'For you, Ben?'

'Yeah, please.'

'Much better wait until it's been quiet for two or three days. My father's right, tongues do wag a lot more than they should – sometimes about absolutely nothing, but the Germans seem to react to it all the same. Seems people just get a feeling something's going on, and – best thing is to lie low, let it pass. We have our quislings too, you know – our traitors, eh?' Switch of subject: 'Ben is Australian, Papa, did he mention it?'

'Australian, eh.' Putting down his mug. 'Will you go back there after the war, d'you think?'

'I don't know. Did have a sort of a plan. Government scheme for ex-Servicemen – in a nutshell, you clear about fifty thousand acres of bush within a certain period of time, and it's all yours. That began to look a bit doubtful when I got a German bullet in this knee, and now – well, a thing that happened recently's sort of—'

Roar of an aircraft's engines. Yet another seaplane, he supposed. You'd have had to be at the window to see it, but it had sounded closer than all the others, could even have been right over the top. Loen said as the racket lessened, 'Your boat's invisible to them down there, don't worry. You were saying – something happened recently?'

He nodded. 'A girl I would have married – she got killed. She was in SOE in France. They're giving her a medal – posthumously, but—'

'What's that – excuse me?'

Anna interpreted the word 'posthumously'. Shook her honey-coloured head then: 'Medals . . .'

'Yeah. Exactly.'

'I'm more sorry than I can say, Ben.'

'When you told us about your husband, I thought – *snap*.' He shrugged. 'Not meaning it flippantly at all, you know, only—'

'I know. Yes.'

'Well, listen to me now.' Loen sat back in his chair. 'I am not – please understand this – *not* match-making. Snap or no snap. That would be stupid, also perhaps offensive to you both, and I'm not a stupid man, at least I don't think I am. On the other hand I don't beat about the bush either. Commander – would you please, when you sail from here, take Anna with you?'

'Papa—'

'Straight answer, sir – yes. If you and she both—'

'No. Thank you, Ben, but *no*. Papa, I don't have the slightest inclination or intention—'

'Listen.' Her father pointed at the window. 'All this that's going on. All right, they're searching for the two you've got now in your boat, maybe. Or for boats that shouldn't be here. Doesn't matter what for, one of these days they find Anna, then they discover she was the wife of Leif Berge who was prominent in the resistance in Oslo—'

'They don't have any way to find that out. At least, not—'

'Don't enough people around here know you married Leif Berge?'

'Some do, sure, but not that he—'

'Anna.' Ben nodded towards her hand. 'You wear a wedding ring, and you use your married name – Berge, you gave us that name when you came on board. If you *were* questioned—'

'It's not an unusual name, you see.'

'But if you were questioned—'

'I'd tell them mind their own damn business!'

He smiled at her. '*I* like that, but believe me the Gestapo—'

'You know much about the Gestapo?'

'My girl did. She was tortured by them – she escaped that time, but—'

'Got caught a second time?'

He nodded. Crazy about her eyes. 'She went back in. *Third* time, that was.'

'As brave as you can get . . . What was her name?'

'Rosie. Actually Rosalie. Her father was French.'

'Listen.' Loen again. 'In Shetland, living there now, is a man by name Per Dalen, and his wife Sissel. He's a skipper with the Shetland Bus crowd – uh? Well, *she* is related to us, and they'd look after you, Anna, they'd take you in and—'

'But I don't *want*—'

'Hush.' He'd gestured, a 'calm down' signal. 'What *I* don't want is to have my daughter taken by the bloody Germans. I very *much* don't want this. Much, much sooner cook my own meals ashore and afloat. And speaking to you very seriously, as your father—'

'I'm over twenty-one, Papa, and I've already been away from home, a married woman—'

'Excuse me.' Ben put his oar in. 'If you decide you *would* like to come to Shetland – or England, for that matter – I'd be very happy to take you with us and – see you were taken care of. I understand your father's anxiety for you too. Not that it'd be exactly dead safe coming with us – as you know. But you've got today and tomorrow to think it over. On the whole I'd like to push off tomorrow night – *tonight* even, if it wasn't for—'

'My advice would be hang on a while.' Loen got up and went to the window. 'Suppose tomorrow it's all quiet.' Nodding towards the anchored trawler. 'That one gone and no airplanes, you'd think maybe they're searching some other fjord, but it could be what they do all this for – so someone will make a move, and anyone who does – see, that's who they're looking for, eh? Bastards just waiting, watching.' He shook his head. 'I'd say wait three, four days after it's gone quiet. A week, perhaps. Whether or not she comes to her senses and goes with you—'

'Whether or not.' Ben nodded – glancing at her, and telling her father, 'I'm sure you're right. But the lads down there are all keen to make a run for it – and they're civilians; in any case I'm not the *Ekhorn*'s skipper. As I said, while we're here we *are* a danger to you. Isn't there a notice they hand out to you saying the penalty for having any contact with the enemy is death?'

Vidlin had told him this. Loen nodding – his back to the window now, fists on his hips: 'What d'you think is the penalty for making a run for it when the bastards are sitting there waiting for you? Ask your boys *that*!'

Chapter 23

Jacqui with her head back and eyes shut, as if to distance herself from her own statement: 'I know *exactly* where the farm is.'

Silence: despite the distant rumble of artillery and closer firework-like popping and crackling of small-arms fire. Rosie on the point of saying something like, 'You're joking', but thinking better of it, asking instead, '*Where*, Jacqui?' although the question hanging most heavily in the air was of course *how*? Expressed by a frozen-faced, cold-voiced Clausen now as, 'Under what circumstances did you come by such knowledge?'

Which was what Jacqui had been expecting, of course. Looking at him tiredly, as if – Rosie's interpretation of it, this – wishing he didn't have to be *quite* so bloody German. She told him, '*Not* in the way that you are choosing to assume, *chéri*.'

'May I have a more positive answer to the question?'

Rosie chipped in with: 'Jacqui – *where* is the farm?'

'Near a small place called Bazoches, about seventy kilometres east from here. I have it marked on a road map.' She started to get up. 'I'll show you.'

'Perhaps I might re-formulate *my* question.' Clausen put a hand out as if to detain her: she stayed put anyway, waiting for it. 'Who marked the map?'

'*He* did, of course. He wanted me to go down there with him. The time you were in Lyon – the very day you left, in fact, he shot round here!'

'You never thought of mentioning it to me?'

'Thought – yes, of course I have. Several times. Often, in fact. It seemed best simply to hold him off. He was pressuring me for quite a long time, you know. If I'd told you, you'd have felt it was obligatory to – I don't know, but you'd have gone after him in some way, and – what sort of a fuss, scandal, repercussions—'

'*Did* you go to his farm?'

'No, I did not.'

'Or anywhere else?'

'I went – as you know – to Rouen, to see to the business. Since you were going to be away—'

'Did you go alone?'

'You know damn well I did!'

'I *thought* I knew. But you've kept this to yourself – what, a month? No – three weeks. Even in the last half-hour said nothing, despite my having explained—'

'I knew how you'd react. And I hadn't thought about this young girl's predicament – not really. Then seeing Jeanne-Marie's distress – while accepting her kindness . . . so you've had a half-hour delay; now you've got it, so get on with it, uh? Before this present situation arose though – you know the sort of influence Lafont wields, if you'd had a real bust-up with him don't you think you might soon afterwards have found yourself recalled to Berlin? Incidentally leaving me *extremely* vulnerable?'

'How do I know you "held him off"?'

'What sort of woman d'you think I am, Gerhardt?'

'An exceptionally beautiful one – and Lafont is well known as an inveterate pursuer—'

'Gerhardt.' Rosie had been exercising patience. 'Jacqui told me – here, last Friday – that Lafont had been chasing her, she couldn't stand him, hadn't told you about it because she didn't want a lot of trouble. In other words, she could handle it – as she's just told you. Jacqui, *he* told me – Monday night, when he'd arrested me – that he knew

Lafont had been chasing you and didn't care because he trusted you. Doesn't sound like it now, I admit – but that *is* what you told me, Gerhardt, isn't it? So neither of you had any surprises coming, what's the fuss about?'

'Answer me one question then. Jeanne-Marie – *your* view please, since for some reason you're making it your business. Would you mark a map for someone if you didn't have reason to believe they'd want to get there?'

'*He* might have. Trying to force the issue. Force *her*. Anyway, the fact is that he *did*. May I see it, please?' Rosie on her feet – in Jacqui's beaded-satin slippers and yellow towelling dressing-gown. 'Because the sooner we can get this moving—'

'Yes.' Jacqui went over to the bookshelves. Rosie asked Clausen, 'You'll still keep your word now, will you?'

Gazing at her as if having difficulty in focusing, or in shifting his line of thought – from Lafont and Jacqui, she supposed. That was the doubt suddenly: that he might decide oh, the hell with her, let her stew here in Paris – so then no deal over Léonie. In which case – do without him. Now, maybe one *could*. Maybe . . . He was frowning, having caught on to what she'd asked him; surprised by it: 'Why should this make any difference?'

'Well – lovers' tiffs, you know . . . Anyway I'll use your 'phone – when I've seen the map. What we spoke of – gendarmes working with the Resistance – so happens I do have a contact. If they'll come in on it, you'll co-operate?'

'Since I gave you my word, and—'

'Here it is.' Jacqui came back unfolding a well-used road map; she spread it on the table while Rosie moved other things aside, and after a bit of searching put the tip of a fingernail to a small pencilled cross.

'There you are. See – Bazoches.'

'Lafont's mark, uh?'

'I told you.'

'I still don't understand why he should have, unless—'

'Hang on.' Rosie, checking the map's scale, and the distance. 'You said seventy kilometres . . .'

'It's what he said – I *think*—'

'I've got to ring these people, need to be sure I have it right.' Behind her as she went to the telephone Jacqui was telling Clausen, 'I suppose because he's the great Henri Lafont and is used to sweeping all before him, doesn't believe the word "no" when he hears it – and that's the only word he ever got from me. But for God's sake, if you *knew* he was pestering me—'

Dialling. But then getting no reply to either of the numbers Leblanc had given her. After this length of time and the effect of solitary confinement, might have got them wrong . . . Thinking now *please*, Adée, *please* . . . And hearing Jacqui's, 'Any case, *how* did you know?'

'Yeah?'

'Adée, hurrah!'

'Jeanne-Marie! Been hearing about you – got Nico here!'

'So he's told you I'm OK. You know it all. Fine. All well with you?'

'I made him eat and sleep, then he'll take your things to you. Oh, he's awake, this thing ringing—'

'My apologies to him. Adée, is it possible to get in touch with Martin Leblanc?'

'Not here. Since they bust in and grabbed *you*. How did they know to find you here?'

'Through the telephone number. Remember I told you I'd had to give it to someone? Adée, if I give you a message for Martin, could you get it to him?'

'Sure. I'll send Nico. Listen, we were so *pleased*, girl—'

'Put Nico on, let me tell it to *him*?'

'OK. We going to see you some time?'

'Damn sure you are. Without fail. Few days, maybe. Look after yourself, Adée. Listen, let Nico start out right away, will you?'

'Here he is.'

Nico's voice: 'Jeanne-Marie.'

'Hi, Nico. Adée said you'd get a message to Monsieur le Professeur for me. Very urgently?'

'OK. How did it go at Rue Lauriston?'

'The birds had flown. But we know where, and there's reason to believe they've got the girl with them. Well, here there's only me and the SD officer you met and a young lady who lives here – at the address I gave you, Rue de Passy. Nico, they've gone to a farm which is owned by Lafont, near a village called Bazoches, seventy kilometres east of here. We have a map with the farm marked on it, and a car – the Citroen you saw – and as it happens a *gazo* too, if we needed it. But one man and two women – against maybe half-a-dozen Bonny-Lafonts—'

'If I may say so, you'd be crazy to go near them.'

'I'm wondering whether Martin might persuade that gendarme who was a soldier to take an interest in it. Maybe bring a squad of his own people with him. I know they must have their hands full, but with a good chance of arresting Henri Lafont – *and* Bonny, by the way, and some others – they'd be keen, don't you think?'

'I'd guess so. Don't *know*, but—'

'So tell Martin all this, ask him can he set it up – and to call me here?'

'Give me the number.'

She did that. Adding, 'They'll need their own transport, obviously. However many of them, and room for prisoners I suppose. But get to him at once, Nico? They won't be hanging around that place for ever, and – if the girl *is* with them—'

'I'll ask Monsieur Leblanc to ring you as soon as he can, and I'll come out either with them or on my bike ahead of them. I've got your stuff here.'

'Bless you, Nico!'

She hung up, found Clausen and Jacqui watching and listening. And not quarrelling – not at this moment. She told them, 'I think they will come. Only hope to God they're quick about it. If we can get there really fast – not find just another empty—'

'Tell me about them.' Clausen, frowning. 'Martin – and some gendarmes, an ex-soldier and the boy Nico—'

'Nico you already met. May come ahead on his bike – bringing my things, remember I asked him? Or he may come with the others. Martin is a schoolmaster who used to teach him. Nice man. Whether he'll come himself I don't know. Or the others for that matter, one can't be absolutely certain.'

'*Résistants*, obviously.'

'Gendarmes. One as you say a former soldier. You don't have to know more than that about them, do you?'

'Not if they don't have to know who *I* am.'

'Well, they *will*. It'll seem to them a very peculiar business, having you in on it. In fact – Gerhardt, you don't *have* to come at all. Except for the car – they won't have room for all of us, and that *gazo*'d be too slow. Could you say the Citroen had been pinched from you – hi-jacked by *résistants* – get yourself to the Continental or wherever in the *gazo*?'

Jacqui said, 'I'm going with you, Jeanne-Marie.'

Clausen spread his hands: 'Then so am I.'

'In case I run off with Lafont?'

'Don't be silly, Jacqui.'

'No. All right. Not the time for it, is it? I know, I'm sorry. Perhaps you'll kill Lafont. I *hope* you will.' She went to him, wrapped her arms round his neck. 'Sorry, my darling. And I forgive you for being silly earlier.'

Jacqui heated a tin of ravioli to keep Rosie going until lunch, which would feature a chicken casserole that was already simmering. The rest of the cold pork she was proposing to use for sandwiches which they'd take with them in the car.

Rosie had almost finished eating when the 'phone rang.

Clausen answered it, said flatly, 'Please wait', and offered the receiver to Rosie: 'Leblanc.'

As she'd been hoping it might be. She grabbed it. 'Martin?'

'Jeanne-Marie. Let me say first how delighted I was to hear from Nico—'

'Yes. Thank you . . . But the rest of it – about Lafont?'

'I've spoken with Fernagut and the answer is very much *yes*. He's collecting a team and a truck and he'll telephone you when he's setting off so you can be waiting in your SD's Citroen – save time, set off as soon as he joins you. You know the way, I understand, so you lead him. It'll probably be a *Wehrmacht* truck.'

'You coming with them?'

'No. I have things here I can't leave. In any case I'd be no use to you. But listen, Fernagut makes the condition that the prisoners will be his own – no question of SD interference. He doesn't like having your German along – but I explained about the car, that you had your own problems and this was the solution. So you take the girl they're holding – if she's alive, eh? – and he takes the Bonny-Lafonts, they're gendarmerie prisoners entirely. Agreed?'

'As far as I'm concerned, he can hang them. How long before he gets here?'

'A few hours. There's a lot going on, and he has to make various arrangements. Oh, but Nico is on his way to you now, with the things you wanted. You won't want him to go with you, will you?'

'Not – especially—'

'And I have work for him here – plenty. So—'

'We'll give him a meal and send him back.'

'That would be fine. And in due course you'll hear from Fernagut.'

'Yes. Thank you *very* much, Martin. I'm so sorry about Georges and the others.'

'The Bonny-Lafonts will pay for it. Thanks to you, and with a bit of luck now. I may say that Gabriel Fernagut is delighted to have the chance of this. There's been no love lost in that quarter, and it'll be a great *coup* for him professionally.'

'Hope he comes soon, that's all.'

'He's aware of the urgency. But – at this of *all* times, huh? Incidentally, his arrangements include having gendarmerie come up to Bazoches from Provins – which is only twenty kilometres to the south.'

'I hope they won't just go charging in!'

'He's asking them to set up road-blocks. So unless Lafont's moved on already – in which case too bad, we've lost him – well, they won't get far. I must go now, Jeanne-Marie. Good luck with the girl.'

'I'll be in touch later through Adée.'

'Fine.'

He'd hung up. She did the same and went back to finish her ravioli. Telling them, 'It's all set – or will be. Nico's on his way, the others will be "a few hours", he says. Their leader, name of Gabriel Fernagut – gendarme I mentioned, the ex-soldier – will telephone when he's setting off so we can be ready downstairs. All right?'

Clausen was frowning. *'A few hours?'*

'Fernagut's getting gendarmerie from some nearby place – Provins – to set up road-blocks, or *a* road-block. So with any luck—'

'At Bazoches, road-blocks?'

'I suppose so. Only pray the Bonny-Lafonts don't get to know it's happening.'

A nod. 'Could be dangerous for your Yvette.'

'Exactly. *Exactly.*' She put down her fork, mopped the plate with bread. When in Rome . . . 'That was marvellous. When's lunch?'

They all laughed. Jacqui said, 'Well, three days, and every twelve hours a mug of – soup?'

'Slop. Pig-swill. Anyway I feel much, much better now.'

Clausen said, 'With lunch we'll have a bottle of the Riesling that you liked.' To Jacqui then: 'Did I tell you that in the cellar at 93 Lauriston he'd had them smash all those great vintage Burgundies and Bordeaux?'

'He's mad, obviously.'

'Yes. But now I'll have a bath. Even if the water's cold. Tell me though, Jeanne-Marie. You don't have to, of course, it's just that I'm – intrigued, a little. We were saying on the way here, you're as concerned for this Yvette di Mellili as I am for Jacqui. So – is it as you might say a *personal* concern – as mine is, obviously – or do you still see a danger of her revealing vital military information?'

'I doubt she'd have much to reveal. As I said, it's more that I simply want to save her life. For one thing it's what I was sent here for, and another – she was kind to me in Nancy, and I liked her. Rouquet too. All right – part of their job and perfectly natural – fellow agents, all that . . .' She was addressing Jacqui mostly, wanting her to understand and see it her way. Clausen was still the cold-faced SD hatchet-man who in his time had sent people like herself and Yvette to unpleasant deaths, only happened at this stage to be pursuing what he saw as his own interests. She finished – to Jacqui – 'And having been there oneself – more or less – makes us – well, sisters, you might say.'

Clausen had listened attentively to that, and looked relieved – that he wouldn't be helping to deprive the Reich of a source of valuable intelligence, she guessed. He was on his feet now, with a hand on Jacqui's shoulder. 'Off to the tub. Then perhaps a nap. Don't want to lunch *too* early, do we? Nap, *then* lunch?'

'Maybe.' Small, private smile at Rosie. 'Didn't get much last night, did we? Jeanne-Marie, the spare room – that door *there* – perfectly good bed in it, mattress that doesn't smell—'

'What luxury! But I'll wait to let Nico in.' She moved her left arm as if to check the time, then remembered – not for the first time – that she had no watch. 'Damn . . .' Shaking her head: Jacqui with an eyebrow raised. Rosie explained, 'No timepiece. Gestapo woman stole it, in that hell-hole.'

Clausen had stopped in the doorway, looking back at her. At Jacqui then, who nodded. 'I've a spare you can have, Jeanne-Marie. *Chéri*, in the dressing-table, top right-hand drawer.'

'*That* one?'

'Yes. Please.'

'Very well . . .'

'What are you up to?'

'Giving you a present. I want to, don't you *dare* refuse it!' Clausen came back with the watch: Jacqui took it from him, told Rosie, 'Left wrist, please, and shut your eyes.'

Gold. By Vacheron – *Genève*.

'I couldn't possibly accept this!'

'I don't like it much. Certain – associations I don't like. Please, take it?'

'It's a fact she never wears it.' Clausen turned away. 'Excuse me.'

'If you don't like it, Jacqui, why not sell it?'

'How could I sell it, when it's yours? Look, I'd be very hurt if—'

'Compromise, I'll wear it until we get to London, and you can sell it there. Meanwhile, thank you *very* much.'

'I was thinking, Jacqui – no need for you to come to Bazoches. Not Gerhardt either. I could drive his Citroen – we need something reasonably fast – if he'd allow that?'

'I don't think he would.'

'But then you could stay here together, he wouldn't have to consort with *résistants* – which might be tricky for him—'

'I might be some help with your Yvette, don't you think?'

'I'd manage.' She added quickly, 'If she's there, even—'

'Don't go on with that. Tell yourself she *is* there, alive and—'

'She won't be – undamaged.'

'There you are, then. The more reason I should go with you. If it was just you alone, if she's hurt, and you had the driving—'

'I might borrow Nico. I could ring back to the man who called, or Nico could when he gets here—'

'How much use would he be, though? You're right, she might have been hurt in all sorts of ways.' Jacqui shook her dark head. 'Leave it as it is. I'll come. I'm happy to. So Gerhardt will come too: no problems with the car, and for Yvette – you and me, between us – much easier. Also, I'll be there to navigate. Map-read, all that.'

'Hardly essential. Looking after Yvette – yes, maybe, but—' a gesture towards the folded map. 'I've got it in my head already – via Porte Vincennes or Porte Dorée – then Joinville – and straight on. At Fontenay-Trésigny we're more than half-way. Map-read if you want to – only need a torch, but—'

'At Bazoches then, which way?'

'Well – the famous pencil cross!'

'That marks Bazoches. Out of which, although it's only a small village, there are several ways one can go.' She'd dropped her voice: Clausen was in either the bedroom or the bathroom, might conceivably be hearing this. 'And a place like that, you stop to ask someone where is the farm of Monsieur Lafont, the best you'd get is "the farm of Monsieur *who*?"'

Mouth open, eyes rolling, dim-witted peasant look: Rosie laughed. 'Surely locals know when a farm's been sold?'

'There'd have been no name on it. Pierre Bonny does all the paperwork for him anyway. Some peasant would have been handed a wad of money and told to shove off, that's all.'

'But *you* could find it, you're saying?'

'I think so.' Eyes wide, thinking about it. A nod. 'Yes, I could.' Slight frown at Rosie's probing look. 'What's the matter? He gave me a very detailed description, that's all – so I could meet him there. Of which, as I have already found it necessary to assure my darling Gerhardt, I had not the smallest intention.'

'Would you have been driving there yourself then? Not driven by him?'

'I suppose . . .'

'Using what car? Gerhardt's? Property of the SD?'

'Look – I have no idea. I wasn't going to do anything about it, anyway. No, of *course* not *his* car!'

Watching her: and just about damn well *knowing* . . . Hardly believing her own conjecture – observation – but recalling recent doubts about leopards changing or not changing spots; and as near as damnit certain this one hadn't.

'I take your word for it, of course.'

'How *very* kind!'

'But how will you handle the so-called navigation without at least re-arousing suspicions?'

A shrug. 'It was as I told you. He was speaking very excitedly about this place. See, you turn left here, then after this little crossing, just about *here* – and oh, it's so *beautiful* . . . when a man's enthusing to that extent, it's rude not to pay attention, Jeanne-Marie!'

'Where did you learn that? Charm school? La Chatte's college of higher education?'

'Now look here—'

'No, Jacqui. I'm amazed you'd even let him in here!'

'In *here*?'

'He'd been here when I met him downstairs, hadn't he?'

'Oh – that time. Yes. Only for a moment. He was hoping Gerhardt might be home.'

'No, he wasn't. No car down there, he'd have known he wasn't. If there had been he wouldn't have come up, would he? Certainly wasn't the time he marked the map for you either. Really, Jacqui – *Lafont*! Of all the *poisonous*—'

'You're jumping to conclusions and you're entirely wrong. And if you let *him* hear any of it – well, my God . . .' She leaned closer, whispered, 'Aren't you ignoring something quite important? If I'd kept quiet – uh? Give me credit for not playing safe and keeping it to myself – which I *could* have, you know?'

'Yes, that—'

'Isn't it what matters most to you? Anyway, leave it now. Please?' Sounds of Clausen's emergence from the bathroom. 'Tell me' – back up to a normal tone of voice – 'this girl's name, di Mellili – of Italian origin, is she?'

'Her father might have been. She was born in Belgium – mother French, father I'm not certain, but he left them and skipped to Venezuela. Mother and daughter then moved to London.'

'Pretty, is she?'

'Yes. Neat little figure, good features, lovely eyes, hair rather like yours—'

'Her bad luck, maybe. In her present company.' Getting up, calling back to Clausen, 'Coming.' Adding to Rosie, 'That was a stupid thing I said. I'm sorry. In any case I'll help any way I can.'

Nico arrived soon after midday. He'd left his bike chained up down below, had Rosie's bag – formerly Léonie's – slung over one shoulder, and was carrying her small battered suitcase. Eyeing Jacqui's bright towelling gown as he came into the hall and Rosie shut the door and bolted it, then kissed him on both stubbly, slightly spotty cheeks.

'Thank you for all you've done for me, Nico.'

'Nothing. Your pistol's still in here.'

'Lucky to get away with that, wasn't I? At the Dog, I mean. How's it going, down-town?'

'A lot of casualties on both sides. Every day. They're burying Catholics at Notre-Dame des Victoires, Protestants at l'Oratoire. At Notre-Dame they say the daily average is thirty to forty – but many more than that are wounded, of course. Anyway' – following her through – 'Captain Fernagut'll be here later—'

'Captain?'

'What M'sieur Leblanc is calling him. I think he likes it. He'll have eight men, he says, in a *Wehrmacht* truck with "FFI" on it in white paint. I was to tell you this so you'll know it when you see it.'

'Right.' Clausen wasn't going to be ecstatic about that, she thought. 'Sit down, Nico?'

'Well, for a moment. Maybe a glass of water?'

'Of course. We're expecting you to stay for lunch, incidentally. A casserole of chicken. You'll stay for that, I hope?'

'Is the Boche major here?'

'Yes, but—'

'I think I won't stay. All right for you, you know what you're doing, but—'

'I like *that*!'

An armband, one of those Leblanc had shown her, on the rolled-up sleeve of his collarless grey shirt. *Vivre Libre ou Mourir*. He touched it, smiling. 'The best choice is *Vivre Libre*, I think.'

'Definitely. Make sure that's what you do. I'll get your water. How about coffee though?'

'No, thank you. Just water.' He told her when she brought it, 'M'sieur Leblanc sends his best wishes for a happy outcome. But he does want me back there – to carry messages, run errands—'

'I'm sure you do more than that.'

'It's enough, in fact – quite exciting, now and then. Well, you can hear it, can't you?'

'Certainly can. *And* the other.'

'I've had a few near squeaks. But also we're making Molotov cocktails by the thousand. And would you believe it' – he took another gulp of water – 'several of the Boche light tanks have been knocked out? You take the Molotov, sneak up close enough and lob it into the hatch. *Whoosh*, it goes up in flames, and inside it they're cremated, eh? So now what they're doing, the Boches, they take a prisoner –

Frenchman – and tie him to the tank's hatch. You think twice then, you see.'

'I'd say you might.'

'Most would. Sometimes the Molotovs are dropped from windows. So Boche snipers watch the windows . . . Oh, I tell you – guess who's running a hospital and stretcher-bearers?'

'Tell me.'

'Comédie Française. All the actors and actresses, the *Sociétaires* – their theatre is now a hospital – Théâtre-Français at the Palais Royal, you know? They have it defended, barricaded, and the actresses are nurses. In fact we've taken over all the hospitals – so if the young lady you're setting out to rescue should need medical attention—'

'I'll remember that. *Sure* you won't stay for lunch?'

'Sure – yes. And' – he got up – 'must go. In fact I'm glad we were able to be on our own like this. No offence, but—'

'Understood. Nico, one thing – my bike, at the Dog—'

'Don't worry – Adée had me bring it inside, it's in her house now.'

'But it was padlocked!'

'Locks can be picked and chains cut. So happened the key was in your bag. Adée has it now, for when you want it.'

'I was going to say, I doubt I'll need it again, so you have it. If I did I might borrow it back from you – so don't sell it right away, that's all.'

'Bikes fetch a lot of money, these days!'

'Yours, anyway.' She wasn't trying to persuade him to stay for lunch, because she could understand his not wanting to fraternise with Clausen. 'Come on, I'll see you out.'

She took her gear into the spare bedroom and laid it all out on the bed. Someone – Adée, obviously – had washed and ironed a few things for her. She selected underclothes, skirt, blouse and a toffee-coloured cardigan. Shoes – no problem in selection, she'd brought only this one spare pair. But great to be shod again . . . The cardigan according to the label in it had been made in France, but in fact she'd bought it in Winchester two years ago on an outing from Beaulieu during the last part of her SOE training course, the part in which one visiting lecturer had been Derek Courtland – who early this morning she'd seen in rigor mortis and drained of blood, but only about three weeks ago had given her the little Beretta .32 automatic. They'd been meeting the Halifax from Tempsford that had flown Marilyn in: Courtland and the elderly *résistant* who'd organised the reception had had Sten guns, he'd lent her the Beretta and then suggested, 'Well, hang on to it, if you like . . .' She took it out of Léonie's bag, removed the clip, thumbed the shells out of it, wiped them shiny-bright and then re-loaded them, pushed the clip back in and replaced the pistol in the bag. Mind still away in that forest clearing: seeing him as he'd been at that time, then contrastingly as she'd seen him ten hours ago. Imagining how it must have been for him, this past week or so. Lafont with his whip – very little doubt of *that*. And Jacqui in those same arms? She took the two spare clips which had been in the suitcase and put them in the bag too. Could be a battle, at Bazoches. Battle *of* Bazoches, might call it. Imagining herself proposing to Ben, in say the Gay Nineties or the New Yorker in a week or a fortnight's time – however long it took him to get back from Norway – 'Tell you about the Battle of Bazoches, shall I, my darling?'

'Bazoches . . . Peninsula War, would that have been?'

'Why, certainly. In which I played an heroic part, as you can imagine. Fighting for my Emperor, of course . . .'

Ben, my *super* darling. Who will not under any circumstances ever be allowed within 50 miles of Mademoiselle Jacqueline Clermont.

Apart from the enormity of the thing itself – cavorting sexually with that odious creature – to have taken such a risk, *vis-à-vis* her beloved Clausen! Because 'Monsieur Henri' was thought of as a catch amongst a certain type of Parisian enthusiastic amateur? One for the collection? Probably how he'd have seen his seduction of *her*: but it was still incredible. To look as sensational as she did, and be such a bloody fool!

Not to mention slut.

On the other hand she was right in what she'd said last – she *had* spoken up when she could have played safe and kept her mouth shut. Had courage, therefore. What else – ethical standards, principles? How then consort with *any* of those people?

They didn't lunch until two in the afternoon and only then because Rosie, expecting Fernagut's call at any minute, banged on the lovebirds' door to wake them.

Still no call, though. Twice she checked that the telephone was still alive. Surprising that it was, with the bullets flying. In mid-afternoon Clausen said he was surprised the fellow had agreed to go chasing out of town in any case, with all that going on. 'That' meaning the continuing – if anything, increasing – sounds of battle in the streets. Fernagut might have found himself trapped in it. Or, having arranged for police action at Bazoches, decided he needn't hurry. What was more – Clausen warming to his theme – might have decided not to approach the farm in daylight. Dark by 9.30, say, and 70 kilometres to cover – with reasonable progress, say an hour and a half, maximum. Departure 8 pm, therefore – or 7.30 to allow for especially heavy traffic on the roads. A glance at Jacqui: 'We could go back to bed.'

She'd smiled, murmured something Rosie didn't hear.

At about 6 o'clock over mugs of coffee on the balcony – alcohol had been voted down – Clausen advanced another theory: that having alerted the gendarmerie at Provins, Fernagut might have decided he didn't need to take any further part in it himself.

'Not likely.' Rosie pointed out, 'He'll want the kudos of personally arresting Lafont. It's why I thought he'd agree to it in the first place. He made a point, by the way – Leblanc did, for him – that the prisoners will be his, nothing to do with you or the SD.'

'Why should *I* want Lafont?'

A *moue* from Jacqui. 'I thought you were going to shoot him for me.'

The 'phone rang soon after that, and Rosie went in to take it. A gruff voice demanded, 'Jeanne-Marie Lefèvre?'

'Captain Fernagut?'

'Gabriel Fernagut, yes. We'll be with you in thirty minutes. Will you be ready, please, in your vehicle?'

'At the front of the house, inside the gates. Drive in, we'll be there. Black Citroen.'

'Of the Gestapo, huh?'

'Actually the SD, but—'

'Same thing. Thirty minutes, then.'

He'd hung up. A man who called a spade a spade. Rosie told them – they'd come in from the balcony – 'They'll be here in half an hour, and he wants us to be downstairs in your car.'

'As the other one said. Yes.' Clausen shrugged. 'Anyway, why not? Tell you the truth, I was thinking he might have been killed. Didn't like to mention the possibility.'

'Considerate of you.'

She checked the time on her beautiful and doubtless extremely valuable gold Vacheron. No – *Jacqui*'s gold Vacheron. She'd wear it for the time being because it was inconvenient not to have a watch, but would greatly have preferred the old luminous job – Marilyn's – which that bitch had stolen. This one – having what Jacqui had said were bad associations – might represent the fruits of some earlier sexual excursion. Farewell present from the colonel of engineers in Amiens, for instance?

Chapter 24

It was a *Wehrmacht* truck such as she'd travelled in on more than one occasion as a prisoner. It came in quite fast – unsurprisingly, having taken a lot more than the half-hour Fernagut had promised – swerving around the nymphs and sending gravel flying as it braked, stopping where it blocked the Citroen's exit. They'd painted FFI in white letters half a metre tall on this side, its driver's door, no doubt on the other side too, and Clausen, hunched forward with his forearms resting across the wheel, was muttering angrily to himself in German. Watching the driver – uniformed gendarme – get out and first reach back in for a Schmeisser: its strap over his shoulder then, letting it hang with his right hand on it, stubby barrel pointing more or less this way. Evidence of the success of Fernagut's raid on the *Milice* armoury on Tuesday night, she guessed. Just standing there, looking at Clausen and at Jacqui who was in front beside him – or at the car generally. Two others had meanwhile jumped down from the truck, while yet another was coming around the front from the passenger side. Fernagut, Rosie guessed; that was a sergeant-major's strut, all right.

He'd politely but very perfunctorily saluted Clausen, but now passed that wound-down front window, came to hers. Unsure, though: looking questioningly at Jacqui too. 'Jeanne-Marie Lefèvre?'

'Yes.' She nodded. He was dressed as a sergeant – and

was wearing a *Vivre Libre ou Mourir* armband. She added, 'Thought you were a captain.'

'Not yet, madame.' Stiff-looking brown moustache, scar on the left cheek, hadn't shaved today. Asking her, 'The major of SD, is this?'

'Yes. Major Clausen. And this is Mademoiselle Clermont. She'll be helping me with the young lady we're *hoping* to be in time to rescue.'

'I share that hope.' He'd moved to Clausen's window now – getting a close look at him. Clausen was dressed as he had been last night and this morning – military greatcoat over civilian shirt and trousers. Fernagut asked him, 'Are you ready to follow us in this vehicle, monsieur?'

'Or you follow *me*. In that stolen vehicle.'

'I should remind you that you and your compatriots stole France, four years ago. Since when the conduct of the SD in particular has not endeared you to us. In fact I would be happy either to shoot you or take you into custody. I understand however that you have been co-operating with Madame Lefèvre in this operation, on which basis a truce may be said to exist.'

'I think Madame Lefèvre would like to get on with it.'

'Do you accept that you are under my command?'

'Well – at the farm—'

'It's a police operation – *French* police. You either accept my authority or we leave you here and I'll have one of my men drive this thing.'

A sigh, and a glance at his watch. 'Very well.'

'Are you armed?'

'Yes. A pistol.'

'You will not use it against anyone other than Bonny-Lafonts. Not even against them unnecessarily. I want them alive.'

'Self-defence and the protection of these ladies, is all.'

Now it was 7.20. Earliest likely time of arrival at Bazoches say 8.30. Rosie urged, 'Please let's go.'

'One other thing – I'd like one of my men to travel with you. If you, mam'selle' – Jacqui – 'would mind moving to the rear—'

Clausen asked, 'What for?'

'Getting through Paris we'll be using roads which your forces are not patrolling. A car of this type is liable in present circumstances to be shot at. An attempt might be made to stop it. There are barricades – could be new ones we might run into. But with a gendarme in the front, and wearing this armband—'

'To Bazoches only, then. I've no intention of becoming your prisoner. After Bazoches, no escort.'

'As it happens, none would be available to you, we'll be getting back as fast as possible. Mam'selle?'

'All right.' Jacqui got out and Rosie opened the rear right-hand door for her. Fernagut beckoning one of the other gendarmes: 'You travel with them, Morice, rejoin us on arrival at Bazoches.' He told Clausen, 'Out of town by way of Vincennes.' He pointed: '*That* fighting is in the south now. If they get into Paris this evening, as some expect, they'd probably enter by either Porte d'Orléans or Porte d'Italie. I mention this for your guidance later.' He'd stepped back. Morice – red-faced, grey at the temples – climbing in after Jacqui had transferred, raised an eyebrow at the insignia of rank on Clausen's epaulettes. 'Might discard the coat, *Herr Major*? If we *are* stopped at some barricade . . .'

Out, and left, downhill. Rosie guessed they'd cross the Seine by the Pont de Passy. After that they'd no doubt be dodging eastward on minor roads through *arrondissements* which she didn't know at all, and re-crossing the river somewhere close to Vincennes. She asked the gendarme – Morice – 'Seventy kilometres – how long will it take, d'you think?'

'More than seventy, madame. Mapped distances out of Paris are given from Notre-Dame. We're starting about six kilometres to the west of that, and our route won't be anything like direct. Seven-thirty now, so – with favourable conditions and no hold-ups, say – eight forty-five, nine o'clock, but . . .' spreading his hands above the machine-pistol on his lap – 'Pouf, how can one be sure?'

Nine o'clock, she guessed. Getting to be dusk by then. The sort of time when they might make a break for it. If they were planning to do so, not simply to separate, melt in all directions, all over France, no doubt with false identities all prearranged. Passing themselves off as *résistants*, maybe. While Lafont with his honorary German citizenship would surely head east. Sickening, to think that even one of them might get away – live on, masquerading as a human being.

She said to Jacqui a minute or two later, 'Isn't it an astounding thought, that the Allies might be in Paris before nightfall?'

'To me, profoundly so.' Clausen, interrupting whatever Jacqui had begun to say. 'It means I go in the bag. That's now virtually a certainty. There'll be no breakout that I could now take part in. Those who've gone have gone, those who are still here – from General von Choltitz downward—'

'That's nothing but the truth, I guess.' Morice turned to look at him. 'You'll be either a prisoner or dead. Despite this you intend returning to Paris?'

'Yes. I have to.'

'Well. Viewing the matter dispassionately, monsieur, since as I heard just now you'll have no escort with you, I ask myself would you not be tempted to drive into Alsace-Lorraine – to the Rhine, or to join your own forces still this side of it?'

'I *could* do that, I suppose.'

'D'you have enough gasoline in the tank?'

'Just about. But – for one thing, there's no certainty one would get through, and for another these young ladies have to be taken back to Paris. That's part of the deal we made, it's why I'm here.' Easing the wheel over: close behind the truck, turning right towards the river. There was other traffic about, but not much. People would either be joining in the fun down-town, Rosie guessed, or staying indoors, clustering around illicitly held wireless sets. If it was generally known that Allied forces were so close, excitement would be intense. A *gazo* lorry with armed civilians all over it jammed its brakes on, coming out of a side-street on the right and stopping well out into this road; the truck and now the Citroen swerving out around it. One of those on top behind the lorry's cab was waving a tricolor. They'd have seen the white letters, FFI – seen this gendarme too. He was giving them a wave. It probably had been a good idea to have him on board. At the bottom of this road, she thought, Quai de Passy – straight over it to the bridge. After that, heaven knew. She thought that Morice, who seemed intelligent enough, might have questioned Clausen about driving east because of his insistence to Fernagut that after Bazoches he'd be on his own again. She'd wondered about that herself: whether she wasn't crazy to be trusting him. He was saying, in what sounded like a friendly, relaxed exchange with Morice, 'I don't suppose my people are doing any more than defending the strongpoints. There are hardly enough of us left in Paris to do more. Even though we have a few tanks and greater fire power . . .' He banged the wheel with the flat of one hand: 'In any case one has to admit it's over. Speaking of which, Jeanne-Marie—' avoiding another *gazo* truck very much like that last one, reinforcements or new recruits being ferried into the centre, she guessed; she cut into whatever he was about to say with, 'You said a week ago you thought it was as good as over.'

'I know. But then we heard of two SS divisions being on their way to us – which surprised me. Probably surprised our general too, since he'd been ordered to destroy the city, burn it, lay it waste – and was ignoring that order . . . What I was going to ask you, Jeanne-Marie – in case we run into trouble and might be separated – if I was prematurely captured, for instance – tell me how at some much later stage I might communicate with Jacqui?'

'Write to me – or to her in care of me – at SOE in London.'

'Address?'

'We've been your speciality for years, you know perfectly damn well—'

'Baker Street, but I forget the number.'

'No, you don't. In any case I'm not telling you, you'll have to work on it.'

'Sixty-two to sixty-four, Baker Street. But that's "F" Section, which I suppose would be closed down by then. Head office is – eighty-two?' Nodding to himself. 'Yes. Eighty-two. And what's your real name?'

She laughed. 'I've forgotten. Had so many.'

'Not *real* ones.'

'I expect it's in my file. But we're looking a couple of years ahead, aren't we?'

'I'd say a year at least.'

'By that time, you can take it I'll be Mrs Ben Quarry.'

'Say that again?'

Jacqui said, 'I'll write it down for you. Scrap of paper somewhere.' Searching . . . Murmuring, 'Story of true love, is this?'

'As a matter of fact – yes, it is.'

'Englishman?'

'Australian. A sailor.'

'Here we are. First name Ben – easy, B-E-N – second name—'

'Q-U-A-R-R-Y.'

'Got it. Good guy, is he?'

'What d'you think?' She and Jacqui both laughing. Rosie thinking – again – *Not so good that I'd let you within arm's length of him . . .*

They'd seen one barricade – hastily backed out of that street and followed the truck on yet another diversion – but apart from that hadn't been stopped or had a shot fired at them. None that had made itself felt, anyway. Had the Seine behind them now, Bois de Vincennes too; the Marne was to be crossed next, at or near Joinville. Clausen, she construed, had quite genuinely accepted what he now saw as inevitable – that he'd become a prisoner-of-war. His tone and attitude – in that last exchange with her, for instance – had been far less stiff and posed . . .

Happy at the prospect of being out of it?

There was also, of course, what he'd said about his experience having been all with France and the French, so that henceforth he mightn't pull much weight. That would be a factor – that he'd virtually be out of a job.

He wasn't talking now, only concentrating on staying close behind the truck. They'd been separated a couple of times by overtaking vehicles, but never for long. Hadn't been doing badly either, she thought. Then thought again – double-take, seeing it was now 8.15 . . . actually 8.17. If ETA Bazoches had been 8.45 or 9 o'clock – Morice's guess – they weren't doing so well at all.

Jacqui had the map. Rosie asked her, 'How far from here, d'you think?'

'Not sure where we are, exactly.'

'Let me see?'

Murmuring, 'Some map-reader . . .' But – about an hour to go, maybe – barring major hold-ups.

'Gerhardt – if you pushed up closer behind, think they might step on it a bit?'

'I'll try.'

Foot down, closing up. Then – it was working. An extra five – ten – kph. She leaned back, closed her eyes. Knowing it wasn't likely that Yvette would be still alive, more probable that the butler Brançion had lied, that Yvette, like Courtland, had been tortured to death and that her remains were in the grounds of the house in Rue de la Pompe.

All of this, therefore, based on – not even hope, more a *pretence* of hope.

Ignore it, though. Carry on pretending. Face it when the

moment came, but until then stick to the pretence. For more positive and pleasurable thinking meanwhile – the bright dawn at the end of all of this – in the shortest of words: Ben. B-E-N. And Q-U-A-R-R-Y. Picturing him, conjuring up his image: promising herself that when she was back and he was too she'd really work on it – tell him let's do it *now*, this bloody minute – post the banns or whatever it is one does – before they drag us apart *again*.

They would have married, if it hadn't been for this job of hers. The intention had been there, all right – for a year, at least. Not before that, admittedly. That waste of time had been *her* silly fault, not his. They'd met in the SOE building in Baker Street in mid-February of 1942, a day and a half after her husband Johnny had been shot down and killed, and the day Singapore had fallen to the Japanese. She'd had her problems, and he'd had some cause to celebrate – oh, getting back to sea, despite injuries sustained in action which for some time had confined him to shore duties – and they'd got plastered together that night, woken next morning in a single bed in the Charing Cross Hotel.

He'd said he'd sleep in the bath. Afterwards denied having even *thought* of it. Then not seen him for a year – had gone to a lot of effort *not* to. Silly cow . . .

She'd jerked awake. Morice had shouted, 'Road-block!' and Clausen had stamped on the brake: Rosie realising she'd been dozing, reminiscing in her sleep or half-sleep. In fact must have slept for quite some time. The light was fading, she had to tilt her Vacheron's dial in close-up to read the time.

Nine-sixteen.

'This Bazoches?'

Jacqui said carefully, 'I think it must be. You had a good snooze, Jeanne-Marie.' There was a cross-roads ahead, Rosie saw. No – only a turn-off to the left. No actual road-block either, only a large blue van parked with its right-hand wheels up on the verge, and gendarmes standing around – drifting aside now while waving a *gazo* through in the Paris direction. Fernagut's truck had stopped close to the van, and Clausen pulled in behind it. He asked Morice, 'You leaving us here?'

'I am, I believe.' He pushed his door open, said to Rosie and Jacqui, 'Good luck, mesdames.'

'Thank you, monsieur.'

'Village up there on the left, I suppose.' Rosie could see roofs and chimneys, houses half-hidden in greenery which like the roadside grass was glowing as it always did in the last of the evening light. Clausen was getting out. Fernagut talking with a group of men from the van; Clausen had the map with him, no doubt to show him Lafont's pencilled cross, and he'd stopped there on his own, waiting for that conference in the middle of the road to finish – none of them even looking at him. To Rosie it illustrated the enormous change that seemed to have come about in a matter of just hours: SD major humbly awaiting a gendarme's convenience. Jacqui murmured to her, 'Through the village there, then to the left, about a kilometre along that lane, and the farm's on the left. There's a little river with willows along its banks.'

'Going to tell *them*?'

'Rather looks as if I might not have to, thank God.'

Fernagut and Clausen were coming back towards the car, the policeman telling him – well, telling *them* – 'We'll wait here until nine-forty – for the sake of the light, you understand. Colleagues have the farmhouse surrounded. They located it quite easily, I gather. It's on the left, a kilometre back in that direction, on a lane we turn into from the village centre. Farmyard and outbuildings come first, then the house which they say is large; one drives in through the farmyard. You'll want to be in there with us, of course – to take care of the young lady, if she's there – but I would ask you to remain in your vehicle until we have established control.'

'Already surrounded?'

'Under observation, say. They're placed where they could

quickly block the exit with their van – another like that one – if the *salauds* tried to break out.'

'I'm thinking mostly of the safety of Yvette,' Rosie told him. 'That's her name, you should know it. They might try to use her as a hostage, for instance. May I ask how you're going to do this?'

'With doors and windows covered by marksmen, we'll smash in at the back – south side, looks down over pasture to a river. It'll be dark enough by then – on that side anyway. The only lighting in the house is from lamps and candles, they say.' He peered at his watch. 'Move from here in – fourteen minutes.'

Clausen tossed the map in to Jacqui, asked Fernagut, 'Want us to follow *you*, or the van?'

'The van. And let the other one get in ahead of you as well. Clear, monsieur?'

It felt more like half an hour than ten minutes. In the course of it Rosie took the Beretta and a spare clip out of Léonie's bag, slid a round into the little pistol's breech, checked the safety-catch was on, then put it in the right-hand pocket of the blazer Jacqui had lent her. Spare clip in the other pocket, along with the map-reader's torch which she'd appropriated. Clausen had glanced back while she was doing it, asked her, 'What kind is it?'

'Beretta thirty-two.'

'Carried one of those before?'

'Sometimes.'

'Used it?'

'That'd be telling.'

'You used a knife on the SS officer you killed, but—'

Jacqui drew in her breath: '*Killed? SS*—'

'The pistol I've carried most often is a Llama.'

'Heavy for you, I'd have thought.'

'It's always suited me very well. This time, though, I'm travelling light, and this is a very neat little job.' She was on the point of telling him it had been Derek Courtland who'd given it to her, but instead pointed ahead – Clausen still craning round, looking back at her and Jacqui during this conversation: 'Gendarmes embarking.'

'Ah. Well, then . . .'

Jacqui still had a hand on Rosie's arm: 'You killed an officer of the SS?'

'On a train. I had help, I must admit. Rather expert help. I still don't know who *he* was.'

Clausen started the car. The sun had sunk in a blaze of glory over Paris, but there was still plenty of light in the sky back there. Too much, maybe. Fernagut's truck pulled out, passing around the blue van which then followed it. Clausen pushed the Citroen into gear. Rosie with her eyes shut, face in her hands, whispering in her mind *Please, let her be there, and alive?* A shiver then – a moment's panic, inexplicable – unless it was the feeling she was asking too much, couldn't have *everything* come up roses. *Ben too, Ben home safe, please?*

On latitude 61 degrees 55 north it was still broad daylight, and from the window in Einar Loen's living-room, using Loen's old binoculars, Ben was watching the armed trawler shortening-in its cable. He had Petter Jarl with him, and they were waiting to see which way the trawler headed when it finally did get its anchor up. If it moved eastward – further up-fjord – they'd take the *Ekhorn* out tonight, in about two hours' time. Most of the day had been spent in argument and discussion; in the course of it Ben had persuaded Loen to come down with him to the launch and give them all his view of the situation – that it would be wiser by far to wait a week or at least several days – but Jarl and most of the others had been unconvinced, remained fairly desperate to get away. To *try* to get away, Ben had amended quietly. Jarl understood and spoke some English, as long as one spoke slowly and enunciated clearly. His argument – Jarl's – was that the trawler had been putting landing parties ashore by motorboat in various places during the day – Ben had seen it from this window too, a couple of times, the motorboat returning to the ship and then setting off again – and before they were through, Jarl argued, they'd surely come for a look in here. It was sheer luck they hadn't already, that this far they'd seemed to have been concentrating on the northern shore; sooner or later that was going to change, and you'd get damn little notice of it.

Bjorn Stang, who'd piloted the *Ekhorn* in, and had all the local knowledge, was very much in favour of getting out as soon as possible. That trawler would shift tonight, he thought – probably before dark: if it did – at any rate if it moved *up*-fjord – he was in favour of making a break for it there and then. He was an experienced seaman and fisherman, had been born somewhere on this coast and commanded the respect of the others – including Petter Jarl who, although young and inexperienced, had somehow inherited the command from Nils Iversen, despite having been more Iversen's trainee than second-in-command, Ben thought. The essence of it was that they felt they were in a trap here: and nobody, not even Anna's father, could say with any certainty that they weren't.

The crucial factor, anyway, was the armed trawler. As long as it stayed where it had been all day there was no question of making any move. None of them disputed this: or that if it moved down-fjord it would still be between them and the open sea. Might steam right out of the fjord – as it had on the night *600* had arrived – but you wouldn't know until you ran into it, *if* you took that risk. Ben had asked Loen earlier in the day what he thought might be the chances of it moving up-fjord – because obviously it wasn't going to stay in that one spot for ever – and Anna had chipped in with a whole list of villages and fjordlets to which it might go next, maybe in preparation for resuming the search tomorrow: 'Gloppe Fjord, Vereid, Rysfjoeren, Utviken – or there's Invik, that's in Inviksfjord – oh, and nearer still of course Alfot . . .'

'A whole lot of fjord, in fact.'

As Vidlin had pointed out, 80 or 90 kilometres of it. Which meant the German could move himself *well* out of the way, if he chose to do so.

He handed Jarl the glasses. 'Your turn. Taking their damn time about it, aren't they? Maybe the motorboat's still away and they're waiting for it. Can't see it – can you?'

They'd shortened-in, and were just sitting there. Loen had gone to visit some neighbour about getting word to the people in Alesund that their stuff was here in his outhouse. He'd been showing signs of ill-temper since (a) Anna had refused his suggestion of a move to Shetland and (b) the *Ekhorn*'s crew hadn't accepted his advice to sit it out, let things cool down. It was 9.30 now, two hours before it would be dark enough to push off – if the trawler did deign to move. Ben had told them OK, if it did – and went up-fjord – fair enough, he'd be with them, but otherwise wait for tomorrow night – and they'd agreed on that. Leaving Jarl at the window now, he sat down at the table beside Anna who was writing a letter on paper torn from a school exercise-book.

'If we do go – you coming?'

She finished the line she was writing, put the pen down and looked at him. Those eyes, at such close quarters . . . With Rosie, if you'd had to single out one feature it would have been her mouth. He'd called it her 'I'll-eat-you-alive' mouth. In a similar way, with Anna it was the eyes. They had a magnetic quality: as Rosie's mouth had had. Magnetic pull which he'd never seen any reason to resist. Same applied here and now – at least, as it felt to *him*.

She'd drawn back a little; glanced away in Jarl's direction then back to him, telling him very quietly, 'The answer is no. I can't leave my father.'

'But he wants you to.'

'He thinks he does. He's forgotten what a lonely man he was.'

'Well, he might be again, but it's what he'd choose, he'd be happier knowing you were safe.'

'Sailing tonight in *Ekhorn* – safe?'

'How long ago did you say your mother died?'

'I was twelve.'

'Ten years ago.'

'A little more.'

'I'll tell you one thing, Anna.' The eyes really did have it; he told them, 'You're lovely. You truly are quite, quite beautiful.'

'I'm staying here with my father.'

'You and Rosie would have hit it off pretty well, what's more.'

'You're what they call "on the rebound", Ben. *You're* lonely.'

'Aren't you?'

'For Leif, of course.'

'I mean it though – you'd have found a lot in common. She'd approve – I mean, of me talking to you like this.'

'Not if she was alive, she wouldn't.'

'If she was alive I *wouldn't* be talking to you like this.'

'No, I don't suppose you would.' Giving thought to that; then asking, 'Are all Australians like you?'

'Hell, no. Lots of 'em are quite ugly.'

The smile. 'You tempt me, Ben.'

'*Well,* now—'

'No. I *can't* leave him.'

Jarl called from the window, 'Trawler moving!'

'Which way?'

'Can't say.' He added some Norwegian which Anna translated as, 'Could be making a wide turn, he says.' Ben was at the window, and Jarl grunted, 'Go *up*-fjord. Here.' The glasses. Ben took them and saw he was right; and that it had its motorboat in tow. He felt Anna beside him, asked her, 'Tell him we'll push off at eleven-thirty? He could go down and tell his mates, if he likes. I'll keep lookout here as long as the light lasts, in case that object comes back, in which case – too bad.'

Jarl listened to that in Norwegian, and nodded. 'OK.'

'How long to warm through her engines?'

The answer came out as, 'Ten, fifteen minutes.'

'OK. Eleven-fifteen. I'll be with you before that, though.'

Anna said when they were alone, 'I was hoping it would turn the other way. That's the truth, you may as well know it.'

They were face to face; he slid his arms round her. Actually *under* the loose jersey – as it turned out. It was a patterned jersey and she had a white shirt under it with a long, lemon-yellow skirt.

'*Won't* you come with us?'

'I can't.'

He kissed her, lightly. 'Not even just to Shetland, to those friends?'

'What good would that do you?'

'I'd know you were safe. As your father would.'

'I'll be safe here, don't worry. Safer than in the *Ekhorn*, what's more. I don't think you should be sailing this soon; I think my father's right.'

'Meet again when it's all over, Anna?'

'If you like.'

'You don't mind *this*?'

His unshaven jaw. She shook her head. Kissing again, much less lightly and for longer; telling her then as she ran her fingers over it, 'It's going to be a beard. Had one before.' A luxuriant growth which he'd shaved off for Rosie. Who *would* have approved, he felt sure. What she would not have raved about exactly was Joan – the Stack girl – who was now in any case a non-starter.

Kissing a lot more and Anna realising that she was indeed *very* tempted – almost as much as he was. Whispering – her mouth just clear of his: 'When the war ends or the Germans get out of Norway – write care of the postmaster in Alfot, will you?'

'Bet your sweet life!'

'Ben?'

'Uh?'

'There's a wider view from upstairs. See past that headland a little way – actually *my* window—'

'But if your father—'

'He'll be an hour yet. Come on . . .'

'Oh, *Christ*!'

'What—'

Didn't need any wider view. The armed trawler was sliding into plain-enough view as it was, from behind that headland. Slowly . . . as if drifting, not under engine power. He'd snatched up the glasses, had them on her. Close into this side of the main fjord, close to its junction with this one – *much* closer than it had been before. And . . . stopped. He muttered, 'Boat's alongside, men mustering on deck. Climbing down into it. Damn and blast and – look, nothing anywhere near here they can be inspecting except the creek, is there?'

Nothing over the other side either. Bare rock. Trees this side, rock that side. And too late to get down there and warn them. Just pray they were alert and keeping a lookout: he'd suggested to Jarl they might do so from the wheelhouse of Loen's boat. Might have, might not. Ben had the glasses in his right hand, left arm around her – as if to support or steady *her* . . . She said, 'They'll hear the boat's engine, won't they?'

'And what? Start running, or start shooting? Then the trawler moves in anyway. They'll have machine-guns as well as that thing on its foc'sl. All the *Ekhorn* has is—'

'I saw. Jarl showed me.'

The boat was leaving the trawler's side now and – sure enough – heading straight in. Seven or eight men in it. They'd have automatic weapons, you could bet on that, would hardly need back-up from the trawler. Run alongside

Loen's cutter, no doubt, and from her deck . . . 'It's slowing. Your father's boat must be in plain sight from there.'

'The *Kari*'s licence is in order. They've only to read the number that's painted on her, and check it on the list they'll have with them.'

'Doing that now maybe. Stopped, and – cox'n's standing with glasses on her.'

Or on the *Ekhorn*. If, after Jarl had given them the message 'Sailing eleven-thirty' they'd begun taking the cam netting off; being so eager to get away, they might have.

'Ben!' Anna let out a squeak of excitement. '*See?*'

Of course he could – did. Better than she could, since he had the glasses. The motorboat was under way again, turning away, bubbling whitish wake curving away from its stern, helm over to starboard. To head *back*. Ben using imagination to make sense of it – trawler on its way up-fjord, skipper realises there's this one place he hasn't checked. He puts his ship about and comes back – not far, only a few thousand yards, sends his boat in, and all they see afloat is Loen's cutter . . . of which the number checks, registration and licence are OK.

Anna hugged him. 'Ben – thank God . . .'

'Looked bad for a minute, didn't it?'

'Very. *Very* bad.'

She was in his arms: he'd reached to put the binoculars on the window-sill. 'Better just make sure that thing does go back up-fjord now.'

'It will do. If it was going westward, wouldn't have stopped just off the headland. Feel how fast my heart's beating, Ben?'

He accepted the invitation; and she was right, it was fairly racing. He supposed his was too, but it was more fun checking hers. Kissing again too; but remembering then, and taking his mouth off hers to ask her, 'Better view from upstairs, you said?'

Chapter 25

Dark enough already, here in Bazoches. In the village, anyway, this narrow main street shut in between dark house-fronts, small huddled houses without as much as a candle visible in any of them, only here and there a gleam of the day's last pinkish light in the glass of a dirty window. Streets empty too: this one was, anyway. Clausen had turned up from the main road at a crawl, following the van's dark bulk; over the hump of a stone bridge, then the houses crowding in on both sides. Watching over Clausen's shoulder, Rosie caught a glimpse of Fernagut's truck as it led away to the left; more space around them then – market square, of sorts – and the van turning now: at walking pace, no more, she supposed to minimise the sound of their approach.

If they did hear the cars' engines, would they react to it?

You wouldn't have thought it would be noticeable. But from the outside, three engines – and the others louder than this, for sure. There was some intermittent traffic hum from the main road – a few hundred metres down there to the left, beyond a certain acreage of pasture and the river – which was the quarter in which one might see the moon rising if there was going to be one. Might well not be: that might have been the end of the old one last night. She *thought* it had been: remembering her first sight of it in the forecourt of Rue des Saussaies – visual memory linked to that of the absolute marvel of fresh, clean air, enjoying that despite being under the impression that one was being taken – bare-footed, on sharp gravel – to some place of execution.

Clausen braking gently. Stopping. The van ahead drawing away, merging into the semi-darkness of the lane, which at this point was overhung by trees. He pointed, and she saw it then: another large police van turning out of a track or field-entrance on the right-hand side. Clausen now reversing 5–10 metres to give it room to turn out ahead of him. About half a kilometre to go, she supposed. Gendarmes keeping the farmhouse under observation would have been deployed from that van, which would have been parked well back off the lane in that patch of woodland – perhaps hours ago. The nearest cover there'd been, she supposed; and risky enough even to have been that close, in broad daylight. If the Bonny-Lafonts had been on their toes and taking precautions, patrolling the farm's surroundings . . .

Slowing again, Clausen muttered, 'Seems we've arrived.'

The truck – Fernagut's – had turned in to the left. Dark enough now for it to have looked black in doing so, hard-edged in silhouette against the sunset's afterglow. There were no lights on any of the vehicles, of course. Rosie had seen Clausen put his Luger on the front passenger seat beside him. He was turning now – over rutted, hard-baked mud and through a gap in a low wall. There were buildings ahead and to the right: barns, cartsheds, cowsheds, whatever; and beyond, an area of what looked like neglected kitchen-garden, a higher wall at right-angles to the lane, and a cottage-sized building of which that run of wall seemed to be a part. That, or the building was very close against it. You wouldn't have called it large – as Fernagut had said the farmhouse was – so . . . cottage, call it . . . Blanked off from sight now anyway, an open-fronted stone shed intervening. One could have branched off to the right there, across that shed's open front, but the vans had held straight on. Similar shed or barn off to the left. But in that one – the end-wall of which they were passing now – at the last moment she'd spotted what might have been two cars closely resembling this one. Brançion had said two Citroens, one van. It had been no more than an impression – afterthought almost, quick glimpse and then imagination maybe playing a part, but if she'd seen what she *thought* she had – well, the Bonny-Lafonts were here for sure, had not flown *this* coop.

Clausen had stopped – abreast the rear left-hand corner of what she now thought of as the Citroen shed. The van ahead had stopped too and for a few seconds had been surrounded by a throng of disembarking gendarmes. One of them was at Clausen's window suddenly: 'Please to pull off that way.' To the right – pointing. 'This one has to reverse so as to block the exit, uh?'

Clausen nodded, started forward again with the wheel hard over, turning along the back of this Citroen shed. There was just room to get round, clearing the rear-end of the van. The open area ahead and to their left now, Rosie saw, was farmyard, with the other van and the truck stopped in the middle of it and the van that had been in front of them backing away now to put itself in the entrance/exit, the gap in the roadside wall. Clausen was edging his car slowly forward on a line parallel to the back of this shed: and Rosie saw the house. The 8- or 10-foot wall she'd seen, before the shed had obscured her view, ran from the lane – probably did form the back or side-wall of the cottage – and continued to the nearer corner of the farmhouse. Which *was* large. Set well back – couldn't see its lower part because of the wall – with a jumble of black roof-slopes and ridges, two stacks of chimneys, windows on the upper floor reflecting the glow in the western sky.

Eyes down to the wall again: to a timber double gateway midway between the smaller building and the main house. Easily visible because it was standing open, a rectangular opening 6 feet high by 8 across. Had one turned right on the lane side of the shed with the Citroens in it one could have followed a track – driveway – that passed on the lane side and led to those doors. Could have driven in there now, even, from here: on round the other end of this shed, off cobbles then on to the drive and through the gateway to the house.

Where Lafont would doubtless have driven, or been driven, on arrival. Deposit personnel and baggage – and prisoner? – at the house, cars then to their garaging in the shed. Presence of the two cars having become by now less speculative than an assumption. But she had *not* as yet seen the Renault van which Brançion had mentioned and might well be the one she and Nico had seen at the Rue de la Pompe house, and which because of the way they'd felt about the place at that time she'd come to associate with Léonie. Obvious form of transport for a prisoner, anyway.

A gendarme, bareheaded and carrying a rifle, not machine-pistol, came trotting from where she guessed he'd have parked that van in the exit to the lane. He was crossing the yard from behind them and to the left, passing between them and the other vehicles and making for the far end of a long, low building on the yard's southern side. Milking shed – and that end of it not far from the house. Exit to pasture in fact between house and shed. He'd be covering windows and any doors in that end of the house, she supposed. Might have been wiser to stay with his van, perhaps. But another of them might have stayed there: and from where that one had now melted into the gloom he'd also be covering any approach to the truck and/or the other police van – if there was a breakout from the house, for instance. One didn't know how many there were in the contingent from Provins: and not having seen anything much of the dispersal from vans and truck at the time of arrival, could only assume that all aspects of the house must by now be covered, with what one might call the assault group somewhere on its south-facing side, preparing to break in.

'Taking their time about it.'

Jacqui agreed: 'What I was just—'

A whistle – double peep, sharp and clear. Clausen grunted,

'Unh?' – translatable as 'Here we go . . .' Action swift and loud then: crash of timber and glass – much as it had sounded at the de la Pompe house but more of it, more than one point of entry – and shouting from the house now. A burst of fire from a machine-pistol: Rosie asked Jacqui, 'Let me out?' Wanting to get out on the right-hand side, where – at least to start with – she'd be out of sight from most directions including the near end of the house. She climbed over Jacqui and slid out, leaving the door for Jacqui to pull shut and running for the nearest point of deep shadow thrown by the wall. Then along it to the gateway. Crouching there, where the drive led into another yard with a grass or earth circle in its centre. Lights flickering in the house – torches. There'd been no more shooting but a lot of shouting. A single shot now – the sound had come from upstairs, she thought, and was followed by a brief snarl of Schmeisser-fire. She was edging through, upright now, holding herself close against the framework of the open door on this right-hand side, to get a look from the inside at the smaller, ancillary building – farm-worker's cottage, or whatever.

Renault van. *Black* van anyway. Yes – Renault shape. Parked this side of the cottage and close to it, close in to the angle it made with the wall. So use that for cover; it was as handy as it could have been, in fact. She crept through and around the timber door itself – which made for greater exposure than she'd have liked – then was close to the wall and running.

Van, first. Bastards *might* be keeping her in it . . .

Weren't, though. Its doors weren't locked, and it was empty. She shut the door she'd opened and edged on round and up between it and the cottage wall, looking for a door or window – but too close, getting no general view of it – and about as tense as she'd ever been. Fleeting memory of the Manoir St Valéry, *that* night's mayhem – forgetting it completely though at the sound of someone smashing through a window, timber and glass going like a bomb-burst, an almost familiar sound now – from the main house, she guessed at its far end or thereabouts. She'd pulled back into the space between van and wall, then saw a man running – in *this* direction, *from* the house – maybe from around that far corner of it. An end window maybe he'd crashed out of. Like a drunk's or an ape's shambling run but actually covering the ground quite fast: he'd hit the edge of the grass circle – some sort of kerb – almost gone flying, but recovering, staggering back on course . . .

Course for this van. Wouldn't know the exit was blocked, naturally. She thumbed the Beretta's safety-catch off. Sighting on him, waiting for a kill at close range: Berettas weren't exactly target pistols. Dark stain on his face – blood from window-glass, she guessed.

He had *not* been making for the van: coming off the grass patch he swerved to his left, came pounding on in that weird splay-footed way and with his arms gyrating – for balance presumably – and now flung himself at a door in this cottage's wall: bursting straight in, Rosie only seconds behind him, other boots pounding the yard's hard surface from the direction of the house, and a shot – rifle-shot, that ricocheted off the stone wall near this door – but she was inside, and – no gestapist. Kitchen table, dresser, coal-stove: then boots crashingly loud on wooden stairs. Straight, steep, narrow stairs from inside what looked like a cupboard, familiar odour from an oil-lamp glowing under a slope of ceiling in the room they led to, and a male scream of, 'Didn't think I'd leave you to them, did you?'

Léonie had one wrist chained to the iron bedstead, and the man had a knife in his right hand, by the look of it was reaching with the other to grab her by the hair. She was off the bed though, on its far side. He had blood all over him, from his dive out of that window. Rosie howled, 'Drop it and stand still!'

Should have shot him there and then: because with the knife, and that close, and his seemingly murderous intention in the first place – unless he'd come not to kill her but to get away with her – but if his intention *had* been to kill her and he'd moved fast—

He'd whirled to face Rosie.

'Who the *fuck*—'

Now – in those few seconds – he looked as if he meant business with the knife. She'd yelled again, '*Drop* it!' and for another second was ready to let him have it between the eyes – an intention which he'd have read, which held him with mouth open, gasping, chest heaving noisily like bellows, eyes showing a lot of white, face and head actually running with blood from gashes. The knife *had* fallen: both blood-stained hands lifting, palms towards her, into the path of any bullet as if they might be enough to stop it. Swaying, feet shifting for balance as on a moving deck. She had the pistol aimed at the bridge of his nose, her hand surprisingly steady, torch in the other hand at least partially blinding him, hearing herself ask Léonie – stupid question, when she thought and told about it afterwards, but asking it in English – 'You all right, Léonie – Yvette?'

'Do I *know* you?' She was pulling back away from *him* as far as she could get, as the length of her arm and the chain would allow: answering the silly question then with, 'All bruised – everywhere. *Literally* everywhere, I'm—'

'He rape you?'

'Christ, *yes!* Lafont *gave* me to him, said—'

'Want to kill him yourself, or I do it for you?'

'You – please, I—'

He was *grinning*, and shaking his head. Imbecilic. Fear – terror – disbelief – or madness? Didn't understand English anyway, couldn't know what was coming – not for certain anyway, but—

'*Where* would you shoot him?'

'Oh' – pointing, with the unchained hand – '*first* shot—'

'Yes.' Downstairs they were crashing in through the kitchen. She knew exactly where to put the first shot. Second and third not far from it in the lower belly where one had always been told it hurt the most. Ears ringing from the whipcrack shots, further deafened by his screaming; he was doubled over, emitting shrieks, now buckling at the knees – hugging himself, on his knees and toppling over sideways just as the first of the gendarmes crashed in. Rosie put the sole of her shoe against the bloody face, pushing him over on to his back: she shot him again but this time in the forehead. Had to find the key then for the padlock on Léonie's chain. She told the gendarmes – there were two in the room by this time – 'It was self-defence. He was coming at me with that knife. I fired one shot – as you see.' Her torch-beam on the bullet-hole in his forehead: 'That one.'

'Yes. Beyond dispute.' They'd both looked, and now exchanged nods and grunts of agreement. Having also seen Yvette, obviously. This one added, 'It was precisely as you say. But now, you search for—'

'This.'

The key. He'd had it on a string around his neck and she'd snapped it off, showed it to the gendarme as she went to Léonie. 'My name's Rosie. We met in Nancy. Are you going to be able to walk?'

'His name – Bernin. Victor. Lafont called him Vic. He – Bernin – once threatened to cut off my eyelids.'

'What a charmer.'

Léonie was hobbling, supporting herself with her hand hooked over Rosie's shoulder, and with one gendarme hovering close behind, ready to assist but not touching her. Rosie wasn't touching her either, leaving it to her to find what support she needed – she'd said she didn't want any arms around her, on account of the all-over bruising. Her face was a patchwork of brown, purple, yellow from it. She was wearing what looked like a man's nightgown – striped, straight-sided and reaching to the ground – and had said she had no idea what had been done with her clothes. Rosie had told her, 'We'll fix you up, don't worry. We'll be driving back to Paris now to a flat in Passy. Girl with me, Jacqui Clermont, lives there and has masses of clothes. They'll be big for you but we'll fix them well enough for getting back to England. Through here now, Léonie – I mean Yvette. Sorry, keep thinking of you as Léonie.'

'I don't mind being Léonie. I still think of Derek as Guillaume.'

They were approaching the gateway in the wall, Rosie pointing: 'Through there, then it's only a few yards. One thing I must explain. The man driving this car – it's *his* car – is Jacqui's boyfriend and he's a major in the SD, but—'

'SD . . .'

'—he's on our side in this, oddly enough. Jacqui's been tied up with him for ages, he knows the Resistance would give her short shrift if she was left here on her own now – Allies may already be in Paris, by the way, they were tipped to arrive this evening – anyway, they'd as like as not do her in, so he's been helping me find *you* in return for my promise to take her to London with us. She was working for SOE, you see, and she's entitled, but he doesn't know that, better *not* know – OK?'

Movement of split and flattened lips: 'OK.'

There was a crowd in the farmyard between the parked vehicles and the near end of the house. By torchlight surrounding them she saw half a dozen men in handcuffs and leg-irons, guarded by gendarmes with Schmeissers. That tall one would be Lafont: she wondered whether Jacqui might have spotted him. The van's doors were open and the other one, which had been moved to block the exit, was growling its way back into the yard at this moment. One of the gendarmes who'd been in the cottage when she'd killed Bernin had trotted over to that large group, reporting to Fernagut she guessed – or maybe to his own *patron* from Provins. One didn't know who was who, exactly. There was a smaller, separate group, she saw – three or four women who were also handcuffed – and some children.

Jacqui came running. Clausen was out of the car too, but waiting for them beside it. Léonie asked Rosie, 'How did you know they'd brought me here?'

'Well – I wouldn't have gone into this if you hadn't asked, but the starting-point was – Guillaume.'

'Lafont whipped him to death. In front of me. Took *days*.'

'I guessed, something like that. I saw the chair and the hook in that cellar.'

'Why Bernin thought of cutting my eyelids off. To make me watch.'

'Is this – *Yvette*?'

'Yes, Jacqui. Don't touch her, she's bruised all over. Yvette – Jacqui.'

'Hello, Jacqui. We're going to your apartment and you'll fix me up with some clothes, Rosie says.'

'Why, of *course*—'

'Jeanne-Marie?'

Fernagut. Rosie called back, 'With you in a moment.' Then to Léonie/Yvette, 'We'll get you into the car – sandwiches and a Thermos of coffee – *real* coffee, if—'

'Brandy too.' Jacqui asked Rosie, 'Said anything about Gerhardt?'

'Yes, I've explained.' She added to Léonie: 'Gerhardt is Major Clausen. Better call him Gerhardt – easier—'

'I feel like Alice in Wonderland, but—'

'Some wonderland.' Jacqui said, 'Listen, soon as we get to the flat, I'll send for a doctor. And if he says hospital—'

'London's the place for her, Jacqui. Hospital there, if necessary. Unless the doctor's adamant she mustn't travel. Her mother's in London, and – anyway, Paris hospitals are going to be packed out.'

'Definitely London, please.'

'Mam'selle Yvette?'

'Yes – Gerhardt. They say you helped find me, I'm – grateful.'

'Charming that you should say so. Now if we use this

door – Jacqui, you might get in the other side, help her in from inside, d'you think?'

'All right, Léonie?'

'If they don't pull me, or—'

'She's badly hurt, Gerhardt. All-over bruising, especially. Best not to touch her, let her crawl in, give her help she *asks* for but – see, I'm not holding her—'

'Understood.'

'I want a word with Fernagut. Won't be two minutes. Yvette would like sandwiches, coffee and Cognac – she'll tell you in which order.'

Fernagut was telling another gendarme, 'You take them then, but they remain my prisoners, I'll arrange to collect them when things have settled down. Keep 'em locked up and incommunicado – and no chances, they're wild beasts, uh?'

'All right. The men in my van, and the women and children in yours, Justin. And Justin – have your lads dig a couple of holes for those two before you start off, would you?'

'Maybe *one* hole? In that cabbage patch – for easy digging. Hey, Philippe—'

'Another thing.' Fernagut again. 'The two Citroens in that shed, and the small van inside there. D'you have men to drive them?'

'Oh, sure!'

'Take all three then, but one Citroen is mine. The best of them – because you get the van as well. Fair do's? Look after it for me and I'll take delivery when we collect the prisoners.'

'As you say, Gabriel – fair do's.'

Fernagut turned to Rosie. 'Forget about the man you had to shoot. There was also one against whom *I* was obliged to defend myself. I'm *very* glad you have the young lady safe.'

'You won't need her evidence, will you? I hope to get her to London within a day or two – she's been through enough without—'

'Don't worry. We've enough evidence to hang every one of them fifty times over.'

'You're leaving them here for the time being?'

'They'll hold them in Provins until we're ready. With Allied troops maybe in Paris already – God knows, it'll be chaotic these next few days. I need to get my lot back there right away, in fact. Could set off together, if you like?'

'Best you go ahead. We have food and drink for her – can't rush her, she's amazingly well in control but—'

'Very well. May I say, the capture of those creatures I owe entirely to you—'

'You did it, *mon Capitain*. Congratulations.'

'There now.' He'd put a hand on her elbow, turning her, pointing. 'That's Lafont, the one embarking. And that small, stocky one – Pierre Bonny. To our shame, once a very senior policeman. That dwarf-like object now – Lafont's nephew, Paul Clavié. And that's Engel – exceptionally vicious. He and Clavié will face multiple rape charges, as well as murders. And Montand – Chauvier – well, they're small-fry, you might say . . .'

One police van and the other vehicles, the Citroens and the Renault, were leaving, while in the back of Clausen's car, between Rosie and Jacqui, Yvette munched sandwiches. She'd started with a swig of Clausen's brandy, and he'd offered her his greatcoat as a rug to cover her, but she hadn't been able to stand its weight.

Rosie muttered, 'Those bastards! That one in particular.'

'Yvette says you killed him.'

'Instinct to do it there and then. She doesn't have to think of him still walking around, she knows he's wiped out.'

'You think of all that at the time?'

'No. Just wanted him dead.'

'Probably a good idea, at that.' Jacqui asked Yvette, 'More coffee now?'

'Oh – if there's more to spare—'

'It's *for* you.' Rosie asked Jacqui, 'What's for midnight supper when we get back?'

'What's left of the chicken casserole – and there's cheese – and Gerhardt's wine of course. I'm sure he'll insist—'

'You see, we've been living in luxury, Yvette.' Remembering her as she had been in Nancy, as Guillaume Rouquet's pianist: neat, efficient, self-possessed, coping with all the pianist's round-the-clock dangers which Rosie herself had known all about; and sympathetic and helpful with Rosie's own then rather special problems – such as having her portrait on the Nazis' 'Wanted' posters, for instance. Now Jacqui had poured a mug of coffee: Yvette didn't want saccharine substitute in it. Asking Rosie, 'How come you were in Paris looking for us in the first place?'

'I'll tell you that as we go along. But look here. Your bag – you gave it to me when I was setting off with Guillaume, remember?'

'Yes, I do—'

'How about this, then? Hey presto – shoes!'

'How on *earth*—'

Clausen said, 'Truck's pulling out.' Fernagut and company. Leaving only the van with the gang's women and children in it still standing there, its rear doors shut and gendarmes with Schmeissers guarding it while their colleagues finished digging a grave for two in the cabbage patch beside the lane. With her head near the open window Rosie could hear that digging going on. Yvette asking her – again – 'Where did you find my shoes?'

'House in Rue de la Pompe.' She didn't mention that they'd had them on a mantelpiece as ornaments; it was a fairly creepy notion and neither necessary nor probably desirable to tell her everything. Not at this stage anyway. She hadn't mentioned the dumping of Guillaume's body either. Clausen was craning round again: 'Coffee finished? Ready to go, are we?'

There'd been lightning-like flashes in the night sky over Paris, but none for some time now. Rosie had been telling

Yvette about her surprise re-briefing at Fawley Court and the news of her and Guillaume's capture having emanated from Boemelbourg via a fellow-pederast who for years had been a wheeler-dealer for SOE. She hadn't mentioned the man's name – Cazalet – because she didn't think Clausen knew about him, and the game wasn't necessarily quite over yet. She finished, 'It was a long-shot chance but a chance of sorts, so they packed me off.'

'You mean you offered. Thanks.' A hand on hers. 'Many heartfelt thanks.'

She'd have liked to do justice all round by attributing to Jacqui the pinpointing of the farm, but felt sure Jacqui would prefer it if she didn't.

Clausen was driving fast, and there was very little traffic. They'd passed a place called Rozay-en-Brie, which Jacqui – who had the map and had reclaimed the torch – said was 26 kilometres from Bazoches. Therefore 44 to Paris: say 50 or so to Passy. It was open country on both sides here. Yvette asked, 'Apart from going to your flat, what's our programme in Paris as you'd see it?'

Clausen said, 'I leave the three of you at the apartment, put on a uniform and report to my headquarters in l'Hôtel Continental. At least, endeavour to. If the Americans are in Paris it's more likely I'll be made a prisoner-of-war. Meanwhile Jeanne-Marie – or Rosie as you call her – will telephone to a Resistance leader with whom she's been doing business, and he'll no doubt make whatever arrangements she requests.'

'First of all, though' – Jacqui – 'I'll send for a doctor to come and see you, Yvette.'

'But then to get to England—'

'The man I'll telephone, name of Leblanc, will fix it: contact some headquarters unit – Yank, maybe – and they'll get on to the British command, who'll buzz SOE in Baker Street, who'll have us flown out – from Le Bourget, I—'

'Hold tight!'

Braking. There'd been some kind of explosion – just seconds ago. A bend ahead of them here, fairly sharp, woodland to the right, and . . . smash-up? Combination of the bend and trees on that side meant one had come on it suddenly: none of the women had been looking out ahead and – shockingly – here it was, up close – a vehicle on its side in flames, and men running – one crawling – black against the brilliance, which now exploded again – a sheet of flame leaping outward – blast driving *this* way – flame higher than the trees, burning pieces flying . . . Clausen had stopped the car in a juddering skid that had left it slewed diagonally across the road – Rosie with her arms loosely but protectively round Yvette – whether she'd have wanted it or not, might have been worse off without it. 'All right, Yvette?'

Clausen said, 'That's the truck. Your gendarmes.'

Had been. Was burning wreckage now, a central heap of it, and around that a general scattering. Also grass burning on the verges. Running men had vanished – they'd be part of that litter, she imagined. Reek of petrol. Clausen said, with the driver's door open – half out of it, shrugging into his greatcoat – 'Tanks. See? That was a shell from the one to the left, I think. There's a staff car back there and I imagine they're escorting it. I'm going to see who and what—'

'Gerhardt, *why*—'

'Because naturally I have to. Calm yourself, *chérie*.'

One tank – one on the left – was coming on slowly, smoke still drifting from its gun, on the wider verge and around the spill of still smouldering, smoking wreckage. The other was stopped on this other side, further back. Clausen was out in the road, had not only his coat on but also a cap which he'd scooped out from under the front seat: was clearly a major in the *Sicherheitsdienst* again. He'd pushed the door shut and moved around the front of the Citroen, was starting up the road slanting left to skirt around the nucleus of the wreckage – would also be passing close to that tank, which had now stopped with its gun pointing this way, Rosie noted. The other tank had its gun trained this way too – she thought. Harder to see because of the smoking debris between here and there. She'd thought of climbing over into the driving seat and moving this car into the side in case those Germans wanted to come on through – one wouldn't want to detain them – but decided maybe better not, better to leave it for Clausen on his return. Fingers crossed that he'd return. At this moment he was passing between that tank and the wreckage of Fernagut's truck. Poor Fernagut, who would *not* be making captain. Clausen, at such close quarters with the tank, raising both arms for the duration of a few paces, signalling peaceful intentions – humorously, perhaps. It was beginning to make sense to her, as initial shock wore off: *Wehrmacht* truck with FFI painted on it, and full of gendarmes, Fernagut maybe not seeing until the last minute the dark-toned camouflage-painted tanks, not having envisaged any such things being on this road – putting his foot down, hoping to get by before they got a close look at that white lettering.

'He's at that car.' Jacqui. 'Oh, please God . . .'

'He'll be all right.' Rosie talking to herself and Yvette as well as to Jacqui, speaking half-formed thoughts aloud more than making sense or logic. 'Talk his way out of it somehow – tell them we're his prisoners or something.'

Yvette had her eyes shut. Had had plenty to keep them shut *against*, in recent times. Could only sit, hope, poor little thing, pray this might resolve itself.

Come to that, it was all *anyone* could do.

Both tanks were at rest, guns trained in this direction, and Clausen was stooped at the rear right-hand window of the staff car. Smoke was thinning from that heap of wreckage although there was still a bit of a glow from it, and one had a clearer view of the staff car now: big saloon, probably camouflage-painted but with lighter patches – rectangles – on its front mudguards. Army or brigade insignia, she supposed.

He was coming back. Picking his way through the litter of it. Had stopped: looking down at the littered roadway to his left.

'Oh, *no* . . .'

He had the Luger in his hand, had half-turned and was aiming downward at – something. Loud crack of the discharge, upward movement of his arm in recoil. A step closer then, peering down – and now leaving it, coming on, circumnavigating the centre of it again. Still with the pistol in his hand, and looking around him quite intently as he came. Yvette still had her eyes shut, wouldn't have seen that incident, but Jacqui had; it was she who'd murmured that 'Oh, *no*', and her window Clausen came to now. He'd re-pocketed his Luger.

'Jacqui – take over as driver, please. Or you could, Jeanne-Marie, but I think Jacqui knows Paris better. The way we followed them through, *chérie* – remember?'

Word *them* accompanied by a movement of the head and high-fronted Nazi cap towards what had been a truck with eight men in it. Jacqui saying, 'I remember it well enough, probably. Most of it. But why, what are you—'

'I have to go with them. A general I never heard of. I told him the story I gave my own people – following up the prisoner who should have come to me, not to Lafont—'

'So what are you doing with three French girls in your car?'

'One is that prisoner – who knows nothing, shouldn't have been arrested in the first place – and you two are SD agents who've been working for me, will continue as agents when we leave Paris – to return before long, one hopes – so it's in SD's interests that you *should*—'

'D'you *have* to go with them?'

'Only hope I have of continuing in the service of the Reich. It's the Free French who are in Paris – French Second Armoured Division, despatched by General Eisenhower to take possession. Advance units broke in via the Porte d'Italie a few hours ago; the rest of the division will be in at daylight, with Americans then to back them up. Jeanne-Marie – you *will* take her with you?'

'Of course. Who did you kill just then?'

'I'm not sure. It may have been the one who travelled with us – Morice. I put him out of his agony, was all.'

Jacqui had gone round and was getting in behind the wheel. Clausen said, 'Everything we've been telling each other, *chérie*. *Everything*. In due course, however long it may be—'

'However long. Take *enormous* care?'

'I'll get a staff job if I can . . . But – I'll guide you through now.' He pointed: 'Around that edge of it.' The general's horn had blared. Clausen said quickly, 'Be *very* careful yourselves. Paris will have gone mad. There'll be small-scale battles all over, I expect. Tank battles and—'

'Don't worry, we'll make it.'

'Start up, then?'

'Yes.' Fumbling for the starter. 'If I remember how . . .'

But no problems. She got the car moving, dragging the wheel hard over then, and Clausen starting back that way – over to the left-hand side, clear of the strewn wreckage. It wouldn't have been the best time to get a puncture. They were going to pass very close to the tank that had done the shooting; and its gun stayed on them as they approached, that turret inching round – until Clausen waved at it angrily and it stopped. Tank commander's little joke? The other tank was in clear sight then: on the move, forging clatteringly ahead with one track on the narrow verge where trees encroached and the other crushing some more of the truck's remains – perhaps bodies too. There'd be other traffic ploughing through or into that mess before long, Rosie thought, these sods weren't going to do anything about it. She had a clear view of the staff car now – it had moved, shifted from the middle of the road to the right-hand side. Clausen touching his hat to the general, then stopping beside the big car's rear left mudguard, turning to wave Jacqui over to the other side where she ought to be now, having got by the various obstructions. He might, Rosie thought, having his back to the general, have stooped to Jacqui's open window, blown her a kiss, called *Au revoir* – or even *Auf Wiedersehen* – but he wasn't risking any such thing, was drawn up stiffly at attention, saluting.

Then – gone, lost astern, as Jacqui straightened the car and began to pick up speed.

Postscript

'So that was Rosie's "finale", as she described it to me.' Marilyn Stuart, tall, white-haired, drew herself up and saluted not as she'd been taught to in the Wrens sixty years ago, but army fashion – maybe even *German* army fashion. This was in Marilyn's cottage in East Sussex – in a long, low room with a timbered ceiling and, on a grand piano, a silver-framed portrait of the Group Captain she'd married just after the war. He'd been quite a bit older than her, and she was now in her eighties. Saying – about Rosie – 'Imagine it – from an SD major, who at any time in the previous four years would have had her shot!'

'It must have been tricky getting back into Paris that night – fighting in the streets, tank battles even—'

'They got through, anyway. And on the way – yes, I remember now – it was the di Mellili girl who had the brilliant idea of contacting Michel Jacquard. Remember, the one-armed Free French paratroop commandant who picked Rosie up out of the field where she'd otherwise have died? Rosie had last seen him in Metz, when he'd been moving to another job: and Yvette di Mellili knew him quite well – he'd had quite a bit to do with her boss, Derek Courtland – and she knew the job he'd been transferred to was Maquis and Resistance liaison on the staff of General Leclerc: French Second Armoured Division, which Clausen had just told them was breaking into Paris. Yvette piped up with, "Then Michel Jacquard must be there!" And they got in touch with him through – oh, what was his name—'

'Leblanc?'

'The Resistance man Rosie had been working with, anyway. Yes. Leblanc. And it speeded everything up for them, of course. Jacquard had a direct line to us, we knew him well. Splendid man. Although he took a bit of a shine, Rosie told me, to that – what was *her* name. Clausen's then girlfriend – I was telling you, she rattled on about him in the car, Rosie said—'

'Jacqui. Jacqueline Clermont.'

'Yes. Michel couldn't have had long to do anything about it, mind you; we had the three of them out of France in two shakes. Rosie really had been through more than enough by then. I was very much aware of it, I hated her going straight back in after the *dreadful* time she'd had.'

'Saved Yvette's life for her, anyway.'

'Yes. In more ways than one. That girl should have been – well, a long-term psychiatric casualty, but—'

'Rosie's spark of genius.'

'You could call it that. Her *instinct*. And the guts to act on it, no messing about or dithering!'

'You don't know whether she's still alive, you said.'

'No. Christmas cards stopped coming, and after a few years I stopped sending them. We'd started off well – not just cards, letters all about the land-clearance contract they'd taken on – then I realised I wasn't getting answers, and it came down to cards, and finally, as I say—'

'Nothing from Ben?'

'No. On the cards it always used to be "from Rosie and Ben" – and for an address, although of course I had one, she'd sometimes put "Beyond the Black Stump". Australian for "back of beyond", I gather. But – as I say – they petered out and—'

'You'd imagine that even in the wilds of Australia, when she was after all mildly famous – books and newspapers, references to her as "Rosie GC", and all that—'

'Think she wouldn't be *allowed* to disappear without trace, wouldn't you? I agree – extraordinary. I did make a few enquiries, but I had very few contacts out there – and didn't know anyone who'd known *them* . . . Ben, though – he only got back from his trip to Norway about a week after we'd got Rosie out of Paris, and – this *is* a point – until he arrived in Lerwick in the Shetlands he was firmly under the impression that she was dead. We'd told him so – *I* had – Lise's story, all that. And then – I don't recall every detail, but when we got the astounding news – from Derek Courtland, wasn't it – that she was alive and kicking strongly, well, Ben was out of reach, perhaps he'd already left for Norway – so getting our news when he docked in Lerwick must have been – oh, *staggering* . . .'

'Must indeed.' I'd had an account of Ben's Norwegian adventure from a Canadian former MTB skipper who'd been a close friend of his. This man had written to me from Ottawa and later we met in London, where he gave me the gist of it as retailed to him by Ben. I told Marilyn, 'He had a hair-raising time getting out of a fjord they were in. There were German patrol-boats prowling, and that launch's engines were as noisy as an MTB's, apparently. The dilemma was whether to creep out very slowly on one engine – which was still fairly thunderous – or go flat out, *bust* out – although with rocks and little islands all over the place . . .' I saw she wasn't following this very closely, and cut it short. 'They made it, anyway. Must have been near enough the same time as Rosie, Yvette and Jacqui were dicing with death getting back into Paris. Incidentally, what happened to Jacqui?'

'Jacqui. That one again.' Fingers to her temples, concentrating . . . 'Oh, yes. She went off with some Yank.'

'Clausen didn't show up then?'

'Not that I know of. He may have, later on. We'd packed up "F" Section long before VE Day, though. No, I have no idea, frankly don't care too much. Rosie and Ben, though – they were absolutely blissful! They got married at Caxton

Hall and – tell you, I've never seen two people so *madly* happy. Really in seventh heaven – and we *all* were, for them . . . I think, you know – I've often thought about it – that if later on anything had happened to either of them, the other might well have *chosen* to disappear . . . Am I barmy, or does that make sense to you?'

Factual Note

Henri Lafont with Pierre Bonny and other members of the Gestapo of Rue Lauriston were arrested on Lafont's farm at Bazoches at the end of August 1944 by French police and FFI. The gestapists offered no resistance. Before leaving Paris Lafont had smashed all the bottles in his wine cellar, ordered Bonny to destroy the files and handed out forged papers to those who wanted them; and a day or two before departure the gang had shot down in cold blood a truckload of 34 *résistants* in the Bois de Boulogne. It is on record that the killers then 'departed singing'. The trial of 12 of them before a special tribunal opened in Paris on December 1st, the defendants including Lafont's nephew Paul Clavié and henchman Louis Engel, both of them outstandingly sadistic rapist-murderers. Bonny, Milton Dank records in *The French Against the French* (Cassell, 1978) tried to save his own neck by informing freely on his fellow gestapists, while Lafont based his defence on his honorary German citizenship, claiming that a 'German' could not be guilty of treason to France. Three defendants who were still in their teens were sentenced to life imprisonment, and the other nine were executed by firing-squad on December 26th at the Fort de Montrouge. Lafont showed no emotion – he had in fact accepted responsibility for all the gang's crimes – but Bonny, having tried so hard to exculpate himself, died in tears.